The Surgeon's Daughter

Also available by Thomas Weldon
from Simon & Schuster:

The Trader's Wife

The Surgeon's Daughter

Thomas Weldon

SIMON & SCHUSTER
A VIACOM COMPANY

First published in Great Britain by Simon & Schuster, 1998
An imprint of Simon & Schuster Ltd
A Viacom Company

Simon & Schuster Ltd
West Garden Place
Kendal Street
London W2 2AQ
Simon & Schuster Australia
Sydney

A CIP catalogue record for this book is available from the British Library

ISBN 0-684-81991-0

1 3 5 7 9 10 8 6 4 2

Typeset in Imprint 13/15 pt by
Palimpsest Book Production Limited, Polmont, Stirlingshire
Printed and bound in Great Britain by
Butler & Tanner Ltd, Frome and London

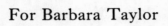

For Barbara Taylor

chapter *One*

She left the city at midday and drove upstate, determined to beat the storm rolling down from Canada. Ninety minutes out of Manhattan, the sky was already the colour of a darkening bruise. On either side of the Interstate fields were ghostly from the blizzard that had struck five days before. A muffled, surly landscape: she'd never liked the funereal nature of winter. She'd always considered herself a spring person, at ease with renewals, green shoots, daylight lengthening.

She passed houses looking hunched against the cold, snow-ploughs parked here and there along the sides of the highway. She smoked – resented herself as she always did for this weakness, this *craving* – listened to the radio, the comforting whoosh of the heater, all the while conscious of the sky losing light by the moment. If the predicted storm blitzed the state while she was still travelling, she'd be forced to leave the freeway and spend the night at a motel. Not a prospect she enjoyed. There was every chance the snowfall would be heavy, and she'd probably be trapped, and one night might stretch into two or more.

She checked the clock. In normal circumstances, this trip took about three hours, but she was driving more cautiously than usual, wary of skidding on an unnoticed ice-slick and crunching into the snowbanks that had been ploughed along the sides of the road.

She thought, *I ought to have cancelled, suggested another time.*

But he'd sounded strange on the phone. 'I want you to come up,' he'd said. 'I need your company. I really do.'

'This is a busy time for me,' she'd told him.

'Please, Andrea. Come see me.'

He'd never been the kind of man who readily admitted he needed anything or anybody. He liked to be self-reliant. He enjoyed the isolation of his house at the edge of the woods, the privacy, the unlisted phone number. He had a stubborn flinty streak that at times belied his more appealing qualities – his impulsive generosity, his kindness, his appetite for life.

She pictured him now in his old plaid jacket with the quilted lining, his ridiculous cap with earflaps. She saw him sip from the flask of single-malt he carried in his pocket when he went on one of his rambling walks through the woods. Whenever he heard the sound of a hunter's shotgun or the roar of a snowmobile he'd shake his head and say, 'Where's the goddam fun in that kind of shit?' He wanted the wilderness to remain pure, even if he believed that its days were numbered and that everything wild would be destroyed eventually by developers and theme-park designers and fast-buck merchants. He despised people who, in his opinion, diminished the world.

'I need your company. Please, please come.'

She wondered why he'd been persistent. Too much solitude getting to him? Cabin fever?

Lamps at exit ramps had already been lit although it was only three o'clock. The wintry gloom was fast-falling and relentless. She was half inclined to turn back, but she knew she wouldn't. Come this far, you go the whole way.

He needs you. You respond. Simple as that.

At three-thirty she left the Interstate and travelled through a series of small towns, where lights burned in the windows of stores and the occasional shopping-plaza created a fluorescent glaze. She found the intersection where she headed east, passing a signpost that read: *Horaceville 14m*. When she reached Horaceville, whose main street was a long strip of shops and fast-food franchises and gas stations, snow was beginning to fall lightly. This was preamble, she thought. This was the advance party of the arriving storm. Soon it would be coming thick and fast.

She stopped at Jensen's Liquor to pick up a carton of Merit Lights and a bottle of Dalwhinnie, the only single-malt the store stocked. A gift for her father: he was fanatical about malts. The air was biting. She drew her scarf up round her chin and hurried back to her car.

Eight more miles. This last leg of the journey always seemed the longest, the blacktop narrow and lonesome, the snow-laden branches of trees forming a skeletal canopy over the car. Eight miles – it felt closer to fifty before she reached the driveway that led up to his house.

She passed between the stand of maples and oaks
that concealed the small wooden house from the road.
The drive was free of snow, which meant he'd been
busy with the blower since the last blizzard, but the
dirt surface was soft under the weight of the car.

She saw his new red Cherokee parked close to the
porch steps. She braked, stepped out, felt the frigid air
hit her face, looked at the house.

Something struck her as not quite right.

Maybe it was the door. Why would he leave it open in
weather this cold, with temperatures expected to drop
way below zero at nightfall? She thought perhaps he'd
gone out back where he kept his stash of firewood but
that didn't make sense because he'd use the rear door
leading from the kitchen.

Or maybe it was the odd lack of light in the windows.
It had to be murky inside, yet the house was unlit.
She shivered as she moved towards the porch and the
dark rectangle of the door. She listened for a sound of
him – he was fond of singing phrases from late-fifties
pop songs in a terrible voice, spontaneous outbreaks –
but there was nothing except the quiet of the forest
behind the house. The sombre isolation of this place
imposed itself upon her as it always did when she
visited, but now in this arctic season it seemed to
have acquired another dimension, a denser membrane
of silence.

From somewhere in the depths of the firs she heard
a sound she couldn't immediately identify, a rustle
suggestive of a heavy garment brushing shrubbery.
What was it – a clump of snow falling from an overloaded branch?

She stepped on to the porch. She'd find him asleep
by the fire, a half-empty shot-glass in a slack fist, a

bottle on the floor beside his chair. His mouth open, a deep contented snoring, firelight on his face.

She entered the house. Strips of newspaper corkscrewed for kindling lay in front of the fireplace. The fire was little more than a dying red glow. The armchair was unoccupied. The room was cold.

Okay. Think. The simple explanation: he went into Horaceville. He had an errand to run. A supply of alcohol, groceries, whatever.

But he hadn't gone in his Cherokee. So somebody picked him up. Somebody drove him to town.

Who? Who had he befriended since he'd come up here to live? He'd never mentioned anyone.

She looked around the room – his desk where a stack of paper was piled in a wire basket, a couple of old prints of nautical scenes on the mantelpiece, his collection of antique mandolins hanging on the walls. She wanted to turn on a lamp, but for some reason she didn't.

He's expecting me, she thought. *He knows I'm coming.*

He's always here when I visit, eagerly waiting, fire roaring in the chimney, the smell of a stew simmering on the wood-burning stove in the kitchen. Fussing round me. Hugging and kissing, touching, reluctant to let go. 'Dear, dear Andrea, you look fantastic, the city air hasn't ruined your complexion, sit down, let me pour you a drink that'll warm you to the bone, and you bring me up to date on your life.'

In the kitchen the stove was unlit. Sliced onions and chopped carrots and crushed garlic lay on a cutting-board. Now she understood: he'd forgotten an essential ingredient for his mysterious stew, the recipe for which he protected like a great secret. He'd rushed into town to track it down and somehow she'd missed him, and

he hadn't gone in the Cherokee because it had broken
down and a neighbour had driven him . . .

But why hadn't he lit the stove – which took an age
to heat up – if he meant to cook?

The back door was open.

The area behind the house was a lake of white
reaching as far as the firs. She saw a plaster birdbath
hung with icicles, and the propane-tank for the heating-
system he never used because he preferred wood fires.
The tarpaulin covering the logs was coated with snow.
She saw a couple of rusted-out old cars, a Buick and
a VW her father had said were on the property when
he bought the place; he just hadn't gotten around
to calling a scrapyard. Eyesores. They were without
wheels, propped up on cinderblocks.

She gazed across the space, bit her lower lip, took
a cigarette from her coat pocket and lit it. She had a
sense of displacement, almost as if she'd come to the
wrong house, a vacation home long abandoned by its
summer tenants.

She shivered, exhaled smoke, scanned the area. Where
was he? She was jumpy. Ridiculous to feel like this
really: there was some rational explanation.

She turned to go back indoors, then stopped. She
wasn't sure why she decided to move toward the stack
of firewood, what instinct compelled her, what voice
it was that whispered instructions in her head, but
she walked through the snow in the direction of the
tarpaulin, hearing her feet crunch, feeling cold seep
through her boots.

She saw a hand on the tarp.

Outstretched, palm turned upward, fingers curled a
little in the dim light.

Her breath froze in her throat. She had a weird

fluttering around her heart. She experienced that unbalanced feeling you sometimes get when your eyes trick you and you misinterpret visual appearances – a shrub glimpsed from the corner of an eye becomes a big rabid dog, a mailbox on a darkened city sidewalk turns into a stalker – and for a moment she thought, *I am seeing things. I am seeing things wrongly.*

But she wasn't. And she knew it.

She walked a few hesitant steps closer to the hand and saw it was attached to an arm clad in the sleeve of a familiar plaid jacket, and her first thoughts were *a stroke, cardiac arrest, he's fainted in the cold*, because these were possibilities she could absorb, clinical explanations she could fit inside an acceptable framework. Stumbling through a shallow drift, unaware of the chill going through her, she reached the tarpaulin and understood that none of these possibilities encompassed the truth, because his face wasn't there, at least not the one she knew so well.

This face was different.

She heard herself gasp. Dizzy, she went down on her knees, sinking through the crust of snow. She turned her eyes sharply aside, but it was too late. The image was already fixed in her brain.

The face, tilted back from the body at an unlikely angle, had been destroyed, the forehead imploded, the scalp blown away. Blood filled what little was left of the eye-sockets. Both cheeks were demolished, revealing fragmented red-white bone, red slime.

If she had any impressions at all beyond the intensity of shock charging through her system, they were of a facial map ruined and unrecognizable and dehumanized.

This was a face she'd never seen before.

*Tell yourself that. Over and over, keep telling your-
self.*

You don't know this person.

You don't know him at all.

But she knew that jacket and she knew that ornate
antique ring on his right hand.

She knelt there for God knows how long, numb and
immobilized, saying to herself that this was a violent dream
she'd entered, soon she'd wake up from it and hear his
voice coming from the kitchen, 'Stew's ready,' or maybe
a phrase from an old rock song, 'I'm in love . . .' but she
didn't hear any such sounds.

And when at last she did hear something it was a
strange unexpected roar that came from a place way
out there among the trees, a whirring, a severe rattling
and strumming of branches. She lifted her face to see
a black helicopter float over the tops of the firs, blades
spinning in clouds of pulverized snow and scared flocks
of crows.

She watched the chopper swing at an angle out of
view and heard the sound fade and then all the raging
silence of the dying afternoon settled back in again.

chapter *Two*

*S*he didn't feel the wind begin to blow flurries through the woods.

She was beyond cold.

She knelt beside the body with her gloved hands paralysed in a clench and her eyes tightly shut.

She didn't remember rising and entering the house. She must have picked up the telephone and made a call, because later – how much later she didn't know, how she passed that time she'd never remember – she heard a car enter the drive and a door slam and suddenly red and blue lights were flashing outside. And then footsteps on the porch and a figure standing in the open doorway, lit from behind by the revolving roof-lights.

The man said, 'Anybody home,' but it wasn't a question and he didn't wait for a response. He stepped into the room where she sat behind the desk with her head lowered. The lamps strobed the dark around her.

'Miss Malle?' he said. 'Andrea Malle?'

She raised her face. This stranger in a blue uniform and coat. This cop. He told her his name was Rick Fuscante. Sheriff Fuscante. He had a deep voice. She thought, *I must have given my name. I don't remember.*

'You mind some light?' he said.

He approached the desk. He reached under the lampshade and tugged on a small chain and when the bulb lit she blinked and turned her face away. She knew grief was rolling inexorably towards her. Only a fragile wall of disbelief held it back.

Fuscante was a tall, lean-faced man with a Mediterranean complexion. He had long eyelashes, dark eyes. 'Your message was . . .' he hesitated '. . . a little garbled.'

Garbled. So was the whole world.

She looked up at him, then rose and walked stiffly into the kitchen, where the back door was still open. He followed. She tried to speak, couldn't. She indicated the stacked logs with a slight movement of a hand. Fuscante had a flashlight hooked to his belt. He flicked it on and went outside and she watched him trudge in the direction of the tarpaulin. She couldn't get any air into her lungs. Her legs buckled and she had to lean against the door-frame.

Falling snow swirled in the beam of the flash. It was coming down thickly now. Soon the body would be buried and then frozen solid when overnight temperatures slumped way below zero. She pressed her fingertips into her eyelids, raised her face beyond the spiked light of the flash toward the trees where the black helicopter had appeared.

Now she wasn't sure if she'd seen any such thing. What was a helicopter doing out there? She understood that if she focused on the curious sight of the chopper she wouldn't have to think of how she'd found him lying behind the logs. You could keep a horror at bay if you knew the right tricks of the mind, if you knew how to send your brain on diversionary little trips . . .

But that doesn't last for long. Sooner or later the reality will come breaking through.

She thought, *Fuscante is going to come back and say there's nothing out there, you must have imagined things, you been smoking anything funny?*

It wouldn't be like that.

She was going to cry. It was just taking such a goddam long time. She felt she had a tumour inside about to burst.

Fuscante was gone for ten minutes before he came back into the kitchen, dusting snow from his uniform. He closed the door. His expression was grim.

'You were the one found him?'

Her mouth was bone-dry, her tongue a strip of leather. She nodded, gestured without purpose, absently removed her gloves, fidgeted with them. Fuscante held her elbow, steered her back into the front room.

'You have anything around here to drink?' he asked.

She didn't answer. Couldn't think. She leaned against the desk and heard him move about the room, the sound of a bottle being uncorked, then he was pressing a glass into her cold hand and saying, 'Go on. Drink this.'

She smelled Scotch. The scent burned her nasal passages. She raised the glass to her lips, swallowed, shuddered. Her eye caught objects on the desk – his rack of old pipes, an onyx paperweight she'd given him a couple of birthdays back, the antique Remington typewriter with the red and black ribbon and the big bold upright keys: and it struck her that the function of these things had been lost altogether, because he was dead and no longer had any need of them; they were orphaned. This was the moment she'd been fighting against, and now she gave way, crumpled, subsided into a chair, hearing the glass fall out of her hand, not caring about it.

Fuscante stroked her arm kindly. 'It's okay, it's okay.'

She was crying, face pressed into her hands. It seemed to her this sorrow came from a source deep down inside her, a place she'd never known before. She'd tapped into a river of grief and it was going to flow and flow until she was empty and raw. She heard herself say to the cop, 'I'm sorry, sorry,' and he made soothing sounds, whispering she had nothing to be sorry about, he understood, it was good to get it all out of your system. Cry, cry all you need. Don't even think about it.

From somewhere he produced Kleenexes and she took them and held them against her eyes. She was rocking back and forth as if this might bring comfort. She recalled something she'd once read about how small infants deprived of all parental affection rocked like this for hours and hours. She thought about the elaborate ring, the plaid jacket, she remembered the old navy-blue cord pants he wore.

It was the face she didn't want to think about.

Fuscante stood close to her. 'There's never a good time for this, but I have to ask a few questions. You understand.'

She lowered the tissues and looked at him. He was out of focus. Questions. That's what cops did. They asked questions. They could be sympathetic like Fuscante, but the questions couldn't wait, no matter what. Death created its own urgency. A man had been killed out there in the snow and somehow sense had to be made out of that. Who to blame? What motive? What kind of weapon was used?

'You know the man who . . . ?' Fuscante didn't finish the question.

'My father,' she said.

The word 'father' felt like a stone she had difficulty expelling from her mouth, the pit of some strange, bad fruit. But that wasn't really her father lying outside, that wasn't the man who sang in a silly cracked voice and criticized the rampant mediocrity at large in the world, who'd given up a successful business and come to live here because he wanted to be close to the heartbeat of the wilderness, feeding birds and painting water-colours of plants and flowers that took his fancy and walking long miles in the woods, the man who'd turned his back on city life and money-making. *Who needs all that goddam stress, anyhow? Give me harmony any old time. I don't want a goddam coronary to shut me down.*

Her world felt empty and weird.

Fatherless.

The word was bitterly resonant, like a single organ note struck in a dark church, and echoing.

Fuscante was kneeling beside her chair now. He sighed and said, 'I'm sorry. Truly sorry.' Then he stood up and wandered round the room, surveying it – for what? Signs of a disturbance? Theft?

She heard herself say, 'He was expecting me. He wanted me to visit.' She wasn't sure why she felt a need to say this. It wasn't informative. It wasn't the kind of remark that would help Fuscante, who'd taken a notebook out of his pocket and was leafing through the pages.

'He lived alone?'

'He likes living alone.' Present tense. Wrong. She'd
have to adjust her grammar. Her thinking. Her *life*. Oh
Jesus. Past, present, she was pinned between the two,
her mind in disarray.

'What did he do? Was he retired?'

She gazed at the damp Kleenexes in her hand. 'Yes,'
she said. Her voice was barely a whisper.

Fuscante scribbled. 'Did he ever have company
here?'

'Not so far as I know.'

'A loner,' Fuscante said.

'He enjoys his own company. He's gregarious when
he wants to be. Which isn't often.' The wrong damn
tense still. She tightened her grip on the wad of tissues.

'And you live where?' he asked.

'Manhattan.'

He scribbled again. 'Any other family that should be
notified?'

'Only my mother,' she said. 'They divorced years
ago. She's in Florida. I don't remember her address.
I've got it written down somewhere.'

'It doesn't matter at the moment,' he said. He wandered the room again. Little slicks of melting snow
dripped from his clothes, his shoes. 'I know it's too
soon to answer this, but is anything missing? Anything
obvious, I mean.'

She looked at him dumbly. What did he think? She'd
had time to look around? She had presence of mind?
Her head ached. Pressure was building in her skull.
She opened the bottle of Dalwhinnie, picked her glass
up from the floor and poured a little into it. She sipped
it; her hand shook. She leaned back in her chair, stared
into space.

She heard him walk towards the fireplace. He examined the mandolin collection. A dozen or so, many with pearl inlays, had been arranged haphazardly on the wall. Her father had collected most of them during his overseas business trips. Fuscante reached up, plucked a string. It vibrated – *ping*.

The sound hung in the room for a long time and irritated her. She stared at him hard. 'Look, shouldn't you be out there hunting for evidence? I mean, goddammit, my father's been *killed*. Don't you need to search for fucking footprints or a weapon or whatever it is you do?'

He walked back to where she sat. He rubbed his jaw. 'Drink the Scotch,' he said. 'Go on.'

She heard a sharp echo of her own brief outburst inside her head. Some kind of necessary release mechanism – that was what had prompted her sudden anger. He's a cop, he has a job to do, he has his own way of doing it.

'Drink it, Andrea,' he said. He had an authoritative manner. She obeyed. She lifted the glass to her lips.

He said, 'Look, I know this is tragic. I know it's damn hard on you. Believe me, I'd rather be a hundred miles from here, and I wish to hell your father was alive and well. But he isn't, and you've got feelings you need to let out, so you just go ahead. I'm the nearest thing around here to a punch-bag anyhow.'

'I didn't mean—'

'Drink,' he said. He moved behind her, put his hands on the back of her chair. 'Did you see anybody or anything unusual? Did you hear anything?'

'Only the helicopter,' she said.

'Helicopter?'

'It came up over the trees.'

'Did you see any markings?'

'I wasn't looking for details. I just remember it was black.'

'It might have been one of those choppers the DEA guys sometimes fly up here,' Fuscante said. 'Lot of grass gets grown in this part of the state. And in winter the DEA trains pilots up here. They might have been flying a training mission.'

She wasn't interested in the chopper or what the Drug Enforcement Agency did. All that belonged in another world. She finished her Scotch. Her attention was drawn to the headlights of a car coming up the drive. It parked out front and somebody emerged and stepped with a heavy tread on to the porch.

'That's Benn,' Fuscante said.

'Benn?' she asked.

'County coroner's office.' Fuscante went to the front door, opened it.

The man named Benn, muffled in long black coat and scarf, came into the room. He had a nasal voice, high-pitched. 'Jesus, these roads are treacherous. So what's the score here, Rick?'

Benn, white hair cut short into his head, had a businesslike manner. Death was what he did. Corpses were his stock-in-trade. They were stats in his ledgers. Fuscante escorted him into the kitchen. She could hear a whispered conversation take place, the word 'shotgun' uttered a couple of times. 'I'd guess a range of maybe three or four feet,' Fuscante said. Benn grunted a couple of times as the cop talked. She understood Fuscante was trying to be considerate, conducting this discussion out of her hearing.

Shotgun. A range of three or four feet. Point-blank.

She didn't want to, but she tried to imagine the scene

– her father going out for firewood, thinking he'd need to get the stove up and roaring, his daughter was due to arrive, he wanted to feed her something hot on a cold day, then somebody entering the house by the front door and stepping out through the kitchen door with a shotgun under his arm, and maybe her father heard footsteps in the snow and turned his face and the intruder fired immediately and Dennis Malle had no chance, probably felt nothing, heard nothing—

There was no consolation in this. None.

She got up from her chair and moved to the bedroom door and opened it. She switched the light on. The bed was unmade, the room untidy with discarded clothing. He'd never been big on domestic order. On the nightstand she saw a collection of everyday things – a clock, a bottle of aspirin, a brier pipe, a hardback book entitled *A History of Cuba*. On the walls hung a few of his water-colours. A forest glade with sunlight slanting through trees. A bunch of wild flowers.

She sat on the edge of the bed and picked up one of the pillows and held it to her face and smelled the scent of her father in its folds and creases, tobacco, skin, the slightest trace of aftershave.

She buried her face in the pillow and wept again. Her heart felt broken in sharp, glassy little pieces like a shattered bottle.

chapter *Three*

*F*uscante entered the bedroom and said, 'Where do you intend to spend the night? I don't think it's a great idea for you to hang around here – if that's what you were planning.'

Plans. She had no plans. Nothing. She stuck her hands in the pockets of her coat.

He said, 'There's a hotel outside Horaceville. It's not the Plaza, but it's comfortable enough.'

She didn't care where she spent the night. What did that matter?

'I'll be glad to drive you there,' he said. He smiled at her a little sadly. She had the feeling that in normal circumstances he'd have a good, generous smile, but not now. 'Fact is, I've got guys coming in to dust for prints and check out the surrounding area for tracks before this snow covers everything. There's going to be a lot of activity around here for a while.'

She heard another vehicle enter the driveway and park out front.

Fuscante said, 'The ambulance.'

Of course.

Men with a body-bag. They'd put her father inside and fasten the zip. She imagined the sound of tiny metal teeth. Then he'd be transported to the morgue, wherever that was. The ice-room.

'You feel up to answering a couple more questions?' Fuscante asked.

She shrugged. She was suddenly listless, and wondered if this was what offset grief, if the system responded to a devastating emotional depth-charge by closing down the valves that supplied adrenalin. She felt suddenly out of touch with herself and her environment.

Fuscante said, 'We can talk tomorrow. It's up to you.'

'Go ahead. I'll try.'

'You said he retired. What business was he in?'

'He designed electronic security systems. He was good at it, always in demand.'

'This is a tough one, I guess – did he have, well, business enemies?'

'If he made any enemies, he wasn't exactly a threat to them in his retirement, was he? He sold the business and came up here. He had a partner, Stan Thorogood, who retired at the same time.'

Fuscante seemed to think about this, then asked, 'What about his personal life? Was there a woman? Anyone special?'

'He would have told me.'

'So you were close?'

'I saw him a half-dozen times a year. We didn't

live in each other's pockets, but sure we were close. Very close.'

'What about his friends?'

'He never seemed to need any,' she said. 'Especially after he came here to live.'

'Before he came here, say?'

'I guess he had friends. Acquaintances, business associates. I can't recall anybody special offhand. Except Stan.' She gazed round the room. Through the window she saw the ambulance. A light-show was going on outside, hallucinogenic, spooky. She heard herself say, 'Any moment now, I'm going to wake up and hear the goddam alarm clock and I'll get out of bed and go brew coffee and smoke my first cigarette of the day and then shower and walk to work if the weather's fine—'

Fuscante interrupted. 'I think the best thing is for me to take you to the hotel right now.'

'And when I get to the office, my secretary's going to put the mail on my desk and a list of the day's appointments and—' She quit talking, placed her hands on either side of her face, wondered what she was droning on about. The need just to *speak*, some form of nervous reaction. A breakdown. Coming apart. She didn't know.

'I'll ask Benn to give you something that'll help you sleep,' Fuscante said. 'You have a bag in your car? I'll go get it, stick it in my trunk.' He left the room. He didn't go outside immediately because she could hear him dialling the phone on her father's desk, then speaking in a soft voice. His tone was questioning, though she couldn't make out what he was saying. She had the feeling he was calling in extra help, bodies to search the area around the house, the woods beyond.

She wandered to the wall and stood with her back

against it, arms folded. She saw shirts and socks, undershorts, crumpled jeans stuffed inside a blue plastic laundry-basket. He must have intended to wash all this stuff. She wondered what else he might have intended, what plans he'd made that would never be accomplished now.

She spotted something on the floor beside the basket and picked it up. His passport. Maybe it had fallen from his clothes, or slipped out of the nightstand drawer. She flicked the pages, skipping past the photograph, gazed at the various entry visas stamped throughout the document. Paraguay, Ecuador, Saudi Arabia, Jordan, Israel. Business trips. He'd been in demand all right. He'd been sought after by clients worldwide willing to pay huge sums of money for his company's expertise.

She slipped the passport into the pocket of her coat without thinking, or maybe because she wanted a memento of her father, something she'd keep, a photograph she'd look at one day when she felt strong enough to face it. Whenever that would be.

Fuscante returned. 'Ready?'

She walked outside with him. She was unsteady in her movements. He opened the passenger door of his car for her. The roof-lights had been switched off now. She got in, saw the ambulance, Benn standing by it. Two men in dark coats emerged from around the side of the house. The body-bag they carried between them was of a silvery material and gleamed like a big landed fish in the light from the house.

She turned her face away from it as Fuscante slid behind the wheel.

He handed her something. 'Benn gave me these. Take them when you get to the hotel.'

She saw two red-and-yellow capsules in the palm of

her hand. She stuck them in her pocket beside the
passport.

Fuscante drove towards Horaceville. He was silent
for a few miles. Then he said, 'He invited you up here.
Didn't you tell me that?'

She said yes.

'How long did you intend to stay?'

'Just for a few days.'

'Was there any special reason he asked you to come
at this time of the year? It's not hospitable weather for
travelling.'

'He just said he needed my company.'

'But he didn't say why?'

'No. He didn't tell me if there was any special
reason.'

'You got any ideas?'

She shook her head. 'Maybe he felt lonely. It doesn't
matter now.' She looked at snow driven against the
windshield. She felt she was being transported through
a bleak white tunnel to an unknown destination. The
road sloped downwards and she could see the thin,
scattered lights of Horaceville in the distance. 'Why
would anyone *kill* him, for Christ's sake?' and she
squeezed her hands into hard fists in her lap and
tried to imagine how the murderer looked, and what
she saw was a squat, brutal face, dark-browed, a rigid
canine mouth.

Fuscante leaned forward over the wheel and wiped
condensation from the windshield. 'Retired guy. Lives
a quiet life, keeps to himself. Doesn't seem to go into
town a whole lot. I never saw him in Horaceville once.
Never met him. So what are we looking at? Somebody
comes to the house with a gun – let's say he's got robbery
on his mind – realizes the place isn't empty, so he shoots

your father out by the woodpile? That doesn't add up.
There's no sign the house was ransacked. And unless
this character is seriously demented and had murder in
his heart from the outset, he'd hardly be likely to shoot
your father. Even an armed thief might be a little more
disposed to take a quick hike than blast away with a gun
when he realizes a place is inhabited . . . Unless there
was some kind of confrontation. Maybe your father told
him to get off the property, threatened him. There's an
axe out there by the logs. Maybe he picked it up. Then
the guy fired the gun, panicked and split.'

Fuscante tapped the rim of the wheel. The wipers
clicked back and forth, smearing snow across the glass.
'What's next? A grudge? Somebody who just didn't like
your father? Somebody who *hated* him . . .'

In her head she heard the roar of a gun. She saw
her father blown back across the logs. Falling. Never
getting up again. 'I can't imagine anybody hating him.
He could be abrupt at times with people he considered
fools, and he probably rubbed some people the wrong
way when he was in business. But he was a good man
and a damn good father.'

'Because he was a good father doesn't mean he was
universally loved, does it?' Fuscante said.

She sank down in her seat. She didn't have the energy
to defend or explain her father. How could she describe
him to Fuscante anyhow? He hadn't known the man.
How could she tell this stranger about those long-ago
Nantucket summers after her mother had walked out,
and he'd taught her to swim and fish, and introduced
her to the intricacies of sailing-dinghies and the mysteries of seashells and driftwood? How could she explain
what it felt like to be the centre of his attention, the thrill
of sharing the world with him? Ice-cream sundaes or

BLTs and the scent of brine on warm breezes and endless conversations and the way he never tired of answering her childish questions and the security she felt when he clasped her hand and the ambition she had to be just like him when she grew up, independent and self-assured and carrying her knowledge with the same quiet certitude he had.

Somebody had killed all that in him. And killed something in her, too.

'This is it.' Fuscante was parking the car outside a four-storey Victorian house with a weathered sign that read: *Glamys Lake Hotel*. He stepped around the car, held the door open for her, then took her bag from the trunk and escorted her up the steps.

Inside the foyer the air smelled slightly damp. A chandelier, converted from candlelight to electricity, hung from the high ceiling. Fuscante walked to the reception desk, rapped the small brass bell.

'You'll be okay here,' he said.

Okay, she thought. What did okay mean? When would she be okay?

A fat man in a black suit appeared behind the desk. 'Lieutenant Fuscante,' he said. He had thick lips and a slight lisp: *'Futhcante'*. 'What can I do you for?'

'The lady needs a room for the night,' Fuscante said.

'A single?'

'At your best rates, Martin.'

'Sure thing.' The fat man looked at her. 'Cash or credit-card?'

She realized she couldn't answer this simple question. It seemed immensely complicated. Cash, plastic, she was fumbling for a response.

Fuscante said, 'We'll settle all that in the morning, Martin.'

'Of course, of course.' The fat man opened a drawer, took out a key attached to a long lozenge of plastic. 'Room Eight would suit. Second floor. Lake view, nice bay windows.'

Fuscante took the key. 'Elevator working?'

'It's still out, I'm afraid, I keep meaning . . . it's that maintenance company, they're so disorganized . . .'

Fuscante was already moving her towards the staircase. Halfway up he said, 'The elevator hasn't been working for the last ten years. It's a joke around here. People in this neck of the woods don't use the phrase "when pigs will fly". They want to be cynical they say, "Oh yeah, right, when the Glamys elevator is working again."' He smiled at her as they reached the landing. 'Local humour. I guess you have to belong here.'

She thought: *He's trying hard.*

She reached her room. Fuscante unlocked the door for her. 'Take the pills. And if you need anything you can reach me at your father's number. If I'm not there, call the desk downstairs. Martin knows how to contact me.'

'Thanks,' she said. 'You've been kind.'

He set her bag down just inside the door. 'You can go back to the house tomorrow if you feel up to it. We'll be finished by then. It's hard, I know, but I guess you'll want to go through his personal effects sooner or later. Bills, legal documents, stuff like that. You might want to postpone it a few days. It's up to you.'

She hadn't considered this task. Somebody had to sift the paperwork of her father's interrupted existence. Life-insurance policies, bank accounts, the slew of documents that accumulated around every person's life, God knows what. She dreaded the notion: a dead man's paper trail. And it wasn't just paperwork. There were clothes, personal possessions. The mandolins, the water-colours. Maybe he had things she didn't know about, things of value. What was she supposed to do with it all? And now another question formed on the edges of her mind. A will – had he left one?

Fuscante said goodnight.

She closed the door. She didn't bother to open her bag. She drew the curtains on the view of the black lake where houses on the far shore glimmered, and then went inside the bathroom and swallowed the pills with some water. She removed her coat and kicked off her boots and lay on the bed, staring up at the ceiling and listening to the clank of the steam radiator under the window. She turned on her side, thought about phoning Patrick in the city, but she didn't have the energy to reach for the handset and she knew she'd come unhinged if she had to talk about her father.

She cried while she waited for sleep, waited for the pills to deaden her brain.

For this day to end.

chapter *Four*

*S*he hoped with all her heart the world might have changed overnight and she'd open her eyes in a different reality. But it was the same. Nothing had altered. Yesterday was history, fixed and immutable, and it couldn't be revised. She stood at the window with the drapes halfway open, the phone cord dangling from her fingers. Snow had been falling all night long and was still coming down across the gloomy lake, concealing the houses on the far shore behind a thick white haze.

Patrick said, '*Killed?* Dennis?'

Killed: the finality of the word. Numbing.

She'd given Patrick the news, and now she wasn't sure what else she could add. She pictured him sitting in the study of his apartment on the Upper West Side, word-processor humming. He was habitually at his desk by seven-thirty a.m. Spurred on to succeed, worried about the competition, younger guys breathing down his neck, guys who could churn out slick scripts at the speed of light, guys with lucrative studio deals.

'I'll come up there,' he said.

'You've seen the weather, Patrick? Look outside. I doubt the airports are open. And even if you had a car and a driver's licence, the Interstate's probably clogged.'

Patrick was quiet for a while. 'Killed. Jesus Christ. And you walked into that godawful situation . . . What are the cops doing? Are they competent? I don't trust these hick law-enforcement officers.'

'You don't trust anything north of Harlem, Patrick.'

'Have they got a suspect? Any leads?'

'I haven't heard. I'll know more later.' She lit a cigarette, thought about Fuscante, cops searching the woods with flashlights during the long, freezing hours of darkness. Had they found anything? Had Fuscante's fingerprint guys turned anything up?

Patrick said, 'Give me the number where you're at, and I'll check the airport situation and get back to you. Meantime, try to sleep. Rest if you can. This is all so awful, so goddam awful. Hang in there.'

Sleep, rest, hang in there. Patrick was sweet, but he dispensed advice like placebos. She told him the name of the hotel, said goodbye, then opened her bag, rummaged through the garments she'd packed for her stay, found her address book, flipped the pages until she came to the entry for Ryman, Meg, and dialled the number. The digital bedside clock registered 8:33.

She stubbed her cigarette out and listened to the ringing tone. I'm the bearer of tragic news, she thought. I'm the messenger nobody wants to hear from.

She got an answering machine. 'You have reached

the number for Meg and Don Ryman. Please leave a
message at the beep.'

Andrea hung up. What she had to tell her mother
wasn't the kind of thing she wanted to leave on a
machine. Meg's husband, Don, was a Florida real-
estate speculator. He was her third spousal venture.
Husband number two, a yacht-builder named Serge
Prosecki, had died of heart failure a few years back.
'Your mother likes rich men,' Dennis Malle had once
said. 'Preferably if they're overweight and don't exercise and they smoke too much. She marries only stroke
candidates.' He'd never said these things in a bitter way,
but always humorously, as if he were still fond of his
ex-wife despite her foibles. Maybe he had been. Maybe
he'd still cared for her in some fashion of his own.

The sleeping-pills had left her woozy and lethargic.
Drained. She needed a strong jolt of caffeine. The
alternative was to crawl back into bed and vegetate.
Be comatose. Forget. She wondered if there was room
service. She called the number for the front desk but
nobody answered.

In the bathroom she brushed her red hair, thought
how anaemic she looked in the mirror. Her eyelids were
swollen, the whites of her eyes faintly pink. She filled a
glass with water and doused them, but saw no marked
improvement. The face that looked back at her had
changed overnight. Those features in which everyone
professed to see great reserves of determination – blue
eyes that could look straight through a person, the
slightly defiant jaw she'd inherited from her father –
had lost an edge. *I don't look impressive*, she thought. *I
don't look like a person who every day of her life goes out to
do battle in the gladiatorial arena of marriage counselling,
the one who negotiates the tricky battlegrounds of marital*

strife, listens to the bickering of spouses, old resentments, animosities, grudges dragged out for an airing, all the toxicity of dead relationships . . .

It was loss. It was another thing grief did to you. It stripped your face down to the bone, eroded the veneer you presented to the world. What you saw in your reflection was somebody who looked pale and vulnerable.

Pull yourself together. But Jesus it was tough and it was going to be tough for a long time, because you were carrying baggage of a kind you'd never had to haul before, and it was filled with boulders.

She tried to phone the front desk again. Still no answer. A hotel in the dead heart of a dead season, what could you expect in the way of amenities? She put on her boots, left the room, went downstairs. There had to be a dining-room somewhere.

She entered the lobby. Nobody manned the desk. She saw a sign directing her to something named the Lake Lounge, and headed down a long, dim corridor to a big room that overlooked the water. There were tables, none of them set. The room was empty. She walked to the bar and called 'Hello', but nothing happened. Just as she was beginning to feel she was alone in the establishment, and the staff had abdicated, she heard a door open on the other side of the bar. A sad-faced woman in a white blouse and black skirt appeared.

'Sorry. Did you call?'

Andrea said she was looking for coffee.

The woman said, 'You're our only guest. Martin ought to close for winter. Why he keeps this place open year-round, you got me,' and she shrugged. 'I'll fetch you coffee. Give me a minute.'

The woman went out the way she'd come in and Andrea wandered to a table at the window and watched rowing-boats tethered to a jetty silently fill up with snow. The pebbled beach was white with drifts.

The woman reappeared carrying a tray, which she set down on the table.

'Enjoy,' she said, and walked away.

The coffee was strong. Andrea drank half a cup, thought about contacting Fuscante, then decided she needed more coffee before she did anything. As she poured from the pot, she became aware of a man entering the room. He was dressed in a black overcoat and had a grey scarf knotted at his neck. She judged him to be about fifty. His hair was black and blow-dried, fluffy, flecked with light flakes of snow. He approached her table tentatively.

'Andrea Malle?'

She nodded.

'We've never had the pleasure of meeting,' he said. 'I was a friend of your father.' He held out a hand, which she took. His skin was cold, his grip firm. 'John Gladd. Did he ever mention me?'

'I don't think so,' she said.

He undid his scarf and she noticed the clerical collar. 'It's Father Gladd, actually,' he said. He smoothed a hand over his hair in the manner of a man to whom appearances are important. His cheeks were rounded and pink, like two small frosted cupcakes. 'I heard the awful news about Dennis. Words don't do much in situations like these, do they? Condolences, regret. They don't add up to a great deal.'

'No, they don't,' she said.

'I liked your father, Andrea. We didn't see eye to eye on many things, so we agreed to disagree. You might say we reached a truce. We had profound theological differences. That's an understatement.'

'He had no time for organized religion,' she said.

John Gladd sat in the chair facing her. 'He made time for me,' he said, and patted his knees with his gloved hands.

She couldn't imagine her father befriending a priest. Sometimes, when too much Scotch had gone down, he railed at what he considered the unconscionable obscenities of the Catholic Church, the grotesque imbalance between the wealth of the Vatican and the millions of impoverished faithful. 'It's all about crowd control,' he'd say. 'That's all the Church wants out of the pious masses. Control. The rest is just so much goddam bull. A real Church would have done something to help the Jews during the war. A Church that had any balls whatsoever would give up its riches and help alleviate poverty. What do they do instead? They invest. They run banks. They get richer all the time.'

'You saw my father often?' she asked.

'Once a month or so,' Gladd said. 'Usually when I was in the mood to put God's case, and he was in the mood to argue.'

'He liked an argument,' she said.

'He was a character,' Gladd said. 'It was an honour to know him. That's what I always felt. Here was a man who'd gone his own way. A touch tired of the world he lived in, so he decided to change his life. That takes courage when you're, what, sixty or so? I admire people who make radical changes like that.'

She didn't want to talk about her father. She wanted to think he was still alive. She needed to float a small illusion in her mind, a way of deferring reality for another few minutes. She pushed her cup aside. 'Your parish is here?'

'It's a very small one, unfortunately. People only turn to the Church at times of uncertainty, I find. Usually economic. When things are going well and there's employment and money coming in, religion takes a back seat.' He leaned over the table and touched the back of her hand. 'I'm surprised he never mentioned me. Perhaps I'm being vain, overestimating my role in his life.'

She was still having a hard time envisaging her father engaged in conversation with this man, arguing about religion. She remembered something he'd once said: 'Never discuss God with one of his agents.' Why hadn't he ever made even a passing reference to Gladd? She wondered if he'd forged other acquaintances here. He'd never talked about any.

She slid her hand away from Gladd's, opened her pack of cigarettes, slipped one out, lit it.

Gladd sighed. 'I can't get it through my head that he's dead. I can't believe the violence involved. I know, I know, the world's filled with violence. But after a while, you feel your compassion is . . . overloaded. It doesn't touch you the way it used to. Maybe you get a little blasé. And then suddenly it strikes in your own back yard and it's devastating.'

She gazed down at the table. She was having a bad moment, a touch of dizziness, coffee and cigarettes and no food. The idea of food nauseated her. She closed her eyes and pictured her father's small home, the woods pressing against it. She said, 'I can't face going back there.'

'Back where?'

'To that house. There are papers I'll have to go through.'

'You can put it off.'

'Sure I can put it off. But it still has to be done, and if I don't do it, who else will?'

Gladd was quiet for a time. 'If it's any help, I'd be perfectly happy to keep you company. You might need some moral support. And I suspect you're going to be busy, because my guess is Dennis wasn't the most organized person in the world.' He looked misty. He drew the sleeve of his coat across his face and turned to gaze through the window. His grey eyes were filled with a sad light. 'If there's anything I can do for you, just ask. You need to talk about all this, unburden yourself, share, whatever, I'm always available.'

'I appreciate that.'

'I'm trained in . . .' he hesitated '. . . grief therapy. I don't know if I approve of that particular expression. It always sounds cold and clinical to me somehow. Maybe because the word "therapy" has unfortunate connotations – as if I'm the shrink and you're the client. I don't mean it that way, of course. But sometimes just talking can be helpful.'

'It's good of you to offer,' she said. How could therapy dissolve this grief? Sharing, dumping feelings on someone else – it didn't make the feelings go away. She knew from her experience with disintegrating marriages that therapy was often futile.

'You don't have the same anti-clerical disposition as your father, do you?'

'I'm your average agnostic.'

'That's something,' and he looked at his watch, then rose from the table. 'I lost a friend yesterday.'

'Lost': the word cut through her like a lance.

'You'll be staying in this hotel for a few days, I guess?' he asked.

'I don't know how long.'

'Let me know when you're going back out to the house,' he said. 'I'll leave you my number.' He took a small notebook out of his pocket and wrote his phone number down. He tore out the page and gave it to her and smiled. 'You look a lot like him, you know. I wish we'd met in better circumstances.' He held her hand a second, squeezed it gently.

'Do I call you John or Father Gladd?' she asked.

'Whatever makes you feel comfortable. Your father always called me Jack. I think it was his way of making sure I didn't get too big for my ecclesiastical boots.' The priest smiled. 'Call me.'

She watched him go. She thought of her father's house, of returning there. Dead spaces, silences. Gladd was right, she'd need supportive company. She got up from the table, and the realization struck her — there would have to be a funeral. She hadn't considered that, either. Suddenly it seemed she was crowded with responsibilities, pressures she wasn't sure she'd be strong enough to carry. You've always been an organized person. You've always been able to cope. What was it Patrick had once said? Your life's like one of those old-fashioned apothecaries' cabinets, all the tiny drawers correctly labelled in copperplate handwriting, everything in its place.

Don't fall apart.

Nothing had ever happened she couldn't deal with somehow.

chapter *Five*

She walked into the lobby. Fuscante was just entering the hotel. He looked bleary. He'd clearly put in a very long night.

'Did you sleep?' he asked.

'The pills knocked me out.'

'I should have taken a couple myself.'

She noticed for the first time that, although his eyes were brown, one was a slightly lighter shade than the other. She wasn't sure if this was just some trick of light and shadow. She was tense, waiting to hear what he had to say. A bulletin. An update. Clues of some kind. A suspect.

'Let's sit down,' he said. He moved toward an old floral couch located under a faded oil-painting of Glamys Lake. Sails billowing in the wind, gulls in the sky, sunlight.

They sat, and Fuscante leaned forward, elbows on his

knees. 'I wish I had more to report, Andrea. The tracks in the snow aren't much help. One set's your father's. Some that are probably yours. My own. And then another set that leads from the logpile into the woods. The trouble is, this new snow's screwed everything up. We've had seven or eight inches overnight. And the wind's blown drifts a couple of feet in places. It's wild out there, believe me. This isn't weather for tracking.'

'The set going into the woods might be the killer's,' she said.

'Yeah. But they're buried, and there's nothing we can do about that.'

'What about fingerprints?'

'Mainly your father's. Probably yours too. A few others we'll run through the computer for possible matches.'

She had an image of somebody with an ink-pad lifting prints from her father's fingers in the morgue. A dead man's hands smudged with black ink.

'Fortunately we had your father's on record,' Fuscante said.

'On record? Why?'

'He had an accident back in October—'

'An accident?'

'You didn't know?' Fuscante said. 'DWI near a place called New Dresden, about fifty miles from here. Ran his car into the back of a pick-up. His alcohol level was way off the chart.'

'He never mentioned this.'

'I guess some things you just want to forget. He hired himself a good lawyer here in town and got off with a hefty fine. It seems he was taking some kind of medication that reacted badly with the alcohol in his system. That was the defence line anyhow.'

Medication. This was also news to her. 'What kind of medication?'

'You'd have to talk with his lawyer about that. Woman called Linda Straub.'

She was silent for a time. She wondered if her father had been sick. He hadn't said so. She had a feeling she was filling in the blanks of his life, joining the dots of his world. A friend called John Gladd. A drunk-driving charge. A court case. A fine. Medication.

Okay, he was probably ashamed of the drunk-driving rap. And maybe he didn't mention the medication because he didn't want to worry her. As for Gladd, presumably the relationship wasn't important to him. That was all. There was no particular mystery in any of these things.

Fuscante said, 'I hate to do this, but I'm going to have you ask for your prints. Process of elimination.'

'Sure. I understand.'

He rubbed his eyes. 'I want to show you this,' and he took a small red-covered book from his pocket. 'Your father kept a diary. Sort of a diary. It isn't the kind of thing where he bared any secrets of his heart. Take a look.'

He handed her the book and she flicked through the pages. There were barely any entries, and they weren't illuminating, simply banal. Reminders. Notes to himself. *March 18 pay insurance premium. April 4 repair loose shingle. June 30 remember Andrea's birthday.*

Fuscante said, 'Go to October twentieth.'

She found the page, looked at what her father had written there. *I heard a prowler outside the house last night.*

'Now November first.'

She turned the pages again. *The prowler was outside*

again last night. Switched on back lights, saw him run into the woods.

Fuscante said, 'That's it. Two references to a prowler. I guess it didn't worry him much, because we don't have any record he ever reported it to us.'

She gazed at her father's familiar handwriting, cramped letters that inclined right in an exaggerated way, as if they were rushing toward the edge of the page. 'This prowler . . .'

'I know what you're going to say. He might be the guy we're looking for.'

'It's a possibility.'

'Sure it's a possibility. But it doesn't take us anywhere. Dennis Malle sees some guy run into the woods. No description, nothing.' The cop shrugged.

She shut the diary, offered it to Fuscante.

'I don't have any further need of it,' he said. 'Keep it. Read it. And if anything in there strikes you as strange in some way, tell me. Given the nature of the entries, though, I don't think you're going to find any great revelation.'

She was disappointed. She realized her expectations were ungrounded, unrealistic. Fuscante had nothing of substance to tell her.

Fuscante rose from the couch. 'Don't look so downhearted,' he said. 'These are early days, Andrea.' He was watching her with a look of concern. She had the odd intuition he was about to touch her face or stroke her hair, some little gesture of reassurance. But he didn't.

'Did you know your father kept a gun?' he asked.

She shook her head. 'No, I never knew that.'

'He had a Browning nine-millimetre stashed under his bed.'

'Maybe he got it because of the prowler.'

'Or maybe he just kept it for security in general. Live alone in an isolated place . . . you never know. We've removed the weapon. You'll get it back later.'

'I don't want it,' she said. 'I wouldn't know what to do with a gun.'

'You can sign a paper authorizing me to dispose of it for you, if you want.' He took a few steps away from her, stopped, turned. 'One thing. This helicopter you saw.'

'What about it?'

'You're absolutely sure you saw it?'

'Of course I did.'

'See, the DEA guys say they didn't have a chopper out yesterday. In fact, they say they haven't flown anywhere near this area since early fall.'

'Then it was somebody else's helicopter,' she said.

'Maybe. But who's going to be flying a chopper around those woods at this time of year? I can't see anybody going up in the face of a blizzard just for a pleasure trip. Can you?' Fuscante massaged his jaw tiredly. 'These federal guys can tell you anything they like. They love having their little secrets. My guess is they're just bullshitting.'

'Why?'

'Because they can, that's why. I call it FWI. Fabricating with Impunity. These characters think they're above the law.'

She stood up. She remembered the black machine whirring over the trees, the powdered snow blown crazily here and there by the rotating blades. She'd seen it. She had no doubt.

'Maybe it was the killer,' she said.

Fuscante seemed to sag with fatigue. 'A killer who escapes in a helicopter?'

'I only said maybe.'

Fuscante said, 'Let's just imagine for a moment that the character who shot your father had a chopper waiting in the woods. Okay? Now that's a whole new scenario, Andrea. One, it's premeditated and damn well planned. It's no robbery attempt that went seriously wrong, is it? Two, you're looking at somebody with enough expertise to land a chopper in the woods while there's snow on the ground and then fly out again. The trees are pretty dense back there. I don't recall any great clearance areas either.'

'Two men, say. One pulled the trigger. The other was the pilot.'

'Two men, three men. Numbers don't matter. All I'm saying is, it's a helluva lot of trouble to go to. Suddenly it's way *out* there, it's left-field and then some. And it brings us right back to the possibility that your father had an enemy, somebody serious enough to go to all the trouble of arranging a chopper. That's pretty elaborate stuff. You know anybody capable of that, Andrea?'

'No. No, I don't. I was just thinking aloud, that's all.'

'I'll check again with the DEA guys. But they're going to say the same thing. Guaranteed.' He looked as if he wished he could tell her otherwise, as if he could deliver the killer to her in chains and say, 'Here, this is the guy, this is the monster.' 'You can go back to the house any time you like now. I figure there's stuff out there you need to do.'

She didn't say anything.

'I'll have people keeping an eye on the house on a rotating basis. So you might run into one of my guys out there. I don't believe in leaving a crime

scene unsupervised. You never know. Some ghoul
wanting to take a look. Souvenir hunters who have the
mentality of grave-robbers. Even in this weather, you'd
be surprised. A little police presence works wonders
at times.'

She hadn't thought about this, the unassailable fact
that murder scenes drew unsavoury people. Sleazoids,
sickos. People who wanted to say they'd seen the place
where a man was murdered. *There was still blood
in the snow, Martha, I swear to God. Look, I got a
Polaroid.*

Fuscante said, 'By the way, I arranged for your
car to be delivered. I also had one of our guys fit
snow-chains.'

'That's kind of you,' she said.

'Part of the service. I don't want you skidding off
the road, do I?' He reached inside his pocket. 'Before I
forget. The house key. I took the precaution of locking
the place up.'

She walked with him across the lobby. 'Do you know
somebody called John Gladd?' she asked.

'The priest? Sure I do. He's at St Peter's Church.
Why?'

'He was here ten minutes ago,' she said. 'He wanted
to tell me he was sorry about my father.'

'I'm not a Catholic, but my general impression is
he's a good man,' Fuscante said. 'The word is his
congregation admires him.' At the door, he paused.
'Come by my office some time before lunch. You'll
find it on Lincoln Plaza, dead centre of Horaceville.
We'll take your prints.'

She said she would. She watched him go out. The
door swung shut behind him, leaving her alone in
the lobby.

chapter Six

She didn't want to go back to her father's house yet. It was too soon. Postpone the inevitable, you're not ready. When will you ever be? She thought of cramped rooms, cold ashes in the grate, chopped food lying where he'd left it in the kitchen.

She went up to her room. The telephone was ringing.

It was Patrick. 'The forecast is shit, pure shit. Huge tracts of the Interstate are blocked. Nobody has a goddam clue when it's going to be open again. Also the airports are shut down. And even if I *could* fly as far as Albany, I couldn't get within miles of you. Not tonight. Probably not tomorrow either. Beyond that, who knows?'

She imagined him adjusting his glasses as he spoke. He'd push the frames up to the bridge of his nose whether they'd slipped or not. She could see his lenses reflect the pale grey glare of his computer monitor, and his stare of hard concentration. At times, lost for a word or phrase, he'd wander absent-mindedly around his small apartment watering plants he'd forgotten he'd doused only half an hour before.

'We ought to live together,' he kept suggesting. 'What's the sense in paying rent on two apartments?' 'When I'm certain,' she'd tell him. 'When I feel it's the right thing.' But she couldn't think of one truly compelling reason why she should share her living-space with Patrick. She was fond of him, sure, but when you got down to the bottom line it was more a matter of comfort and familiarity than anything wild and kickass, it wasn't neons going on and off in her head and angels singing whenever he came in view. She was thirty-two and had gone through one marriage to a professor of sociology called Lionel Wright, who'd traded her in for one of his students, a pert little number with a tiny ass and firm tits – and so she wasn't ready for any big commitments.

'Anything new to report?' Patrick asked.

'This snow hampers everything, Patrick.'

'I take that as a no. I told you, these bumpkin cops, they still look for clues with fucking magnifying glasses. How are you bearing up?'

How to answer that? Not very well. Miserably, if you want the truth. 'I'm all right, Patrick.'

'The hell you are.'

She didn't want to be drawn into conversation about her feelings. Leave them unanalysed in some remote corner of her head. What good would it do to talk about what she felt, anyhow? You might as well pick at an unhealed wound and watch it bleed.

She had a sudden memory of her father, something

she couldn't fix at any point in time or place. She's
sitting in a swing and he's pushing her and laughing
and the sky is coming nearer the higher she goes. She
feels a strident panic, wants the swing to stop, doesn't
want to go any higher. She grips the chains, she can
smell the scent of iron recently rained on, a little rust
in the palms of her hands, the sun is growing bigger
and bigger, she screams, 'I want to get off, I want you
to stop,' and he grabs the seat of the swing and brings
it to a sudden halt and picks her up in his arms. 'I'd
never hurt you,' he says. 'I'd never let you fall off. You
have to understand that, babe. I'm here to look after
you, not to cause you pain.' She grasps this concept
in a flash – trust me, kiddo – and clambers down out
of his arms and climbs into the swing again and says,
'Push me, push me, I'm okay now.' And she is, she's
okay, safe, her father is her gravity. And the swing rises
higher and faster and the sun gets big again, only this
time she's beyond fear . . .

Three years of age. Four. It's gone, she can't remember, it's a wisp in the mind like a dream fading. Her eyes
filled with tears. She was angry all at once. Grief was a
conundrum that had all kinds of twists and contortions.
Withdrawal, despondency, bitter ice in the heart, and
now this: anger.

Patrick said, 'You're crying. I can hear you crying.'

'I'm okay,' she said.

'Jesus, you any idea how frustrating this is, not being
with you?' he said. 'Is there anything I can do for you
from here?'

'You can call my office,' she said. 'Tell Jacquie I
won't be in for a few days. Tell her why. She can cancel
my appointments. I'll contact her at some point.'

'I'll do that.'

'I can't think of anything else. I'll call you later.'

She said goodbye. Patrick made a kissing sound: love you. She put the handset back in place. She walked up and down for a time. Stuck in this box of a room and pacing, remembering her father – this wasn't going to accomplish anything. She thought of calling her mother's number again, decided against it. She was in no mood to go through the whole narrative for Meg, who'd want details. And Stan Thorogood too – he had to be told. That could also wait. Another postponement.

Channel this anger. Do something constructive with it. Go see this lawyer your father hired, see what she knows about his affairs, this business of the medication, see if there's a last will and testament. Begin sifting through the leftovers of Dennis Malle's life. Make a checklist, structure your movements.

She looked in the phone directory, found Linda Straub's office in Horaceville. She dialled the number.

A woman answered. 'Straub and Straub. How can I help you?'

'I'd like to make an appointment to see Linda Straub,' Andrea said.

'Who's calling, please?'

'Andrea Malle.'

A silence on the other end of the line. Just a beat. 'One moment please, Ms Malle.' There was an infusion of holding-pattern muzak, a synthesized 'Greensleeves'. The voice interrupted. 'When can you come in?'

'Any time. Now, if that's okay.'

'That's fine. We're located at 37 Hewlett, just east of Lincoln Plaza.'

'I'll find it.'

She put on her coat, left the room, went downstairs. Martin was behind the desk reading *Newsweek*. 'You

going out in this?' he asked. 'Ttchh. I wouldn't re-
commend it. The roads are lethal. Your car's parked
out front if you really want to take the chance. A cop
delivered it five minutes ago. I've got the keys right
here,' and he rummaged in his desk for them.

She took the keys from him. He said, 'I heard about
your father. I want to say I'm sorry. I hope they find
the person who did it.'

'So do I,' she said.

'An animal,' Martin said. 'Not a person – a goddam
animal. This country, I don't know, it used to be you
could leave your house unlocked at night. Not now.'

She rattled the keys in her hand and stepped toward
the door. Snow blew against the glass. Martin came out
from behind his desk and held the door open for her
with one fat hand. Visibility was poor, maybe a hundred
yards at best, half that when the wind thickened the
patterns of falling snow.

'Remember, drive carefully.'

'I will.'

She bent her head against the wind and walked to
her car, unlocked it quickly. She turned on the wipers,
shivered. The tyres, wrapped in chains, churned snow
as she edged the car out into the road. She flicked her
lights on, concentrated, felt the car slip every so often, a
yard this way, a yard that. A couple of ploughs worked
the highway on either side, red warning lights blinking.
It was stop–start the three miles to Horaceville, men in
orange coats carrying flags and stop signs barely visible
in the onrushing snow flurries.

In downtown Horaceville, pop. 19,407 according
to the sign, she drove along the main drag, passing
Jensen's Liquor where less than twenty-four hours
ago she'd stopped to buy Scotch for her father. Less

than a day. That's all it takes for your world to disin-
tegrate.

A few hardy pedestrians struggled along the sidewalks. Here and there vehicles that had been parked
on the street overnight were invisible under fuzzy car-
shaped carpets of snow. A cop, harassed and blinded by
the blizzard raging into his eyes, was directing traffic
because of a signal failure. He wore luminous yellow
gloves. Christmas decorations, coloured lights strung
from wires, plastic reindeer, swayed.

She reached Lincoln Plaza – City Hall, the DMV
building, police HQ, the usual regulatory offices of a
small town – and then discovered Hewlett, a narrow
street of two-storey buildings and storefronts. She
parked and made her way along the sidewalk to number
37, which turned out to be a hairdressing salon called
Tess's Tresses. Straub & Straub was located over the
salon. She went through a doorway at the side of the
hairdresser's, into a narrow corridor and up a flight of
steps. The air smelled of shampoos and scents and the
slightly burned aroma of hairdryers. At the top of the
stairway was the reception area for Straub & Straub, a
desk, a couple of chairs, Legal Aid pamphlets strewn on
a coffee-table, a ficus browning in the corner. Nothing
fancy. Basic.

The receptionist was a thick-waisted woman of about
forty with a plump lipsticked mouth and glasses hanging from a gold-plated chain round her neck. 'Are you
Ms Malle?'

Andrea nodded.

'Linda's office is the first door on your right.' She
pointed with a yellow pencil. 'Go straight in.'

The door had Linda Straub's name painted in small
black letters. Andrea opened it, stepped inside an

overheated room cluttered with papers, legal briefs, law-books stuffed with ragged markers of coloured paper. A tiny woman in black jeans and a red polo-neck sweater was half hidden behind a pile of documents on the desk.

'Excuse the mess. I'd be lying if I told you this place was ever tidy, because it's not. Sit. If you can find a chair.'

Andrea couldn't find a chair that wasn't stacked with books or folders. Linda Straub, who was probably four feet nine or ten, a skinny, angular little thing, picked up a bunch of folders from a chair. 'There.'

Andrea sat. Linda Straub perched herself up on the edge of her desk. She had glossy pink varnish on her fingernails and long ruby earrings and a bunch of bracelets dangling from each wrist that chinked whenever she moved, which was often. She was a bundle of quick little mannerisms, flutters of the hands, expressive shrugs, rapid blinking, eye-rolling.

'I read about your father,' she said. 'Jesus. It really shook me up. I'm still feeling wobbly. You see the morning paper?'

'No, I didn't. I'm not sure I want to.'

'I can't say I blame you. This has got to be *unbelievably* rough on you. You want a drink? Coffee? Something stronger? I got a nice Armagnac around here someplace. If I can find it.'

Andrea declined. She gazed at the steamed-up window. She imagined the killer long gone in the vast stretches of white countryside. She thought about the chopper again. She pictured the pilot's view. She could see him looking down at her, a small figure kneeling in the snow beside the tarpaulin.

Linda Straub said, 'One plus. Fuscante's a pretty

good sheriff for a small town. Also quite pleasing on the eye.'

'He said you defended my father on a drunk-driving rap a couple of months ago. I'm curious about that.'

'Dennis ran up the ass of a pick-up.'

'He was on some kind of medication, I understand.'

'Right. Fluoxene. It's a no-no with booze. And he'd been drinking copious amounts of Scotch the day of the accident.'

'Fluoxene?'

'It's prescribed for anxiety disorders,' she said.

'*Anxiety* disorders? My *father*? He was probably the least anxious person I ever knew.'

'Apparently not. He'd been taking the drug for some time, I believe.'

'He never told me this.'

'Maybe he didn't want you to know.'

'Anxiety.' She was bewildered. She'd always thought her father had found serenity, especially after he'd sold the business. Even before that, he'd given the impression of a man who worried about very little in life. 'Why would he hide it from me?'

Linda Straub shrugged. 'You think you know somebody, suddenly they're strange, they're doing things you wouldn't have believed. Is this medication business really such a big deal?'

'I guess I'm blowing it out of proportion. I'm not in a great frame of mind. Everything just seems so . . . fragile and confusing.'

'Hardly surprising,' the attorney said. 'In your shoes, I'd be falling to pieces.'

'Maybe I'm headed that way.'

'Or maybe you're made of sterner stuff,' Linda Straub said. She was quiet a moment, running a hand across her very short black hair. Her bracelets rattled.

'Did he ever strike you as anxious or nervous?' Andrea asked.

'Hard to say. He was kind of . . . uh, preoccupied? I figured the case was getting to him. I'll say this. He didn't want any press. He was worried about the story making some local rag.'

'And did it?'

'Not so far as I know. Some upstate sheet might have picked it up, back-page stuff, an inch or two. But not the good old *Horaceville Standard*. I had the feeling any publicity would have mortified him.'

'I never knew him to give a damn what people thought about him,' Andrea said.

'This was one time he obviously did.'

Andrea wondered about this for a second. But her thoughts, which she couldn't get out of second gear, weren't going anywhere. Her father was moving ever so slightly out of her focus. It was an unpleasant feeling. 'Should I talk with his physician?'

'That's up to you. He got his prescriptions from a guy called Wallace who has a tiny practice in Kayserport, which is about sixty miles from here. Wallace also happens to be county coroner, but I guess he likes to keep his hand in with some GP stuff on the side. For some reason I never figured out, Dennis didn't go to a local doc.' The attorney studied her fingernails and frowned. 'Want me to be honest with you? I got the impression your father just didn't want anybody around here to know a goddam thing about him. Okay, so he was into this hermit existence, long walks in the woods and let's get it on with nature and what have you, but why make a round trip of more than a hundred miles

just to get a script written? All he had to do was drive
eight miles or whatever it is from his house into town.
And why get so steamed up about a drunk-driving case
in some butt of a place nobody's ever heard of? I mean,
New Dresden, really. We're not talking about a federal
court here.'

'You make him sound like a man in hiding.'

'Uh, I didn't say that.'

'Implied then.'

Linda Straub fidgeted with an earring. 'It could be
he just wanted complete privacy. You know, just pull
the shutters closed in every window and leave me alone.
Make the world go away type of thing. That's all. As
simple as that.'

The attorney didn't sound altogether convincing, as
if she was back-pedalling from a judgment, distancing
herself from her previous remarks. Andrea thought
about the priest, John Gladd. If her father had wanted
to guard his privacy with such diligence, he'd made
an exception in at least one case. So she didn't know
every little detail of her father's life – was she supposed
to? No human being was ever completely known to
another, right? It didn't work that way. There were
varying shades of knowledge and intimacy, even within
the parameters of love.

She looked around for an ashtray. *A man in hiding*.

'Just flick it on the floor,' Linda Straub said. 'Avoid
the papers.'

Andrea forced a weary smile and tapped ash on
the wood floor, changed the subject to something
more tangible. 'Did he ever mention anything about
a will?'

'Not to me he didn't. Maybe with some other
attorney.'

'How can I find out?'

'I can do that for you. No problem.' The lawyer closed her palms round one knee and tilted her body a little way back on her desk and looked thoughtful. 'It's funny you should ask about a will, because I remember once when we were discussing his court case he said something *totally* out of the blue. He told me that if anything ever happened to him, I was to make sure he had a very simple ceremony. No hymn-singing. No wailing and gnashing of teeth. No priests, no church, no eulogies. He didn't want any kind of theatre. That was how he put it.'

'He wasn't big on ceremonies.'

'He didn't say it any kind of morbid way, you understand. I got the feeling he was being a touch flippant. But kinda serious underneath, you know? I didn't think much of it at the time. He sometimes went off at little tangents. Now I halfway wonder . . . uh, this is going to sound silly . . .'

'What do you wonder?' Andrea asked.

'If he had a premonition.'

'You believe in premonitions?'

Linda Straub shrugged. 'I've never experienced one personally.'

Andrea lapsed into silence. The cigarette had smouldered down to the filter, and smelled bitter. A premonition. People claimed to have them, feelings of foreboding, insights into their futures from inscrutable sources. She wondered if such a shadow had fallen across her father's mind. Something that made him sense his own ending. She felt a strange little fury directed toward him at that moment. *Why the fuck did you have to get yourself killed? Why did you leave me with these goddam fragments?* She resented herself for allowing her anger to turn against her father. It wasn't his fault he'd been killed, he wasn't to blame for having been blown to death by a shotgun.

Suddenly she was very tired, fading.

Linda Straub said, 'I liked Dennis, you know. I can't honestly say I ever got any deep insights into him. But I liked him anyway. He had his own kind of charm. Hidden maybe. So you had to dig for it, which made it all the more interesting. I can't believe this thing happened to him.'

'I can't believe it either,' Andrea said, and got up from her chair.

'Where are you staying?'

'The Glamys.'

'Fawlty Towers,' Linda Straub said. 'Elevator still on the fritz?'

'Yeah.'

The attorney smiled. 'I'll get in touch about the will. And if you want some company while you're here, pick up the phone.'

'I appreciate that,' Andrea said.

'Any time.' Linda Straub walked with her to the door. 'You take care.'

Andrea, wondering again about premonitions and anxieties and shadowy recesses in her father's life, stepped out of the attorney's office. A draught blew up the staircase, and she raised the collar of her coat.

chapter Seven

She walked in the direction of Lincoln Plaza, thinking about the fingerprints she'd promised Fuscante. She was in the neighbourhood, she'd do it now. The snow deadened sounds. Traffic struggling past at hearse-like speed seemed to make no noise. The world was leaking sound: she felt as if she'd lost some part of her hearing. And the wind, dear God, was polar and cruel, slashing through her heavy coat.

She climbed the steps of the greystone Police Department building, where a guy in a ski-mask and goggles was working a snow-blower. He wore a big padded jacket and thick mittens. He raised his face and glanced at her as she passed and shrugged as if to say, 'Why the hell do we put up with this crud every goddam winter?'

She went inside. She asked a cop at the desk for Fuscante. The cop, a short man with a Zapata-style moustache and a badge that identified him as *Gomez, V.*, told her Fuscante was out and wouldn't be back for a while.

'He asked me to drop by,' she said. 'He wants my fingerprints. My name's Andrea Malle.'

'Malle?' Gomez said. 'Oh yeah. Sure. He mentioned you might come in. You're the daughter, right?'

She thought, *That's how they know me around here. The daughter. The murdered man's daughter.* If the blizzard lasted for ever and she couldn't get back to Manhattan and was forced to settle here in Horaceville for the rest of her life, she'd always be the murdered man's daughter, never her own identity.

Gomez was solicitous, moving out from behind his desk and guiding her across the floor. 'I'll take care of it,' he said. He led her through a door and into an office, open-space, about twelve desks, telephones ringing, a few cops moving around, laughter, banter. He directed her into a small room away from the hubbub. 'You're new to this, I guess.'

She wondered what he was referring to – having her father murdered or her prints taken. Suddenly she didn't want him to offer any token of commiseration. She didn't want to hear another expression of sympathy from anybody. She'd had them from Fuscante, Father Gladd, Martin at the hotel, Linda Straub. The words were well-intended, but there was a limit to hearing them and a limit to the number of times she could respond with a remark of appreciation or a muted little smile of thank you.

'Now this is no big deal, only take a minute,' Gomez said. He opened a drawer, removed a small box and a sheet of paper. He took the lid off the box. She saw an inkpad.

Gomez winked at her. 'It's a little messy is all. You wanna give me a hand? Left or right, you choose.'

She took off a glove, offered her left hand. He had a gentle touch. He pressed each fingerprint in turn into the inky surface and then on to the appropriate little box marked on the paper. Thumb here, ring-finger here. This, that. He did the same with her right hand. 'Done. You'll want to wash that ink off. There's a toilet over there.'

She went inside the toilet, locked the door, washed her hands, watched a blue-black stream run down the drain. She had an urge to stay inside this tiny room, bolt herself in and never come out, never face the world again, ignore police negotiation teams and shrinks sent to persuade her out of her self-imposed imprisonment.

She sat on the toilet and lowered her head. What made you suffer anxiety, Dennis Malle? Did you have attacks, dizzy spells, palpitations, whatever? What made you drive a hundred miles or more to see a doctor and get a prescription? Why were you so shy of publicity?

What the fuck were you doing in this godforsaken place anyhow? Your woodland strolls, your amateur water-colours, what kind of life were you trying to lead?

She reached inside her coat pocket, took out the passport. Her father's photograph was about seven or eight years old, she figured, taken during that period of his life when he wore a beard: 'I'm tired of all these clean-shaven business types I have to deal with. I'm tried of all those buttoned-down assholes. This is my way of making a statement. Even if it's only a feeble one.' And so he'd grown the beard and stopped wearing a suit and necktie and he'd gone around in blue jeans and T-shirts, and when it became briefly fashionable to go barefoot inside your shoes and sport loose linen jackets, he'd jumped on those things like a man starved of freedom.

Were you really so sick of your work, Dennis Malle? Were you *that* tired of everything you had to retreat to this nowhere corner of the country? Why didn't you travel in your retirement? Why didn't you find something more active to do with your life?

And now you're dead.

And maybe if you hadn't come up here to live you'd still be alive instead of shotgunned behind a goddam pile of fucking logs, for Christ's sake.

The face in the picture looked back at her. The eyes were keen and smart. There was nothing jaded in them. The mouth was firm, with maybe the suggestion of a tricky half-smile, a little secretive — it was difficult to say for sure. The hair was swept back. A few years ago he'd grown it long enough at the back for a ponytail, but then decided he didn't like that look, it was too obviously modish, self-conscious. And somewhere along the way the gradual transformation had taken place from Boss double-breasted linen jackets to a wretched old plaid thing with a quilted lining, and a cap with goddam earflaps.

Earflaps.

She flicked through the pages. So many visas, stamps, dates of entries and departures. Places he'd been he'd never mentioned visiting. Ecuador, Colombia, Latvia, Lithuania.

She plucked tissue out of the dispenser and blew her nose. She was choking up. *This isn't good enough*, she thought. *This is doing nothing. Shut inside this room with the white walls and the air-freshener stink.* She couldn't mope or lock herself away, she wasn't the type. Keep busy. Get out your mental checklist of things to do. Otherwise, you stagnate. Mope.

'You okay in there, Ms Malle?'

'Just fine,' she called out. She crumpled the tissue, dropped it in the trash, then unlocked the door.

Gomez was standing on the other side. 'Anything I can do for you?'

'I don't think so.'

Gomez, who wore a big pistol on his hip, escorted her back to the front door. 'Look at that, willya. Look at that.' He nodded at the wintry scene outside. 'Tell you, makes me long for faraway places.' He drew out the word 'faraway', so that it sounded like 'faaaaha-way'.

'Me too,' she said. She stared into the snowfall and waited for him to tell her to drive carefully. That's what they did in Horaceville. They said, 'Take care, drive carefully, watch how you go.' What would they have to talk about in this place if it wasn't for the ravages of winter?

She pushed the door open.

Gomez said, 'There's a skill to driving in this stuff.'

'Really,' she said.

'Yeah.' He winked and laughed from the back of his throat. 'Stay home in front of a fire.'

I wish.

She went down the steps and along the sidewalk. At the corner of the street she found a payphone and took John Gladd's number out of her coat pocket.

A woman answered. 'Father Gladd's unavailable at the moment.'

'You expect him soon?'

'I'm sure I'll hear from him before too long. Is there a message?'

'Tell him Andrea Malle called. Tell him I'm going out to the house now and ask him if he'll meet me there.'

'I will,' the woman replied.

chapter *Eight*

It took her an hour to drive the eight
miles to her father's house, sixty minutes stuck in
the wake of a snow-plough working the blacktop. The
big mechanical scoop banked great piles of snow along
the edges of the road. She didn't mind slow progress.
She even enjoyed the idea of the plough as some kind
of company on this lonely road. She was in no hurry
to reach her destination. At the back of her mind was
the possibility that when she got to the house she'd be
snowed in for the night.

She didn't want to be imprisoned out there.

She was tempted to turn back and retreat to the
Glamys, but she thought, no, she'd come this far,
she couldn't sit in her hotel room and just watch the
dreary lake. Besides, she assumed Gladd would get her
message and meet her at the house. She even hoped he
might be there before her, but when she turned into

the driveway the only vehicle parked outside was the Cherokee.

And no sign of any cop presence, either. Fuscante had used the expression 'rotating basis', so maybe one cop had just left and another was due to arrive. Or maybe snow had caused delays. Whatever.

A desolate vista, she thought. This glacial world. She couldn't imagine anybody coming out in this weather to gawk at a homicide scene. You'd have to be a serious murder-freak to make such a trip. She sat in her car for a time. The siege of winter had diminished the house. It was frail and abandoned, roof piled under, elaborate icicles hanging from the small porch.

She realized she had another task at some point in the future: she'd have to put this property on the market. There was no way in the world she'd keep it. The location wasn't altogether desirable – unless you wanted to be perched on the edge of gloomy woods two miles away from your closest neighbour – three small rooms, a rudimentary bathroom, a couple of acres. A summer house was all this place was good for. Not a permanent dwelling, just somewhere you could escape the city for a month or so every year.

And yet he'd managed to live here for almost two years, almost eight seasons.

Tape was strung across the front door, an orange strip stencilled with HPD and CRIME SCENE. UNAUTHORIZED ENTRY FORBIDDEN. She got out of her car and walked up on to the porch, ducked under the tape. She took the key from her pocket, unlocked the door. She was about to go inside – reluctant, heart going a little too fast, all this solitude unnerving her – when she heard a car crunch into the driveway. It was a grey Ford with big ribbed snow tyres. Gladd emerged from it, and she

realized she was pleased to see him. Somebody to keep
her company inside the haunted house. Another human
presence.

Beating his hands together, he picked his way carefully through the snow. His pink cheeks glistened. She
thought of Christmas tree ornaments. 'I came as fast I
could,' he said. He climbed the three steps to the porch,
clutching the handrail.

'I'm thankful you're here,' she said.

He waved her gratitude away with a gloved hand.
She stepped inside the house and the priest, knocking
snow from his rubber boots against the door-jamb,
followed.

'Brrrr,' he said. 'This place needs heat.' He busied
himself with sticks and the old newspapers her father
had twisted for kindling.

She looked at the desk, the wire tray filled with
papers. She felt stalled suddenly, her inner clockwork
silenced and still. *It's too much too soon. I shouldn't have
come here. I should have waited another day, longer. But
maybe this is the best way to deal with the horror. Your
defence mechanism.*

Gladd piled sticks and newspapers in the grate,
then applied a match. Smoke and sparks, little licks
of flame. He added a couple of small logs he took
from a brass bucket at the side of the fireplace. He
angled them in a pyre-like formation. 'There's an art
to building a good fire. You have to get the architecture
just so.'

She slumped into the chair at the desk. Saw her
breath hang in clouds on the air. Where to start?
Fuscante or his people would have gone through the
drawers of the desk already. Procedure. Dust for prints,
then search – for a hint, a tell-tale mark, anything that

might be useful. And they'd found nothing except an uninformative diary and a gun.

She opened the middle drawer of the desk. Paper-clips, a bunch of Bic pens, rubber bands, a pack of envelopes, a scratch-pad still wrapped in cellophane. Nothing of interest here. She opened the side drawers. One was filled with manila folders. The other contained the desiccated corpse of a small mouse, around which mould had formed. Abandoned spiderwebs clung to the pale blue fuzz. She shut this drawer quickly, hauled the folders out of the other drawer, placed them on the desk.

'There. I think we're in business.' Gladd was gazing into the flames. He spread his hands for warmth. Logs hissed, released gases. 'It's sad. A few times I've had the task of going through the personal papers and belongings of my parishioners – usually old people who died alone and no relatives could be found. I never like doing it. I always feel like an intruder. I'm sure you feel the same.'

She wasn't sure what she felt. She was operating on automatic pilot, trying not to think, not to feel. Each folder had been marked with a black felt pen. BNK. INS. AUTO. INVEST. HOUSE. She opened them one at a time.

She found a life-insurance policy issued by Standard Assurance of Ohio in the amount of $500,000. She turned more pages, saw that she was named as benefici-ary. A half-million dollars. Death money. Half a million bucks for her father's life. Sudden wealth for her, big deal: it was a pathetic equation. As compensation for the loss of his life, no sum of money could ever have been appropriate. She imagined her father setting this policy up, talking to the broker, spelling out his daughter's name, making sure the guy got it down properly: Malle, double l. She noticed he'd given his own name as D. J. Malle. Dennis Judge Malle. He never used that middle name, because he'd always said it was dumb, an old family name his mother had imposed on him. Maybe he kept it only for official documents.

A sadness overcame her. *What does it take to deal with the fact that he's gone?*

She set the policy aside, found another issued by an organization called Sun Life Care Inc. A health-insurance policy, a list of benefits. She didn't read it. She opened the folder marked AUTO, which contained insurance documents for the Cherokee. She didn't bother to read these either. The folder inscribed BNK held a bunch of financial statements, checking-account, savings. She glanced at these, then looked inside the folder on which her father had written INVEST, where she found a number of share certificates, and more financial statements, all of them in the name of D. J. Malle.

Gladd said, 'It looks like he was a little better organized than we gave him any credit for.'

'I guess so,' she said.

'His files appear quite tidy, in fact.' Gladd poked the fire. Snow melted on his hair, the collar and shoulders of his coat. 'Would you like some tea? Heat you up a little.'

'I'll make it,' she said.

'No, you stay right where you are.' He went into the kitchen. She heard him fill a kettle with water. She turned her attention back to the folders, opened the one marked HOUSE. Home insurance. Deeds to the property. She gazed at them without much interest. There was also a map of the property and a couple of letters from a law firm called McMullen, Shren & Barque of Albany confirming details of the purchase. D. J. Malle had bought the house and land from somebody called Jeremiah Ealing for the sum of $42,500 in 1990.

1990, she thought. What was odd about that?

He'd still been running his business then. He hadn't sold MalCon until the summer of 1996. He hadn't even mentioned the idea to her until the spring of that year. He'd been in Manhattan, taken her out to dinner at an Indian place on West 57th, discussed the downward trend of her marriage to Lionel – 'Dump him,' her father had advised. 'He's an unworthy shit' – and then during coffee he'd said, 'Incidentally, I'm calling it quits. I'm taking myself out of the business loop.' The news didn't entirely surprise her. She remembered asking him what he planned to do with his time, and he'd been unusually vague. 'Maybe I'll play for a while,' words to that effect. 'I've worked too hard too long.'

And then he'd come up here to a place he hadn't ever *mentioned*. A place he'd bought six years *before* he announced his retirement. Had he been planning to retire here all along? Why hadn't he told her about this house back then? So many things he'd left unsaid. So many things, tiny in themselves, but they added up to a lack of candour on his part . . .

Why didn't you confide in me? You locked me out. Kept me away from certain aspects of your life. And I don't know why.

She reached for the wire basket. Bills, an invoice from Statler Bros of Horaceville for a lube job on the Cherokee, junk mail, a seed catalogue, a mailer from L. L. Bean. She sifted through all these wearily, then got up and walked to the fire and leaned close to the flames. She heard the electric kettle whistle and the sound of Gladd moving cups around.

He appeared in the kitchen doorway. 'Real tea or herbal?'

'Real's fine.'

'There's no milk.'

She said it didn't matter.

'Sugar?'

She shook her head. Gladd came in carrying two cups in his leather-gloved hands. He sat in the armchair to the side of the fireplace.

She tasted the tea. 'How well did you really *know* my father?'

'Oh boy. That's a tough one. Our only substantial topic of conversation was religion – and you, of course. He talked about you. Nothing very specific. Conversational crumbs. He never talked about himself, never discussed personal details of his past. Your mother, for example. He never told me if he was divorced from her or if she'd died or what had become of her.'

She remembered she needed to call her mother. She'd been postponing it. She couldn't keep pushing the prospect away.

Gladd blew on the surface of his tea. 'Why do you ask?'

'Because I keep coming across stuff that's new to me,' she answered. She mentioned the house he'd bought quietly years ago. She told him about the Fluoxene, the car accident, the prowler.

Gladd sipped his tea, then said, 'I didn't know about the drugs. He certainly never struck me as a man who had bouts of anxiety. Quite the opposite. And he didn't say anything about an accident. As for a prowler, I don't remember him ever talking about that. I thought of us as friends, but never *intimate*. He didn't confide in me. And I wouldn't have dreamed of bringing any of my personal problems to him. It wasn't that kind of relationship.'

'How did you meet?'

'Pure chance. I was out in the woods with some of my parishioners last summer. There's a small group of elderly people in my church who collect wild flowers they dry and arrange – quite attractively, I have to say – and then sell for charity at our annual fund-raising function.' He paused and looked into the fire in the manner of a man struck by a fond memory. 'Your father was out walking. We met. We talked. He invited me to visit his home next time I was in the vicinity.'

'And that's it.'

'That's the story,' Gladd said. 'I took him at his word. I dropped in for the first time a couple of weeks later. We took it from there.'

She sat motionless for a time. 'I'll keep his water-colours, and maybe some odds and ends of a personal nature. I don't know yet. The mandolins . . .' She looked at them hanging on the wall. She'd always thought this a peculiar hobby, given the fact her father had been tone-deaf. '*They're pretty to look at*,' he'd said. '*There's some intricate woodwork, some fine pearl inlays.*' 'I might keep them. I might auction them. I don't know.'

Gladd said, 'Don't make decisions you may regret later. Take your time.'

She nodded as if she agreed, but she didn't want to take much time over any of this, she wanted to get it done, walk away from this house, away from the echoes and the ghosts, and begin the process of healing, of forgetting how she'd discovered her father.

If amnesia was possible. The image might assault her in dreams for the rest of her life.

She scanned the surface of the desk. 'It's funny. There's no address book. No Rolodex. No list of phone numbers. I guess there weren't many people he ever needed to call.'

She looked at his itemized phone bill. No long-distance calls except for a couple he'd made to her. The persistent ones: *I need your company. Please come up*. She put the phone bill back in the envelope. 'Did he tell you I was coming to visit?'

Gladd said, 'No, he didn't. I hadn't seen him for about three weeks.'

'I keep getting this feeling . . .' It was vague, whatever it was, and she groped for the correct words. 'It was important to him that I make the trip. He wanted to see me about something.'

'And you don't know what?'

'No.'

'Perhaps he had something he needed to say to you. Some kind of father–daughter thing.'

'I won't ever know that now, will I?'

Gladd tossed another log on the flames. He dusted his gloved hands together, then picked up his tea. She watched him for a moment, this unlikely acquaintance of her father. The fluffed-up hair, the mound of the cheeks, the benign features. She imagined Dennis Malle and the priest arguing about God in this very room. And then she thought about the diary, the dry factual entries: her father had never written anything about Gladd. He'd never written: *The priest came and we argued*. But there hadn't been anything of a personal nature in any of the scant entries. So why had he kept the diary in the first place?

A diary that yielded nothing, a gun under his bed . . .

Time to phone Meg. No more delays. Her address book was in her purse out in the car. She stepped outside, hugged herself in the hope of a little warmth, went to her car, retrieved the purse. She hurried back indoors. Gladd had taken the cups into the kitchen. She heard the sound of water running.

She turned the pages of her address book to Meg's number. She dialled, listened to the ringing tone, half expected the answering-machine, half *hoped* she wouldn't get through.

But she did.

'It's me. Andrea.'

'Andrea? Not my daughter Andrea by any chance?'

'You're being sarcastic,' Andrea said.

'Me? I'm never sarcastic. Caustic, sure. I do caustic. Sarcastic's beneath me.'

'It's not the time, Mother.'

'Goddam, you phone what, twice a year in a good year, and you expect me to be bowled over with appreciation?'

'Not now,' Andrea said.

'Oh hey hey, you're in *serious* mode. You getting married again? You pregnant or something? Or is this the obligatory Christmas call?'

'It's Dad.'

'Your father the hermit? The latter-day bohemian? Our very own Thoreau? My. What's he been up to now? What big things are happening at Walden Pond?'

Andrea heard herself blurt out the story exactly the way she'd done with Patrick, running her words together, finding it impossible to create a coherent narrative. All she had were impressions in no particular sequence.

Her mother said, 'Oh God. Oh my God.'

Don Ryman's voice was audible in the background. 'What is it, honey?'

'I just don't believe it, I *can't* believe it. A shotgun? You did say a shotgun?'

'Honey, what's the matter?'

A whispered conversation took place between Meg and her husband. Andrea heard Don say, 'Jesus Christ! I'll be damned.'

Meg asked, 'Where the hell are you, Andrea?'

'A place called Horaceville.'

'And where exactly is that anyhow?'

'Upstate. About two hundred miles from the city.'

'Where have they taken the . . . you know?'

'The morgue, Mother.'

'The morgue. God. I don't want to *think* about him lying in the morgue. I don't want to *picture* that. Have the police made an arrest?'

'No.'

'I'm coming up there toot sweet. I'm on the next flight.'

Don said, 'Yeah, damn right we're on the next flight.'

'There's a storm, Mother. A blizzard. The airports are closed.'

Meg never allowed forces of nature to interfere with her arrangements. Tropical storms were trifles, hurricanes a mere inconvenience, blizzards a matter for sheer indifference. She sailed through the world like some smooth gilded ship fuelled by an energy source only she could tap. 'Don's already on to his secretary about making flight arrangements, so we ought to get into New York some time this afternoon, maybe early evening, then we'll fly up to this place, what is it, Henrysville, did you say?'

'Horaceville. Mother, listen to me, the airports are shut. And even if they weren't, there's no airport in Horaceville. Albany's about the closest.'

'Okay, we'll go to Albany, Don can arrange some kind of limo to Horaceville.'

'I'm not getting through to you, Mother.' She felt weary all at once. She didn't have the energy to deal with Meg.

'Where are you staying? A hotel or what?'

Andrea told her the name of the hotel. She heard Meg call it out to Don Ryman. Somewhere in the distance, Don Ryman said, 'Okay, honey, I got it, the Glamys Lake, fine, fine.'

Andrea said, 'Look, why don't you call me back at the hotel when you've made arrangements. Okay?'

'I can't believe this,' Meg said. 'He was always so goddam *indestructible*. And now you're telling me some bastard with a shotgun . . .'

'Call me later, Mother.'

'I never stopped caring about the man, you know that? I know we fell apart as a couple, but that doesn't mean I stopped *caring* about him. I want you to understand that, Andrea.'

'I understand.'

'I don't think you do. I really don't think you do, Andrea. I always had the feeling you blamed me.'

'Mother, please. I'm hanging up. We'll talk later.' She put the phone down. She walked into the kitchen. She needed water. Meg jangled her, she *always* jangled her. She filled a glass at the sink, drank. The water was ice-cold. She found herself looking through the window at the tarpaulin. *A man approaches with a shotgun and blasts away. The noise roars and echoes around the trees.*

The nearest neighbour is two miles distant and probably hears nothing.

She gazed at the thick white woods. Impenetrable and secretive.

The killer goes between the trees. A chopper rises into the sky. And then . . . Then what?

Where was Gladd? she wondered. He'd been in the kitchen before, but now he wasn't. She walked back into the front room. She heard the toilet being flushed. She moved to the bedroom door, looked down the short, dim passageway to the bathroom.

Gladd came out and said, 'I gather that was your mother?'

'She's planning to come up from Florida immediately. She does *everything* immediately.'

'It's not going to be that simple.'

'Meg goes from point A to point B and she doesn't give a damn what obstacles might be in the way.'

'She's probably not thinking too clearly in the circumstances,' Gladd said. He walked to the door of the bedroom and looked inside. 'I was never in this room.'

She gazed at her father's clothing, the unmade bed.

Gladd walked into the room. He studied the water-colours on the wall, his expression thoughtful. 'He had a nice soft touch,' he said. 'Good sense of composition and light.' He sighed and turned to her. 'The police don't have any idea who was responsible for your father's death?'

'Not yet,' she said.

'You know, it might have been a stranger with robbery in mind. I hear stories about people who go around checking out isolated houses because they think they're easy game. They watch a place, they learn the occupant lives alone, then they strike. Maybe your father fought back.'

She'd gone through similar conjecture with Fuscante, and she didn't want to go over the same terrain again.

Gladd patted her arm. 'They'll find the killer. I'm sure they will. It's only a matter of time.'

She noticed that the closet was open: all her father's shirts and jackets were visible on hangers. She'd have to sort through the clothes, she thought. She dreaded the task. She had a sudden urge to get herself and Gladd out of this room and seal it the way tombs were sealed, and do the same thing with the whole house—

The telephone rang. The sound was unexpected, harsh. She could only think it was Fuscante, or her mother calling back, but she couldn't imagine why Meg would have the phone number. Her mother and father didn't keep in touch – as far as she knew. She walked to the desk, picked up the handset.

Before she could say anything, a man asked, 'Dennis?'

'No, this is Andrea,' she said.

'Andrea?'

She realized she recognized this caller. '*Stan*? Stan Thorogood?'

Stan Thorogood coughed, a deep unhealthy sound. 'I don't have time to talk with you, kid. Just get me Dennis. I need to talk with Dennis.'

She said nothing for a moment. She hadn't spoken to Stan in three or four years, but he'd always been friendly, always cheerful. She'd always liked him. This wasn't the usual Stan, not even remotely. She listened to the strange way he breathed, as if he were choking. And there was background noise, traffic, somebody almost out of range saying, '*I asked for a cherry Coke and this ain't it.*' He had to be calling from a payphone.

'Stan, is something wrong with you?'

'Just get him,' he said. 'Jesus *Christ*, how many times do I have to ask?'

'I can't get him, Stan.'

'Why? Is he out? When's he due back?'

She told him. Her father wasn't coming back.

Stan Thorogood said, 'Aw, Jesus Christ, no. He was secure there, he was safe, he always claimed—' and hung up before she could ask him what he was talking about.

chapter Nine

She took all her father's mail and folders back to the hotel. She went directly to her room and, dropping everything on the floor beside the bed, lay down. She smoked a cigarette, pondered Stan Thorogood's call, the abrupt termination. She couldn't make sense of what he'd said, nor the manner in which he'd said it.

She rose, walked up and down, looked at the lake. The snow had eased enough for her to see the grey expanse of water and the frozen white houses on the far shore. It was all too gloomy, too dead, to resemble any Christmas-card idyll. She thought, *I want to go home. Shake this glum town out of my system and leave.*

What had Stan actually said? 'He was secure there, he was safe.'

She pressed her forehead against the pane. Secure and safe from what? What did that mean?

'. . . he always claimed—' Then he'd hung up, leaving the sentence unfinished.

What was Stan talking about? And the way he'd sounded, unhealthy, rude, urgent, panicky even, nothing like the man she remembered as her father's long-time partner in MalCon. 'Stan's a quiet genius,' her father had once said. 'You explain the problem and give him the specs and in a couple of hours he's worked out a whole security system right down to the dimensions of the last deadbolt, the last little electronic circuit.'

She'd call Stan back, ask for an explanation. Not now. She was draggy, whatever energy she'd been running on depleted. The sleeping-pills hadn't been such a terrific notion. She couldn't assemble her thoughts in any working order. She was slipping, giving in to emotions she'd been holding back, and a sudden onslaught of loneliness was one of them.

She turned from the window. She couldn't just yield to fatigue and loneliness. That was too easy. Don't succumb. She'd phone Stan immediately. She took her address book from her purse and found his phone number in Pleasantville. She dialled. A recorded voice said, 'The number you have called is no longer in service. If you think you have dialled in error, please hang up and try again.' She dialled a second time, got the message again. Okay, simple, he'd changed his number for some reason. She called Directory Assistance, gave the operator the name and address, waited.

'I'm sorry, caller. I have no listing for that name.'

'Could it be unlisted?' she asked.

'No, there's no listing at all.'

'Nowhere?'

'Not in the Pleasantville area. I'm showing a Stanley Thorogood in Buffalo. Another in Oswego.'

'Let me have those please.' She wrote down the two numbers, thinking Stan must have moved. And then she remembered the impression she'd had that he'd been calling from a payphone – maybe he'd given up his phone when he'd retired. Why, though? That made no sense. She'd call the two numbers anyhow.

She tried the one in Oswego first and found herself talking to a grumpy young woman with a serious head-cold who told her that Stanley Thorogood was her husband and worked with the local power company and what business was it of a total stranger to ask questions anyhow. Andrea thanked her and hung up. Buffalo next. The man who answered called himself Stan Thorogood, but he didn't sound anything like her father's former partner. His voice was young and breezy, suffused with confidence.

So where did that leave her? More to the point, where did it leave Stan?

Think. He'd moved from his home in Pleasantville. He'd retired and, like her father, needed a change of life, of scenery. Where in this vast continent had he gone? She sat on the edge of the bed. Smoked. Thought. *This habit's got to stop. Put it on your checklist.*

She set the question of Stan's whereabouts aside, and although she had a feeling she was missing something, some vague memory of him she'd misplaced, she picked up her father's folders and leafed through them, looked at his bank accounts. He had $2,307 in one checking account, $4,568 in another. The most recent statements indicated very little checking activity: $35.90 to Jensen's Liquor, $18.28 to Horaceville Food Mart, $200 cash. In his savings account he had the sum of $193,565.

He'd told her he'd sold MalCon for something in

the region of $2 million, which he'd presumably shared
with Stan – so where had he deposited his $1 million or
what was left of it after tax? She searched through his
investments folder. Five hundred thousand dollars had
been placed in an entity called Barlow Park Properties,
which appeared to own a number of rental properties
across the country. Santa Fe, San Antonio, Cleveland.
A further $230,000 in a company named Green River
Enterprises, which owned trailer-parks in Alabama
and Arkansas. She looked at the Green River fiscal
statement: *The company is anticipating at least 85%
occupancy in the coming year. Continued expansion is
predicted given favorable market conditions.*

These had the look of safe investments paying a
regular return of about 5 per cent per annum. Low-risk,
low-yield. He'd been conservative with his money. He
hadn't wanted to speculate. No junk bonds, no precious
metals, just good old-fashioned bricks and mortar,
rentals. Safe and certain. Dull and predictable. She'd
have guessed he would have been more adventurous
with his money, maybe even a little cavalier with some
of it – but no. Dennis Malle had settled into a humdrum
existence in a lonely place. The quiet investor. The
amateur painter. The solitary walker in the woods.

A man growing old. But destined never to get there.

She checked his mail for any sign of credit-card statements, but found none. In the old days, he'd carried Diner's Club, a Platinum Amex, Gold Mastercards. He'd
obviously given them up too. Maybe they reminded
him of the life he no longer wanted to lead.

She remembered now. Stan and her father had had
a place where they retreated when they were brainstorming, when they had a deadline to meet sub-
mitting tenders for security projects and were burning

the midnight oil and didn't want to be disturbed.
Her father had taken her there once when she was
about twelve. She couldn't recall why, only that it
was intended as some kind of treat. He was giving her
a little insight into his work, sharing a secret aspect
of his life with her. She couldn't remember the exact
location of the place, just that they'd driven through
Cooperstown and her father had pointed out to her
the Baseball Hall of Fame. The rest of the recollection
was fuzzy.

But why should she imagine Stan was *there*? It was
a rundown old farmhouse with rotting floorboards
and tiles hanging from the roof and bees buzzing
around impenetrable thickets of wild flowers outside the
kitchen door. No telephone, no plumbing, no amenities,
electricity supplied by a generator, a great throbbing
device situated out back somewhere. Only one room
was functional, and she recalled it as a place cluttered
with notebooks and papers strewn across a plain wood
table. 'This is the brain of MalCon,' her father had said.
'This is where it all happens. Forget that ritzy office on
Thirty-second. This is the true soul of MalCon.' Her
memory was of a dump of a place with nothing very
interesting actually happening, and so – bored, a little
disappointed because she'd been expecting something
intriguing – she'd spent the afternoon chasing an undo-
mesticated cat through long stalks of grass and weeds.
She remembered something else she hadn't thought
about in a long time, an abandoned windmill that had
obviously caught fire years ago, a sad black stump of a
thing, arms charred and broken, birds nesting in what
slats remained of the roof. Creepy, she'd thought.

Stan wouldn't have had any reason for keeping that
old house after MalCon had been sold. Unless he sought

isolation too. Unless he wanted to live a life similar
to her father's. She remembered Stan as an outgoing
man, fond of little conjuring tricks he'd first shown
her when she was a child, pulling pennies out of her
ears, making small objects vanish in front of her eyes.
Every time she encountered him he'd still perform one
of his routines for her, and it didn't matter a damn to
him that she could see through the trickery, that the
sleight-of-hand which had so impressed her as a kid
was amateur and obvious. It was a ritual between them.
The last time she'd seen him – in the company of her
father on New Year's Eve 1993 or '94 at a restaurant
on the Upper West Side – he'd performed a stunt with
her wristwatch, pretending to crush it under a napkin
with the base of a wine-bottle. 'Hey presto! You think
your fancy Rolex is smashed, right? *No way*,' and he'd
produced the watch, intact, from under the table. And
she'd laughed because the ritual was just a dumb,
harmless thing they shared.

She closed the folder.

He always claimed— Why hadn't Stan finished his
sentence?

Because he hadn't wanted to. Because he couldn't.

She remembered what she'd said to Linda Straub
about her father: 'You make him sound like a man
in hiding.' Did this apply equally to Stan? After the
sale of MalCon, had both men decided to retreat to
separate isolations? It didn't make sense. It was a
line of speculation going nowhere. Two friends build
a successful company. They spend a long time doing it.
Then they sell out. Go into seclusion. One is murdered,
the other makes a manic phone call because he has a
message that's too late to deliver.

She was restless, needed to get out this room. She

was also hungry and light-headed and her mind was racing. She'd go and see if there was any food available, something light and preferably bland, a sandwich to provide fuel. She couldn't remember when she'd last eaten anything. She walked downstairs – there was nobody at the desk – and headed toward the Lake Lounge. The big room was still empty and bleak. The counter was unattended. She'd have to go through the rigmarole of calling out for service, and presumably the dour woman would emerge from the back with a look of impatience.

'Miss Malle?'

She turned. She hadn't heard the man come into the room. He was massive, big-bearded, wore an old-fashioned beige duffel-coat and carried a battered leather briefcase. Her general impression was of a shambles of a man, paper sticking from coat pockets, clasp of the briefcase undone, ungainly movements. He approached her, held out one hand, which she took. For such a big man his handshake was limp and slack.

'Wallace. George Wallace. County coroner. No relation to the former governor of Alabama and hapless presidential aspirant,' he said. 'Shall we sit?'

chapter *Ten*

*W*allace slapped his briefcase down on a table and sat. His cheeks were a road-map of small broken red veins and he had copious nasal hair. Andrea's main impression was of hair flowering everywhere – the beard, the nostrils, the great shrubs of eyebrows, little wires growing from his earlobes, thick grey-black streaks falling almost to his shoulders. He was somewhere in his mid-forties, she guessed, and his appearance suggested someone who has never graduated from college, the perpetual student, a man in pursuit of one academic degree after another, absent-minded and sloppy, his brain focused on arcane matters.

'You shouldn't smoke,' he said. 'The stats are horrendous.'

'I know I shouldn't.'

'I'm being very serious. I've seen lungs that would strike the fear of death into you.'

'One day I'll quit,' she said.

Wallace said, 'What's wrong with today?'

'It's not the time,' she said.

Wallace sighed. 'Smokers procrastinate like no other class of people. But I'm not here to scold. I'm sorry about your father.'

'I understand you knew him.'

'A little.'

'You prescribed Fluoxene for him.'

Wallace fidgeted with one of the wooden toggles of his duffel-coat. Andrea realized she hadn't seen a coat like that in years.

He said, 'I had a message from Linda Straub. She said you were concerned about the fact your father was on medication.'

'More like surprised,' she said.

'And because I was in Horaceville on official business, I thought I'd drop in and see if I can clear up any questions you might have.'

Coroner's business, she thought. Maybe her father's body. She pushed the image away.

'The drugs were for anxiety, I believe,' she said.

'Right. Fluoxene's used in the management of anxiety disorders.'

'And that's what my father had – an anxiety disorder?'

'He came to me saying he was insomniac, fretful, he had some nervous problems. I prescribed what I thought was best, given the symptoms he talked about.'

'Was he specific about these . . . nervous problems?'

'No, he wasn't. I'm not a psychiatrist, Miss Malle. I'm not trained to scythe my way through the jungles of people's minds. An educated guess? I'd say he'd come to a stage in his life where he was going through a kind of malaise – what was my life all about? What did I achieve? what did I contribute? is this all there is? That kind of thing. It's not uncommon. A man closer to the end of his life than the beginning is sometimes plagued with a variety of doubts and often these lead to depression, anxiety . . .' Wallace wafted the smoke from her cigarette away, then tapped his fingers on the table with displeasure.

She looked at Wallace for a time. He had eyes the colour of the lake outside the hotel. Despite the appearance he gave of disorder, she suspected he was sharp and insightful. She stubbed out her cigarette in an ashtray. 'Why did he choose you as his physician?'

'You ask that question as if you've heard a horrible rumour that I have a bad reputation, I do illegal abortions and write scripts for junkies.'

She smiled. 'That's not what I meant. I'm curious why he didn't see a physician in Horaceville, that's all.'

'Why did he travel all the way to Kayserport just to see me?' Wallace raised one of his big, fibrous eyebrows. 'I happen to own some land adjoining his property. I go out there every now and again, because for years I've had a half-assed notion I might build a house on that plot one day. I met your father by chance and we talked a little, and I guess when he needed a physician he decided to call me because we'd become slightly acquainted. I don't run a full-time practice. A handful of longtime patients, that's all, old reliables who for some unknown reason trust me implicitly. And I'm not out there beating the bushes for new clients. Quite the opposite. But I agreed to see him. I was being neighbourly, you might say.'

'Did you prescribe regularly? Or just one time?'

'He had a couple of refills, I remember.'

'Was he . . . improving?'

Wallace shrugged. 'Hard to say, really. He had his ups and downs. Don't we all?'

She played with her cigarette pack. 'Here's what bothers me. I never detected any depression in him. Never any anxiety. Absolutely nothing like that. So what was he doing when I came to visit? Putting on a bold face? Hiding his feelings? Playing games to mislead me?'

'Maybe you only saw him on his good days,' Wallace said. 'Or maybe you had a positive effect on him, and your presence raised his spirits. I could understand that.'

'Are you involved in my father's . . .' She wasn't sure what the word was. Case? Death? 'Corpse' was what she was looking for, but she couldn't bring herself to say the word.

Wallace nodded. 'Yes, I'm involved. It's my job.'

She imagined Wallace standing over a stainless-steel slab on which the body of her father lay. She saw him examine the remains of Dennis Malle under a hard, merciless light. Cold white flesh. Blood dried on the skin. Nothing left of the face. *Compile your official notes, Dr Wallace, sign the cause-of-death certificate, gunshot wounds, file it away. And life goes on. And next week, next month, whenever, there's always another corpse to be dissected, organs weighed, traumatic injuries to be detailed. And death goes on.*

She placed a cigarette in her mouth, didn't light it.

'Abstinence,' Wallace said. 'Every time you want to smoke, the trick is really simple. Don't apply a flame.'

'I'll keep that in mind,' she said.

'Do you have any other questions?'

'I don't think so.'

Wallace pushed his chair back. 'Again, I'm sorry about your father.'

She wasn't listening.

'I want his ring,' she said.

'Ring?'

'He wore a ring. I'd like to have it. For sentimental reasons. It belonged to his father. It's been in the family a long time and it's important to me. He always said I could have it one day.'

He stood up. 'Of course. I'll make sure you get it.'

chapter *Eleven*

She ate a ham sandwich and then went up to her room and slept for an hour. She dreamed she was inside her father's house sifting through the clothes in his closet, and each item was sodden with blood that ran down her fingers, then slid across her hands to her wrists. Wallace was also in the dream, standing just behind her in the doorway, a shrouded presence who kept saying, 'I can't help you, I can't help you.'

She woke dry-mouthed at 4.30 and the sky was black and for a second she wondered if it was p.m. or a.m. She sat upright in the dark room and looked at the red digital numbers on the bedside radio, saw that it was p.m., then she went into the bathroom and filled a glass with water. She drank it quickly, examined her pale, sleep-puffed face in the mirror, ran fingers through her hair, which looked dull and unhealthy. She stripped, showered quickly, dried her hair, then rummaged through her bag for fresh clothes, settled on a pair of black jeans and a black cashmere sweater. She thought about the fading dream, how she'd been going through her father's shirts and jackets and the blood streaming across her skin.

Her telephone rang. She went back into the bedroom to answer.

Meg said, 'We'll be in New York tomorrow. Don's got us on a flight to JFK. It seems they've managed to get a couple of runways operating.'

'How will you get up to Horaceville?'

'We'll worry about that when we get to New York. Don says that if they've cleared a few runways at JFK they'll probably do the same thing at Albany. If they don't, then we'll arrange to drive up.'

'Assuming the Interstate is passable.'

'They can't just leave the Interstate buried, can they? If they haven't dug it out, we'll think of something else. Don's a genius at arranging transportation.'

Andrea couldn't imagine what this 'something else' might be. A magic carpet? Even Don the fixer couldn't arrange that.

Meg said, 'I'll phone you from JFK. How are you doing? How are you bearing up?'

'So-so. I've been going through Dad's papers.'

'He wasn't very good with his records, as I recall.'

'That's what I always thought. But these seem quite well organized.'

'I'm surprised,' Meg said. 'Then again, he was always full of surprises. Poor man. Poor poor man . . .' She paused, but before Andrea could ask what she meant about surprises, she went on to say, 'Just keep your head above water, dear. Don't sink. I'll be there before you know it. Now tell me. What are the police doing?'

'They don't have any suspects. They don't have a motive.' She wondered what Fuscante was doing. She hadn't heard from him since first thing in the morning.

'So this is just some random act of violence? Is that their official line?'

'There isn't an official line, mother.'

'Don knows a very good private detective in Albany—'

'Tell Don the police are handling it, Mother. I don't think they'd take it very well if you dragged some private eye into the situation.'

'I can honestly say I don't give a damn how they'd take it. If they don't make progress quickly, let's give them some goddam competition.'

'It's only been twenty-four hours, Mother.'

'And crimes of murder go cold very fast, Andrea.'

Whatever you say, Meg. You're the expert in homicides all of a sudden. 'Call me from New York, Mother. And have a safe flight.'

'Take care of yourself.'

'Wait. One last thing. Do you know how I can contact Stan Thorogood?'

'Old Thorobad? There's a blast from the past. The last I heard he was on an ocean cruise of the Far East or something. That was a few years back, maybe longer. But we didn't keep in touch. We never really had much in common apart from your father.'

Andrea said, 'Thanks anyway, Mother.' She added a goodbye and put down the handset. She picked it up again almost at once and dialled Patrick's number. No reply. She wondered where he'd gone. He sometimes took long, contemplative walks when the work wasn't flowing the way he liked. She imagined him strolling through snow in the Village and maybe stopping for espresso or rummaging the stacks in some used-book store downtown or wandering the fluorescent aisles of a video rental place.

She couldn't stand another minute in this room on her own. It was confining, stuffy. She put on her overcoat and scarf and her knee-length brown leather boots and went downstairs, walked out of the hotel with no particular destination in mind.

Lamps lit the steps. Although no fresh snow was falling, the air was bitter and stinging. Before long the night would freeze, creating a hard carapace of ice. She didn't see how her mother and Don would be able to drive up here from the city tomorrow. The Interstate was certain to be slick and treacherous, unless there was a sudden thaw. But thaw brought other problems – slush, slicks, hazardous road conditions.

'Going out?'

She turned. Martin, looking bloated inside a fur-lined parka, appeared in the doorway. He came down the steps and, like some overweight animal sensing prey, peered out into the darkness and sniffed. 'I guess you're going a little stir-crazy in that room.'

'Something like that.' She remembered the dream again. Her father's clothes. The dread she'd felt standing in his room and looking at the closet and thinking she'd have to go through his garments, and now it occurred to her that there was a way round this prospect, one so obvious she wondered why she hadn't thought of it before. 'You know St Peter's Church?'

'Sure I do.'

'How do I get there?'

'You head towards Horaceville, but before you hit the main drag you'll see a sign for the church. Follow that sign. You'll go a couple of blocks down a

street called Broad, and the church is on your left.
You can't miss it.' He looked at her with a serious expression. 'Sometimes religion's the only thing
you can turn to when things are bleak, and you're
feeling bad about life in general . . . I have those
moments myself. I feel this urge to get on my knees
and pray.'

She didn't say she had no intention of praying.
Martin's face had taken on a slightly beatific look and
she had the feeling she'd disappoint him if she said she
was only going to drop in on Father Gladd and see if he
could arrange to dispose of her father's clothes, perhaps
give them to some charity he favoured.

Martin said, 'Light a candle for your father. Do that
on my behalf, if you don't mind.'

'I will, Martin.'

'Father Gladd lives right next door to the church, by
the way. So if you don't find him inside St Peter's, just
go to the house. He's always home.'

She thanked him, walked to her car. She drove in
the direction of town, keeping an eye open for the sign.
Maybe John Gladd wouldn't know what to do with
the clothes, but this was unlikely: priests were used
to accepting charitable donations. They always knew
of needy causes. It was passing the buck, she realized
that, but it would spare her a task she didn't have the
heart for.

She passed under orange street-lamps: the world
glistened and sparkled around her. The road was empty,
eerie. She found a snow-streaked sign that read, *St
Peter's Roman Catholic Church*, and turned left carefully. She drove down a narrow street, houses on
either side, kids building a snowman in a front yard
illuminated by a white porch light. Kids and life and

laughter. A long way removed from her world, her feelings. The sight cheered her a moment.

She saw the church. A disappointment – she'd expected something old and steepled and traditional. But St Peter's was of recent vintage, rectangular and squat, built of beige brick, and the stained-glass windows depicted no Christ, no lambs, no Virgin with halo – only a series of designs that consisted of interconnected cubes of different colours. She wondered what they were supposed to represent: harmony?

She parked alongside a snowbank and got out of the car. She approached the church. It was lit by a couple of globed lamps on either side of the doorway, but the interior, as far as she could tell, was in darkness. She made her way up the path to the door, tried the handle. Locked.

A sign of the times, she thought. What happened if some troubled soul wanted a moment of solitary prayer or contemplation? Too bad.

She turned away, walked the path back to the sidewalk. The air around her was positively brittle: had the night been a leaf, it would have broken at her touch. She moved, picking her way with great care, toward the house next to St Peter's, an old greystone heap with Gothic windows.

She came to a wooden gate, pushed it open, looked up the drive. A gloomy light burned in a downstairs window. The drive had been dug clear of drifts, but the snow was still two or three inches thick. She shivered. The temperature was dropping rapidly. Perhaps zero now, even less. The chill penetrated her coat, her jeans, slipped through her flesh to her bones. Maybe Gladd would offer her some tea, a Scotch, anything hot. She stepped on to the porch, which ran the length of the house. She pressed the doorbell, heard a chime deep inside.

A narrow-faced woman answered. She was around thirty and wore her brown hair in braids suggestive of a design on a harvest loaf. She had a thin voice. 'Can I help you?'

'I've come to see Father Gladd,' Andrea said.

'Is he expecting you?'

'No, but I think he'll see me.'

'Your name?'

'Andrea Malle.'

The woman reached inside a pocket of her cardigan and took out a pair of spectacles. She put them on, peered at Andrea. 'You're the . . .'

'Yes,' Andrea said.

'I read about that terrible business. You poor woman. It must be . . . Forgive me. I'm forgetting my manners. Come in. I'll call Father Gladd for you.'

Andrea stepped into a drab, narrow hallway. The walls were grey, the light dim. She imagined the inside of a submarine felt like this – claustrophobic, unwelcoming. John Gladd needed some advice on interior decorating, obviously.

'Please wait here,' the woman said. She vanished into a room at the end of the corridor. The housekeeper, Andrea thought. Housekeeper, social secretary, cook, guardian. Andrea looked at a crucifix on the wall, and then her gaze roamed to the foot of the stairs. The carpet was worn and shabby, the handrail in need of fresh paint. She remembered what her father had said about the Church: 'They invest. They run banks. They get richer all the time.' Clearly none of that wealth was filtering down to the level of the local priest in Horaceville.

The woman reappeared. 'Come this way, please,' she said.

Andrea walked down the hallway.

'Just go in,' the woman said, and opened a door.

Andrea stepped inside the room, and the housekeeper closed the door quietly, leaving her alone. The room, plainly furnished, shabby as the hallway, was warmed by a log fire. The air was musty. A huge striped cat lay on a rug in front of the fire and regarded her without much interest. A newspaper lay open on the floor beside an armchair, and a jumble of books had been stacked on the mantelpiece and a pair of grey socks were drying in front of the fire.

A door on the other side of the room opened. The man who came in was short and bald and rotund, and wore a black sweater over his clerical collar. He smiled at her and said, 'Forgive the mess, I wasn't expecting visitors,' and he waved a hand vaguely round the room.

'I'm looking for Father Gladd,' she said.

'I'm John Gladd.'

'No,' she said. '*Father* John.'

'I'm Father Gladd.'

'No, this isn't right,' she said.

'What isn't right?'

'I've made a mistake, I'm in the wrong place.'

The priest said something about stress and the delicate balance of the human heart at times of great sorrow, and then he stepped toward her and held her elbow and steered toward a seat, and she thought, *I've come to another St Peter's*, and her mind was filled suddenly with bizarre notions of alternative universes, the duplication of names and identities, but these made no sense, they were illogical ramblings, disconnected thoughts, complications.

She sat down and closed her eyes.

When she smelled the brandy the priest poured into a glass and held to her lips, she felt something give in the core of her brain.

chapter *Twelve*

The priest telephoned Fuscante, who arrived within ten minutes of the call. She was turning the brandy glass around in her hands when the cop entered the room. She told him about the man who'd called himself John Gladd, and he listened with a look of concentration, sometimes glancing at the priest, who was plainly distressed by the entire situation.

Fuscante said, 'You invited him out to the house.'

She felt short of breath, a small flutter in her chest. Nerves, nicotine. The edge of distress. 'I couldn't see any reason not to. I didn't want to go there on my own, and he said he was a friend of my father.'

'What did he do there?'

'In what sense?'

'Anything out of the ordinary. Anything that struck you as strange.'

She tried to think. He'd made tea. He'd lit a fire. He'd

looked at her father's paintings. He'd shown very little interest when she'd been going through the folders. 'No, nothing I can remember.'

'He didn't seem to be sniffing around for anything in particular?'

'He was only out of my sight a couple of times. Once when he went to the toilet. Once when I went to my car. You're talking a matter of only a couple of minutes total. Do you think he was scoping the place out for something worth stealing?'

'It's a consideration,' Fuscante said. 'I can't dismiss it out of hand.'

'We left the house at the same time,' she said. 'I'm sure if he took anything I would have noticed.'

'So if he wasn't a thief, why did he go to the trouble of pretending to be a priest?'

'Maybe he was one of those ghouls you talked about,' she said. 'Maybe he got a weird kick out of dressing up and hanging out at a murder scene. I don't know. He seemed perfectly okay to me at the time.' She looked into the half-empty glass. The brandy she'd drunk had left a sensation of molten brass in her stomach. She was flushed – the heat from the fire, the alcohol, the reaction to the fact that somebody posing as John Gladd had lied his way into her life.

She said, 'He was pretty accurate when he talked about my father's feelings toward organized religion.'

'Then you think he *might* have known your father?' Fuscante's expression was intense, focused. She wouldn't like to be interrogated by this man.

'He might.'

'But it doesn't explain the goddam charade,' Fuscante said. 'Why didn't he just say he knew your father and ask if he could be of some assistance to you? He didn't have to dress up, did he?'

She looked at the priest. 'Do you mind if I smoke?'

'Go ahead,' the priest said.

The cat suddenly leaped into her lap. She stroked it a couple of times, then nudged it aside and lit a cigarette. The priest lifted the cat and held it against his chest.

She said to Fuscante, 'Maybe he'd never met my father at all. Maybe he'd just learned some things about his attitudes and opinions.'

'How?'

'He could have done some background research, I guess.'

'Research,' Fuscante said in an unconvinced way. 'Where? Why?'

She admitted she didn't know. She realized she was flying kites to see if they caught the wind. She pictured the man she'd known as Gladd stick a poker in the fire. Saw him fetch tea from the kitchen. Saw him sit with the cup in his hand. There was one tiny constant in all these recollections, and she mentioned it now to Fuscante. 'I just remembered . . . he never took his gloves off all the time he was there. I assumed it was because of the cold. Now I'm thinking—'

'He didn't want to leave prints,' Fuscante said. 'He knew you'd find out sooner or later he wasn't who he claimed to be, and he took the precaution of leaving no clues to his real identity.'

She nodded. 'Perhaps.'

'And he stole nothing. He didn't go snooping around. He was convincing.'

'He had the priest act down pretty well. Talked about his congregation. His wild-flower club.'

'His what club?'

She explained this to Fuscante.

The priest said, 'Funny. We happen to have such a club at the church. And they *do* make arrangements of wild flowers for our annual fund-raiser.'

Fuscante said, 'So he knew something about this church as well.'

'Apparently,' the priest said.

'Describe him, Andrea,' Fuscante said.

She did her best. She mentioned his pink cheeks. She could see him clearly enough, but she couldn't remember any distinguishing characteristic – mole, wart, anything that would single him out. She described his car, a grey Ford with snow-tyres.

Fuscante said to the priest, 'Ring any bells, Father?'

The priest shrugged. The cat squirmed and clawed into his shoulder. 'I can't say it does.'

Fuscante turned back to Andrea. 'What about his accent?'

'It's hard to say. He just sounded like most people around here.' And then she remembered him saying, 'I'm surprised your father never mentioned me. Perhaps I'm being vain, overestimating my role in his life.' *You had no damn role in his life*, she thought. *That's why he never mentioned you, Jack*. She'd been trespassed upon, he'd intruded into her life at a terrible time, tricked her, *cheated* her, and she'd welcomed him because she hadn't any reason to suspect he was fake. And even if she had been, would she have noticed anything out of place about him? She doubted it.

Fuscante stood with his back to the fire, hands clasped behind his long overcoat. 'I don't get it. Here's a guy prepared to run the risk of discovery – and for what? I just missed him by a few minutes when he came to your hotel. I could have run straight into him.

He obviously thought it was worth taking chances just to get into the house. He used you as cover. He knew you had genuine business at the house. He knew if he was in your company and you encountered one of my people out there he wasn't going to be stopped and asked for ID. The question is – are we dealing with a harmless loony here? Can we write it off like that? I don't think that's a chance I'm prepared to take. I'll get guys out looking for him, I'll issue a description—'

'Such as it is,' she said.

'It's better than nothing,' Fuscante said.

Barely, she thought. 'Wait. I almost forgot. I have his phone number.' She fished in her pocket, found the sheet of paper lying against her father's passport. She took the paper out, gave it to Fuscante. He looked at it, then walked to the desk and dialled the number.

She watched him. She felt tension running through her. She wondered about connections – the bogus priest, her father's secretive life, Stan Thorogood's phone call: it was as if these things were linked in some strange way, like different-shaped knots along the same length of string. But she had no compelling reason for believing this. The world was all at once stripped of sense, shedding its form. Solids turned to liquids, liquids to gas, nothing was firm, nothing grounded in certainty. A man is shotgunned to death, gravity doesn't apply, facts are in free-fall. You don't know what the hell is going on, and it sends little shocks through your system.

Fuscante talked softly into the phone for a few minutes, his back turned to Andrea. He replaced the handset and looked at her.

'That number's an answering service here in town,'

he said. 'It's a small concern run by a couple called Jim and Mary Grattini. I know them. They're good people.'

'Then they must have seen the alleged priest when he was setting the service up,' she said.

'No, they didn't. It was done over the phone. And the first month's service was paid in cash, which they received late last night. Hand-delivered to their mailbox in an unstamped envelope.'

'And they didn't think it odd that Father Gladd would need an answering-service?'

Fuscante said, 'You're in that business, you don't last long by being indiscreet and asking awkward questions. They accepted him as a client. Simple as that. They'd assume he had reasons of his own. They wouldn't probe. The timing bothers me. This character opens an account with the Grattinis five or six hours after your father's body has been discovered. Why? Because he already *knows* he's going to introduce himself to you, he *knows* he's going to offer you his services as a companion in grief, and he needs a local telephone where you can get in touch with him because it lends his masquerade a certain authenticity. So it's planned. It's carefully thought out. He wants to meet you. He wants to accompany you to that house. Why?'

She got up from the sofa. Her legs were stiff, cramped. She walked to the fire, thinking of John Gladd again. She had no idea why he would have gone to such lengths. She looked at Fuscante, whose expression had become one of exasperation.

She said, 'How did he learn last night my father was dead? The news didn't hit the newspaper until this morning, did it?'

'Bad news travels fast in small towns,' Fuscante said.

He drew his hand down his firm jaw. 'I'm lost. And I don't like that feeling.'

'And I can't think of anything else I can tell you,' she said. 'I wish I could.' She gazed at the priest, who was still holding the cat. 'I'm sorry you got involved in this.'

'It isn't your fault,' he said. 'I have to say, it's a spooky feeling to think somebody's impersonating you.'

She moved toward the door. Fuscante followed her out into the hallway. They said goodnight to the priest and went into the freezing dark. Fuscante walked beside her down the drive, the surface of which was glossy and tricky. The sky was clear of cloud now, the full moon hard and white and alien.

As they went through the gate Fuscante said, 'If you hear from him again, don't think twice, call me immediately.'

'Somehow I don't think I'll hear from him again,' she said.

'You never know.' He stared out through the dark in the direction of the church. He plunged his hands inside his coat pockets. 'I'll be honest with you, Andrea. This whole thing's going nowhere. I don't have a lead. I don't have a witness. I don't have a goddam motive. The DEA are still denying they had a chopper in the vicinity . . . And this impersonator business doesn't help any. I feel like I'm treading water. Very chill water. I wish to God I could get a break. Something. Anything.'

'It might happen when you least expect it,' she said.

'I hope so,' he remarked.

She reached her car and Fuscante held the door open for her.

He asked, 'How are you doing? How are you holding up?'

'That's hard to answer. Sometimes it feels like I'm trapped inside a seriously bad dream. Sometimes I think I'm just going to unravel and collapse. And then I have moments when I fool myself into thinking I'm coping all right, just so long as I don't stand still.'

Fuscante was quiet a second. 'I wish I knew what that goddam fake priest wanted. I'll circulate a description anyway, see what happens. Part of me wants him to be nothing more than a morbid crank with a warped taste for deception.'

'What does the other part want?' she asked.

'The other part . . . I think the other part would like him to be implicated in your father's death, because it would give me something to work on. But that's the part that worries me.'

'Why?'

'Think about it,' he said. 'If he's whacko enough to return to the scene of his own crime with the victim's daughter, then you've got to question his intentions. And I don't like the answers I'm coming up with.'

She stared at him. 'Meaning I might be in danger?'

'It's a possibility.'

It hadn't occurred to her that the man impersonating John Gladd might be dangerous. A fraud, sure. A weirdo, maybe. But dangerous, no, she hadn't even considered that. And it was hard to do so, even now, it seemed abstract and remote, because she couldn't square the idea of menace with the pink benevolence of the man's face. But killers, she thought, come in all shapes and sizes. No one physical type has a monopoly on murder. The quiet man next door who prunes his roses and mows his lawn fastidiously. The lonely guy you see at midnight in the supermarket loading his trolley with microwave dinners for one. The old fellow who sings in the church choir and is out doing good deeds in all kinds of weather.

'I can't think why he'd want to harm me,' she said.

'And I can't think why he'd want to harm your father either, Andrea.'

She got in behind the wheel and looked at him. 'Maybe he's just a sick person who's harmless, maybe that's all there is,' and she put the key in the ignition, wondering why she'd uttered those words with a confidence she suddenly didn't feel.

'Just be careful,' he said.

'I'll be careful.'

'I mean that. Don't take it lightly.'

'I don't intend to.'

'And I don't intend to let you.'

'You'll keep an eye on me, is that what you're saying?'

'As a precaution.'

'You're a cautious man, Sheriff.'

'Call me Rick.'

'You're a cautious man, Rick.'

'I have to be. So if you happen to see a cop hanging around the hotel now and again, you'll know why.'

'I appreciate your concern,' she said.

She watched Fuscante recede in her side mirror under the icy moonlight. He dwindled to a tiny figure motionless on a snowbanked sidewalk, and then he was gone and she was heading back to the hotel along the empty road.

chapter *Thirteen*

*I*nside the hotel, she went directly to the Lake Lounge. The big room wasn't deserted this time – men sat on stools at the bar and music issued from a jukebox in the corner she hadn't noticed before. Heads turned as she entered: she was registered, noted, filed. Martin, dressed in a white apron, was working the bar and smiled when he saw her.

'What can I get you?' he asked.

'Scotch.'

'Any particular brand?'

She shook her head. It didn't matter. He poured from a bottle of Johnnie Walker Red. 'Ice? Water?'

She wanted it straight. Martin said it was on the house. She thanked him, took her drink to a table, lit a cigarette. She noticed Martin lean across the bar in a confidential manner and say something to a double-chinned man hunched over a beer. The man turned, glanced at her, then looked back at Martin. Information conveyed and digested. She was an object of curiosity. The news of her identity would go from one drinker to the next until all seven men who occupied stools would know who she was. She tossed back half of her drink, and thought about the man who'd passed himself off as John Gladd.

A mystery. But so was the prowler her father had mentioned in his bland diary.

And so was Stan Thorogood's phone call.

And, above all the rest, so was her father's murder.

She pondered the imposter, his possible motives. Think. He wanted to get inside the house without anyone being suspicious. But for God's sake, why?

If he didn't want access to the house for the purpose of theft – then what? She let this question simmer at the back of her mind. She had the feeling she was approaching this problem in the wrong way, only she couldn't think how.

'Gladd' had known *some* things about her father. That much was indisputable. *We didn't see eye to eye on many things, so we agreed to disagree. You might say we reached a truce. We had profound theological differences.* Her head ached. She took a couple of aspirins from her purse and swallowed them with her Scotch.

He was a character. It was an honour to know him. She remembered asking, 'How well did you really know my father?' But his response, which she couldn't recall verbatim, had been vague. *No real intimacy, I wouldn't have brought Dennis my personal problems* – words to that effect. And then she remembered him standing in the bedroom, looking at the pictures: *Good sense of composition.* He'd patted her arm and said something like *The police will find the killer. It's only a matter of time*, and there had been a quiet certitude in his words, a quality in which she'd found a small, transient comfort.

Goddam you, she thought. *For whatever purpose, you used my grief. Pretending, lying, doling out your phony sympathy, your concern. Fuck you. Whoever you are.* And she felt anger at herself for failing to see through the man's fraudulence.

She pushed her unfinished drink aside, turned her thoughts to Stan Thorogood. In the old days, before the company had been sold, MalCon had rented a small suite of offices on West 32nd Street. She remembered her father occupied a room that adjoined Stan's and that the door between the two offices had always been open. No secrets between partners. *'Stan and me, we share everything.'*

She remembered the decor, glossy black desks and filing-cabinets, brilliant white walls, spare prints predominantly red. The place had always struck her as stark. The reception room had been dominated by the only other employee of MalCon, a big, assertive woman called Irene Passmore. Irene, all high platinum hair and glossy plum nail-polish and low-cut peasant-style blouses that gave her an imposing Teutonic look, had guarded access to the partners with the ferocity of a Doberman. You needed a cast-iron reason and a brave heart to get beyond Irene's desk to the inner sanctum. Andrea had secretly nicknamed her Irene Passless.

She hadn't thought about Irene since the company had been sold, and now she wondered what had become of her. Retired? Pensioned off? Working elsewhere? Her father had never said. Maybe whoever had bought the company had retained her, but Andrea couldn't

imagine Irene working for MalCon under new ownership. An easy camaraderie, a smooth familiarity, had
existed between Irene and the partners. And nothing,
nothing, happened inside MalCon that Irene didn't
know about.

It was possible, she supposed, that Irene might know
where to find Stan. An outside chance, anyhow. How
to locate her, though? Andrea finished her drink. As far
as she could recall, Irene had lived somewhere on the
West Side: she walked to work every day, no matter
the weather. Dennis had once referred to her as his
dedicated angel. So where did angels go when they
were made redundant?

She was aware of someone climbing down from one
of the stools and approaching her table. She raised
her face, saw the double-chinned man Martin had
whispered to: he wore a fringed suede jacket and a
denim shirt buttoned to the throat, no necktie.

'Name's Filly, John Filly,' he said. 'Spelled like in
the horse.'

She half-smiled at him. She wasn't in the mood for
the company of a stranger.

'Knew your dad,' he said. He rested his hands on her
table. They were big and callused, black dirt under the
fingernails.

'Did you?' She was interested now.

'Sure did. I got a breakdown truck, see. Hauled his
old wreck back from New Dresden when he had that
accident.' John Filly had thin, oily hair, parted to one
side. 'Damn old mess that Chevy he had. Lucky he
didn't do himself an injury. 'Course, the car was a
write-off.'

'What was he doing in New Dresden?' she asked.

'Drinking, for one thing.' John Filly smiled shyly. He

hitched his thumbs inside his belt. 'Nice enough guy. Paid his bill right off. I liked him for that. Some folks string you along. Or they argue about the charges.'

'Why don't you sit down?' she asked.

'I don't mean to intrude.'

'No, please. Tell me some more about the accident.'

Filly sat, looking uncomfortable. 'Guy called Strumm, an onion-farmer out to New Dresden, going along minding his own business, carrying a load of two-by-fours and rolls of chicken-wire, when your father banged into the back of his pick-up doing about sixty, sixty-five. Drunk as all hell. Didn't know the time of day, is what I hear. Crumpled the shit outta that pick-up.' He hesitated. 'Lookit, I don't want to speak ill, hell, you know.'

'It's all right. My father enjoyed his drink. You're not telling me something I don't already know.'

Filly leaned across the table. 'What I hear is your daddy was drinking that day in a place called the Eight Ball. It's a bar in New Dresden. New Dresden, now, well, it ain't much of a place. About one tenth the size of Horaceville here.'

'Was he drinking alone?'

'Wouldn't know a detail like that, miss.'

'It's strange he'd travel all that way to drink.'

'Yep. It's a long haul just to get smashed. A hundred miles round trip about.'

She tried to imagine her father drinking alone in this place called the Eight Ball. He could handle liquor – she'd sometimes been astounded by his capacity – so it was safe to assume he'd consumed a sizeable amount that day. And unless he was drinking quickly, which he never did if single-malts were involved, it would take him more than a few hours to get drunk enough

to become truly careless on the road. Blind drunk. So
what had he done? Sat hour after hour in the Eight
Ball boozing in solitude? Okay, he enjoyed drinking
on his own, tracking thoughts that became less and
less lucid the more he drank. But still. Why had he
chosen that place?

Her father's life: it was beginning to resemble a
crumpled map left too long out in the weather, and
some of the place-names and road-signs had been
bleached beyond legibility.

'Can I buy you a drink?' Filly asked.

'I think I've reached my limit,' she said. She didn't
have her father's ability to hold drink. She was a
lightweight. Already she was experiencing a slight
fuzziness around the edges of her awareness.

John Filly said, 'Could be he didn't want to get
himself liquored up around here. You-don't-shit-on-
your-own-doorstep principle.'

She thought, *He travels long distance for his medication. He goes even farther away to drink.* Wallace had
explained the former. But that left the latter unanswered. 'He might just have gone for a drive, stopped
at this bar.'

'Sure. He might.'

'Is there anything of interest in New Dresden?'

'Interest? Like what?'

She shrugged. 'Historic monuments. Museums. Anything like that.'

He laughed at the idea. 'New Dresden? Christ, no.
It's strictly one-horse and dull as paint drying.'

'If it had an art gallery, I could just about see him
going there. He enjoyed art.'

'*Art* gallery? It's got two bars, church, post office
and a general store. It don't even have a school as

I recall.' He raised his glass. 'Anyhow, here's to his memory.'

'His memory,' she said.

'What happened to him is a downright disgrace. Stuff like that don't happen in Horaceville. Maybe you get a little rowdy business some Saturday nights, but hell, that's harmless, that's just folk letting off steam. Nobody gets hurt. Sure as hell, nobody gets *killed*.'

Her thoughts, still turning in all kinds of directions, rushed away from her. But one particular idea kept coming back, and she couldn't push it aside entirely. Persistent little thing.

What if? she wondered.

She looked at John Filly and said, 'It was nice talking with you.'

'Likewise,' he said.

She got up, just a little light-headed. The notion that had occurred to her was one she probably wouldn't have entertained if she'd been a hundred per cent sober, but sometimes alcohol turned your mental processes around in such a way that you experienced a flash, a little sizzle of illumination – almost always wrong-headed but arguably plausible at the time of conception. Like the one presently ringing in her mind. The one that congealed, the one that wouldn't be budged.

Filly stood up politely. 'You go easy now,' he said.

But she was already walking toward the exit, and didn't hear him. She went into the foyer, picked up the phone at the reception desk and dialled the emergency number for the police. When her call was answered she asked to be connected with Rick Fuscante.

chapter *Fourteen*

*F*uscante said, 'You've been drinking.'

'I had a Scotch, that's all.'

'A Scotch and a weird brainstorm.'

'Okay, maybe it's a brainstorm. But it's worth thinking about.' She looked from the window of the Bronco.
Moonlight gleamed on snow. She felt the blast from the
heater of his car.

'It's cockeyed, Andrea. You're saying I'm looking
at this impersonator's purpose from the wrong perspective.'

'I'm saying it's an idea worth exploring, that's all.'

Fuscante stared at the road ahead. Ice had formed
on the windshield, translucent patches here and there.
He flicked his wiper switch, sprayed water on the glass,
but it froze immediately in streaks. 'Somebody wise once
said to me that if anything sounds like a good idea and
it's after nine o'clock at night, it probably isn't one.'

'Is it nine?' she asked.

'Eight-thirty.'

'So it's not a bad idea yet.'

'It's not a great idea at any time,' he said.

She had the feeling she'd let the Scotch carry her away, and that the little bubble of a notion she'd come up with in the bar would suddenly pop and seem far-fetched. But for the moment that hadn't happened. The bubble might have a thin membrane, but it was still floating. Only just. 'He wants access to the house. And we've been assuming all along it's because he wanted to steal something. All I'm suggesting is you have an open mind about the alternative – he didn't want to *steal*, he wanted to *leave* something behind.'

'That's precisely where you lose me,' he said. 'What in God's name would he gain by leaving something behind?'

'I don't know.'

Fuscante emitted a long sigh. 'He was out of your sight for a few minutes. He went to the toilet. You're asking me to imagine he might have left something in the john?'

'We won't know until we look, will we?'

Fuscante glanced at her. 'How many Scotches?'

'I told you. One.'

'Plus the brandy the priest gave you,' he said. 'Overload.'

Overload, she thought. *Cockeyed*. 'Do you think I'm looking forward to going back to my father's house? If you do, you're way off. All I'm saying—'

'Yeah, I know what you're saying. Don't tell me again. I hear the cry of wild geese.'

She tilted her head against the back of her seat. 'Linda Straub said you're a good cop.'

'If I'm any good as a cop it's because I'm methodical. I'm logical.'

'Logic's a straitjacket.'

'It's worked for me in the past,' he said. 'What are you suggesting? Is this some kind of lateral thinking thing you're into?'

She didn't like his tone. She lapsed into silence, watched the snowbanks piled against the side of the road. She thought of icebergs on a black ocean. What had seemed to her a bright notion in the warmth of the lounge — certainly one she'd felt worth sharing with Fuscante — had begun very slightly to diminish in the light of his scepticism. *You're out here on this lonely road. Welcome to the real world.*

He'd said, 'You're asking me to imagine he might have left something in the john.'

Like what? An early Christmas present?

They'd go inside the house and search the bathroom and find nothing and she'd have to admit her idea had been dopey. And Fuscante, although he'd be too polite to crow and say, 'I told you so,' would certainly give her a quietly bemused look. Goddam.

She wanted to turn to him, say, 'Okay, it's a wrong-headed notion, I admit it, let's just get the hell out of here and go back and you can drop me off at my hotel and I can sleep my delusions off.'

But the house was only a half mile away and Fuscante would say, 'We've come this far. Let's check your brainstorm out, let's put it to bed once and for all.'

He drove the last short stretch in silence, then turned the Dodge into the driveway. She saw the house, windows silvered by moonlight. She imagined shafts of cold light illuminating the rooms inside, and shining on icy rivulets trapped in the folds of the tarpaulin out back. She thought of food frozen solid on the chopping-board in the kitchen, a knife lying to one side where her father had left it. Grainy snapshots taken round the edges of a murder scene.

The house looked ghostly and utterly uninviting, as if it had never been occupied, or as if its only tenants were spectres.

Her father's Cherokee was parked near the steps of the porch. Another vehicle, a four-wheel-drive of some kind, idled alongside it, exhaust making dark plumes. She saw on a side panel the triangular insignia of the Horaceville Police Department.

'Jerry Lime,' Fuscante said. 'He's on watch. I told you I didn't want to leave this place unattended for any length of time.'

Fuscante stopped the Bronco, opened his door. Jerry Lime came out of his vehicle and called, 'All quiet on the western front, Rick.'

Fuscante acknowledged his colleague with a wave of his hand. He stepped down from the car and looked at Andrea. 'You ready?'

She wasn't. She didn't want to go inside that house. She didn't want to move. She stared at the yellow crime-scene tape.

'Well?' Fuscante said.

'I didn't say I *personally* wanted to go inside.'

'Let me remind you. This is your idea, Andrea.'

'I *know* that.'

'So? Are you coming in or are you staying here?'

Jerry Lime called out again. 'What's happening?'

'The lady can't decide if she wants to go inside the house or stay out here,' Fuscante replied. 'She's vacillating.'

'Yeah, I've been in situations where ladies vacillated,'
Lime said, and laughed.

Vacillating, she thought. *Cold feet. Chickening out.*
That sad unappealing house. She couldn't go in there.
This whole thing was dumb. She should have stayed
in the bar or gone back to her room.

'Well?' Fuscante asked. 'This is what you wanted,
Andrea. This was your notion.'

His breath hung in the air. She imagined his words
might appear in these foggy little clouds like dialogue
in comic-strip balloons.

He stretched a hand out to her across the driver's
seat. 'Changed your mind?' he asked. 'Had second
thoughts?'

'Okay,' she said. '*Okay*. I'm coming.'

She was aware of Jerry Lime climbing on to the
porch. She heard him say, 'Allow me, I've got a key,'
and then he reached for the door.

The blast – fierce and vicious, violating the silence
of the place – rocked the house.

Windows blew out, frames shattered, a rolling globe
of red-yellow flame exploded in a rush through the
front door and engulfed the porch and the crime-scene
tape curled and disintegrated instantly. Andrea saw a
volcano of snow, heard the crack of wood igniting,
saw the porch collapse, flame sear whatever was in
its path. She opened the passenger door of the Dodge
and dropped into the snow and crawled away from the
house, her heart stop–starting, breath frozen in her
throat. She glanced back, the night was lit by fire
shooting through the rooms and rising up and curling
round the roof. She tasted a chemical black smoke in
her mouth. A slice of broken glass that seconds before
had been part of a windowpane pierced her palm.

She heard somebody scream, saw Jerry Lime with his coat on fire rolling around in the snow in a desperate attempt to douse the flame, and she stumbled towards him, thinking she could help in some way, wasn't sure how, she picked up handfuls of snow and tossed them over him, but that was useless, what she needed was to pack him in great layers of snow and ice, she needed a spade to shift the stuff in sufficient quantity, but the heat from the house was too intense and drove her back, and Jerry Lime's gloves were spitting licks of flame. She stepped away, lost her balance, saw thick smoke obscure the moon as she fell, then she raised her face and saw flame spurt under the chassis of the Cherokee and the air was rich and sickening with the stench of rubber burning and Jerry Lime was still screaming and Fuscante had vanished God knows where. She got to her feet and tried to get back to help Jerry Lime again. His screams were horrifying, piercing. The drifts impeded her movements and the blow-torch effect of the burning house forced her back. The intensity of heat melted snow and turned it to icy slush under her.

The burning house crackled with the sound of a pig carcass on a spit. Timbers in the roof creaked, slates slid loose from joists, the house was buckling as it burned. She knew she couldn't leave Jerry Lime to suffer in the snow like that, fuck the heat, she'd haul him clear somehow, even if he was dead she'd pull him away. She stepped forward again, pawing smoke from her eyes, and then she was aware of somebody grabbing her shoulders and dragging her to the ground and drawing her through drifts away from the house.

She thought she heard Fuscante say *The propane-tank out back's gonna blow for Christ's sake.* And it did, a *swoosh* of fire that illuminated the sky with a red electric intensity. Somehow she didn't *hear* the explosion, she felt it as one might an earthquake, the ground shaking and rumbling under her body as if something had cracked in the crust of the world.

Fuscante said, 'Stay here.'

She watched him rush into the flame and smoke and for a while he was lost to her and she felt alarm, as if she were suspended in a place where her oxygen supply was running out too rapidly and a constriction had locked her lungs – and then he emerged again, pulling Jerry Lime away from the heart of the conflagration, turning him over and over through layers of snow as he did so.

chapter *Fifteen*

Horaceville General, built in the 1930s, was a place of funereal dirt-brown corridors and cumbersome old air-ducts and radiators that gurgled with sounds suggestive of people drowning. Andrea had a silver of glass removed from the palm of her hand by an ER physician called Asquith, a brisk little Australian who worked in silence. He gave her a shot that made her feel loose-limbed and spacy. She guessed some kind of tranquillizer for shock. Afterwards, she went out into the corridor, where Fuscante was waiting. She had a sense of seeing him through slightly discoloured water. He had smoky black circles under his eyes. His lips were stained dark. She wondered in a vague way how she looked.

She sat down beside him on the bench.

'They've airlifted Lime to a hospital in Albany,' he said. 'They don't have the facilities here for burns like his. They don't know if he'll pull through.'

She wasn't sure what to say. *I hope he does. I hope he's going to be okay.* She remembered what 'Gladd' had said to her on their first meeting: 'Words don't do much in situations like these, do they?' She gazed the length of the corridor. Her hand ached. Fuscante got to his feet. He massaged his right shoulder, grimaced.

'Are you okay?' she asked.

'A pulled muscle, a couple of bruises I got when the blast knocked me out for a few seconds. Nothing compared to Lime. You?'

'The doc gave me a shot. A downer.'

Fuscante stood up, touched the buttoned flap of his holster, as if he wished he could pull the gun loose and shoot something, anything, any target that presented itself. His jaw was clenched tight. The bone structure of his face seemed different, harder, more sharply defined. He ran a hand through his hair, walked round in a circle for a few seconds, then stood directly over her.

'Tell me something I don't know,' he said.

She looked at him. 'Something you don't know?'

'Tell me what the fuck is going on.'

'I wish I knew.'

'Gimme more, Andrea. Somewhere in that pretty head of yours I figure you've got to know something, and maybe you don't even know what it is, but I want you to concentrate, I want you to think goddam hard. Think about what happened out at that house. Why somebody would blow it up. Why somebody would murder your father. Think. Just *think*.'

He gripped her wrist tightly. She felt confused. The drug kicking in, her brain scrambling. Fuscante's steely attitude surprised her, even though she could understand it. He had a colleague almost burned to death, a man who might not make it. And if Lime did survive he was facing the prospect of months of painful grafts, months of restoration, but never a full recovery. He wouldn't look the same. He wouldn't think or feel or be the same again.

'Are you trying?' he asked.

'I'm trying,' and she was, sending her blunted mind here and there, as if she might by chance stumble on the spoor of whatever it was Fuscante sought, but she was hunting on rocky terrain, and it was tough not to stumble.

'Try harder,' he said. 'Let's go through it step by step. Your father retires. He lives a reclusive life. Nobody seems to know him except in the most superficial way. He doesn't encourage friendships. The people he does business with in town know nothing about him. Why? Why does he want all this privacy and solitude, Andrea? And please don't tell me he's just a guy jaundiced by the world and looking for serenity in his old age, because I am not in the fucking mood to hear that. People get killed, okay. People are murdered, okay. But in my experience they don't usually get their houses blown up after they're dead and lying in the goddam morgue. So why does his house get blasted out of the landscape? Why the fucking lethal light-show spectacular?'

She dragged her arm free. She was woozy, off-balance. She felt a weight in her eyelids. Fuscante drew her to her feet and marched her along the corridor and stuck coins in a vending-machine. He handed her a cardboard cup. 'It's not great coffee, but it's going to keep you awake just a little longer. Drink.'

The cup was hot, hard to hold, the coffee stewed and bitter. 'He plants an explosive device,' she said.

'And?'

'He rigs up some kind of booby-trap that poor Lime

set off. He doesn't care who triggers it, it might have been you, me, he doesn't care a damn about who he kills, he just wants to destroy the place—'

Fuscante brought his face up close to hers. 'Destroy? Oh, big understatement. *Majestic* understatement. *Pulverize* is the term you want. Blow off the face of the earth. Reduce to ash. Why does he want to do that?'

'I don't know,' she said.

'Drink the coffee, Andrea.'

'I am drinking the goddam coffee.'

Fuscante had her cornered between the vending-machine and the wall. She could smell smoke on his coat and the scent ferried her back to the house, Lime's screams, the destruction.

'What are we talking about here, Andrea? Exactly what are we looking at? Let's say this impostor is the guy that killed your father. Let's also say he decides for some reason that the death of Dennis Malle isn't enough. It doesn't accomplish everything he wants to accomplish. So he goes back, he plants a device he knows will wreck the place. Why? Because he wants to wipe out any trace of . . . what? Something he believes your father might have concealed in the house? Something stashed away in a hidden cubbyhole he doesn't have time to search for? Papers, say. Documents. Maybe something your father had that his killer didn't want him to have. Something incriminating. I don't goddam know. What could your father have had that was so important?'

'If I knew I'd tell you. Believe me.'

He lost energy all at once, slumped forward a little, his face almost touching her shoulder. She had a tiny urge to comfort and calm him, perhaps touch his cheek, the back of his hand. She could practically taste his fatigue and his anger and his frustration. He shoved a lock of black hair off his forehead. A muscle in his jaw worked.

'Yeah. I know, I know you'd tell me,' he said quietly. 'The trouble is, this whole thing is beyond me. I get the feeling I'm playing in a different league with this one.'

'*You're* in a different league? My world is advising married people how to avoid choking each other to death, for God's sake! I spend all my working hours applying tourniquets to marital wounds. It's not a world that includes explosions and murder, Rick. It's rough at times, but it's a walk on the beach compared to this whole nightmare.'

He stepped back from her, massaged his eyelids with the thumb and index-finger of his right hand, then looked at her. 'Come on, I'll drive you back to the hotel.'

They walked outside. Fuscante escorted her across the parking-lot. It was midnight and the air was as cold and cutting as a blade dipped in ice. He held the passenger door of his Dodge open for her. The panels were smeared with smokestains, the windows blackened. One of the headlights had been blown out.

He got behind the wheel and drove in silence and she stared at the road, thinking about the blast, the flames, the flying glass, the ambulance whining in the snow, the sirens of the fire-truck, but the medication had already begun to distance her from the devastation.

Not far, but just enough.

Fuscante said, 'You told me he worked in security. He designed systems.'

'It was a team thing between my father and his partner, Stan Thorogood. Design and installation. They did the houses of the rich and famous. Big corporations. A lot of their business was overseas. They installed systems for Saudi princes, Korean industrialists, bankers in Hong Kong, Singapore.'

'What happened to this partner?'

'He retired when the company was sold.'

'You keep in contact with him?'

She felt a twinge in her hand. 'No, I don't. Strangely enough, he phoned me at the house this afternoon.'

'And?'

'He wanted to speak to my father. When I told him what had happened, he got upset, hung up.'

'You think your father kept in touch with Stan regularly?'

'I checked my father's phone bills. If he called Stan recently, he didn't do it from his home phone.'

'Where is this partner?'

'I've lost track of him.' She looked at Fuscante. She thought about telling him exactly what Stan had said on the phone, but she didn't, because Stan had been vague, and because she was experiencing a certain fade. She wanted to sleep. Deeply and dreamlessly. No deaths. No explosions. She needed the quiet of total oblivion.

'You don't think it strange he called the day after your father's death?'

'I didn't give that any thought.'

The cop was turning the Dodge into the driveway of the Glamys. 'Do you think all this could be connected in some way with your father's work? Security's a sensitive area. Your father must've had access to a whole load of information. Electronic schemata, alarm systems. He knew how to design and install them, so presumably he also knew how to surmount them. Didn't the Pharaohs kill the slaves who knew the locations of the tombs?'

She turned this question round in her head. She

remembered Fuscante asking yesterday if her father had made any enemies. 'You're suggesting a former client might be behind everything?'

'I'm not suggesting anything. I'm just tossing out whatever crosses my mind. Which isn't in the best of shape at this moment. I keep flashing on Jerry Lime.'

He parked outside the hotel, got out, helped her from the vehicle. 'I'll walk you up to your room,' he said. 'You look like you're about to collapse.'

She was. The drift inside was deepening. Shadows flitted around the edges of her awareness. The stairway seemed endless. She was sluggish in her movements.

Outside the door of her room Fuscante said, 'Some specialist guys are coming down from Albany in the morning to rummage through the wreckage. They'll look for fuses, detonators. Maybe we'll get a clearer picture then. Of what – God knows.'

She took her key from her pocket, opened the door.

The room was icy and for a moment she wondered if the heating had broken down but then she saw the window was wide and the curtains shook gently and that all her father's folders were gone from the surface of the bed where she'd left them, her pillows had been stripped from their cases, her mattress shifted to an angle, and her overnight bag upturned, her clothes spilled across the floor.

chapter *Sixteen*

Fuscante drank a glass of water in the bathroom. He'd already explored the ransacked bedroom and now, leaning wearily against the sink, he finished his drink. Andrea stood in the doorway, arms folded against the cold that had penetrated the place. She watched him examine himself in the mirror, then splash water on his face. He doused a washcloth and approached her and with a surprisingly gentle touch applied it to her face and forehead, and when he'd finished she saw the cloth was darkened with streaks of smoke.

'I've been wanting to do that since the hospital,' he said.

'Thanks.' She was a little embarrassed. She hadn't looked at herself since the explosion. She had no great urge to go examine her reflection. Vanity was a low-priority item. She turned, went back inside

the bedroom, stared at the disarray of her clothing.
'Everything's gone. All his papers. All his records.
Everything.'

'But nothing of yours.'

'Apparently nobody's interested in my stuff.'

Fuscante walked around, stepping over her spilled
clothing, then going to the window, which he'd closed
earlier. He'd already probed the scene, so what he was
looking for now? Something he might have missed? A
thorough man, who plugged away despite his fatigue.
Also a brave man, who'd endangered himself to drag
his colleague clear of fire. And she wasn't forgetting
that he'd pulled her down into the snow just before
the tank exploded and hauled her back to a position
of safety. She wondered if he had a personal life, a
wife, kids, a fiancée, or if being a cop limited his social
activities. Did he go home to a darkened apartment
or some big frame house filled with children and a
devoted wife?

'What now?' she asked.

'Good question.'

'All I want to do is get the hell out of Horaceville,
go home, get involved in the conjugal strife of other
people. I'm beginning to feel this town's like one of
those ships that get icelocked and you're stuck for
weeks with the same passengers and the same crew.'

'You go home, you'd have to come back at some
point for your father's funeral,' he said.

Events had blown that prospect out of her mind.
But it might be a long time before her father was
buried, because the ground was frozen and nobody
dug graves in chilly climates until a thaw. They kept
bodies in cold storage during the winter. She thought
of her father lying in an icy drawer week after week

after week. She wasn't looking forward to the funeral
no matter when it took place.

She sat down, lit a cigarette. She didn't want to
think how easily her room had been accessed. She
didn't want to put a face to the person who'd stolen
the papers, although it was 'Gladd' – who else? – who
crossed her mind.

Fuscante said, 'These stolen documents, they were
just financial records? Insurance policies?'

'Stuff like that. Not very interesting.'

'Somebody imagined otherwise.'

'Somebody's going to be very disappointed,' she
said.

'You read through them, didn't you?'

'Yeah, I did.' She ticked the items off on her fingers
as she itemized them for him.

'And absolutely nothing of a titillating private nature?'
he said.

'Unless you get excited looking at car-insurance
policies and bank statements and such. I don't.'

'Presumably the burglar was worried there might be
something else in the folders.'

'You're back to the possibility of incriminating
material.'

'I'm thinking that way, sure. I don't know what
else to think.' He picked up the telephone, punched
in a number. 'Jonah . . . yeah, this is Rick. Yeah, I'm
okay, it's Jerry I'm worried about . . . Yeah, I know
. . . I asked for a man to keep an eye on the Glamys
. . . What? That's great, that's just great. Sometimes
I think I'm speaking into a goddam vacuum . . . Have
him call me.'

Fuscante slammed the phone down. He looked at
Andrea and smacked his right fist lightly into the palm

of his left hand. 'The officer I detailed to keep an eye on this place was called away on account of some dumb bar brawl, and nobody had enough brains to arrange a replacement. Which pisses me off more than a little. If somebody had been cruising the area around the hotel, he might have seen something. Now we've got nothing. This is what happens when you try to run a department on a budget that wouldn't be enough to operate a Little League ball team. I've got twenty-one cops, and three of them are part-time. I need about thirty or forty.' He walked to the door, where he paused. 'After I leave, lock up. And please don't say anything about stable doors and bolted horses, okay? I've already locked the window. You'll be fine. I'm going down to have a word with Martin. You want him to send somebody up to make the bed and tidy the place a little?'

She shook her head. 'It's not worth the trouble.'

'Sleep,' he said. He opened the door. 'Remember, lock it.'

'Why would anyone bother with me? I don't have anything left to give. They got my father's papers.'

'You're using the plural,' he said.

'He. They. Gladd. Whoever.' She shrugged.

'He. They. Somebody might just think you're keeping something back, Andrea.'

'They'd be wrong.'

'They don't know that. They might do more than break into your room next time.' He stepped out into the corridor.

She wanted to thank him for his swift action at the house, but he'd already closed the door. She locked it. She drew the curtains, didn't look out across the dark lake. She'd seen enough of it. She adjusted the mattress, smoothed the sheets, replaced the pillowcases. She lay down, thinking of somebody scaling the wall outside her room, climbing through space.

She switched off the lamp, closed her eyes: irritatingly, sleep wouldn't come. Her mind was bucking, if only feebly, against the drug in her blood. She kept seeing Lime burning, kept remembering how she'd scratched and scraped up snow and tossed it over him before she'd been driven back by the inferno . . .

Sleep. Come on.

She was shivering and nervy and her limbs were cold. Aftershock. A reaction to the explosion kicking in only now.

She sat up, turned on the lamp, blinked.

She lit a cigarette. It soothed her a little.

She reached for the telephone, called Directory Assistance, and in a voice made dry by smoke and medication, asked for a listing for Irene Passmore in New York City. The operator gave her the number and she scribbled it down on the bedside note-pad. Then she dialled it.

A man answered. 'Yeah?'

She said she wanted to speak with Irene.

The man said, 'Who is this?'

She told him.

'You're Dennis Malle's daughter,' he said.

'Right.'

'I'm Leon, Irene's husband.'

She hadn't known Irene was married. She said, 'We never met.'

'No, we never did.' She heard him strike a match, inhale smoke from a cigarette. 'And you want Irene.'

'If it's not inconvenient.'

Leon Passmore said, 'You obviously haven't heard.'

'Heard what?'

'She left me. After nineteen years of marriage, she upped and left me. And I didn't see it coming. I didn't have a clue. You'd think I'd pick up on the signals, right? Hell, I didn't hear that train coming down the track.'

'I'm sorry to hear that.'

'Yeah, well, I've accepted it. That's what you do. You accept . . . And you want to find her, you say.'

'If you know where she is,' Andrea said.

'I heard a rumour from a niece of Irene's that she was living someplace upstate. She had no phone listing. But I never looked for her. I didn't have the heart for it. I thought – what's the point?'

Andrea felt sleep roll toward her again. This time it was more persistent, a clammy, thickening fog. 'I'm sorry if I disturbed you, Leon,' she said.

'No sweat,' he said. 'Wait. Irene's niece told me the name of the place. I'm trying to remember what it was. It's on the tip of my tongue. Maybe I just want to block it out, huh?'

'I'd understand that.'

'Anyway . . . it's gone.'

'If you remember, I'm upstate at the Glamys Lake Hotel in Horaceville. Goodnight, Leon.'

She hung up. She lay back. She drifted. She dreamed she was that kid on a swing and the guy pushing her kept saying, 'Trust me, trust me,' but the voice wasn't Dennis Malle's, and the shadow that fell across her from behind belonged to somebody else, a total stranger, and she wasn't unhappy when the sound of the telephone roused her from the weirdness of the dream.

'I just remembered,' Leon Passmore said.

'Remembered . . . ?'

'The name of the place Irene's niece mentioned.'

'Yeah, right.'

'New Dresden,' he said. 'I'm sure that was it.'

chapter *Seventeen*

*P*atrick telephoned at 8.30 a.m. 'I tried to call you last night a couple of times.'

She was groggy from the injection. 'I tried you too.'

'I couldn't work,' he said. 'I went out and had a couple of beers.'

She struggled upright, rearranged her pillows.

'You okay?' he asked. 'Hanging in there?'

She didn't want to get into a prolonged narrative of last night's events. She was thirsty and hadn't fully surfaced from sleep. She felt she was rising through brackish water to a light-source a long way above. 'Hanging in,' she said.

'Here's a traffic bulletin, and it's dismal. They've cleared a couple of runways at JFK. But Albany's frozen solid and they don't know when it's going to be operational. Maybe this afternoon, maybe tonight. And there's a travel advisory warning people to avoid

the Interstate because of the overnight freeze. Which
of course means no buses. Goddam, I wish I'd done
the American thing and learned how to drive when
I was a kid, because at least I'd be able to make the
effort.'

'You don't *have* to come up, Patrick,' she said. 'I'll
be home in a couple of days, maybe sooner.' She
kept uncertainty out of her voice. She had no way
of knowing when she'd leave Horaceville. The very
name of the place had begun to feel like a weight she
was carrying.

Patrick said, 'I *want* to come up. I want to *see* you.
I miss you.'

Wintry sunlight came through a narrow slit in the
curtains. Severe and blood-red and chilly.

Patrick's voice brightened. 'Incidentally, I had a call
from Seymour Stein and he wants to get together some
time this afternoon.'

Seymour Stein was a well-known West Coast director
who'd been dickering over one of Patrick's screenplays
for months.

'Stein's *interested*?' she asked.

'He wants to discuss some revisions before he takes
it to what he calls the next stage. And he's only going
to be in New York for one day. I hate to tempt fate,
but it sounds promising. He mentioned how much he
liked the basic concept. He said it caught the mood of
– get this – the *Zeitgeist*. Which I guess is his way of
saying it might work.'

'That's terrific, Patrick.'

'I'm not getting my hopes up. I've been here before.'

'You're an old pessimist.'

'In this business optimism's a self-inflicted cruelty,'
he said. 'We'll see. I've arranged to meet with him at

four at his hotel. By that time I expect I'll know about
the general traffic situation . . . Listen, are you sure
you're okay? You sound a little . . . off.'

'I just woke up. I need my coffee.'

'Go get some. I'll call you later.'

'Good luck with Stein,' she said.

He made his characteristic kissing sound. She realized he hadn't asked anything about the murder investigation. She knew that as soon as he was off the
phone he'd forget all about her. He'd sit down and
eagerly re-read the screenplay Seymour Stein wanted
to discuss. He'd dangle one leg over the edge of an
armchair and hold a blue pencil at a belligerent angle,
as if it were a scalpel he meant to probe deep into his
own words. Maybe it was best he stay in the city. What
would he do here, anyhow? Hold her hand? Utter words
of sympathy?

She got out of bed, remembering what she'd learned
about Irene Passmore. She wondered if it was simple
coincidence that her father had been drinking in New
Dresden on the day of his car wreck. She didn't think
so. There were scores of small towns and hamlets
scattered around this part of the state – why should
her father choose New Dresden out of all the rest?
He went there to meet Irene Passmore, say. Why?
Talk about old times. Do a little bullshitting. But
he'd never mentioned anything to her about Irene.
Why should that surprise her? She was becoming
sadly resigned to the fact he'd lived much of his life
at a subterranean level she couldn't excavate. That she
hadn't really known him – depressing.

She showered, shampooed, recalled the rather pleasant way Fuscante had taken a washcloth and applied it
to her face. A nice touch. Gentlemanly and concerned

and, yeah, okay, intimate – but without being intrusive, without being suggestive or pushy.

She dressed in jeans and a wool sweater, put on her coat and boots, left her room, locked it, went downstairs.

Martin was standing behind the desk. 'Rick Fuscante told me about the burglary. I don't know what to say. Nothing like that ever happens at the Glamys.' He rubbed his fat hands together apologetically. 'The intruder must've climbed a drainpipe that runs close to your window. I guess you didn't have the window locked from the inside.'

'These things happen,' she said. 'It's not your fault.'

'Was anything of value missing? Jewellery, anything like that? Because we're fully insured, you know.'

She shook her head. She wondered if Martin had heard about the explosion. Probably. The whole town would know by this time. She waited for him to mention it and inevitably he did, coming out from behind his desk and lowering his voice in the manner of a man who knows good gossip is even tastier when whispered. 'I heard about that business out at your father's.'

She said nothing. She picked up a couple of tourist leaflets from the desk and scanned them idly. *The Catskills, An Enduring Joy. Explore The Finger Lakes.*

Martin said, 'People are saying it was some kind of dreadful accident.'

'Really.'

'Yeah, a propane-tank leaked and that poor cop Jerry Lime probably tossed a cigarette away, and . . .' He shrugged. 'Great shame about Jerry. Nice fellow.'

An acceptable cover-story, she thought. She wondered if Rick Fuscante had encouraged this fiction. An accident was easier for the locals to digest than the idea that anyone had deliberately blown up the house. It was also less alarmist, less sensational, it wouldn't have some dogged reporter from the *Horaceville Gazette* snooping around in the hope of a terrific scoop. An exercise in damage limitation. Keep the citizens serene. They already had a gruesome unsolved murder too close to their quiet community for peace of mind – why give them something else to scare them? Why make them believe a bomber had been in their midst?

'Were you out there when it happened?' he asked.

She told him no. It was easier to lie than to subject herself to an interrogation. 'Can I get some coffee?'

'Sure you can.' Martin picked up the phone, punched a button, talked to somebody. 'If you go to the lounge, Jeanette will bring it to you. Is coffee all you want?'

'I don't eat breakfast.'

'Unhealthy way to start the day,' he said. 'People should always eat breakfast. I always do.' He patted his huge stomach. 'As you can see.'

She turned away from him, then changed direction, returned to the desk. 'Do you have a map of the state?'

He produced one from a stack in a drawer and gave it to her. 'Thinking of going somewhere?'

'Not really,' she said. 'Can I keep this?'

'On the house.' He smiled and his eyes vanished in folds of white flesh.

She thanked him, went to the lounge, where the woman called Jeanette had already set coffee on a table for her. Although she hadn't asked for food, there was toast and jelly. She sat down, ate the toast, poured coffee, then spread the map open. She found New Dresden, inscribed in letters so tiny she could hardly see them.

Getting there was the problem, given the conditions. If she decided she'd go at all . . .

She knew she'd try. She didn't have to think about it. It would be hazardous, and slow going, but if she left now she might make it before nightfall. And when she got there, *if* she got there – what then?

She'd go to the Eight Ball, of course. She had no other point of reference.

And then what?

No, the prospect was wrongheaded. Even if she managed to locate Irene Passmore, which was far from guaranteed, would Irene know Stan's whereabouts? There had to be a simpler way – except she couldn't think of it. She stared at the map, gazing at the thin veinwork of roads and hearing an echo of Stan Thorogood's phone call: 'He was secure there, he was safe, he always claimed—'

Safe. Safe from what? Tell me what you mean, Stan. Speak to me.

She stared hard at the map as if she might somehow divine Stan's location simply by the act of fixing her eyes on the roads and rivers and lakes.

New Dresden.

She ran an eye down the map. She saw Cooperstown, five miles from New Dresden.

She remembered the Baseball Hall of Fame, that trip with her father more than twenty years ago. That sunny afternoon behind the rundown farmhouse and the tall stalks of grass and wild flowers and the wild cat she kept trying to catch and how she'd snagged her jeans on brambles, and it occurred to her that maybe Irene had gone to that old house, but she couldn't think why she'd retreat to such a forlorn place, couldn't envisage Irene, outgoing and brassy, a devout New Yorker, becoming a hermit the way her father had.

New Dresden. No, it was too far.

But worth a shot.

She supposed she'd have to tell Fuscante about her intention. He'd try to talk her out of it, of course. It was a risky trip on bad roads. She'd end up skidding into a ditch and stranded. He wouldn't be able to keep an eye on her and he didn't have the manpower to send somebody with her. There was always the chance of 'Gladd' turning up again, and that might be unpleasant, worse than unpleasant. And so on.

He'd have a hundred reasons, all of them solid and reasonable.

She felt an obligation to tell him.

She put her cigarette out, folded the map and stuffed it in her purse. She walked into the lobby, used the desk phone to call the HPD. She asked for Fuscante. A voice she recognized as that of Gomez said, 'He's out at the moment. Say, is that Miss Malle?'

'Yes it is.'

'Thought I knew that voice. How ya doing?'

'I'm all right. When do you expect him back?'

'When it comes to the sheriff, you can never tell. You got a message for him?'

'No, no message.'

'I think he's out at your father's house with some guys I never saw before – if you want to call him on his cellphone.'

'It's not important.'

Okay, she'd tried to reach him. She'd done her duty. She walked out of the hotel. She moved towards her car. Low in the sky the sun was as cold and disapproving as a prosecutor's eye. The parking-lot was empty, no sign of a Horaceville PD car. She scraped ice from the windshield with the edge of a credit-card, making a spyhole. Then she hesitated before unlocking the door.

She thought: *Go. This is my business. It was* my *father who was murdered.* But even as she settled behind the wheel and fastened her seat-belt a voice in her head said, 'This isn't totally sensible, Andrea.'

But she was going anyhow. Because she had to. Because too many things didn't gel and too many questions hung unanswered and while Fuscante was going through the charred rubble of the house with his explosives experts, she'd explore the outer edges of the mysteries – if she could.

She turned the key in the ignition.

chapter *Eighteen*

*S*he couldn't drive much more than ten mph most of the time. She listened to the tyre-chains grind over the iced surface of snow, but even with the chains to prevent slippage, the car slithered now and again and she had to think, *Do you just float into the skid, or do you brake lightly and hope for the best?* She saw no other traffic and thought, *How sensible people are to avoid these conditions.*

But not you, Andrea. Not you. She held the wheel as if her hands were welded to it. Her fingers became stiff, her wrists ached, the cut in the palm of her hand throbbed.

White fields stretched to an arctic blue horizon. Telephone poles were glossy constructs of ice. Icicles dangled in fantastic coruscating configurations from wires. She had the sensation she was the only person in the world. She wished now she'd persisted in contacting Fuscante to say where she was going.

She'd underestimated isolation.

At noon she stopped in a small town called Govanville where she hurried out of the cold – it was below zero, it had to be, her skin was chilled, her joints frozen – and went inside a diner. She ate vegetable soup and Saltines and checked her map. She was twenty miles from New Dresden and already stressed from the concentration of driving. She smoked a couple of cigarettes, drank coffee, peered from the steamed-up window across the parking-lot. Hers was the only vehicle out there. She was the only customer in the diner.

She remembered what Fuscante had said about the Pharaohs killing the slaves who knew the locations of the tombs. Had her father known something he wasn't supposed to know? A security job he'd done for a paranoid client, say. Somebody who didn't like the idea that Dennis Malle had the blueprints and knew the passwords and the electronic codes of a certain security system. Somebody crazy enough to kill to protect this secret, crazy enough to blow up a house in case secret material might be concealed in a hiding-place.

She ransacked her head for memories of her father's clients, but she'd never met any of them personally, and he'd never dropped names. He'd mentioned places he'd been to, and he always brought presents back from Malaysia or Egypt or wherever he'd travelled – but that was as far as it went. He didn't talk about his work except in broad terms. He might say he'd done some work for a Kuwaiti oil billionaire, or he'd completed a project for an industrialist in Italy, but he never identified these people. MalCon survived in a competitive industry because it was run with absolute discretion.

And *if* he'd died because of some knowledge he

possessed, and *if* he shared all aspects of MalCon's business with Stan, then it followed that Stan was in danger too.

If. The world was all ifs. You couldn't build bridges with ifs. Ifs spawned only perplexities.

She rose, went to the cash-register, paid. Then she walked outside, rushed to her car, switched on the heater. She drove through Govanville, which was decrepit and gloomy, faded storefronts, abandoned sidewalks, one set of traffic signals at the town's only significant intersection. And then she was back on the narrow road, dead trees pressing in on her and the wintry sun beginning its early decline. Only once did she see another vehicle, a jeep driving in the opposite direction.

She calculated she had about four hours of daylight remaining. She tried to drive a little faster, but when she gave the car more gas it tended to fishtail. At fifteen miles an hour she had some control – beyond that she felt nervous and uncertain. Eventually she saw signs for Cooperstown, the Baseball Hall of Fame, the Corvette Americana Hall of Fame, the Cooperstown Dreams Park, whatever a Dreams Park was.

Three miles before Cooperstown she came to the intersection for New Dresden and she took it. The last five miles.

This road was worse than the one she'd just left. Narrower, even more icy, it had apparently been ploughed cursorily. Drifts banked against the shoulders allowed a clearway of about six feet, so that she had the sensation of driving through a tunnel. And now she was heading directly into the sun and had to adjust the visor. Dead of winter and you need sunglasses. She leaned forward over the wheel, concentrated, wondered what

would happen if a car came toward her unexpectedly.
But no other vehicle appeared.

She had the road to herself all the way to New
Dresden, where she parked in the main street – the only
street – and sat for a moment, massaging an ache out
of her shoulders. She looked around. A hardware store
called Stoddard's, a grocery named the New Dresden
Food Mart, a shop with the unlikely name of La Scala
that appeared chintzy, as if it had been decorated with
stray tourists in mind, maybe people who got lost on
their way to the attractions of Cooperstown. It was
the kind of shop that sold Crabtree & Evelyn soap and
Laura Ashley fabrics and hand-made scented candles,
and it had a CLOSED sign hanging in the window.

She couldn't imagine her father in this place, couldn't
picture him walking along this street; any images she
managed to conjure up were spectral. But then she
couldn't envisage him in Horaceville either, which
compared to New Dresden was a metropolis. *You
haunt me, Father*, she thought, *even as you elude me*.

The Eight Ball. She couldn't see it from the car.

She got out, tightened her scarf, walked to the end of
the block. She passed a drycleaners, a lawyer's office, a
bar called MacEnroe's Tavern. At the end of the block
she paused. New Dresden was a one-block burg. She
looked at the other side of the street. A post office. A
thrift store. A café by the name of Sally's Ham'n'Eggs.
She watched a man come out of the post office and go
into the café and she realized this was the first sign of
life she'd seen so far in this place.

Beyond the café was a red-brick two-storey building
outside which hung a big black ball with a white figure
8 inscribed on it. She crossed the street, arms extended
a little to maintain her balance on the ice, which she

noticed had been spread with rock-salt and was melting here and there to slush. She reached the sidewalk and moved down the block towards the Eight Ball.

You came this way, Dad, she thought. *You passed through this same door I'm about to push open . . .*

The room was small and dark. A cigar burned in an ashtray on the bar although there was no sign of the smoker. A muted lamp with the word Pabst printed on the glass shade illuminated the area behind the counter. She had an impression of tables and chairs, but her eyes hadn't grown accustomed to the shadows here. She didn't like the place, an instinctive reaction – it was typical of thousands of smalltown bars where only locals drank, where tight cliques grew and calcified over the years, and strangers were regarded with a certain hostile wariness.

She wished she hadn't come. She wished she hadn't surrendered to impulse. This curiosity was a by-product of grief and anger. Did she *really* think she'd learn *anything* in a place called the Eight Ball in New Dresden? What did she imagine she was doing, playing goddam detective? Her world had tilted and been blown out of focus, that was it, her normal patterns of behaviour had short-circuited. The tidy arrangements of her life had come unglued, and there was too much spillage, and it was going out of control and suddenly she couldn't manage it, couldn't get the spillage back inside the appropriate compartments, couldn't impose order on things. Leave this place, she thought. Go back to your car. Drive away. Return to all that stuff you did before, applying Band-Aids to bust marriages, listening to the grievances of husbands and wives and tales of emotional cruelty and physical violence, broken china and busted heads, kids becoming neurotic under the weight of their parents' mutual animosities, work you used to consider useful and constructive, marriage guidance, counselling the bruised, the walking wounded.

Face it. You couldn't counsel a goddam beaver on log-chewing in your present state of mind, Andrea. You couldn't guide a blind man across a street.

'Help you in some way?'

The man was .sitting at one of the shadowed tables just beyond the reach of light. He rose, walked to the bar, picked the cigar out of the ashtray and sucked on it.

'A Scotch,' she said, 'please.'

The man went behind the bar. She saw him clearly now in the lamplight. He was maybe forty-five, bulky, needed a shave. He wore a dark-blue crew-neck sweater with a beige reindeer pattern. 'Perfect day for a Scotch,' he said. 'Warm them bones.'

She approached the bar, climbed on to a stool. 'They need warming,' she said.

He poured from a bottle of Bell's. 'Ice? Water?'

'Straight,' she said.

'Coming up.' He slid the drink toward her.

She felt the heat at once, back of her throat, her chest. She lit a cigarette just as the guy took another long drag on his fat cigar. He propped his elbows on the bar and leaned toward her. His thick eyebrows were unruly but his dark hair had been cut close to the scalp.

'Passing through?' he asked.

'You could say that.'

'Picked a great time of year,' he said.

She fingered her father's passport in her coat pocket. Then she took it out and opened it, placing it down on the bar with the photograph up. She pushed it toward the guy, who reacted more with suspicion than with curiosity, as if the sight of an official document of any kind suggested a world he didn't welcome – Feds, Revenue officials, any of that gang down there in DC who ran the whole show. Bullies with warrants and badges.

'You know this man?' she asked.

He picked up the passport as if it were a dead fish. He squinted at the photograph, then raised his eyes to Andrea. 'Couldn't say for sure.'

The secrecy of smalltown bars. The discretion of bartenders. She imagined his thoughts. *She's the guy's wife maybe and she's asking questions and what we do around here is we protect the confidentiality of our customers. We're guys and we look out for one another and we don't give shit away.* He handed her back the passport.

'He was here in October,' she said.

'October, huh.'

'He drank here and then he went out and ran his car into the back of a pick-up truck.'

'You with the law?'

She shook her head.

'The state liquor-licence people?'

'No,' she said. 'I'm not going to bust you for serving an inebriated man, if that's what's worrying you. He's my father. *Was* my father.'

The guy crumpled out his cigar with one deft stab. 'Last October, you say.'

'Right.'

'He's the guy that ran into Artie Strumm's pick-up.'

'That's the one.'

The guy shrugged. 'Yeah, I remember it. Fact, he sat

right where you're sitting now. He was here for maybe
three of four hours, I guess.'

'Alone?' *You sat on this same stool, Dennis Malle.*

'So far as I can remember.'

'Did you speak with him?'

'The weather maybe.'

'He was here for four hours and the weather was the
only topic of conversation?'

'He didn't look like the kind of a guy who wanted
conversation.'

'And nobody came to meet him?'

The barman shook his head. 'I remember he used
the phone a couple times.'

'Did you hear him talk with anyone?'

'Nope. I think whoever he was calling wasn't answering. So he just went on drinking. Then he left. Next
thing I heard he'd driven up the exhaust pipe of Artie's
pick-up. Which didn't please Artie none.'

'I can imagine,' she said. She closed the passport.

'You said he *was* your father?'

'He died.'

'That's too bad. So you're like looking into his
background or something?'

'Something,' she said. 'Was that the only time you
saw him here?'

'Yeah, it was.'

She took off her gloves, studied the tiny cut in the
centre of her palm. She raised her eyes, looked at the
bottles of liquor lined up on glass shelves. She spotted
two single-malts, a Macallan and a Bowmore. She
thought of her father sitting on this same stool hour
after hour. He'd have chosen the Macallan. Between
drinks he'd tried to contact somebody by phone. Who?
She left her Scotch unfinished. The ghost was heavy

suddenly, the air around her weighted with her father's presence.

'Tell me,' she said. 'Does a woman ever come in here – a woman with dyed platinum hair she wears piled up on her head? She's what you'd call . . . full-figured.' *Probably you'd say big tits or humungous hooters*, she thought.

'I can't think of anybody matching that description,' he answered.

'You're sure?'

'I know my customers. Matter of fact, we don't get many women in here.'

I bet. She tapped the passport on the bar. Think think. Go back down the years, back to that old farmhouse and the long grass and the cat you couldn't catch and that burned structure surrounded by a riot of weeds. She stuck the passport in her pocket and looked at the barman, who was picking cigar flakes from his teeth with the edge of a playing-card, a jack of Diamonds.

'You know the countryside around here pretty well?' she asked.

'Born and raised in ND,' he said.

'Is there an old windmill somewhere?'

'A windmill?'

'Yeah. A burned-out old thing.'

The barman smiled for the first time since Andrea had entered the place. 'Jeez, that takes me back a few years. You must be talking about the Logan property. It's the only windmill I ever heard of in this neck of the woods and she burned down . . . must be twenty-five years ago, maybe longer.'

'How far is it?'

'Three miles roughly.'

'Can you give me directions?'

'Now why would you be interested in a ruined old windmill?'

'Sentimentality,' she said.

He looked doubtful. 'And you want to go there? Down to the old Logan place and look at this wreck of a windmill? You sure?'

She nodded. He took a paper napkin from a stack and plucked a ballpoint pen from a drawer. 'You can't take a car down there in this weather,' he said. He drew a few quick lines on the napkin. 'You'll get maybe as far as the Oak River Bridge on wheels. After that, you're looking at a quarter-mile walk. And I'm talking a difficult quarter-mile – drifts out there can go ten feet high, maybe more, depending on how the wind blew them. If I was you, I'd junk the idea. There's nothing down there except an empty old house and that windmill.'

She tugged the napkin out from under his hand and looked at it. She saw she'd have to take the main road out of New Dresden as far as the Oak River Bridge – which he'd marked as ORB – and then walk a line he'd drawn from the bridge to the windmill, which he'd indicated with a pattern resembling crossbones.

'Don't say I didn't warn you.'

'I won't,' she said.

'And don't get stuck out there, for Christ's sake. Because nobody's gonna find you if you do.'

'I won't get stuck,' she said.

'You say that now.'

She paid for her drink, stepped down from the stool. Outside, the sun was turning from crimson to a frigid orange as it died. She had an hour of daylight, maybe ninety minutes. She crossed the street to her car and noticed a pale moon emerge in the darkening blue. And she wondered if there wasn't some old omen associated with the sun and the moon in the sky simultaneously.

A bad or a good one?

She couldn't remember.

chapter *Nineteen*

The bridge was an old wood structure straddling a stretch of fast-flowing black water. Andrea had left her car about a hundred yards away where the road had become impossible to drive, and now she gazed across the bridge to the other side. All she could see were dead trees and drifts. She couldn't remember crossing a bridge twenty years ago, and for a moment wondered if this was in fact the place her father had brought her back then, or if there was another burned-out windmill somewhere else nearby, one the barman didn't know about. She thought it highly unlikely. In twenty years memories mildewed, small details faded. In any case, the time her father had brought her here he'd driven through Cooperstown first, so there had to be another access road to this property from the Cooperstown side. She might never have crossed this river at any time in her life.

She clutched the icy handrail, didn't look down at the water some twenty feet below. Halfway across she considered turning back. She could find accommodation in New Dresden and start out again early in the morning, but she'd come this far and she couldn't see the sense in retreating. Besides, she was impatient, and although the idea of trudging quarter of a mile through this awful terrain in failing light wasn't exactly a joy, she wasn't about to turn back now.

She reached the other side of the bridge. There was a pathway of sorts through the trees, where recent winds had created drifts that might have been wondrous things if you were a nature photographer but were wretched for anyone on foot. She trudged, finding herself at one point waist-deep and struggling. The snow was less deep the closer she got to the edge of the smothered path, where the strength of the wind had been blunted by trees. She moved for a while through mounds that reached as far as her knees, then paused.

Hard going. Quit smoking. Her lungs felt like seared meat.

She moved again, feeling as if she were locked in combat with the forces of nature, conspiratorial and always overwhelming. Whirlwinds, tropical storms, blizzards. Nature had all the ammo.

She was chilled and miserable and breathing hard. An old windmill and an abandoned farmhouse. *You're out of your head*. She imagined an oil-painting: *Crazy Woman in a Winter Landscape*. She tried to think warm thoughts – an electric blanket, a log fire. Her head was like frozen tundra and the tiny voice in her skull that told her, 'It's not too late to turn around,' spoke in a foreign tongue. How far had she come from the bridge, anyhow? She had no way of knowing. The sky was dimming. The idea of darkness caused her a flutter of unease. She should have brought a flashlight. A cellular phone might have been useful also. Too late to think of such things. She moved a little faster, not much.

And then she smelled smoke, a faint whiff coming from somewhere in front of her. Burning wood, she thought. Then she lost it a moment and the air smelled only of cold – if cold had a smell, and it seemed to her by this time that it did, sharp and clinical, like a mix of eucalyptus and menthol.

She caught it again, definitely wood burning, and it had its source somewhere ahead. She'd been flagging, but the scent lifted her. A fire, a hearth, life . . .

Life. Somebody had lit a fire. But who?

There was only one way to find out and, although she felt a little jolt of uncertainty, she started forward again. The path rose gradually. Breathless, she reached the top of the incline.

And there it was below her some five hundred yards away, the old farmhouse, but different, altered by winter into an ice-structure, an angular igloo. Smoke rose from a chimney. On the far side of the field way beyond the house stood the weird wreck of the windmill, hunched on the skyline like a big, dilapidated snowman. She started down the slope, remembering how this place had been in that long-lost summer, green and alive with butterflies and crickets clicking in the long grass, and her father sitting at the table with Stan Thorogood, the litter of paper, notebooks, beer stashed in a Styrofoam cooler, a bottle of Macallan on the floor. 'This is the brain of MalCon.'

She felt a tweak of sadness for everything that was lost. But she didn't have time for sorrowful indulgences, she kept moving, heading down the slope, drawn by the rich blue-black smoke. The windows of the place were unlit: they reflected the enfeebled sun like light from some distant foundry. Despite the smoke, she had the feeling the house had recently been abandoned. She wouldn't know that for sure until she knocked on the door, would she? Was that the approach to take? Go straight up, rap on wood, see if anybody answered? And if a stranger opened the door – what then? Sorry to trouble you, I happened to be passing?

The house was surrounded with the clutter and junk of years – old tyres, a rusted car raised on cinderblocks, the intestines of a tractor that had been stripped down and left to rot, antique farm equipment that lay in the snow like skeletons. She couldn't imagine anyone as vibrant and citified as Irene Passmore surviving in this place.

Coming here is a mistake, she thought.

She reached the porch. The roof hung at a slanted angle, worse than she remembered from before. A broken windowpane was covered with brown paper cut from a grocery bag. She could read the lettering: *esden Food Mar*. She remembered her father saying, 'It doesn't look like much. But never be fooled by appearances, kid. Now why don't you play outside while Stan and I do some serious brainstorming?'

She raised a hand to knock. She hit the wood with her knuckles and waited, shivering, trying to distance herself from the way her jeans pressed cold and damp against her skin and her feet froze inside her boots.

Nothing happened. Nobody answered. She knocked again, waited some more, then decided she'd just turn the handle and go inside, what the hell, she wasn't going away from here empty-handed, she'd come too far and she was in a hurry, she had a long return trip

to Horaceville in front of her. She turned the knob,
pushed the door a little way, then took two steps into
the room.

Smoke smouldered darkly in the fireplace. The chimney wasn't pulling properly and clouds swirled back
inside the room. She saw a heap of wadded papers
slowly burning, some in flames, others red and curling
around the edges. She noticed this on the periphery of
her vision, because her attention was drawn to the far
side of the room where a door was open and a man
appeared in the adjoining room, watching her, his face
hidden in shadow. She stood very still.

She didn't know what to say. She'd intruded. She'd
come where she wasn't wanted. The man moved forward a couple of steps.

She felt her breath coagulate in her throat. He
was familiar, the way he stood, the slight slump of
shoulders. The clothes were wrong, he wasn't wearing
the three-piece suits he always favoured – he was
dressed in jeans, a thick sweater, a cracked leather
jacket.

'*Stan?*'

He stood in the threshold. 'Go back where you
came from.'

'Jesus, Stan, it's me, it's *Andrea.*' She had a powerful
urge to hug him, and maybe find in his touch a small
connection to her father. The recovery of lost times. But
his manner kept her back, and the tone of his voice.

'Go, just go, you hear me?'

'Stan, what is it? I don't understand.'

'Go, for God's sake.'

'Stan—'

He held a hand up in a say-no-more, I-don't-want-
to-hear gesture. He came a little closer. He'd changed

since she'd last seen him. His thinning hair was more grey and lifeless, but there were deeper changes in him, the sunken cheeks, the lack of colour in his lips. His skin was grey. He was clearly unwell. This wasn't the joker with the feeble magic routines. This wasn't Stan, the Abracadabra Man who'd found silver dollars in her ears.

'What the hell is going on, Stan? For Christ's sake, tell me.'

He approached the fireplace, stabbed some smouldering papers down into the flames with the sole of his boot. Sparks flew out into the room.

'What is it, Stan? All this hiding, all this . . .' She didn't have the words.

He had a sudden coughing attack, made a funnel of his hand and held it to his lips. He bent over, spluttered. 'This is no fucking place for you. You hear me?'

'Stan,' she said. 'An explanation. That's all I ask.'

'The fuckers got Dennis. They're not getting me. No goddam way are they getting me. I told him we should have left the country altogether, but no, he figured that was too obvious. Lie low where they least expect it, he said. Right. Sure. Smart.'

'Who, Stan? Who are you afraid of?'

He stamped on the bundled papers in the fire again. 'Leave. Do yourself a favour. The less you're involved the better.'

'I'm already involved, Stan. Who the hell killed my father?'

He turned to her and his face was hard. She'd never seen him look this way before. 'I'll throw you out of here physically if I have to. Don't make me do that.'

'Is it somebody you did some work for, is that it? A former client? Tell me, Stan.'

'Yeah, yeah. That's what it is. That's exactly it.' He was flat and unconvincing, a bad actor.

'You're a goddam liar,' she said.

'You asked, I answered. That's all you're gonna get,' he said. 'The door. Go the way you came in. For your own good.'

'I'm not leaving until you tell me the truth.'

He caught her by the arm and steered her toward the door, but she broke free from him. 'I told you, Stan, I'm not leaving.'

A figure appeared in the doorway. Andrea's first impression was of a shotgun. Then her eyes were drawn up to the face – unadorned and white and strained, hair silver and cut very short, mannish. But there was no mistaking the wide mouth, and the big heavyweight plaid jacket failed to conceal the large breasts.

'You better listen to Stan,' Irene Passmore said.

Andrea wondered at transformations, disguises. She had the feeling that everything in the familiar world had slipped away from her, she'd fallen through space and time into some other reality where people had altered beyond recognition and nothing gelled.

'You don't have to point a gun at me, Irene.'

'Call it enforcement,' Irene said. The looks might have changed but the deep voice was unmistakable. 'Just do what Stan tells you. Get the hell out of here while there's time.'

Andrea still didn't move. 'You and Stan . . .'

'You surprised? Dennis didn't tell you about us?'

'My father didn't tell me about *anything*,' Andrea said.

'You get close to somebody after seventeen years,' Irene said in such a way that the subject was closed, no further explanation was going to be given.

Stan said, 'This is wasting time. We've gotta move.'

Andrea couldn't imagine Irene being with Stan. The big woman with the flamboyantly dyed hair, the slightly built balding man with the sharp suits and the expression of a spaniel eager to please. An attraction of opposites. A longtime office affair maybe. But now they were both dressed in drab winter clothing and there was no more flamboyance about Irene and Stan was no longer so keen to please.

'How did you find us, anyhow?' Irene asked.

'Some niece of yours told Leon you were up here.'

'That goddam Charlotte,' Irene Passmore said.

'Charlotte?' Stan asked. 'The one you sent a get-well card?'

'Don't say it, Stan.'

'I told you, I told you at the time that was sheer goddam folly,' Stan said.

'Yeah, well, it's too late to get into an argument now,' Irene said. 'The main thing is to get the hell out. I got everything in one backpack.'

'And I burned every piece of paper I could.' Stan's voice was weary. 'That's it. Finished.'

Andrea listened to this exchange and felt her presence had been momentarily overlooked. These people had a fugitive life of some kind to lead, and it meant leaving few traces, moving to new places where they might settle into deeper anonymity. She was watching a tableau involving two highly stressed people whose world was one of tension and anxiety – but mainly what they projected was pure fear, concentrated fear, the kind that prompts a manic urgency to move, to stay one step ahead of whatever it was that pursued them.

Stan looked at her. 'You won't leave?'

She said, 'I want some straight answers, Stan.'

'Oh, kid,' he said, and just for a moment he sounded like the Stan she remembered. She half expected him to produce a deck of cards and tell her to pick one and it would turn up in his inside pocket. 'Kid, kid. You don't want answers, believe me. Straight or otherwise. You just don't want them.'

'Wrong. I want them badly, Stan.'

Irene slung an olive-green backpack over one shoulder, handed the shotgun to Stan, and stepped in front of her. 'Some other time, babe. Do yourself a real big favour and split.'

Andrea watched her move towards the front door. Stan turned, followed her out to the porch.

'Wait,' Andrea said.

But they were already descending the porch steps.

'Wait!' Andrea walked to the doorway. Irene's backpack struck and snapped the spine of a long icicle, a crack suggestive of glass breaking. Stan and Irene reached the foot of the steps and moved along the side of the house.

Andrea hurried on to the porch. Stan, scanning the landscape as he moved, followed Irene toward a pick-up truck that lay under a black tarpaulin. Irene whisked the tarp off, opened the passenger door, threw her backpack inside. Stan opened the door on the driver's side. The truck was four-wheel-drive with huge tyres that lifted the chassis about five feet from the ground. Even so – how could it get out through the drifts? No way, Andrea thought, then remembered there was an alternative track to the house, one that took you not back through New Dresden but towards Cooperstown instead, and maybe Stan had already cleared the worst of the snow or salted the ice and he knew the truck could make it.

Andrea heard the truck roar to life and she raced toward it, calling Stan's name, seeing exhaust sully the air as the pick-up groaned and crunched forward through snow. She chased it some twenty yards, thinking she could catch it up, force it to stop, drag answers out of Stan somehow, but the vehicle – sliding a little – was pulling away from her and she lost her footing and slithered face down beside the old tractor, and when she looked back up she saw the tail-lights burn red, the truck ploughing through snow, powder and ice spraying the fuel-tainted air. She beat her gloved fists into the snow in frustration. Goddam, the truck was getting away from her, and whatever secrets Irene and Stan knew were going with it. She watched the vehicle skirt the edge of the field where the windmill stood – that had to be the path out of here, and Stan must surely have cleared it earlier, because now the pick-up wasn't labouring quite the same way it had been before.

And then she heard something else, a rasping, distinct and harsh, coming from the vicinity of the windmill where the very last of the sun laid a pale red patina over everything. She saw two snowmobiles roar into view from behind the windmill, black shapes buzzing across the white surface. Instinctively, she told herself not to move, to stay very still on the ground and make herself invisible, if it wasn't too late for that. The air around her was charged with the static of menace and she no longer felt the cold, she was one step outside herself, an observer watching two snowmobiles speeding toward the slow-moving pick-up, seeing the riders' visors glint and white vapour trails of snow rush away.

She wanted to shut her eyes but couldn't.

Even as the snowmobiles approached the tail of the

truck she continued to watch, sensing that something terrible was about to happen, and she was powerless to do anything to prevent it. The pick-up was trying to gather enough speed to shake off the two pursuers, but it couldn't get away. Andrea saw a shotgun emerge from the passenger window and heard the blast, but the riders were undeterred because Irene's aim had been bad. The gun went off again, and again Irene missed, and now the truck sashayed to one side as if Stan had lost concentration behind the wheel. The two black hornet-like vehicles dropped back a couple of yards and one of the riders, with a gesture that was almost casual, produced a weapon, an automatic of some kind. He opened fire.

Rap rap rap rap rap. The flat hard sound was reminiscent of a woodpecker a long way off.

She saw the pick-up skid to a halt and tilt at a bizarre angle: one of the tyres must have been blown out. Stan and Irene got down from the cab and began to hurry away, stumbling as they rushed. Irene was trying to reload the shotgun and Stan was shouting in a strident voice, but he was too far away for Andrea to hear what he was saying. Before Irene could get the shotgun loaded, Stan went down in the snow like a tree axed in one stroke, and Irene stopped to bend over him. *Rap rap rap rap.* She turned a moment and screamed at her assailants, but then she was struck and fell in such a way that her body covered Stan's.

Andrea thought: *No. Not Stan and Irene. No!*

A jeep approached from the direction the pick-up had been travelling, and came to halt. A man emerged and stood, hands in his coat pockets, some fifty feet from where Stan and Irene lay. The snowmobiles zoomed toward the man. He took off his hat and ran a hand across his black hair. He spoke to the riders, then gestured toward the house.

Andrea flattened herself in the thick snow. She didn't know if she'd been seen or if the snow-blasted shape of the old tractor concealed her from view. She moved backwards slowly, reverse crawling. She heard the snowmobiles idle, then the sound of the jeep starting up. And for a moment she thought everyone was leaving.

Instead, they came down towards the house.

She kept back-tracking on her knees, slithering, hearing the frantic rush of her blood and the sound of her heart thudding. She was praying now for darkness. She wanted the sanctuary of nightfall. She shuffled back, and back, labouring, barely able to breathe. *They'll see me. If they haven't already. They'll see me and they'll kill me.* Backing up, face to the ground, like an animal burrowing.

She sensed she was was close to the porch without daring to raise her head and look. And then she was under it, but still she felt too exposed, and so she kept going back until she was below the house itself, concealed in a cold, dark crawl-space filled with frozen cobwebs and stiff old newspapers and hardened sheets of fibreglass insulation that tickled her face and frigid muck that might have been the abandoned nests of rats. She lay more motionless than she'd ever done in her life. She turned herself to clay, a statue stashed and forgotten in the foundations of the place. She thought: *I don't exist.*

The snowmobiles and the jeep parked close to the porch. The jeep door slammed.

She heard heavy footsteps on the porch.

Somebody said, 'A quick look-round and we're out of here.'

The voice was one she recognized.

It belonged to the man who called himself Gladd.

chapter *Twenty*

*S*he felt she was trapped inside a tiny cavern. The air reeked of dead things, mould. 'Gladd''s voice was a mumble over her head. He was standing directly above her, separated only by a thickness of wood and a layer of rotted insulation. The fibreglass made her skin itch. She removed a glove, scratched her face and scalp.

Another voice, this one high and fluting, said something like 'Burned every scrap of paper they had . . .'

The sound of – what? Drawers being opened and shut? Closet doors slammed? Something made of glass fell and broke on the floor. She heard it shatter. What were they looking for? What did they expect to find? More footsteps. More rummaging, breakage.

She moved her head. She had maybe two inches' clearance between her body and the underside of the floor.

'Gladd' said, 'I don't think he'd have kept anything anyhow.'

The man with the high voice said, 'You didn't feel that way about Malle.'

'Gladd': 'Dennis was way smarter. Plus he had stronger survival instincts. Stan was never in the same league when it came to self-preservation.'

She changed her position and a portion of insulation slid out of place and a rotted slat of wood slipped to the ground as she turned on her side. She wondered if the sound carried up through the floorboards and so she held her breath and shut her eyes and pretended she was someplace else a long way from here. A nail dangling from the wood scratched the back of her hand, and any pretence she might have maintained was gone. *You're underneath this goddam house and there are killers just over your head and you're not going anywhere, not even in your mind.*

The man with the penny-whistle voice said, 'You want to do this house just in case, Hal?'

Hal, she thought. The impostor had a name.

'Wouldn't take a minute to rig it. You did the other one.'

Hal said, 'This is different. If Stan kept anything here, it's already ashes.'

She realized they were talking about a demolition job, they were pondering the idea of blowing this house up like her father's. She'd be incinerated if they did that. She'd die in smoke and flame with a burning house collapsing all around her.

There was a long silence from above.

What were they doing? Setting up an explosive?

I have to get out of here. Crawl away. How could she do that without being heard or seen?

She thought, *No, don't, don't destroy it.*

'It's your call, Hal.'

Another silence.

Hal: 'I guess we'll leave it as is.'

'I just noticed some kerosene. We might've had ourselves a real nice blaze if you didn't want to go with the explosives.'

Hal: 'You worry me sometimes, Jimmy.'

Somebody else spoke, presumably the second snowmobile rider. He had a low, throaty voice. 'I always said doing a number on that other house was fucking crazy.'

Hal raised his voice angrily. 'A chance I had to take. I took it. Sometimes that's what you have to do. Take chances, Falco.'

He no longer sounded kindly. He'd shed the priestly role like a serpent sloughing off an old skin. She wondered what his last name was. Hal who?

'What about the daughter, Hal?'

Andrea felt something flap against her face. It had the texture of decayed velvet. Strands of ancient dust tangled with dried-out webs. She pushed it away.

Yeah, Hal, what about me?

The high voice: 'I still think we shoulda grabbed her a while back—'

Hal: 'You don't make these decisions, Falco. You don't make any fucking decisions.'

'She coulda told us where Malle was located. Instead you let it drift and drift.'

Hal: 'Did it ever cross your mind she might've found some way of warning her father? Huh? You ever think about that? We pressure her, she makes a quiet call to Daddy and Malle takes a hike. It's a fuck of a big country and you can lose yourself for a long time if you try hard enough. Christ knows, Dennis managed it. You don't think straight, Falco.'

'We coulda made sure she didn't contact him—'

'Oh yeah, sure, we could've finalized her, and then what? Say Malle tried to contact his daughter, only she hasn't been seen in a while by anybody, she hasn't shown up for work, her friends are missing her, and so he thinks the worst and what does he do? Huh? I'll tell you. He splits, Falco. He splits again. And we're back where we started. Looking for the fucker. Hunting through God knows how many hick towns, deeds of sale, property tax records—

Silence.

Finalized, she thought. It was an appalling euphemism.

Falco said, 'We didn't need to ice her, Hal. We coulda just followed her, that's all I'm saying, woulda saved us a whole bunch of time—'

Hal: 'She's not stupid, she notices somebody trailing her. Then what? Little warning lights flash inside her head and maybe she goes to the cops. I'm being stalked, she says. So the cops love stalkers and they get interested, and that's another whole can of worms – you don't think, Falco. You just don't fucking think.'

With resentment in his voice Falco said: 'So we leave her alone? We don't concern ourselves with her now?'

Hal replied, but she couldn't hear his answer because he'd moved beyond her range, crossing the floor, perhaps stepping inside another room, and his words were muffled.

Falco said: 'You sure that's the right idea, Hal?'

Hal returned from wherever he'd been and came back within earshot of Andrea. 'I don't usually just say stuff for the good of my health, Falco. I think it's the right idea, otherwise I wouldn't have said it, would I?'

She wished she'd heard Hal's initial reply. She wished

she knew what he'd said to Falco. 'I think it's the right idea.' Meaning what? She didn't like to speculate.

Falco said, 'She's kinda cute, I think.'

'Cute doesn't come into the equation, Falco.'

Andrea listened to footsteps, then the sound of what might have been a poker shoved into the fireplace. Maybe it was the man called Jimmy stoking the flames in disappointment because Hal had rejected the idea of destroying the property. Then Hal said something about the bodies. Something about snow. How the bodies wouldn't be discovered until spring. This isolated place, you wouldn't get many visitors out here. And it was a damn sure thing that neither Thorogood nor his woman had made friends in New Dresden, for Christ's sake. Look at the way Malle had managed to hide out near Horaceville for what – nearly two goddam years? Jesus. So nobody was going to come looking for them. You could bet your ass on that.

Hal's voice was flat and cold. He was talking about two people who'd been murdered – on *his* orders, because he was the one in charge of the killers – and he spoke as if he were reciting multiplication tables. She thought of Stan and Irene dying in the snow, and how she'd found her father dead, and her mind was filled with images of bloodstained crystals, red ice. Lives snuffed out. And she had absolutely no doubt that if they discovered her concealed under this house she'd receive the same fate.

Maybe that was what awaited her anyhow. Maybe that was what Hal's idea amounted to.

She heard them move on to the porch. She heard Hal say, 'It's damn cold. I hate this shit season.'

Jimmy laughed. 'That's why we need a fire, Hal.'

Then Hal said, 'I'd like to know who the fuck killed Malle.'

Falco: 'I don't see it matters. Guy's dead.'

Hal: 'You're talking shit, Falco. Sure it matters. Somebody shows up out of nowhere and does the job and you think this information isn't important to us?'

Falco: 'It might have been this prowler character.'

'It might. I want to know. I want certainty.'

A silence. Somebody shuffled his boots on the porch and made an exaggerated shivering sound. 'Brrrrrr.'

Hal: 'I'll go back to Sky—'

The rest of what he said was lost to her amidst the sound of them clambering down the porch steps. Their feet crunched as they walked back to their vehicles. 'Skysomething.' She didn't move for a long time. She heard the sound of engines fade in the distance and silence came back and still she didn't move. Only when she was completely certain she was safe did she emerge from under the house.

Her back ached. She had a crick in her neck and a pain in her heart.

It was night now, and the countryside lit by an icy moon.

The silence around her was profound and unsettling, a fragile skein drawn over the landscape. She glanced towards the windmill, saw the pick-up illuminated as if by fluorescence.

She thought of the two bodies stiffening as the temperature dropped and dropped. And she wondered what all this death meant, what these fugitive lives signified, where Hal fitted in the framework.

She stumbled through snow into the clear chill night, without once looking back.

chapter *Twenty-One*

She drove through moonlight all the way back to Horaceville, glancing time and again in the rear-view mirror, half expecting to see Hal's jeep or some other vehicle, but there was nobody behind her. When she reached the hotel she wanted to sleep – better yet, to black out – but knew she couldn't. She walked through the empty foyer and climbed the stairs to her bedroom. She needed to contact Fuscante, but first she stripped off her wet clothes, which smelled of stale detritus from the crawl-space. Her hair was filled with tiny threads of pink fibreglass. She showered quickly, found a clean pair of jeans and a sweater in her bag. When she stepped out of the bathroom the telephone was ringing.

Meg was on the line. 'We're here at JFK and it seems we're stuck. Don's gone off to see if he can scare up some kind of transportation to take us up to Henryville—'

'It's Horaceville, Mother.'

'Horaceville, then. I can never keep these backwater place-names straight in my mind.'

Andrea was about to mention the condition of the Interstate, but she wondered what was the point. Meg was in her inconvenienced-traveller mode, and had probably argued with ticket clerks and airline personnel, blaming them personally for the weather and the delays.

'Don usually finds somebody he can bribe,' Meg said. 'God, I hate airports. I hate this hanging around. All these arrival and departure boards and signs that say Cancelled or Delayed. I've been up since the crack of dawn. The flight we were supposed to catch from Miami this morning was cancelled, *of course*. I'll keep you posted, anyhow. It's been a very long day already and I'm exhausted.'

'I think you should find a hotel in Manhattan and start all over again in the morning,' Andrea said.

'We may be forced into that.'

In the background Andrea could hear Don's voice: 'Seems nobody wants to work in this country any more, goddammit. Little bit of ice and the whole state comes to a standstill. Lawd.'

Meg said, 'Oops. Don's having a row with somebody. I'll be in touch.'

Andrea said goodbye, hung up. She didn't want Meg's company at this time. She didn't want to relate events to Meg, because she'd react with hysteria. Your father's house *blown* up? Stan and Irene *killed*? She'd rant at the cops and pressure Don into making phone calls to the influential people he reputedly knew. 'Get something done, Don. Call that guy you know in the FBI. Call that senator, whatsisname. The world's coming to pieces and you're just standing there. I want to see some goddam action here!' Meg wouldn't be good in this situation.

She sat on the edge of the bed, dialled the number for the Police Department. She asked for Fuscante and was put through to him immediately.

He sounded aggressive or worried, she couldn't decide which. 'Where the hell have you been? I've been trying to reach you for hours.'

'I took a drive.'

'A drive? Where?'

'New Dresden.'

'New *Dresden*?'

'I need to see you.'

'Likewise,' he said. 'I'll come to the hotel. I'm leaving now. Next time you decide to take a hike, let me know beforehand.'

'Why?'

'Because I don't want you out there running around, that's why.'

'It worries you, does it?'

'Yeah, frankly, it worries me. In the circumstances, don't you think that's a normal response?'

Normal. She didn't know normal any more. 'I'll meet you in the lounge.'

'No, not the lounge. It's too public. I'll come up to your room.'

'Fine,' she said.

He hung up a little sharply. She brushed her damp hair without enthusiasm. She looked at her face in the bathroom mirror. Her shiny red hair emphasized how pale she'd become. But make-up, no, she wasn't interested in painting her face, applying lipstick, eye-liner, whatever. She didn't have the inclination. She smoked

a cigarette, tried to shove events at the farmhouse out
of her mind, but they wouldn't be exorcised – she could
still hear the ugly rasp of the snowmobiles and the sound
of automatic gunfire.

She walked to the window. The lake was glassy
under the moon and the small boats at the jetty were
ice-locked. It might have been serene in a wintry way,
but it wasn't, because Hal was out there somewhere.
Hal and his cronies. And she didn't know what they
were doing, what they planned, or what compelled
them to kill. She felt exposed suddenly in the window
– as if a sniper were watching her through an infra-red
scope attached to a high-powered rifle – and stepped
back, drawing the curtains, blocking the night out. She
smoked another cigarette and just as she finished it she
heard Fuscante at the door.

She let him into the room. He looked and sounded
cranky. 'It smells like an ashtray in here,' he said.

'I smoke. I'm an addict. I'm working on it. Don't
lecture me.'

He unbuttoned his overcoat and sat in the chair by
the dressing-table and stretched his long legs. 'You go
to New Dresden without telling me. Why? You like to
do things solo?'

'I tried to reach you.'

'You didn't try very hard.'

'Because I knew you'd talk me out of it.'

'Damn right I would.'

'By the way, I didn't see any of this surveillance you
talked about,' she said. 'I wasn't conscious of any of
your people keeping an eye on me.'

'I told you I don't have the resources I need. By the
time my man turned up at the hotel this morning, you'd
already disappeared. I've had guys out looking for you,

you know. The idea you'd go to New Dresden or anywhere else for that matter never crossed my mind.'

'Call it impulse,' she said.

'I wish you'd harness your impulses. I didn't know
what had happened to you, where you'd gone. Martin
said you asked for a map and then you just took off.'

She sat on the bed and looked at him. She thought he
seemed weary. And concerned. Worried for her welfare.
She was touched by this.

'I'm waiting. You're going to tell me something,'
he said.

She compressed her story. He listened without any
expression until she reached the part where Stan and
Irene had been gunned down, at which point he sat
upright and shook his head, the gesture of a man
troubled by the way she'd placed herself in a dangerous
situation. He reached out unexpectedly and grabbed her
hand and held it, as if to impart comfort. She looked
down and saw how his big hand dwarfed hers, how
pale her skin seemed enclosed in his, and then she slid
her fingers away and reached for her cigarettes on the
bedside table – more because his touch flustered her
than from any urge to smoke. She lit the cigarette
anyway and finished what she had to say, and it was
only when she reached the end of her story that she
felt the full impact of the events she'd described. She
lowered her face because she thought she was going
to break down and didn't want Fuscante to see this
happen. He obviously sensed her distress, took her
hand again and stroked the back of it, saying nothing
for a long time.

Then he stood up, as if slightly embarrassed by the
uncop-like act of touching her. He walked up and down,
an expression of concentration on his face. He had one of

those faces that concealed very little. He lived very close to the surface of himself. She could hear him thinking, sifting her information, trying to make connections, looking for explanations, but they were eluding him as much as they'd eluded her.

'This character Hal doesn't know who killed your father?'

'That's what he said.'

'But he'd like to know.'

'Yeah. That's the impression I got.'

'Okay. Let's say he had reasons, whatever they were, to wipe out anybody connected with MalCon. Let's also say he wanted to remove all trace of MalCon – documents, records, everything. He hunts down the people who worked at the firm. Stan Thorogood and the woman, he gets them, but he was a little too late when it came to your father. And now it puzzles him. Or maybe it does more than just puzzle. It worries him. He's troubled by it. And he isn't going to go away.'

'No, I don't think he's going to go away,' she said.

'He's interested in you.'

'He said something to his guys about me, but I didn't hear what.'

'I wish you had.'

'So do I, Rick. So do I.'

'Maybe he's thinking your father left you something at the house among his papers, and you stashed it in a secure place without telling anybody.'

'That's not a possibility I want to dwell on. The implications downright scare me. If they imagine I know something I'm not supposed to know, it doesn't exactly bode well for my future peace and contentment, does it?'

Fuscante stared down at her and was silent for a

moment. 'You got an impression he knew your father personally?'

'I can't be one hundred per cent sure.'

'What we *do* know is that the people who worked for MalCon had some reason to hide the way they did.'

'Some reason,' she said. 'But what?'

'We keep missing something. What is it? What are we missing? Think.'

'I've tried that until my head hurts.'

'When you went to that old house years ago with your father, do you remember him and Stan Thorogood talking about anything in particular?'

'That's going back, Rick. I was a kid. I played outside. I don't remember eavesdropping. The place bored me. I don't know what I was expecting when he took me there, but I remember it was a big-time let-down. They had a cooler of beer and a bottle of Scotch and bunch of notebooks and papers on the table. I wasn't paying attention.'

'What about other times? There must have been occasions when you were together with Stan and your father. Did they talk business?'

'If they did, they were vague.'

'And you can't remember.'

'No. Even when I visited their office – which happened maybe twice – I don't remember them talking shop.'

She had the feeling he was suddenly going to turn on her the way he'd done at the hospital, pin her against the wall, demand answers she couldn't give – but he didn't. Instead, he sat beside her on the bed and gazed into her face, his look devoid of aggression. In a quiet voice he said, 'I'm worried.'

'I share your concern, Rick. Believe me.'

'I don't know who Hal is or why he's doing what he's doing. Okay, he was involved in the two murders, but he's ruled himself out as the person behind your father's slaying. So we're at square one where that's concerned. I just don't have anything I can get my teeth into. I know there's meat somewhere, but I just can't get to it. It's all bone. Goddam. *Goddam.*'

He looked lost and vulnerable, as if he'd just been stripped of rank, demoted without reason. She understood she was attracted to him, that she'd found him attractive almost from their first encounter, but she'd stifled the thought. In another time and place maybe – who knows what might have arisen, who could predict the chemistry between any two people? – but not now and not here. She thought of Patrick busy pursuing his career in Manhattan. She thought of him alone, hunched over his work. She felt a tiny pang of guilt, as if her conscience had just been tested and found inadequate. Dear God, she was straying off at tangents. There were killers in the darkness, her father was dead, and here she was gazing at Fuscante's long eyelashes and his downhearted expression and thinking how pleasing he was to look at. Get real. This is coming out of your emotional shakiness, your uncertain condition, your loneliness.

He interrupted her wayward thoughts. 'Who bought MalCon?' he asked.

'My father never said. But I never asked him, either.'

'It might be useful to know. There might be something helpful in old company records.'

'It shouldn't be hard to find out. It would only take one phone call. Look them up in the book.'

'I already looked this afternoon. There's no such company.'

'Then the new owner changed the name, I guess.'

'To what?'

'There should be a record of the sale. The State Corporations Commission would be the obvious place to start.'

'I'll try first thing in the morning during office hours,' Fuscante said, and glanced at his watch. He rose from the bed, rubbing the side of one leg vigorously. 'Getting old.'

'You hide it well,' she said.

'Is that a compliment?'

'I guess it must be,'

He smiled at her. He had a good smile, like a light brightening a dark room. 'I meant to mention the explosive,' he said. 'The guys who came down from Albany found the remains of a timing-device.'

'Is that going to be useful?'

'They don't think so. There's nothing special about it. So they say. They think the explosive used was something called C-4. Czech origin. Again, not very useful. It's in this country in abundance. A dead end. Like the fingerprints. I haven't had a chance to tell you about them yet. Aside from yours and your father's, we found prints we don't have matches for. They could be anyone's. The former owner. The people who moved your father's furniture. The realtor who showed the house. It's a lost cause.'

'I hate lost causes,' she said.

'Good. Because I don't want to see *you* become one,' he said. 'Next time you have some bright idea and feel like taking a trip, consult me first.'

'I swear,' she said.

'I better contact the county sheriff about that business over in New Dresden. He'll have questions. I'll try to field them for you.' He was quiet for a few moments. 'You can't stay here. You know that, don't you?'

'Is that an order?'

'I want you where I can keep an eye on you. This hotel's too damn easy to access. I don't feel good about you being here.'

'What have you got in mind?'

'I'll show you. Why don't you get your things together?'

She got up from the bed and started to pack her stuff. She didn't ask any questions. She went along with his suggestion willingly. She trusted him. If he said he knew a safer place, she accepted that.

While she tossed her belongings inside her bag, he asked, 'Is that what you really do for a living – counsel married people?'

'For my sins,' she said.

'I bet you're good at it. You'd be sympathetic. Patient. Candid. I can see that.'

She'd never been good at accommodating compliments. They always sent a hot sensation to her scalp and made her feel awkward. She crammed her clothes inside the bag, wrapping the damp stuff in a towel.

He said, 'Pity I didn't run into you a year ago. You might have been able to help me.'

'Why? Martial problems?'

'Cops aren't good conjugal risks, I guess. Ask my former wife.'

She zippered the bag and looked at him and the thought crossed her mind that she should telephone Patrick and tell him she was moving out of the hotel. But it was eleven o'clock, and she was drained, and she didn't know where Fuscante was taking her. Besides, Patrick was probably hard at work, engrossed in his own little world – and she hated to disturb him because she always felt like an intruder, a real person gatecrashing a private party whose only invited guests were Patrick's fictions.

'Ready,' she said.

'Fine. Let's go.' He took the bag from her hand.

She followed him out of the room and downstairs.

As she walked outside into the cold air, she found herself looking around, checking the scene for anything strange or out of place, a shadow, somebody loitering, whatever.

This is the way my world has become, she thought. *Looking, checking, making sure. This is new behaviour, and I don't like it.*

She walked to Fuscante's vehicle. He held open the passenger door for her and stuck her bag on the floor.

'Buckle your seat-belt,' he said.

She watched him walk to the driver's side and noticed that he too looked around as he moved, assessing the darkness, weighing the night, one hand stuck inside his unbuttoned coat and touching the pistol he wore in a holster.

chapter *Twenty-Two*

He drove her to the edge of Horaceville, down streets that would have been leafy in summer. Small frame houses, old trees, porch-lights. It was the kind of neighbourhood where she felt there was a sense of stability. People didn't move away from here. They raised their kids, lived and died in the same homes where they'd been raised themselves. A continuity of experience, history.

He parked in the driveway of a one-storey pale-green frame house where a yellow porch-light burned. He unlocked the door, turned on a light, ushered her inside. The living-room was untidy in a superficial way — books and newspapers scattered on a coffee-table, mugs with dregs of coffee in them, a pair of discarded jeans slung across the back of a sofa. The walls were dark red, and prints hung here and there, mainly English landscapes. Fuscante began to pick things up.

'It's a mess,' he said. 'I don't get time.'

'You live here alone?'

He gathered up a bunch of newspapers. 'After the divorce Cathy went to Chicago.'

She wondered what she'd expected. That he lived with his ageing parents? She sensed that the subject of his marriage was a no-go area, that there were residues of pain. 'Any kids?'

'No, that's the one bright spot. Kids would have made it rougher.' He stacked the papers to the side of the fireplace. Basically he was moving the mess from one place to another, but she didn't remark on this. She decided she'd help, the least she could do, so she gathered the empty mugs.

'You don't have to,' he said.

'In lieu of rent,' she said.

He gathered the books, arranged them on the mantelpiece. His reading material was eclectic. *The Sun Also Rises. Chess Problems Volume 3. Principles of Economics*.

'Where's the kitchen?' she asked.

'I'll show you.' He led her out of the room and through another doorway. The kitchen was filled with plants in need of water; there were a couple of empty pizza boxes on the counter, eggshells in the sink. The red and black tiled floor was in need of polish.

'Like I said, I don't have time.'

'You don't have to apologize, Rick.'

He picked up the pizza boxes, stuck them in the trashcan, which was already overflowing. 'This was my parents' house. I was brought up here. Went to school at the end of the block. My mother died when I was thirty. My father didn't think much of the world after that. He lost heart, I guess. Died six months after her.'

'Sad,' she said.

'He doted on her.'

She noticed a chessboard on the table. 'You play?'

'I used to. My father enjoyed a game,' he said. 'Now I just do problems. Brain aerobics.'

She took the eggshells out of the sink, stuffed them in the trash. She filled the sink with warm water and a squirt of washing-up liquid, then put the mugs in it.

'You like organization,' he said.

'Habit.'

He opened the refrigerator. 'Want a beer?'

'Is there anything stronger?'

'There's some JD.'

'Fine. No ice.'

He opened a cabinet, took out a bottle of Jack Daniels, poured some into a glass and set it on the table between the chessboard and a salt-shaker. He popped a can of Miller's and sat down, and she sat in the chair facing him.

'I need this,' and she picked up the drink. 'Is it okay to smoke here?'

'I don't mind. My ex-wife smoked.' He twisted in his chair, reached behind, opened a drawer, found an ashtray pilfered from the Mark Hopkins in San Francisco. 'Souvenir of a honeymoon.'

She lit a cigarette. 'So even cops steal, huh?'

'Cathy was the light-fingered one,' he said. He stared at her in silence for a time. 'You feel okay being here?'

'Sure.'

'You're not uncomfortable with this situation, I hope.'

She shook her head. She picked up a chess-piece, a rook, and looked at it idly.

'There's a spare bedroom,' he said.

'That's fine.' She replaced the rook.

'Is there somebody in your life?'

'Yes.'

'Serious?'

She didn't know how to answer. 'Serious, half-hearted.'

'What does that mean?'

'He thinks he'd like a commitment. I don't want to make one. I'm not sure he's really worked it through in his head. Living with somebody – it sounds good to him, I guess. The right move. Except I don't want to live with him.'

'What does he do?'

'He writes screenplays. He earns good money, but they never get made into movies. Not so far.'

Fuscante drank some beer. He rose. 'I have to call Jack Black. The county sheriff I mentioned.'

'Yeah, sure.'

'Be right back.'

He went out of the room. She heard him on the telephone, although she couldn't make out what he was saying. She looked at the chessboard, sipped her drink. She felt at ease here. The house was lived-in, comfortable. You just knew people had been happy most of the time behind these walls. Christmases, Thanksgivings, Labor Day barbecues out back, burgers sizzling and hot dogs bursting open. She'd missed out on a whole lot of that stuff. Her father was often away at the wrong time and her visits to Meg in Florida were few and far between because Meg was always in the throes of marrying or divorcing, and so she'd been shuttled off to spend too many holidays with Sam Malle, her grandfather, in New Paltz. Dennis made up for his absences lavishly when he returned – those long summers in the rented house on Nantucket, camping trips, whitewater rafting. He'd never stinted. He didn't want to be a Disneyland kind of dad. He'd never been frugal with his time or his attention. It was just that she'd lost too many damn Thanksgivings to count. It wasn't his fault. He had to work. MalCon was the core of his life, his other baby . . .

The sadness came welling up. She drained her glass. The balm of booze. How it simplified things, defused the mind.

Fuscante came back into the kitchen. 'Old Jack's pissed off. Doesn't like corpses strewn around his fiefdom. I can't say I blame him. He's making arrangements to have the bodies removed.'

'Does he need a statement from me?'

'He'd like one. I said I'd take it and fax it to him over at his office in Kayserport. It saves him the trouble of coming all the way here to see you. Jack sure hates to be inconvenienced. Basically he's bone-lazy . . . Are you hungry?'

'No, not really.'

'I'm quite good at whipping up a quick feast.' He had that eagerness to please of a man who wants company but rarely has it.

'I'm really not hungry.'

'I'll do a great breakfast, then.'

'Just pour some coffee into me, that's all I ask.'

'You're an undemanding guest,' he said. 'Are you tired?'

'I think I can sleep after the JD.'

He said he'd show her to the spare room. She followed him out of the kitchen along a hallway. At the back of the house he led her into a room furnished with a double bed, a nightstand, an armchair, a goose-necked lamp on an old rolltop desk.

'My father slept here after my mother died,' he said. 'It hasn't been used in a while. I ought to find some clean sheets.'

She waved the offer aside. 'I'm sure it's fine.'

He pulled back the quilt, a patchwork of red and burgundy velvet squares, and then he fluffed up the pillows. He drew the curtains. 'The bathroom's two doors down,' he said. 'If you need anything from the kitchen in the middle of the night, just help yourself.'

'This is kind of you, Rick.'

'It gets quiet around here,' he said.

She understood. By quiet he meant lonely. 'Are you sure me being here isn't going to cause some gossip?'

'Like I care,' he said.

'And it's not some breach of protocol, is it?'

'None that I know of. It's nice to have somebody in the house. And you'll be safe here. I promise you that. The windows are wired into a central alarm system which goes off if anybody so much as *touches* a pane of glass. Back door and front, exactly the same. My father installed it after Mother died. He was beginning to grow suspicious of the world towards the end of his life. He imagined thieves and cut-throats everywhere.'

He stood in the doorway a moment. A strand of hair that gave him ongoing problems fell across his forehead and he whipped it back.

'I'm three doors along if you need me. Just past the bathroom. Okay?'

'Okay,' she said. 'How's Jerry Lime doing?'

'He's tough. He's hanging in there.'

He said goodnight, and shut the door. She listened to him walk back down the hall and the sound of a door opening somewhere. She sat on the edge of the mattress, which was lumpy. It didn't matter. The room was comforting. The house emitted good feelings. She'd sleep here in safety, knowing Rick Fuscante was just down the hall. She undressed, put her robe on, tied the cord. She turned out the light, then lay down under the patchwork quilt.

She listened to the silences of the neighbourhood, felt how one house huddled close against another. People borrowed cups of sugar from each other around here. They baked pies for the people next door. They went in and out of one another's houses, drank coffee, talked, babysat the neighbours' kids. A gentle rhythm to life, a place where nothing much ever happened.

Until Dennis Malle had come to the vicinity to hide. And be killed.

She opened her eyes. She was thinking of his ring and wondering why it hadn't been returned to her yet. Tomorrow she'd call Wallace and remind him.

chapter Twenty-Three

She woke. For a moment she didn't recognize her surroundings. The moonlight against the curtains, the smell of old furniture wax in the air. Fuscante's house. Of course. She got up from the bed and switched on the lamp. She'd been dreaming, she couldn't remember what. Whatever, it had left her uneasy.

She stepped out into the hallway and walked to the bathroom, moving quietly. She filled a glass with water and then, feeling a pang of hunger, found her way to the kitchen. She rummaged inside the refrigerator, retrieved a half-empty jar of salsa and a bag of jalapeño chips from a closet. She sat at the table and dipped the chips into the salsa and ate a few. The clock on the stove read: 4.25 a.m. She looked at the chess-pieces. She imagined Fuscante sitting here on his own, working out chess problems. A picture of solitude.

The telephone rang.

There was something ungodly about a phone ringing between midnight and dawn. It was never great news during these hours. She wondered if she should answer it, then decided no, it wasn't her phone. Fuscante would have an extension in his bedroom. It stopped after four rings. She replaced the salsa in the refrigerator, put the bag of chips back in the closet. Tidy. She stepped out of the room. Fuscante was coming down the hallway, wearing a navy-blue robe. He looked sleepy.

'It's for you,' he said.

'For me?'

'Give me a few seconds, then pick up in the kitchen.' She heard him hurry along the hall to his bedroom.

Inside the kitchen, she lifted the handset on the counter and said, 'Yes?'

'You've changed your address, I see. One place or another, it doesn't matter. The sheriff is listening, of course. He'd be foolish not to. Are you there, Fuscante?'

She knew this voice.

She heard Fuscante say, 'Yeah, I'm here. And I'm pissed off at being wakened at this time of morning.'

'Let's say I'm just a man plagued by insomnia. I get my best ideas in the wee small hours.'

Andrea said, 'The priest routine was pretty good,' and she tried to infuse diffidence into her voice, *you don't scare me*, but there was turbulence inside her.

'I did some amateur theatricals as a boy. I guess the greasepaint's in my blood. I enjoyed being a priest. I was really getting into it. I was even on the point of asking if you wanted to make a confession, Andrea,' and he laughed. It was a curious laugh. He seemed to inhale air swiftly, rather than expel it. A sucked-in, wheezing sound. It was as if his whole laughter mechanism worked in reverse.

Fuscante broke in. 'Either you have something to say or you don't. Which is it, buddy?'

'What a direct guy you are. Straight to the point. No diplomatic detours for you, huh?'

'Life's too short for bullshit,' Fuscante said.

'The point's very simple,' the man said. 'We want little Miss Malle to know we're around. We're like the weather. Ever-present. Some days calm, other days stormy. Often unpredictable.'

'Who's we?'

'Oh, you're asking too much, Rick.'

'Sheriff,' Fuscante said.

'Forgive me. Rank, right. The hard-won badge. You're a proud man. Also a brave one. Some might say a little foolhardy. I won't split hairs. It's a matter of perspective.'

Andrea said, 'And what's your perspective?'

'That's debatable, and might take too long to explain.'

She said, 'We've got all night, Hal—'

Oh shit! She caught herself too late. As soon as she'd said this she knew she'd given away something she should have kept to herself. She wished she could retract her words, but it was too late: whenever you said something, it no longer belonged to you.

There was a long, nervous three-way silence. She twisted the phone cord round her wrist. She listened to the quiet whir of the electric clock on top of the refrigerator. She heard her heart.

'Funny,' the man said eventually, 'you knowing my name like that. You fill me with curiosity.'

She didn't know what to say. She wished Fuscante would intervene, but he was silent.

Hal said, 'Been doing some research, huh? Been snooping about, turning over stones? That's a sneaky thing to do, Andrea, and it makes me very unhappy. But I don't have a sunny disposition anyway. I was born under a bad sign. My mother always claimed there was an eclipse of the moon the night she gave birth to me.'

Fuscante said, 'Where the hell is this going?'

The man said, 'We all have problems, Sheriff. Yours is the identity of Dennis Malle's killer. Mine runs along somewhat similar lines. With a difference or two.'

'What I hate is this goddam mystification,' Fuscante said. 'Why don't you come right out and say what the fuck you're doing? I mean, if you're capable of that.'

'Don't try to goad me, Rick. I'm impervious to that ploy.'

'What do you want with Andrea?'

'The truth.'

And there was that laugh again. That quick, strained drawing-in of air, the way it seemed to get trapped in the back of the man's throat. She hated that sound. She hated the way it made her feel. Shivery, uneasy. She saw she'd tightened the phone cord so hard around her wrist that her circulation was impeded. Her fingers tingled.

'What truth?' she asked. 'What damn truth are you after?'

'Andrea, there's only one truth ever. You can surround it with half-assed stories, you can build a fortress of lies – but in the final analysis, sweetheart, there's still only one truth. Think it over.'

The connection was cut suddenly.

Andrea put the phone down.

Fuscante came into the kitchen, carrying a sheet of

paper torn from a note-pad. He sat at the table, shook his head.

'I screwed up,' she said. 'I really screwed up. He knows I have his name and it's going to bug him and he doesn't sound like the kind of guy I'd want to bug.'

'No, he doesn't,' Fuscante said. 'And he obviously saw me bringing you here. I didn't notice anyone watching. So he's good. I have to give him that.'

She felt she was standing on a ledge and the drop was a long one. She'd suckered herself into imagining she was safe in this house. But she wasn't. The menace, the amorphous thing that lay in shadow, was all around her. She couldn't define it. Couldn't pin it down. She didn't understand it, therefore couldn't analyse it. It was just *there* the way Glamys Lake was just *there*. The way snow was just *there*. It was a law of nature. A fact.

Fuscante said, 'I can't keep moving you around from place to place. They'll always find out where you are.'

'I could go back to Manhattan, I guess.'

'And you'd be left in peace there?' he asked.

'No, I don't think so.'

'Neither do I. So you stay here. I wonder what he wants when he says it's the truth he's after?'

'Welcome aboard,' she said quietly.

He rose and moved towards her. He put his arms round her and stroked her hair. She liked the feeling of his strength. It was an illusory security, but for the moment it was reassuring. He didn't say anything, just held her, kept running the palm of his hand lightly across her hair.

She said, 'Why did he telephone? Why not keep quiet? Why does he want me to know he's out there?'

'The fear factor,' he said.

'If that's it, it's working.'

'I have the number he called from. I'll check it out.'

He stepped back from her and looked awkward, as if he'd forgotten his manners and transgressed a rule of etiquette by holding and trying to comfort her. He picked up the telephone. She turned away from him. A man calls at 4.30 a.m. and tells you he wants the truth. What truth? She thought about his peculiar laugh: it was as if he wanted to stifle mirth, not release it.

Fuscante was speaking into the phone. 'Did I wake you, Jonah?' he asked. 'Yeah, it's important . . . I want you to locate a number for me. It's six two four nine seven eight three . . . Physical location, right. Get back to me.'

He put the phone down and turned to her. She could read it in his face: he wanted to touch her again. She stood very still. It was one of those finely balanced points in time where you either yielded to an impulse or turned away from it. She wondered what she'd do if he gave in to the impulse.

He said, 'You think you can get back to sleep?'

'I have serious doubts.'

'Okay. Sit down. Let me do my chef thing.' He busied himself, skillet on the stove, scrambling eggs, peeling strips of bacon from a package. She watched him cook. He did it with such enthusiasm she didn't have the heart to tell him she didn't feel like eating. He worked quickly. He set a plate in front of her. She looked at the bacon, the scrambled eggs, the toasted English muffin.

'Eat,' he said.

She picked up a fork and got through a couple of bites. Then she watched him devour his own food.

Her mind drifted back to what the caller had said: 'We all have problems, Sheriff. Yours is the identity of Dennis Malle's killer. Mine runs along somewhat similar lines.'

The telephone rang. The sound startled her. Fuscante picked it up quickly, listened a moment and then in an urgent voice said, 'Okay . . . okay. Here's what I want you to do, Jonah. Check around, see who's new in town, see if any strangers have turned up in the last twelve hours or so, check gas stations and see if there have been any unfamiliar customers, check any cars you don't recognize, see if any of the B and Bs have new business, which I doubt. Also check empty houses, especially those with For Sale signs. Have you got that? Use all available officers . . . I don't care if you have to get them out of bed, Jonah . . . Overtime? Don't give me that shit.'

He hung up, and looked at her. 'Our friend called from a payphone on Docherty and Fifteenth,' he said.

'Where's that?'

'One block down from this house,' he said, and pushed his plate away. 'This is 827 Docherty.'

'*Jesus*,' she said.

'"Jesus" is right.'

chapter *Twenty-Four*

It was six a.m. before she managed to get back to sleep, and even then she slept only three more hours. Time had collapsed around her, and she couldn't remember how many days had passed since she'd first arrived, and she felt as if she'd been in Horaceville, inside this same nightmare, all her life. She didn't even know what day it was.

She got out of bed and found a note on the kitchen table that read:

Be back in a few hours. Look out the front window. Take care. Rick.

Taped to the sheet was a key which he'd tagged with a slip of paper: *Front door.*

In her robe, she walked into the living-room. She parted the curtains. A patrol car was parked in the driveway. She could see an officer seated behind the wheel. He looked at her, waved. She raised a hand in reply, then went back to the kitchen and brewed coffee, thinking of the cop out there in the cold. She returned to the front door, opened it, gestured to the officer, and he got out of his car. He was a big, broad-shouldered man with a red face and ginger sideburns. The temperature was numbing, zero at most. The sky was the grey of an aircraft carrier.

'Coffee?' she asked.

'I dunno. Rick didn't say I should come inside.'

'You have my permission,' she said. She wanted company, another physical presence.

'Uh, well, I guess that makes it okay.' He followed her into the kitchen. She poured him coffee, which he sipped standing, as if sitting down might be considered too much of a liberty. He looked uneasy enough just being in the house. He clutched the mug in his thick red hands. They were bricklayer's hands, she thought. She could see them stacking bricks, mixing mortar. Strong, trustworthy hands.

'What's your name?' she asked.

'O'Hanlon. Joseph O'Hanlon. Joe.'

'Irish.'

'Long ago,' he said. He scanned the kitchen. She wondered if he thought she was sleeping with Fuscante. Maybe he did. Maybe the gossip was already buzzing through the Department. She realized she didn't mind the idea of such speculation. It made her feel she was harbouring an intimate secret.

He declined her offer of a cigarette. She lit one, drank some coffee. 'Your brief is what – to keep me in sight at all times?'

'Something like that. Anything you want to do, I have to clear it with Rick first.'

'Anything?'

'Except obvious things around the house, I mean.'

'Like taking a shower and getting dressed?'

'Stuff like that. Personal.'

'Has he told you why?'

'I don't ask him questions, Miss.'

'You just take orders.'

'Especially when he's not in a real terrific mood. Which between you and me, he's not.'

She sat in silence for a time, then she looked up Linda Straub's number in the phone directory and called it.

'I tried to reach you at the hotel,' the attorney said. 'They told me you'd checked out. I guess the charms of the Glamys didn't do it for you.'

'I guess not,' she said. She didn't want to tell the attorney where she was calling from. In a town like Horaceville, she'd probably find out sooner or later anyhow.

'I heard about that explosion. Wow. They're saying it was some kind of gas leak.'

'That's what I understand.'

'Too bad.' There was a shuffling of papers. 'You're calling about the will, I suppose. Okay. Dennis made no will with any of the lawyers in town. I checked around. Nothing. And he didn't file anything with the state. Now it's possible he made a will in some other state, but that's going to take time to check.'

'I don't know why he'd write a will in another state,' she said.

'We could be talking about something he did years ago. Passing through some place, took it into his head

to write a will. Some people get the urge to do it before
they step on an airplane. You just never know. I've
had clients who made wills when they were visiting
their grandchildren out in California or Hawaii. I'll
keep checking. Say, how are you doing, anyhow?'

'I'm fine.'

'Uh-huh, I'm hearing notes in a minor key,' the
attorney said.

'Do I sound that way?'

'A bit.'

She glanced at O'Hanlon, who was making a big show
of not listening. He'd found an old newspaper and was
turning the pages.

'How much longer are you staying, Andrea?'

'I don't know.'

'You want a drink or some company, call me.'

Andrea thanked her and then hung up. *No will*, she
thought. *A life of loose endings and hidden compartments.
Come back to life just for a moment*, she thought, *and
tell me the truth. If there is a truth. Or is it all obscurity
without end?*

She told O'Hanlon she was going to get dressed.

She went into the bedroom. She put on the clothes
she'd been wearing yesterday. Her wardrobe was seriously depleted. She dragged the damp stuff out of her
bag and wondered if Fuscante had a washing-machine.
She gathered together all her laundry and went back
down the hallway. She found a washing-machine and
dryer stacked in a small cubicle at the back of the
kitchen. She stuffed the clothes inside the washer,
pushed a button. Domestic chores, automatic pilot.
But she couldn't postpone indefinitely the fact she
wanted to go out, even if it meant O'Hanlon checking
first with Fuscante.

She asked him, 'Where can I find the coroner's office?'

'He's down in Lincoln Plaza. The basement of the PD Building. Why?'

'I want to see him.'

'Now, I'm not so sure, Miss Malle.'

'It's no big deal, Joe. You can drive me down there.'

'I'll need—'

'Permission. I know.'

O'Hanlon looked flustered. 'Isn't it something you can do by phone? You *have* to go out?'

'What I want to do I can't accomplish over a phone, Joe. Call your sheriff. Tell him.'

'Ask him, you mean. You don't *tell* Rick. You tell him, he doesn't listen. You ask him nicely, you got a shot.' O'Hanlon picked up the phone reluctantly. Watching him, Andrea thought about Meg, wondered if she'd managed to get out of New York. Meg would leave a message at the Glamys one way or another. It was something to check later. She listened to O'Hanlon, who was one of those people unhappy with phones. He was all mumbles and little grunts.

He turned, handed the receiver to her. 'He wants to speak to you.'

She took the phone from him. Fuscante asked, 'Why do you want to see Wallace?'

'He has something I want.'

'Which is?'

'My father's ring.'

'I can pick it up for you,' he said.

'I want to do it myself, Rick.'

'Why?'

'Because I get stir-crazy. Because I don't like my

movements being impeded. And because it's *my* father's ring.'

'It's risk I don't like,' he said.

'Don't you trust O'Hanlon to look after me?'

'Sure I do, he's solid and reliable—'

'So what's the problem? It's broad daylight. I don't see any shadows out there. The people I worry about are the ones who come in the dark, Rick.'

Fuscante sighed and said, 'Put O'Hanlon back on the line.'

She passed the phone to the cop, who said, 'Uh . . . okay . . . uh,' then replaced the receiver. 'He says as long as I don't leave your side. And as long as we're quick. Also I'm to make sure the house is locked up.'

She put on her coat while O'Hanlon checked the back door, and then plodded from room to room examining the windows. When he came back she followed him outside. The front door was self-locking. Just the same, O'Hanlon twisted the handle to be sure.

She had to sit in the back of the car because O'Hanlon explained there was a departmental regulation against civilians sitting up front with the driver. He drove down the block.

'Slow a moment,' she said.

He braked. 'Some reason for this?'

'Nothing special,' she said.

She leaned forward and stared at the payphone. She tried to imagine Hal standing there in the chill dark of four-thirty a.m. She wondered if he'd disguised himself, if maybe he'd worn Coke-bottle glasses and a crumpled overcoat, drab and anonymous, nobody you'd turn your head to look at twice. The greasepaint in his blood. She pictured him standing inside the

glass booth, his gloved hands holding the receiver.
She heard his peculiar laugh. She sat back and realized that she'd assumed a hunched position, as if
for protection, as if to conceal herself. But nobody
was out there. Nobody was watching – so far as she
could tell. But how far was that? The houses were
quiet. Chimney-smoke drifted lazily into the grey air.
It was all so damned ordinary. And last night Hal
had come down this everyday street and used that
payphone and he'd said, 'We want little Miss Malle
to know we're around.' He'd intruded on this calm.
He'd stepped out of some other sphere, an altogether
darker place where violence and murder were the
norms.

She didn't look back when O'Hanlon reached the end
of the street.

It was just a payphone. Just an instrument of com-
munication.

The car was heading down the centre of town now.
A couple of trucks dumped rock-salt on the streets.
Snowbanks piled along the curb had frozen solid and
were blackening already from exhaust fumes. In a short
time they'd look ugly, sidewalk fixtures nobody wanted.
A few people went in and out of stores, huddled against
the chill, hurrying even as they tried to stay upright on
slippery concrete.

At Lincoln Plaza O'Hanlon parked outside the Department building. He opened the door for her, looked this
way and that, his expression one of serious vigilance,
then escorted her up the steps. Inside, the air smelled
of disinfectant. He led her past the front desk and along
a corridor to an unmarked door.

They went down a flight of stone steps to the basement. She wasn't sure what she'd expected – tiled

walls, a laboratory atmosphere, stark lights. Whatever, it wasn't this long, dim hallway, ancient heating-
pipes overhead, paint flaking from walls. Obviously
this underground facility didn't have a high-priority
budget. She was a little surprised by the dankness of
the place – but where else would you store and dissect
the dead? It was apt somehow.

There was no sign to tell you this was the morgue. It
was as if somebody wanted to keep it secret. She wondered where her father lay, behind which of the several
doors along this corridor. She pushed the thought aside.
She didn't need it, didn't need to clutter her head with
more bad thoughts: she'd bottled her grief and shelved
it and she didn't want to reach up and take it down again,
because she'd disturb the sediment of the feeling.

O'Hanlon stopped outside a door on which the word
Inquiries was painted in white letters. He knocked.

A voice said, 'Come.'

O'Hanlon opened the door, Andrea directly behind
him. 'Miss Malle wants a word, Dr Wallace,' he said.

'Ah. Miss Malle, of course.' Wallace wheeled his
chair away from his desk. He wore a white lab coat.
His metal desk was stacked with folders and papers.
On a shelf an organ Andrea couldn't identify hung in
a jar of murky liquid. A lung, a liver. She didn't know.
She smiled at Wallace, who didn't get up from his chair.
He tugged at his beard and asked, 'How are we?'

She shrugged, wasn't sure what to say. This place
depressed her.

'Time,' he said. 'Everything takes time. Remember
that. Old platitudes are like old wines. They're usually
the best ones.'

She realized she must look sad, the bereaved
daughter.

'What can I do for you?' he asked.

'I came for the ring,' she said. 'It probably slipped your mind.'

Wallace wheeled his chair back against the wall. 'Ah, yes. The ring . . . I don't quite know how to tell you this.'

'Tell me what?'

'It's gone, Miss Malle.'

'What do you mean, it's gone?'

'Exactly what I say. I looked for it. It wasn't there.'

'Somebody – are you saying somebody *stole* it?'

'I'm not saying that. It might have slipped off in the snow when your father was being carried to the ambulance. It might have been lost in this building. I don't know.'

'You don't know. How can you not *know*?'

'I'm sorry. Truly I am. I questioned the ambulance attendants. They don't remember seeing it. I had this place searched top to bottom. Nothing.'

'That ring belonged to my grandfather. He got it from his father. My father promised it to me. It's not the ring, for Christ's sake. It's not the object. It's what it means to me.'

'I understand,' Wallace said.

'No, I don't think you do.'

'I can assure you—'

'I don't want assurances, I want the goddam ring,' she said.

'And I'm telling you with my deep regrets that it's gone.'

'It was precious to my father, who didn't have any great interest in material possessions, but this one thing meant a whole lot to him.'

'I don't know what more I can say, Miss Malle.'

She was flustered and incredulous. How could they lose the ring, for Christ's sake? The house, her father's clothing, the paintings even – she could take the loss of all that stuff. But not the ring. Not that.

She didn't know what to say. She felt raw emotion swell inside her, something of anger, something of despair. She clenched her hands and stared at Wallace as if she meant to strike him for his carelessness. He didn't know her sense of loss went deeper than the ring. She wanted to say 'Don't you see, it's not the fucking ring, it's not just a decorative gold band and a tiny emerald, you asshole. Don't you get it? It's everything that's happened since I came to this godawful place.' She was on a downhill slope suddenly and couldn't see where it ended.

She caught herself. She wasn't going down into that quagmire. No way.

'We'll keep looking,' Wallace said.

O'Hanlon said, 'I'm sure it'll turn up somewhere. Right, Doc?'

'Don't be so goddam patronizing, Joe,' she said. She looked at O'Hanlon, whose big face was flushed.

Wallace got up from his chair. 'Do you . . . can I get you something to help?'

'What have you got in mind, Doc? Fluoxene? I don't need mood-altering drugs,' she said. 'I'm going back to the car.'

She went out of his room and into the corridor. She raced up the stairs, O'Hanlon climbing behind her.

Rick Fuscante appeared at the front desk. 'Get your ring?' he asked.

'No, I didn't get my ring.'

'Why not?'

She told him.

'It's got to be somewhere,' he said.

'Oh sure, it's *somewhere*. Obviously.' She felt her eyes water and she thought, *This is silly, perfectly silly*, but she was imagining the ring on someone else's finger now, or lying in a pawnshop window or in a jeweller's safe, anywhere except where it was supposed to be. Which was on her father's hand.

She brushed her sleeve across her eyes and Fuscante said, 'Go back to the house. I'll be there when I can.' And to O'Hanlon, 'Take damn good care of her, Joe.'

Yes, Joe, take care of me. I'm sailing too close to the edge.

Fuscante touched her shoulder. 'I'll see you later.' He looked and sounded exhausted. She knew he and his officers would have been checking Horaceville since early this morning, stores, gas stations, bed and breakfasts, looking for – what was the term? – anyone suspicious. Anyone strange. And it was because of her they were doing all this leg-work. Because she wasn't safe.

She felt weighted down.

She smiled thinly at Fuscante, and then she was out in the flesh-numbing street under a sky of solid lead in a small town where she didn't want to be.

chapter *Twenty-Five*

*S*he unlocked the door of Fuscante's house, thinking she'd call the Glamys and check to see whether Meg had telephoned or if there was a message from Patrick. O'Hanlon followed her into the kitchen and stood with his arms folded, watching her as she dialled the number. Martin told her there were no messages. Presumably Meg and Don hadn't been able make travel arrangements yet. As for Patrick, he'd be stuck in the city like Meg. Her head had begun to ache in the aftermath of her anger with Wallace.

She took off her coat, wondered about dragging some kind of chitchat out of O'Hanlon, but the prospect seemed unlikely. She checked closets for aspirin, eventually found a pack in a drawer and swallowed a couple of them.

'I think I'll lie down for a while,' she said.

O'Hanlon nodded. He stepped into the hallway

behind her and watched her walk as far as her bedroom
door. O'Hanlon the Vigilant, the Keen. He wasn't going
to let Fuscante down. He'd croak first. She went into
the bedroom, closed the door.

The gloved hand clamped hard round her mouth
before she had time to react. The pressure of palm and
fingers against her lips was powerful. She was shoved
on to the bed and pressed flat on the mattress, and the
weight of her assailant on her body was overwhelming,
forcing air out of her lungs. Something was thrust
against the side of her neck. Metallic, smelling of an
oily lubricant.

'Don't turn or I'll blow your lovely head off. We're
going to have a very quiet little chat, Andrea.'

She lay still. She wasn't breathing well. The man's
weight was suffocating. Her face was squashed into the
patchwork quilt. The gun barrel indented her flesh.
Small coloured flashes jigged in front of her eyes.

'The alarm system here's antiquated,' he said. 'Fuscante
ought to be ashamed.'

She wanted to resist – it went against the grain of
her impulses just to submit like this – but what filled
her mind was the weapon and what might happen
if his finger twitched or some crazed notion possessed him.

'We whisper, because we don't want to disturb that
nice cop, do we?'

She thought of O'Hanlon in the kitchen. Maybe
he'd come down the hall and look in on her, but that
wasn't likely. He was too polite, or perhaps too socially
awkward, to enter a woman's bedroom uninvited. And
then she realized she didn't want him walking through
the door, because there would certainly be gunplay,
and he'd be unprepared for it, unable to reach his

holster in time. She imagined gunfire rumbling through the house.

She shifted her head slightly. He immediately forced it back down into the quilt. He had great strength in his hand. 'No sudden moves. Are we clear on that, sweetheart?'

She mumbled a muffled sound of assent into the velvet quilt.

He asked, 'Let's get this question out of the way first. How do you know my name?'

He released her slightly, so that her face was freed and she could speak. She wasn't sure what to say. She couldn't think of an instant lie. She wondered where the truth would get her. *I was under that house. I was in the crawl-space.* She cursed her careless tongue, the way she'd slipped on the phone, but half past four in the morning wasn't the best time of day for thinking clearly.

He shoved the gun hard into the nape of her neck. She made a small sound of pain.

'I don't like the gun—'

'Don't like the gun? You're not *supposed* to like it. It's not here for your pleasure, sweetheart. It accomplishes two things. One, to instil total fear. The other is to encourage a certain acquiescence. Am I getting through to you? I hope to God I am. Because I kill. I kill and it doesn't matter a damn to me. I'm not burdened with a conscience. So let's hear your sweet voice. But keep it soft and low.'

'I can't remember how I know your name.'

'Don't ask me to buy that one. *How the fuck do you know my name?* Simple question.'

The gun dug into her, serious pressure on the base of her neck.

'Okay. *Okay*. I was there.'

'You were where, sweetheart?'

'At that farmhouse.'

'Ah. Hiding somewhere. Eavesdropping.'

'But I didn't see anything.'

'I'm taking that with a pinch of salt, Andrea. Let me guess what you saw. Blood on the snow. Carcasses. I'm not interested in that, anyway. So a couple of losers are dead and stiff, big deal. What I want to know is, what did you *hear* apart from my name?'

'Nothing else.'

'Just Hal, eh? That one word just sort of popped up. You expect me to believe that?'

His face was close to her hair. His breath smelled fresh, peppermint. She heard him remove one glove with his teeth, a quiet gnawing sound, then his bare fingers rested on her cheek.

'I'm asking a fucking question. What else did you hear?'

'Somebody called Jimmy. Another called . . . I can't remember.'

'Try.'

She remembered the crawl-space, words drifting down. 'Falco,' she said.

'See how easy it can be. I ask and you answer. Why put yourself and me through these little difficulties, huh? Accommodate me.' He moved his body a little. He was pressed against her buttocks, a forced intimacy she found distasteful. She closed her eyes, tried to distance herself.

'What did we talk about?' he asked. 'Refresh my memory.'

'I couldn't hear you most of the time.'

'Is that so?'

'That's the truth.'

'Truth's a funny thing, Andrea. People bend it and twist it. Sometimes they just downright lie. Are you lying to me now? Make up your mind. The safety is off.'

'I swear I'm not lying,' she said. 'I can't breath. Jesus.'

'This isn't *supposed* to be pleasant for you. I don't go around making people merry. I don't go away leaving them all cheerful and thinking they've just had a day in a fucking sauna. Now what about a last name?'

'Falco and Jimmy just called you Hal.'

'Just Hal. What else did you hear?'

'Nothing.'

'You're sure about that.'

'I'm sure.'

'See, it's real a problem where I'm concerned. You can identify me. That unsettles me. I don't care for that. It's something I need to ponder. Meantime, let's move along quickly. Let's talk about Daddy. He wanted you to visit. He insisted on it. Why? Why was he so pushy?'

'I never found out, did I?'

'You're not talking to some fucking counterfeit priest now, sweetheart, pretending to be all kind and fatherly. *What did he tell you?*'

'He was dead when I got there. You know that.'

'Before that, Andrea. He asked you to visit. "Come up. I want to see you." Why?'

'I don't know.'

'He gave you some hint on the phone.'

'He didn't give me a hint of anything, Hal.'

'Okay. Something physical. Something he couldn't give you over the phone.'

'Dammit, there was nothing, no hint, no physical object, nothing. He asked me to come, I came.'

'Gee, Daddy's little girl just drops everything and runs when he calls, huh? Devoted to Dennis. Mr fucking Wonderful. You worshipped the ground he walked on.'

'I loved him.'

'Love's a mirror you can see any reflection you care to see, Andrea. Daddy Wonderful. Daddy's a saint. Daddy's a good man. Hot-shot with alarm systems. Big man with a wealthy clientele. Just jetting off to see some fucking sheikh in the Gulf, the guy wants an electric fence around his harem. Bye, Andrea. Kiss on the cheek, see you real soon. Off to wire the conjugal compound and make sure nobody slips inside and pokes one of the Arab's wives. Ha fucking ha.'

'What are you trying to say?'

'I only want to know what he told you. And I don't have all fucking day.'

A sound from the hallway. She heard O'Hanlon go into the bathroom. Hal pressed her face deep into the mattress and whispered, 'Play dead or you will be,' and she lay there, heart hammering, a world of enforced silence. The cistern flushed. O'Hanlon came out of the bathroom and his footsteps faded down the hall and a door closed.

'Okay. So Daddy told you shit. And I'm to believe that?'

'Believe what you like. I don't give a damn.'

'My my, there's spirit in you. Backbone, huh? Admirable.' He pressed down on her harder. She felt squeezed. She couldn't move. 'Imagine a harem, having your pick every night of a different woman. I'm in the mood for a twelve-year-old virgin tonight, Abdullah. What

a life. What a rich lovely life . . . So Daddy was the
cat's fucking pyjamas, wasn't he? You just don't have
a fucking clue about your precious daddy, do you?'

'I don't know what you're talking about.'

'You're a good-looking woman, you know that? In
other circumstances . . . Hey-ho, the story of my life is
a saga of missed opportunities and lonely motel rooms
and you don't want to hear all that crap, I'm sure. Don't
cry for me, Argentina.' He bent forward with his lips to
her ear, one hand holding the gun, the other, stripped
of its glove, sliding up her spine under her sweater. His
skin was clammy, greasy.

She said, 'You sorry bastard. Is this how you get
your thrills? Holding a gun to a woman's head? Are
you getting off on this?'

'I'm immune to insult, remember? Criticism's water
off a duck's back. It takes all kinds to make up this funny
hideous world we inhabit, Dennis Malle included.'

'My father,' she started to say.

'Your father. He was blessed. He could walk on
fucking water, right?'

'What do you mean?'

'I'm not in the business of telling children there's no
Santa Claus, sweetheart. But I'll say this – your daddy
was a great man with stories. A truly great man.'

He moved a few inches away from her, relieving the
pressure. She wanted to turn her head and look at him.
But she didn't.

'Who killed Dennis?' he asked.

'Nobody knows.'

'The last word was some prowler with robbery in
mind. Has that changed?'

'Not as far as I know.'

'I can't imagine a prowler getting the drop on Dennis.

He was too sharp for that. He had eyes in the back of his head. So who the fuck shot him, huh?'

'Why is it so damned important for you to know this?'

'Because I'm distressed, Andrea. I'm very territorial. I don't like the notion that somebody might have shot Dennis and then started sniffing around looking for goodies.'

She had a sense of being trapped inside one of those tiny puzzles where you rearranged sliding plastic tiles to make a sequence of numbers from one to ten, and she couldn't get it right because one of the tiles was missing or she'd forgotten the key to the sequence.

'You stole his papers, didn't you,' she said. 'Did *you* find any goodies?'

'Your father's papers made for totally humdrum reading. Unless, of course, you removed the really hot stuff and shared it with Rick Fuscante. Sorry, *Sheriff* Fuscante.'

'There was no hot stuff.'

He was quiet for a moment. 'The thing is, I can't make up my mind about you. One minute I want you dead, then I change my mind. I think you might have passed something along to your friendly sheriff, something Daddy Wonderful told you, or some document you took from his files. I go back and forth on the matter. This way, that way. Kill the fucking bitch, don't kill her. You see my problem?'

A sound from the hall, the front door opening, Fuscante's voice, O'Hanlon saying something to him.

'Oh-oh,' Hal said. 'Time for a hasty retreat, sweetheart.'

She thought, *I'll call out, I'll scream.* She felt a movement close to her face, saw him sliding his hand back inside his glove, which was of soft brown leather.

He said, 'Hush. Not a sound, Andrea. Remember the gun. I'll be around.'

She heard him cross the floor, the sound of the window being opened. She turned to look at him, but all she saw was a black coat, a shadow against the grey sky, a curtain flapping as he pushed it aside. She rushed to the door and looked at Rick Fuscante at the end of the hallway and her expression must have alarmed him, because he hurried towards her.

'What is it?' he asked. 'What's wrong?'

All she could do was point to the window.

Fuscante ran across the room, climbed out.

She didn't notice O'Hanlon pass her and head in the same direction. Light all around her dimmed, and she stuck her hand over her mouth, fighting back nausea. She could still feel the intruder's touch on her spine, as if he'd left behind a hand-shaped Vaseline print.

chapter *Twenty-Six*

Fuscante returned with O'Hanlon after fifteen or twenty minutes. She wasn't keeping track of time. She'd wandered into the living-room and was walking up and down, restless and nervous. She couldn't harangue Fuscante for the inadequacy of his alarm system, because he'd gone beyond the limits of his responsibilities by inviting her into his home. He'd shown her hospitality and concern. He was under no obligation to do that. He might just as easily have suggested she spend a night in the local jail for her own safety.

'Did you see him?' she asked.

'Not a goddam trace,' Fuscante said. 'Thin air.'

She looked out into the street. The sky was growing darker. More snow was in the air. 'How could he vanish so quickly?'

Fuscante said, 'I don't know. We checked all the

nearby houses. Nothing. Wherever he went, you can
bet he travelled on foot. A car would be too slow on
these streets. He might have run off toward the old
railroad tracks. Beyond that there's about sixty acres
of woods. Good cover.'

O'Hanlon was busy on the phone. He'd clearly been
given instructions by Fuscante to arrange road-blocks
in the neighbourhood. She heard him say he wanted cars
and uniforms at certain intersections immediately. He
wanted a cop presence along specific streets – Docherty,
Fifteenth, Sixteenth, Ames, McAlister, Froggat. He
also wanted a search of the woodland Fuscante had
mentioned, which he called Hackett's Wood. There
was urgency in O'Hanlon's voice. Now, get it done
now, get off your asses.

Fuscante led her out of the room, hand on her elbow.
They went inside the kitchen. He poured her a glass of
Jack Daniels and told her to drink it, and her mind
went back to that first meeting at her father's house
when he'd given her a shot of Dalwhinnie and ordered
her to down it. They had a little bit of history going
now, shared experiences.

'Look, I'm sorry,' he said.

'Don't be. It's not your fault. He knew how to trip
your system.'

'Tell me what he said, what he wanted.'

She went through it hesitantly. Fuscante sat at the
table, focusing hard on her words. His brown eyes had
become darker and more intense: they were the colour
of bitter chocolate. His mouth was a thin determined
line, like a single crayon-stroke.

'You must have been terrified,' he said.

'It's one word that comes to mind,' she said.

He reached out and took her hand. There was no

awkwardness in the gesture this time, just a natural spontaneity. She had the sudden thought *I'd go to bed with him*, then dismissed it as an irrelevance. Carnal flashes had no place in this situation.

'At least now we're sure Hal thinks you know something. And he believes you've told me what it is.'

'That's going to wear thin real soon, Rick. Hal's going to say, "Goddammit, let's not hang around, let's just put her lights out."'

'And mine too,' he said.

'Possibly.'

'Plus you witnessed two murders.'

'Sure I did. But I didn't see the killers' faces. I can describe Hal, but what good's that going to do? Even if you locate the man, he'll deny he was anywhere near the place at the time. So what could you charge him with? Impersonating a priest? There's no evidence linking him with the explosion at my father's house. He just comes over as some weirdo who likes to wear a dog-collar. That's not exactly big-time crime, is it? As for him invading your home, he can deny that too. His word against mine. You didn't see him. O'Hanlon didn't see him.'

He got up from the table. He took a carton of milk from the refrigerator and drank some.

She sipped her JD and watched him. *Yeah, I would*, she thought. *It wouldn't take much to have an amnesia attack about Patrick.*

He stuck the milk carton back and drew a hand across the white moustache of milk above his upper lip. 'Who the hell is he?' he asked. He wasn't really directing the question at her but at the world in general, as if he half expected an answer to come from the walls.

She thought about what her assailant had said: '*You*

*just don't have a fucking clue about your precious daddy,
do you?*' 'I don't know who he is, and I don't think the
question is why he wanted to kill my father, or why
anyone else wanted him dead, for that matter. I think
the real question is something else, Rick, and I've been
too goddam dumb and deluded and sad to ask it. Never
mind Hal. Who the hell was Dennis Malle? – that's the
real question. Who *was* he? I don't think I know any
longer. I haven't a clue. And that hurts. That really
hurts. You believe you know a person. You give your
love unconditionally. And it's a boomerang that comes
back and smacks you right in the face.'

'Hal might just have been blowing smoke. Trying to
rattle you by running down your father.'

'I'd give a lot to believe that.' She walked to the sink
and washed her hands in washing-up liquid, then dried
them in a paper towel. She could feel the gun still, she
could feel a spectre of the hand against her bare skin.
She lit a cigarette and went back to the table.

'One thing I know for sure. He was pretty well
acquainted with my father. He said he couldn't imagine
anyone getting the drop on Dennis because he had eyes
in the back of his head – you don't say that kind of thing
about somebody you don't know. Now I'm wondering,
did they work together in the past? Maybe they did,
and it all went wrong and my father and Stan had
to do a disappearing act. Maybe there was betrayal
involved. Somebody was cheated. There are scores to
be settled.'

O'Hanlon came quietly into the kitchen. He looked
downcast. 'I should've done better,' he said.

'Nobody's blaming you,' she said.

'I should've done better anyway.' He flattened his
big hands against the sides of his overcoat and looked at

Rick. 'I phoned the orders through the way you wanted. Anything else?'

'I'll stay here with Miss Malle,' Fuscante said.

'You want me out there?'

'I want everybody out there I can get, Joe.'

O'Hanlon turned to Andrea. 'I'm sorry, Miss.'

'Forget it,' she said.

Fuscante said, 'Joe, for God's sake. Leave. You're not to blame.'

O'Hanlon nodded but seemed unconvinced.

After he'd gone, Fuscante said, 'He's more sensitive than he looks.'

She went to the coffee-pot and poured two cups, although it was bitter by this time. She gave one to Fuscante and tipped the shot of Jack Daniels into her own. It was too early in the day, but what the hell. Call it medicinal, a tranquillizer. She needed something to settle her nerves.

Fuscante undid the buttons of his coat, gulped some coffee down. She understood he was impatient to be out hitting the streets, doing the real job, but he was stuck here with her in the role of protector.

I should disappear, she thought, *step out of his life. Do what my father did. Hide away. Find a safe place, if such a thing exists.*

Your father hadn't found one, had he?

She tilted her chair back and said, 'Was it all play-acting, Rick? If there was another side to Dennis Malle, a dark side, he never showed it to me. So what do I do? Go back and re-examine everything he ever said? Poke around in the ashes for a little cinder of certitude or truth? Why the hell should I feel any need to salvage his honour, anyway, assuming he had any?' She paused, caught her breath. 'The stories he told when he came back from his business trips. I mean, were they all just a bunch of crap? "You should've seen the guy's house," he'd say. "Everything made of marble and gold. Place cost him thirty million bucks." Or "You should've seen the Arab's palace, kid. The guy had a small private army and a thousand peacocks on lawns sprinkled with distilled water imported by the tanker-load from Europe." Stuff like that. Never any names, never any identities. Maybe they just didn't exist.' She banged a hand on the table. 'If he was a fake, I have to accept it, don't I?'

'If it's true,' he said.

'If it's true,' she said, and couldn't keep scorn out of her voice.

'You don't know for sure, do you?'

'And maybe I don't want to find out. Preserve the illusion. Except I'm not good when it comes to living in cloud cuckoo land, Rick. I prefer truth every time. It might be tougher, but in the long run . . .' She clenched a hand in a gesture of frustration. 'And MalCon. What about MalCon? Was that all some kind of elaborate fiction?'

He snapped thumb and middle finger together. 'Shit. I meant to phone the Corporations Commission about MalCon. I've just been too goddam busy this morning. We've been turning this town over. Nobody's seen anything unusual. No strange cars, no strange faces. You'd think somebody would have noticed something in a place the size of Horaceville, but no. This Hal's like the wind passing through. You feel it, but you don't see it. He comes. He vanishes. And what about his two buddies at the farmhouse? Where have they gone? Are they still around?'

She was quiet a moment, remembering Stan and

Irene, not wanting to bring all that back again. *The fuckers got Dennis. They're not getting me. Who, Stan? Who were you afraid of?*

'I get the feeling they're not too far away,' she said.

'If they're here in Horaceville, why hasn't anyone noticed them?'

'I don't imagine they'd be in town. A few miles away, an isolated house, there must be plenty of those around here.' Something turned and shifted at the back of her mind and she had a difficult moment bringing it into focus, and even when she remembered what it was the recollection shimmered and finally eluded her. Something Hal had said in the farmhouse. A place where he said he was going. But it was ash now, and she couldn't get hold of it.

'Most of them are inaccessible at this time of year,' Fuscante said. 'Not just farmhouses. There are about a dozen hotels you can't reach in this kind of weather.'

'Unless you have some unusual means of transportation.'

'A chopper, for instance,' he said.

'Yeah, a chopper.' She thought about it again, the black shape rising out of trees, and somebody looking down, seeing her slump to her knees beside her father's body.

'You think it might have been Hal in that chopper you saw?' he asked.

'It's a possibility.'

'You remember you also suggested another possibility, that it might have been the killer flying it?'

'I remember.'

'And since Hal isn't the killer . . .' He let the sentence go.

She thought: *The mysteries are like snowdrifts. They*

pile up inside your head and sometimes a random thought will blow them one way, a vague instinct blow them another. It was a world of infinite possibilities and patterns. 'I don't know,' she said. 'I don't know anything any more. I have a serious need to deal with something tangible and boringly practical right now. Why don't I call the Corporations people?'

'It might be better coming from a cop.'

'Why? The kind of information I want is usually a matter of public record. They'll tell me anything they'd tell you.'

'Go ahead,' and he massaged the sides of his head with slow circular movements of his fingertips, a man tired of bafflement.

She checked the phone directory, found a number, punched it in. The line was busy. She put the handset back and said, 'Civil servants. They're always tied up. I'll try again.' She finished her drink, then strolled the room with her arms folded, her body tense.

He caught her in mid-stride and held her close. The silence between them was strangely vibrant. A current.

'This isn't going to help,' she said.

'I know, I know.'

'You and me. It's a side road.'

'It might be more. It might be the scenic route.'

She was trembling just a little. But not with fear this time, not with anger. Anticipation. Desire.

'Do you want to travel it?' he said.

'I think so,' she said.

Maybe this was the hiding-place. Fuscante's body, his sex. His lips touched hers very lightly, a tentative kiss that changed key quickly, moved up a tempo. She slid her hands inside his coat, laid them against his hips.

She heard his heart beat. Or was it her own? She parted her lips, felt his hands gather and bunch her sweater and pull it up a little. She wanted him, on the floor, the kitchen table, up against the wall, it didn't matter. She was aware of his urgency and hers in collision.

She unbuckled his belt, lowered his zip, curled her hand round him. This was a place where she didn't need to think about the mysteries, where she was set free from menace. They slid together to the floor, a tangle of limbs and clothing, an undoing of restraints. She'd never wanted anyone quite this way before, with this kind of abandon, and the frantic nature of her urge amazed her, and even as she arched her back to simplify for him the task of sliding her jeans from her hips, she realized this was going to be frenzied, sweet and quick and deep and overwhelming. She'd said, 'This isn't going to help,' but she'd been wrong, very wrong. This was obliteration and oblivion, an ascent to another level, a place of light where the shadows couldn't reach. Patrick, she should have been thinking of Patrick, but he was jettisoned somewhere in the wake of all this, ballast. She felt no guilt, she was beyond that, she wanted this man inside her as deep as he could penetrate, and she raised her knees on either side of him, and he made love to her as if they'd known each other a long, long time, but were strangers still. There was flow and rhythm and madness. She cried out loud when she came, and she shuddered, clinging to him, holding him as hard as she could, not wanting to release him. Not now. Not in the next minutes. Stay this way as long as you can.

He lay with his face against her shoulder.

For a long time neither spoke.

She closed her eyes, wanting him again. That depth. That sense of being carried away.

'Was it scenic for you?' he asked.

'It was a journey all right,' she said. 'I'm wondering if there's a round-trip ticket.'

He smiled, placed his hands on either side of her face. 'The bedroom might be the next stop,' he said.

'Anywhere,' she said. But she didn't want to move. There was a mood here she didn't want to break.

Then the telephone rang, a sound from an external world she had no need for.

'I have to answer that,' he said.

'I know you do.'

'I really don't have a choice.'

She disliked his withdrawal. She hated the empty feeling. She covered herself with his overcoat because she felt cold. She heard him pick up the phone, then he turned to her and said, 'It's for you. Somebody called Meg.'

chapter *Twenty-Seven*

*F*uscante drove her to the Glamys Lake Hotel, where Meg and Don were waiting in the lobby surrounded by luggage. Meg, in a white fur coat and matching hat, hugged her, and Don smacked a kiss on her cheek before he melted into the background the way he always did in Meg's company. Nobody ever upstaged Meg, who was fussing around her daughter now, touching, stepping back, then looming forward for yet another embrace.

'Let me look at you,' she said. 'Let me take a good long look at you.'

Andrea felt winded by the sheer force of her mother's attention. She glanced at Fuscante, who'd been relegated, like Don, to the background. Meg tugged off her fur hat and shook out her long hair, which had been dyed a kind of burgundy, and turned to look at Fuscante. 'Who's this, Andrea?'

Andrea said, 'Sheriff Fuscante. Rick.'

'Rick,' and Meg seized his hand. 'Are you the one hunting down this goddam killer?'

'Working at it.'

'Hard, I hope.'

'Hard as I can,' Fuscante said.

'You've got nice honest eyes. Good strong face. I like your hands—'

'Mother,' Andrea said. 'You're embarrassing him.'

'Oh, nonsense. Show me a man who doesn't enjoy a little flattery and I'll show you a eunuch. If you think somebody has attractive features, you say so.'

Meg linked a steely arm through Andrea's and took her a few yards to one side. 'Something between you and this hunk?'

'You're jumping to conclusions,' Andrea said. How annoyingly effervescent Meg could be. But sometimes she had very sharp perceptions, a knack of tuning in to situations, and her insights were surprising.

Meg ran fingers, much adorned with rings, through her long hair. 'Is there a cup of coffee to be had in this dump? The trip – my God, the *trip* Don and I have had. You wouldn't believe. The flight to Albany was a *nightmare* with the plane rocking and pitching, and you know I get nausea. And then Don had to bribe some shady Turk – or was he Armenian? – with a totally filthy limo to bring us down here, and that took an age. Two things I hate in a limo, threadbare carpets and a scruffy driver. I need coffee.'

'There's a lounge,' Andrea said.

'The lounge it is. Don? You coming?'

Don scurried forward in his ankle-length camel-hair coat.

Meg said, 'You too, Rick.'

Fuscante said, 'I'll take a raincheck, if you don't mind.'

'Too busy to take five minutes out for coffee?' Meg fluttered her long false eyelashes at Fuscante. She flirted without thinking.

'We'll talk again,' Fuscante said. He smiled and looked at Andrea. 'You'll stay here until I come back for you?'

Andrea nodded. She watched Fuscante go outside, saw him cross the parking-lot. He got into his Dodge. A patrol car wheeled into the lot just as Rick pulled out. The car flashed its headlights at the Dodge. *Protection*, she thought. Fuscante wasn't a gambling man.

Meg said, 'You look at him like he's something wrapped in shiny paper under a Christmas tree and you can't wait to get it open.'

'You're absurd,' Andrea said.

'I know drooling when I see it. Where's this lounge?'

Andrea led the way down the corridor. The lounge was empty. Meg gazed around and said, 'You checked out. I don't blame you. This joint has seen better times. That fat clerk had to track you down. Moved in with the cop, have you?'

Andrea didn't want to get into explanations yet. She didn't say anything. They sat at a table by a window and Don went off in search of service.

Meg reached out and seized her hand. 'What progress has been made in this godawful matter?'

How to answer? Andrea wondered. She said, 'It's slow.'

'In other words, nothing's changed since we last spoke.'

'That's about it.'

Meg lost some of her sparkle for a moment. Her

mood dipped. A light went out of her blue eyes. Even her wine-red lipstick seemed to lose its lustre. Andrea wondered how much effort it cost her to maintain her exuberance.

'I find it so damn hard to believe he's dead.'

'I know,' Andrea said.

Meg looked out at the lake, fidgeted with a ruby pendant at her neck. 'I told you, I used to think he was indestructible, big and strong, fearless. He was the kind of man you couldn't imagine anyone ever harming. Of course, when it came to harming me, well, different matter *altogether*.'

'That's history,' Andrea said. She didn't want to hear about marital warfare, the wounds inflicted.

'And what version of this history have you heard? His. Not mine. You were always closer to him, anyway.'

Closer, Andrea thought. *To a stranger*.

'Oh, he could dish it out,' Meg said.

'Please, Mother. Not now.'

'You think I'm here to bury Caesar without a word of some kind?'

'There isn't going to be any burial, Mother. Not until the ground thaws.'

'Burial? What burial? He never wanted to be *buried*. He said if he died before I did – this was back in the days when we were still quote unquote in love and in heat – "Make sure they burn me. I don't want to lie festering in the ground. Just put me in a box and send me straight down the chute and into the furnace." His very words.'

Andrea thought about flame, cinders. 'Was he serious?'

'I guess he was,' Meg said.

Don came back, carrying a tray he set down on the

table. Coffee-pot, cups and saucers. 'You two girls want some time alone?' he asked.

'That's very sweet of you Don,' and Meg patted the back of her husband's hand.

'I might stroll down to the lake,' he said.

Meg said, 'Do. Just don't get your feet wet. I don't want you coming down with something.'

Don smiled a little bleakly at Andrea. He had expensive implanted teeth and his face had undergone cosmetic surgery. His cheeks were smooth and flat and his eyes unnaturally large. 'Sad situation, Andrea. Very sad. I'll leave you to talk.' He drifted away from the table.

Meg said, 'He's a dear man. He has this thing about water. Always wants to buy a boat. He knows I get seasick. He'll be happy out there staring at the ripples. He can spend hours doing it, God only knows.'

Andrea was silent a moment. 'This cremation business. Are you sure he said that?'

'A woman never forgets a man like Dennis Malle, sweetie. What he does and what he says. Especially what he does.'

'Why?'

'Frankly? The best sex I ever had. Does that embarrass you? We were at it morning noon and night and in-between times too. We couldn't get enough of each other back then. We were carnivores.' Meg slid away into a memory and was silent a second. 'Give me one of your cigarettes.'

Andrea pushed her pack across the table. Meg took one of the cigarettes, lit it, sipped her coffee, made a face. 'That is vile.'

'It's the boondocks, Mother. You can't expect French roast, Jamaican Blue Mountain.'

'Why did he come up here to live, for Christ's sake? I never bought into that back-to-nature craparoony, you know. Your father had about as much interest in nature as I have in what happens under the hood of a car. Big change of heart, he said. Civilization's a pig. Who needs the fumes and the stress? No, he didn't come up here to enter into some holy communion with Mother Earth, sweetie.' Meg smoked theatrically, cigarette held far away from her face, hand bent slightly backward. When she puffed, she did so as if nicotine were a habit she'd inherited, a genetic fault.

'Why do you say that?'

'I knew the man. The move up here – no, there's more to that than swooning about in the woods and listening to birds.' She looked at Andrea and her eyes were sad. 'You still blame me, don't you? You don't have to deny it. I know you think I just abandoned you. One day I just packed my case and voilà – Momma Houdini. Well, it wasn't quite like that, sweetie.'

'Does it matter?'

'Dammit, it matters to *me*. I want to set the record straight. I left your father because I couldn't take it any more. Simple as that.'

'What couldn't you take?'

Meg stubbed out her cigarette. The filter was smudged with lipstick. 'He was never there when I needed him. And I'm not just talking sexual needs. It was everyday things. Sit down, let's have a martini, how were things at the office, darling. Oh, I screamed for the ordinary sometimes. I wanted banality. I needed a home life. Sweet domesticity. Surprised?'

'A little.'

'I could have stood it, I believe, if he'd been square with me.'

'And he wasn't?'

'Square? Your father's life obeyed no regular rules of geometry. He was more quantum physics. Black holes. He kept disappearing inside them. I wouldn't have minded if he'd been truthful.'

Andrea leaned across the table. 'He lied to you?'

'Oh, sweetie, he was a *master*. An absolute master. But some of the lies were pitifully unnecessary. Like one time he brought me a sandalwood box he said he'd bought in Java or some such place. He was always terrific with the details, you see. He'd been to a bazaar, haggled with the toothless merchant, the place smelled of flies and tainted meat and incense – he'd pile it on. He could talk a great picture. A few days later I saw his American Express bill and the sandalwood box he'd haggled so fiercely over in Java had actually been bought at a gift-shop at JFK.'

'That doesn't sound so great a lie,' she said. She wondered if she was defending Dennis Malle even now. After everything that had happened, was she still rallying to protect his name? He was always terrific with the details, she thought. The colourful struts that supported lies, gave them plausibility. Was that what he'd done up here? Created details – the isolated house, the shy retiring life – to support another kind of fabrication? This way to the maze. Step inside the hall of mirrors. Your daddy was a great man with stories.

Meg said, 'Why not just say where he bought the goddam thing? Lies pollute your head. You catch one, and next thing you know you're looking for more, and pretty soon everything's a lie, or a potential lie anyway. You start to think paranoid thoughts. Was he really in Java? Did he really go to Helsinki like he said? Was he really and truly in Jakarta or Kuwait? Did he buy these gifts he lavished on me at airport shops on US soil? There's more if you want it. Or do you think I'm speaking ill of the dead? Maybe you do.'

'I'm not sure what I think.' *Yes, you are.*

'Here's a cute one for you. This was just before your thirteenth birthday. Dennis had to go on one of his infernal trips. South Africa, I remember. Cape Town. Then he phoned me saying he was in London because the aircraft had developed some kind of electrical failure on the way home and had to be rerouted. He'd be delayed getting back to New York. By this time, I'd begun to develop a certain reluctance to believe his stories. What did I do?'

'You phoned the airline,' Andrea said.

'Great minds,' Meg said. 'I phoned the airline.'

'And there was no failure.'

'No failure. No delay. No detour to London. The flight had arrived quite safely, thank you, in New York.'

'Why did he lie about that?'

'I used to think he had women all over the place. It's the first thing you jump to, I guess. But I never found any evidence of that. I did all the usual soap-opera things. Checked his pockets for those tell-tale matchbooks, theatre-ticket stubs, whatever it is the betrayed wife is supposed to find. Studied his credit-card statements with all the care of a proctologist. Checked his laundry for lipstick. Sniffed his shirts for any unfamiliar scent. And, yeah, I admit, I looked for unsightly sexual stains. I was quite the spy, sweetheart. Quite the investigator.'

'Did you find evidence?'

'Absolutely none. So why did he lie, you ask? I reached the conclusion he couldn't help himself. I think if he had a choice between a simple truth and a pointless lie, he always opted for the fib. And that's when I packed my suitcase. You see, the ground just kept shifting. Nothing made sense. I'd fallen down the rabbit-hole. My husband was a pathological liar. I didn't want that kind of marriage.'

Andrea turned the word 'pathological' over in her mind, then said, 'Did you ever think he was hiding anything?'

'I always thought he was furtive, if that's what you mean. I don't know if he was hiding something specific. I assumed he just couldn't tell where truth left off and lies started. The lines were fuzzy.'

Fuzzy lines. Dennis Malle kept changing shape. Andrea concentrated on bringing an image of him to mind and what she saw was a blurred Polaroid, a man in a sailboat against a blue sky. But look closer – no distinct features, no distinguishing marks, just a face obscured by hard sunshine.

'Did he tell you I wanted to take you with me when I left?' Meg asked.

'No.' She was surprised.

'See? He also lied by omission. He kind of threatened me, you know. Touch the child and all hell. The threat was all the worse because it was so goddam vague. When I walked, I walked without you. Later, things improved a little. Distance was a great help. If he had a reason to phone me, usually when it had something to do with you spending time with me, I felt pretty glad he was in New York and I was in Coral Gables. We were capable of a certain restrained dignity. But the harm had been done. The lies. The threats. And some things still bleed no matter how tight you tie the tourniquet, sweetie. When he sent you down to Florida now and then, I wanted to keep you there. But I didn't want the havoc I felt Dennis would create, you see. Besides, and this is damnably selfish, I had made a small career out of getting married, and I didn't have a great deal of room for you. I'm sorry about that.'

'I'm sorry too,' she said. 'I believe he was fond of you, anyway. I don't think he actively disliked you, Mother. If there was any rancour, I never saw it.'

'You may be right. The last few times we spoke, he was very civil.'

'He phoned you?' she said.

'From time to time.'

'I didn't know. What did he say?'

'This and that. He was doing some painting. He was contented. We reminisced sometimes. The places we'd been. He liked to remember the time we spent in Venice. That's where he first mentioned cremation. We were walking along the Lido at the time and he came out and said it: "I want to be burned." It was one of those bitter wintry days and there was fog. We were discussing death the way people in love sometimes do. You know, the big drama of it. I wouldn't want to survive you, etcetera. Yackety-yack. Of course, you think you can't possibly live without each other. It's just too bleak to consider. But things change.'

'When was the last time he called?'

Meg said, 'Two months ago. Maybe longer. He was in a nostalgic mood.'

'What did he talk about?'

'Our travels. Do you remember this? Do you remember that? Now he's dead and none of it matters, does it?'

Andrea looked through the window. Don was standing on the shore, a camel-coloured stick-figure at the water's edge. Now he's dead and none of it matters – no, that wasn't true. It mattered. More than ever. Because the lies were mysteries, and the mysteries were lethal.

She wanted to tell Meg the whole thing, the deaths of Stan Thorogood and Irene Passmore, the explosion, the threats, the whole story, but she didn't. He was hiding, Mother. He was a fugitive. Later, when she felt the time was right. Whenever that would be.

Meg said, 'He was a lover like no other. I'd make that his epitaph, if it was up to me.'

'Who did he sell MalCon to?' Andrea asked.

'I didn't keep *au courant* with his business dealings, Andrea. Why?'

'Curious.'

'No, you're more than curious. What's been going on up here in Harpersville that I don't know about?'

Andrea didn't bother to correct her. 'There was some vague speculation that he might have been killed by an enemy he made in his business.'

'A business enemy,' Meg said. Her eyes suddenly filled with tears and she lowered her face and took a napkin out of the dispenser. She blew her nose and tried to force a smile. 'Sorry. I'm still coming to terms with all this. Or trying to.'

Andrea touched her mother's hand. 'Easy. It's okay.'

'I'm the one should be telling you that,' Meg said. 'But you inherited his strength, I think. It was some of his character you got.'

'I wonder,' Andrea said.

Meg crumpled the napkin. 'A business enemy. Is that a solid line of inquiry?'

'It's a line, I don't know how solid.'

'He never talked business with me. From the day he and Stan started up MalCon, it was like living with a clam. MalCon was a whole other life he led, and I wasn't any part of it. I guess I accepted that, and maybe I shouldn't. "Discretion is what I get paid for," that's what he used to say. It was a holy word. I always half expected him to go down on one knee and face Mecca when he said it.' She twisted the napkin in her fingers, then dumped it in the ashtray. 'Before MalCon, when he was employed by Gridiron Security, it was different.'

'Gridiron. God, I'd forgotten that,' Andrea said. The memory was vague.

'Back then he was more open. It was only when he started up on his own that he stopped being specific about his work. Discretion, you see. Protect the client. Did I ever tell you I went to his office one day?'

'No, you never said.'

'I was feeling sneaky. This was when things between us were coming really unglued. I was having serious doubts about everything. Did he even *have* an office? Was there really such a thing as *MalCon*? This gives you some insight into my state of mind at the time. So I turned up on the doorstep. There was that Nazi in reception, of course.'

'Irene Passmore.'

'Right. Once I'd told her my blood-type and had my orifices searched for contraband, she buzzed Dennis. He looked a little startled to see me. Stan was there. Stan the shadow. Oh, I know you liked him and his stupid tricks, but frankly he gave me the creeps. I always thought he was an illegal immigrant from Transylvania I should report to the Immigration people. So I said I was in the neighbourhood, because that's what you say when you turn up unexpected and uninvited, isn't it?'

'What happened?'

'I felt like Typhoid Mary. There was this stunned silence and a certain amount of hasty folder-closing. Dear God, what did they imagine I'd see? And even if I saw anything, was I likely to understand it? Heavens, no.'

'Did you just leave?'

'No way. I was obstinate. I could see they were all in a tizzy. So I thought, what the hell, I'll just linger until they throw me out. So I checked out the decor and I listened to the Nazi's heavy breathing and Dennis fidgeted and looked at his watch and Stan was highly uneasy and I thought, God, this is enjoyable, I'm having a ball wandering around the inner sanctum.'

'I can imagine,' Andrea said.

'Dennis started edging me to the door, he's busy, workload up to here, and so forth. And then I realized what it was – they were expecting somebody they didn't want me to meet. Christ only knows why. Like it would make a difference to me? Then a guy came in. It was one of those situations you could cut with a knife. I was filled with mischief and feeling great. I looked at the guy and I introduced myself as Dennis's wife and I gave him my best handshake – the really strong one, you're not going to let go, you're pumping away, you've got the initiative, big smiles – and I asked him, "So I've given you my name, what's yours?" Dennis is clearing his throat like this is the most enormous gaffe since the Garden of Eden and the Beast of Belsen is just fuming and Stan's cringeing, and the guy, who's caught off-guard, smiles and introduces himself. And I thought, yeah, all right, a triumph, way to go, Meg. Score one for me.'

Andrea said, 'I always admired your nerve.'

'Sometimes I think it's all God really gave me,

honey.' Meg smiled at the memory. 'Dennis was as close as I ever saw him to losing his cool that day. Funny thing, the guy didn't seem too fazed by it all really. "Nice to meet you, Mrs Malle," he says. What was his name? It's on the tip of my tongue. Dammit. I hate when something slips my mind. It was an odd name. What the hell was it?'

'Does it matter?' Andrea said.

'Honey, at my age you want to think your memory's still functioning. Hal. Hal something.'

'*Hal?*'

'Got it. Hal Hapsky. It stuck. I can still see him.'

'Describe him,' Andrea said.

'Why?'

'Just describe him, Mother. Please.'

'I remember thick black hair. Nice speaking voice. Soft. Like his hands. He had a sweet sort of face. Kind of chubby here,' and she touched her cheeks. 'And rosy. You wanted to pinch them . . . Something wrong?'

'Wrong? I don't know.'

'You're pale, sweetie. Quite pale.'

chapter *Twenty-Eight*

Meg and Don checked into a double room on the second floor. The air smelled stale and Meg huffed and complained, but Don – who looked weary – said the room was just fine.

Andrea said, 'It's the only game in town, Mother. Unless I can find you a B and B.'

'I hate B and Bs. I always feel I'm intruding in somebody's home. The shelves are always filled with family heirlooms and photographs of dead relations. This place,' and she surveyed the room with a frown, 'will just have to do.'

Don tested the bed and said, 'Comfy.'

'Good. Because I need a rest,' Meg said. She looked at Andrea. 'What plans do you have?'

'Rick said he'd pick me up.'

'Right. Rick.' Meg opened one of the three suit-cases. She never travelled light. She came prepared for every possibility. Formal clothes, casual, everything in between. Her array of garments always astonished Andrea.

'Say, how long are we planning to stay?' Don asked.

'Until Andrea leaves,' Meg answered. She appeared to have a tone of voice she reserved entirely for her husband, one of patience, as if she were speaking to a child. 'That's what we came for, Don. Support. Emotional help. When she leaves, we leave. I can't imagine she'd want to hang around Hopkinsville too long. Unless, of course, she has good reasons. Personal ones.'

'I've already gone through Father's papers,' Andrea said.

'That is not what I meant, sweetie.'

'I know what you meant.'

'I have a sewer in here,' and Meg tapped her skull. 'Don't tell me.'

Andrea was thinking of the name Hal Hapsky, impatient to pass it along to Rick. It might be a different Hal altogether, but the description sounded close enough to make the name worth checking.

'Don't think me morbid,' Meg said. 'Is your father . . . I don't know how to put this . . . Can I see the body?'

'The *body*?' It seemed to Andrea a tasteless notion to want to look at the dead. Remember them as they looked in life, leave it at that.

Meg asked, 'Is it viewable?'

Don said, 'Honey, *really*, you think that's a good idea?'

Andrea said, 'You don't want to see him, Mother. Believe me.'

Meg shrugged. 'I thought maybe one last time, pay my respects . . .'

'He was shot in the face. There's nothing to look at.' She was back in the snowdrifts behind the house. She was on her knees, paralysed beside the woodpile. The slack hand, the ring that had so carelessly been lost. The head blown away.

Meg said, 'I was wondering, that's all. I didn't realize . . .' She touched her daughter's hand. 'I didn't mean to upset you, sweetie. Now I feel like a ghoul.'

'Don't.'

Meg began to sift through her clothes, eventually finding what she was searching for, a robe. 'I hope the showers work in this place.'

'They work,' Andrea said, and moved to the door.

'We'll see you later,' Meg said. She covered a yawn.

'I'll call, Mother.'

Andrea stepped out into the corridor, went towards the stairs. In the lobby she'd hoped to find Rick Fuscante, but he hadn't returned yet. She looked out through the glass doors at the parking-lot where the patrol car was parked. The sky was grimmer than before: fresh snows were coming. She felt exposed standing so close to the doors. She backed away, sat down near the unoccupied desk, remembered the Corporations Commission. She picked up the phone from the desk and, because she couldn't remember the number, called Directory Assistance. She scribbled the number down on the edge of a tourist leaflet with photographs of the Adirondacks.

She dialled it, and a woman answered.

'I need some information,' Andrea said.

The woman had the kind of voice Andrea always associated with people who had access to fat rubber stamps and seals − officials of the DMV, clerks in government offices, Revenue inspectors. It was cold and nasal. 'It depends on the information.'

Andrea explained, gave the woman the name MalCon.

'And you want to know what exactly?'

'The name of the owner.'

'You could look up this information in any reference library, you know.'

'I'm not near one.'

'Hold, please.' Sigh. The office martyr. She probably resented everybody and everything and was overlooked every year for promotion.

There was bad music, a synthetic rendition of 'Hark! The Herald Angels Sing'. Three weeks until Christmas, and even the bureaucrats knew it. Andrea waited a long time. She was about to hang up when the woman came back on the line.

'MalCon. How are you spelling that?'

Andrea went through the letters. Cap M. Cap C in the middle.

'Fine, fine. I've found it.'

Andrea felt a moment of relief, as if she'd half expected to hear that there was no record of any such company.

The woman said, 'Ownership of MalCon was transferred to a corporation called Hawk's Nest Inc. MalCon is no longer registered as a corporation.'

'Meaning what?'

'Just what I said. It's no longer a corporation.'

'The new owners bought it and shut it down?'

'Yes. But they may simply have absorbed MalCon's function and dispensed with the name, which happens. You could get more information from Hawk's Nest office, at 303 East 42nd Street, New York.'

'Who owns Hawk's Nest?' she asked.

The woman had a whine in her voice. 'The directors are listed as James Thompson and Anthony Falco.'

Falco, she thought. *James Thompson*. *Jimmy*.

Names on corporate papers.

Men on snowmobiles. Visors in the sun. An automatic weapon. Stan and Irene falling in the snow.

She wondered what it all meant, these links, the connections between two killers and her father's old company.

'Will that be it?' the woman asked.

'Yeah, that's all.' Andrea put the phone down.

She wandered to the other side of the lobby and sat on the sofa under the oil-painting of Glamys Lake. Think. *Think*. What was it?

She raised her face to see Martin enter the lobby.

'Miss Malle,' he said. 'There was a message for you earlier.'

She watched him go behind the desk and retrieve a piece of paper. He read from it. 'Patrick called. Wants you to phone him this afternoon. Sounded quite anxious.'

Patrick. How very far away he seemed. She wondered if she'd somehow already dismissed that relationship as dead. It's best we go our separate ways, Patrick. I can't commit. And in your heart of hearts you don't want to either. The prospect of saying these things depressed her. But she had to contact him at some point. She couldn't just leave him hanging. It wasn't fair.

'I didn't tell him you had checked out,' and Martin looked smug: *I know where you've gone, Miss Malle.* He lowered his voice. 'Confidentiality is very important at times. Don't you agree?'

She agreed.

Martin busied himself behind the desk, humming. She watched him, not really seeing him. Thinking. Thinking. Getting nowhere. Going in circles. She was pleased when Fuscante came through the door and slumped beside her on the sofa.

'Got your mother settled?' he asked.

'Upstairs,' she said.

'She's . . .' Fuscante struggled for a word.

'You don't have to be polite, Rick.'

'I was going to say she creates a kind of a buzz.'

'You mean overbearing?'

'That's your word,' he said. He touched her hand.

'Let's go somewhere we can talk,' she said.

chapter *Twenty-Nine*

As they talked, they drove around Horace-ville in Fuscante's Dodge. At one point he used his cellular phone to call his office, then parked in a small square near the centre of town, a kids' playground surrounded on all sides by Victorian houses. Swings and roundabouts lay iced and idle, a small pond was frozen over. Here and there children blasted one another with snowballs and the air was alive with laughter and screams. She watched this for a time. The activities of innocence. She thought it looked like fun. The Dodge's engine was idling and the heater blew with a low whining sound.

Fuscante said, 'I used to come here as a kid. I used to wonder what it would be like to live in one those big houses.'

'You enjoy Horaceville, don't you?' she said.

'Home town. I went to Boston for a couple of years,

worked in the PD. I came back. City living's not my thing.'

She played with Fuscante's hand, absent-mindedly stroking his fingers. She looked at the houses, thinking that they suggested a bunch of strict old aunts watching the park for errant children to reprimand. She was conscious of windows, of glass darkened, and she was beset by the sudden notion that somebody in one of those rooms was watching her. She turned the thought over in her mind, then let it slip away, and focused on what she really needed.

She said, 'Why did my father sell MalCon to people who later killed Stan Thorogood and Irene Passmore and wanted to kill him too?'

Fuscante wrapped his fist round her thumb. She liked the touch, the easy intimacy of it. 'My best guess? There's money involved, lots of it, because massive sums of cash can be counted on to bend most people seriously out of shape. Dennis and Stan scammed these guys. Promises were made and broken, or MalCon wasn't worth what they paid for it, or some creative accounting took place and the books were cooked. Whatever it was, it seriously pissed off these guys Falco and Thompson. And maybe this Hal Hapsky as well, if he turns out to be *our* Hal.'

'But that doesn't explain why Hal is so worried about who killed my father. If I wanted to murder somebody, I don't think I'd give a shit if somebody else pulled the trigger before me. I'd just say, "Hey, what good fortune, some prowler or some random killer did the job for me. It's one task less," and I'd go home smiling. Wouldn't you?'

Fuscante scratched the side of his jaw. 'Unless he wants it all neat and tidy before he closes the books and sticks them on the shelf. An unsolved murder is a loose end. Hal and his friends don't care for that.'

She lit a cigarette. Fuscante cracked the window a half-inch.

'It helps me think,' she said.

'Nicotine really oxygenates the brain, I hear.'

'I hate sarcasm,' she said. She sucked smoke into her lungs. 'Say there's another party involved.'

'And?'

'What if this other party – somebody who isn't associated with Falco and Thompson and Hal – *also* wanted my father dead. He got there first. And that really gets up the other guys' noses.'

'Why would it annoy them to the point where they're prepared to take the risks they take? Breaking into my house . . .'

'I don't know. Maybe you're right, and it all comes down to money. A huge sum of cash my father had stashed, say.'

'If he had cash hidden away, why would Hal blow up the house?'

'Because my father didn't keep it there. He had another hiding-place for it.'

'If Hal knew that, why was he so interested in visiting the house in the first place? Look, you can go in circles with these questions until your head's spinning. In the end it's all speculation. The first law of any investigation is: keep it simple. Discard complexity. Trim the branches so you can see the trees. Occam's Razor.'

'But this is not simple, Rick. This is like trying to play Pick-up-Stix with a catcher's mitt.'

'Listen, all we know right now is we've got three guys working in conjunction,' Fuscante said. 'Out of those three, we have at least two names. We take it from there. Why clutter it up with conjecture? Let's see what we can learn from these names before we get bogged down in more complications.'

He had the kind of mind, she thought, that liked straight pathways, destinations he could work towards gradually. One step at a time. Patience. He was the sort of man who signed on for the whole voyage.

She saw a patrol car. It passed the Dodge, and then kept going round the square. It did this a couple of times before parking directly opposite the Dodge.

'Something you arranged?'

'Another little boost of security,' he said. 'You realize I can't let you out of my sight. You go where I go. And vice-versa.'

'I like the idea. I don't like the reason behind it.' She flipped the ashtray open, stubbed out her smoke. She'd been trying to follow a line of thought, but now she'd lost it. She'd imagined that acquiring information about MalCon might have helped, but it had only thickened the mud. Now she was knee-deep and going nowhere and when she looked back the way she'd come she saw the same dark terrain, a heath of secrets and silences.

A second patrol car entered the square from the north side. It drew up alongside the Dodge. A cop Andrea had never seen before got out. He was a tall man who wore glasses and walked in great stiff strides, intent on covering large distances quickly.

Fuscante rolled down his window.

'Rick,' the cop said. He looked past Fuscante a second at Andrea. It was a neutral grey-eyed gaze, no evidence of assessment in it.

'This is Andrea Malle,' Fuscante said. 'Andrea, Sergeant Jonah Peabody.'

Peabody stuck his head in the window. The tip of his sharp nose was red from the cold, and moist. 'Nice to meet you, Miss Malle. Been hearing your name a lot lately.'

'In connection with trouble, no doubt,' she said.

Heat from the car steamed Peabody's glasses. 'I guess you could say that. Still, that's what we're here for. Trouble.'

Fuscante said, 'What have you got for me, Jonah?'

Peabody wiped the cuff of his coat across his lenses. 'Those names you called in, Rick. I ran them through the usual records. The crime computer, Social Security—'

'Cut to the chase, Jonah.'

'Okay. First name you give me. James Thompson. You any idea how many of them there are? In this state alone, you're looking at hundreds, Rick. Nationwide, God only knows.'

'Leave him aside. What about Anthony Falco?'

'There's a few of them as well. I limited the search to New York for purely practical reasons. Narrow it down where it's manageable, you know? There's an Anthony Falco doing time in Attica for homicide. Another on parole for drug-dealing. He's in Queens. There's also one who did time for passing bad cheques and running various paper scams involving abuse of the US mail for the purpose of fraudulent property deals.'

'Tell me about him,' Fuscante said.

'Last known address . . . I got it on paper here. Hang on,' and Peabody dug inside the deep pocket of his overcoat, from which he produced a folded sheet. 'Twenty-seven Broad Street, Saratoga Springs.'

'What about Hal Hapsky?' Fuscante asked. 'You're

not going to tell me there are hundreds of people walking around with that name, are you, Jonah?'

'There's only one Hal Hapsky I came across.' Jonah Peabody took off his glasses. He had little pink indentations on either side of his nose. 'Take a look at this, Rick.' He took a computer print-out from his pocket, a single perforated sheet. He handed it to Fuscante, who read it and shook his head before passing it to Andrea.

At the top of the sheet was the word CONFIDENTIAL. *Hal Hapsky, DOB 2/2/50, POB, Baltimore, Maryland.* It wasn't a rap-sheet because there was no record of arrests.

Her eye wandered down the paper. *Subject of Federal Grand Jury investigation, Washington, DC, 1984, in connection with the murders of Josef Brodsky and others. No indictment. Subject of Federal Grand Jury investigation, Detroit, Michigan, 1990, in connection with the murders of Anton Lakas, Ellis Kivirrani, Stanislav Melsbakis. No indictment. Subject of Federal Grand Jury investigation, Boston, Mass., 1992, in connection with the murders of Stefan Schwarz, Angelica von Geffering, and others. No indictment.*

She raised her face and looked at the kids in the square a moment before she turned to Fuscante. 'What does all this mean?'

'Simple. Either Hal Hapsky is in the wrong place an awful lot of the time,' Fuscante said, 'or else he's getting away with murder.'

chapter *Thirty*

*I*nside the Police Department building, she followed Fuscante to his office, situated at the rear of a large room filled with desks and smelling faintly of sweat and old coffee. Heads swivelled as she went past: the sheriff's brand-new squeeze – was that the speculation already, the scuttlebutt? Fuscante's office was behind a half-partition, and contained an old mahogany desk and two chairs and a framed citation on the wall.

While Fuscante picked up the phone and dialled a number, she examined the citation. It was an award from the mayor's office, issued for an act of 'unselfish bravery'. In 1994, he'd rescued two kids from drowning in Glamys Lake when their canoe capsized during a summer squall. She thought: *He dashes into flames, he plunges into deep waters. The hero.* She watched him work the phone. His eyes connected with hers and held them a moment. Every so often she'd hear him

use the name Hapsky, or say, 'Yeah, Billy . . . Yeah
. . . I got it.'

When he put the telephone down he pushed his chair
back from his desk.

She said, 'I like the citation.'

He looked a little embarrassed, shrugged. 'Instinct,'
he said.

She gazed at the surface of his desk. Nothing of a
personal nature. No photographs. No souvenirs. No
cute desk ornaments or fanciful pencil-sharpeners or
paperweights. It was a functional space. Computer
terminal, old-fashioned IN and OUT trays made from
blond wood, some paperwork.

She was able to see over the top of the partition.
Cops at desks. FBI Wanted lists on walls. Fugitives
At Large. A big aluminium coffee-pot. Bulletin boards.
Friday Night Basketball Practice. Alcoholics Anony-
mous Hot-Line. Phones ringing.

A female cop with fair hair held back by a yellow
rubber band glanced at her quizzically. Andrea wondered if there was some animosity in the look.

She said, 'I think your people are curious about me,
and maybe a little wary. Especially the woman.'

'That's Millie. We went out a couple of times after
Cathy split.'

'What happened?'

'There was no chemistry, I guess. And I think Millie
had ideas of her own I didn't encourage.' He got up
from his chair, looked at his watch. 'I'll be right back.
There's a fax coming through I want you to see.'

She watched him go from the partitioned space. She
sat, gazed at the phone, then picked it up hesitantly and
dialled Patrick's number, not absolutely sure what she
wanted to say to him. 'I'm stuck here for a few more

days'? 'Don't bother trying to come up'? She got his answering-machine. She recorded a simple message, 'Just checking in. Call you later.' A little relieved, she put the handset back, rose, looked over the partition into the main room.

Fuscante was standing beside a fax machine. Millie, tall and big-breasted, was laughing at something and nudging him familiarly with her elbow. She wondered if they'd slept together. She watched a moment, thinking how strange it was to become unexpectedly involved in the rhythms and relationships of a small town that a few days ago had been completely unknown to her. She had a life of her own somewhere else, but it seemed to her she'd misplaced and couldn't locate it, like this was all some form of illusion she was just wandering through. Horaceville, for Christ's sake. A dot on the map. A small town miles from the big reassuring grey vein of the Interstate. She felt she was a traveller who'd become lost, and subsequently entangled in events that were not of her own creation, that this was a drama of limited duration and pretty soon a curtain would come down and she'd pack up and go back to her former existence. And Horaceville would fade until she could barely remember ever having been here in the first place.

Fuscante came back, carrying a sheet of fax paper. He handed it to her. She found herself looking at a darkened copy of a photograph of a man's face.

'It's not a great image,' he said.

'It's him, anyway,' she said.

'You're sure?'

'Positive. This is Gladd all right. Or Hal.'

'Bull's eye,' he said. 'You're looking at an official photo of Hal Hapsky.'

She stared at the picture. He didn't resemble the kind-hearted priest with his offer of grief therapy. The tone of the image darkened his features, making him sullen. He was unsmiling. She could hear him say, *'I can't get it through my head that he's dead. I can't believe the violence involved.'* She handed the sheet back to Fuscante.

He said, 'According to the guy I just talked with, a homicide detective called Billy Dee in Boston who was once a close colleague, Hal Hapsky was a suspect in at least five murders of German nationals in the Boston area.'

'German nationals? What is he? An old Nazi-hunter? Or just your basic xenophobe? America first, Krauts go home?'

Fuscante examined a note-pad on which he'd scribbled during his phone call to Boston. 'Stefan Schwarz, Angelica von Geffering, a couple of others – members of a German crime syndicate based in Massachusetts. Dee says their main activity was shipping Burmese heroin into Boston via Hamburg. Hapsky is suspected of having plotted their deaths. These were not pleasant deaths, either, Andrea. This was no gun in the back of the skull stuff and let's be quick about it. We're looking at torture, mutilation, dismemberment.'

'Dismemberment?' Her head was filled with images – headless corpses buried in landfills, limbs dredged out of rivers, a whole horror show.

'Exactly. Dee has tapes of phone conversations between Hapsky and various unidentified associates, in the course of which these slayings were apparently planned. The only reason no indictment came down is because of – how did Dee phrase it? – a certain ambiguity in the language of the tapes. In other words, Hal and his buddies used a code. Dee has no doubt Hapsky set up the murders. Proving it turned out to be something else.'

She absorbed this information, but still couldn't see any connection between her father and Hapsky. It was as if Hapsky were a three-prong electric plug you couldn't force into a two-hole socket. It wouldn't fit, no matter how hard you shoved it, how much force you used.

'He's not a nice man,' Fuscante said.

'I already had that impression, thanks.'

'Dee mentioned photographs of the victims. He offered to send me a set. I declined.' Fuscante examined his pad again. 'One other thing about Hapsky. It seems he's got a genuine affection bordering on the obsessive for explosives. Billy Dee says he was once a munitions expert employed in some murky freelance way by a clandestine research branch of the army – the kind of thing where his name wouldn't appear on any payroll, and his services were paid for in such a way the source of the money couldn't be traced. Hal belonged in that category of people the military call "reliable deniables". Who? Hal Hapsky? Never heard of him? His nickname, surprise surprise, was the "Demolition Man".'

The 'Demolition Man', she thought. A secret branch of the army. What kind of reality was this? She turned away from Rick Fuscante and stared from the window out across a parking-lot behind the building. A light snow was falling. Frail flakes fluttered over cars. The normal world.

'What about those other Grand Jury investigations?' she asked.

'Seemingly the same story, Dee says,' Fuscante

replied. 'In Detroit, Hapsky was suspected of organizing the murders of various Lithuanian nationals involved in a massive fuel fraud operation. Again, no indictment.'

'Fuel fraud?'

'It's a complex rip-off scheme where fuel pumps are rigged, and additives – alcohol, say – are mixed into diesel, which creates a low-grade fuel that can be sold to unsuspecting customers as premium. There's a whole black market in this stuff, costing the government millions of bucks in tax revenues. It also forces legitimate operators out of business. Sometimes, when these operators resist, they "disappear".'

She said, 'So Hal Hapsky didn't like these foreign-run operations.'

Fuscante nodded. 'Apparently not.'

She turned away from the window. The sight of more snow was depressing. 'Are we talking about a misguided kind of patriot? Is that what Hapsky is? If there's going to be crime, keep it in American hands?'

'We're talking about a killer. I don't know and I don't care about his patriotism. What I do know is I don't like the idea of him being anywhere *near* my area of jurisdiction. This is a small town, for Christ's sake. We don't get big-time killers. We don't get major criminals. Before your father was murdered, the biggest crime I can remember around here was a couple of Canadian college kids trying to transport two kilos of cocaine from New York City to Montreal. That's amateur hour. Kiddy stuff. Hapsky doesn't do kiddy stuff, Andrea.' He stepped from behind his desk. 'I don't have the manpower or the expertise to deal with a guy like this. That's what worries me. Especially when it comes to protecting you.'

He laid a hand on her arm. 'I can keep you at my place and beef up the personnel.'

'House arrest. For how long?'

'Tell me an alternative.'

'I could just go away,' she said.

'We've been here before, Andrea.'

'I know. But I'm thinking I could leave the country for a while. Europe maybe. The Far East. I don't know. I've got enough money. My father's insurance . . .' She stopped. She realized she didn't want to run. Didn't want to be forced into flight. Goddamm it. She drew a fingertip across the window-sill, leaving a trail in the dust. 'How in God's name did my father come to be connected with a guy like Hapsky? Where did their lives converge, Rick? Where did they overlap? You're telling me Hapsky *arranged* for people to be mutilated and dismembered, and I can't grasp what connection a person like this would have my father. I can't see it at all.'

'Just don't leap to conclusions,' he said, and rubbed her arm, a relaxing gesture.

'I'm trying not to,' she said. 'So obviously I'm still hanging on to the idea my father wore a goddam halo some of the time. Which is beginning to seem absurd. But I can't help it.' She forced a smile although she could feel her eyes watering. 'Maybe Hal and his friends will just go away. Maybe they'll evaporate and we'll never hear from them again. We'll wake up one morning and they'll be gone and life will be livable again.'

Fuscante said, 'Come on. I'll drive you to my place.'

She allowed herself to be escorted back through the main office. Fuscante paused on the way, carried on a lengthy conversation she couldn't catch with a couple of cops, then walked with her out to the front desk, where he said, 'I just checked. Nobody's reported seeing a chopper in the vicinity. So my guess is Hal isn't using one. Or if he did, he's not using it now.'

She wasn't really listening. She felt bleakness descend on her. The Demolition Man. Corpses cut and butchered. She wanted to draw a line in her head, with Hapsky on one side and her father on the other, a kind of border neither of them had ever crossed, Hapsky here, Dennis Malle there, and they'd never met. Hapsky had never gone to the offices of MalCon all those years ago. Her mother had dreamed that one. Daddy was a great man, a good man. This way to denial.

Wallace appeared, crossing the floor by the front desk. He wore a lab coat and an ID badge.

She felt confrontational. 'Found the ring yet?' she asked.

Wallace said, 'Ring? I'm in a foul mood, Miss Malle. I had your mother on the phone ten minutes ago. She wondered if she could see the body.'

Oh Christ, Meg, we went through that. 'She shouldn't have called you.'

'She's a very persistent woman,' Wallace said. 'She wants one last look at – I quote – "the first love of her life".'

'She said that?'

'She said that. I told her she was welcome to see the body any time she liked – if she was prepared to be horrified. I described the extent of cranial and facial injuries. I was specific and I was graphic, which gave me no pleasure. But some things people shouldn't have to see. I don't think she's going to persist any more. You saw the body. Would you want your mother to look at it?'

'No, no I wouldn't.' Andrea let the matter of the

ring slide. Meg, pushy Meg, what was she playing at?

Wallace said, 'She also wanted to know when the body would be available for disposal. Has she talked with you about that?'

'She mentioned cremation,' Andrea said. Disposal was what you did to garbage.

'I told her your father's body is available any time.'

Meg, you come up here and immediately you're planning a cremation. This rush was crass and distasteful. On the other hand, you could argue that Meg was being practical. Why should a body be left to lie in a chilled drawer? There would be a quick service of some kind, the coffin would slide down into a furnace, the end. Except it wasn't the end. Burning a corpse to cinders wouldn't answer any of the questions.

Wallace said, 'If you and your mother want to go ahead with this, there's nothing to stop you. My work's done. Call an undertaker.' He turned and walked briskly away.

Andrea watched him go. She couldn't come to terms with the finality of fire, even if that was what her father had wanted. Besides, Meg was basing her decision on a conversation that had taken place in Venice years ago – maybe he had changed his mind since then. Death wasn't something she could remember ever discussing with him. What did it matter, anyhow? Flame or burial, what difference was there?

Fuscante was moving her towards the front door. Snow tugged by wind blew against the pane. 'You don't like him, do you?'

'Wallace? I find him a little cold.'

Fuscante stared into the street. 'The real enemy's out there, Andrea.'

She looked at how wintry light shadowed his face, how the darkening afternoon shaded his strong features. 'You want to jump into the lake and rescue me, don't you? I'm just like those two kids you saved. With one significant difference. I can give you something you'd enjoy more than a citation.'

'Yeah, I know that. But could I hang it on my wall?'

She smiled at him as he pushed the door open and walked ahead of her into the street.

chapter *Thirty-One*

There were two Broncos parked one behind the other in the drive of Fuscante's house. In the first sat a young cop she'd never met before, a keen-eyed guy Fuscante called Dave Rosen. The other was occupied by Millie, who had her cap pulled down low across her forehead and glanced at Andrea as she passed.

Was that a little look of hostility? Andrea wondered.

Fuscante led her into the house, where O'Hanlon was in the living-room.

Beefing up the protection. Making sure I'm safe.

She'd inherited her father's sins, she thought. His misdeeds. Whatever they were. Whatever you called them. This was what he'd bequeathed her. Not a half-million bucks in insurance, but this — living in the deep shadow of his passing, a prisoner of his past. She resented it. She wanted her own life. It was a simple requirement, surely: but because of Dennis Malle she was being denied it.

He'd left her shackled to a ball and chain.

He'd left her to deal with a crazy called Hal Hapsky.

She walked into the kitchen and Fuscante followed her. Through the window she could see a patrol car parked in the alley at the bottom of the back yard. The cop in this car was a kid called Caskey, Fuscante said. He switched on the electric kettle and said he was going to make some tea.

'At this rate you'll soon have half your force stationed around the house,' she said.

'It's getting to the point where I might have to call in some outside assistance,' he said. 'Maybe some state cops. If I'm going to instigate a thorough search of the outlying areas, which I intend, I'll need all the bodies I can get. Also more snowmobiles. The Department here only has three. Normally that's enough.'

'But we're beyond normal.'

'Way beyond,' he said. 'The trouble is, if I call in the state guys, sooner or later the feds are going to know and they'll be crawling all over the place too, because they're not big fans of Hapsky. And I don't get along with the feds. They come in, take over, and suddenly you're just a gofer for them. I don't like that idea. They throw their weight around.'

He brewed tea, brought the cups to the table. She sipped hers in silence for a time, watching Fuscante over the rim of her cup. He was looking pensive, withdrawn.

'You're thinking you don't need this?' she asked.

'No, I'm thinking I'd like to nail that fucker Hapsky. That's all.' There was determination in his voice. He pulled the tea-bag from his cup, spooned sugar into the tea, stirred.

As she watched him perform this simple domestic act, she thought how the investigation of her father's murder had become part of a wider business that reached out from tiny Horaceville to Boston and Detroit and God knows where else, involving dope-smuggling and fuel-tax scams and the slayings of people unknown to her. It was as if the killing of Dennis Malle were a stone dropped in a quiet pool, and ripples spread from the place where the stone fractured the surface, and they kept spreading. The question 'Who killed him?' had become almost secondary now. If they ever found his killer, would he turn out to be some passing stranger, somebody with no previous connection to her father, just the perpetrator of a random act of violence one wintry afternoon that had set everything else in motion?

Snow fell in the back yard. White gloom. White silence. She finished her tea, lit a cigarette, wished she and Fuscante were alone in the house. But that would be another world, one where she didn't need all this protection, where she was safe.

The motion of snow hypnotized her. She thought about Meg. She'd need to call her soon, because she was certain to go stir-crazy in the Glamys: 'I didn't come all this way to sit in a goddam hotel and twiddle my thumbs. I came to be with my daughter, for Christ's sake, only she's too busy with her hunky cop.' And so on.

She rose, wandered the kitchen. She thought of Venice in winter. Meg and Dennis in love. Dennis saying: 'I want to be burned.' Why was she having a hard time with that one? She'd tried to shove it aside, tried to argue it away, but it came back to her now. She imagined the pair of them walking hand in hand,

wrapped in heavy coats against the cold fog, discussing
the finite nature of relationships. Everything ends in
death. I can't imagine going on without you, my love.
I hope I don't survive you. Had he expressed some wish
for the disposal of his ashes? she wondered. 'Throw
them in the sea. Scatter them to the winds. Just don't
stick them in a vase on the goddam mantelpiece because
that's sick and morbid. I don't want that.'

She stopped at the window. The cop in the car parked
out back lit a cigarette. She saw the flare of his lighter.
He turned on his wipers and they slid back and forth
against the new snow.

Fuscante had unfolded a huge map of the region on
the kitchen table and was bent over it, a pencil in one
hand. He was drawing circles round various locations.
She studied the map. She saw whorls and clumps
indicating woodlands, the curving lines of streams,
figures marking the elevation of the land in places.
Horaceville, in the dead centre, was a conglomeration of
streets beyond which the old railroad line ran nowhere.
Where the town faded out into countryside, tiny squares
and rectangles marked the locations of houses. How
isolated they looked, places you could reach only by
narrow roads. She imagined these homes buried in
snow and wondered how many of them were inhabited
and how the occupants managed when blizzards cut off
their narrow lifelines to the main highway leading to
town. Hardships, she thought. People huddled around
wood-burning stoves. Some of the places had names
in tiny print – *Dover Point Lodge, Smucker's Inn, The
Homestead Resort*.

Fuscante was writing on the map – question-marks,
crosses, asterisks. The crosses, he told her, were to
indicate unoccupied places, the inns and rustic hotels

that did only a seasonal business. Question-marks indicated homes mainly used in summer, but sometimes
their owners travelled up in winter and stayed for
an extended Christmas vacation. These were mainly
retirees, he explained, people with leisure time who
didn't much like the commercialism of Christmas in
cities. They yearned for log fires and freedom from TV
jingles; independent souls, hardy characters. The asterisks were for farmhouses he knew were inhabited.

'Where do you begin?' she asked.

'Good question. Hapsky has quite a choice of places
to hide. I'm trying to think of a place that would be
both secluded and accessible. But not too accessible.
Also, he's not going to go for anywhere obvious. And
we know he has access to snowmobiles, so that widens
the scope a little.' He tapped the tip of his pencil on the
map. 'I'll send people out at first light, see how far they
can get along some of these back roads. I already put
people to work the phones. You never know. Somebody
sees smoke from a place that's supposed to be empty.
An unfamiliar vehicle. We might hear something.'

She walked to the counter. 'I better call my mother,'
she said. 'She'll be chewing the drapes by now.'

'Go ahead.'

Before Andrea could pick up the phone, it rang.

Fuscante turned, reached for the handset. 'Hello,' he
said. A pause. He handed the phone to Andrea. 'For
you. Patrick.'

Patrick? How did he know to find her here? She felt
a sudden little spasm of guilt. She said, 'Patrick, I tried
to call you before. Did you get my message?'

'I had a hell of a time tracking you down,' he said.
'Finally I got Meg at that hotel, and she told me you'd
checked out, but she sounded mysterious when I asked

why. She gave me the name of Sheriff Fuscante, so
I got the number from Directory Assistance. What's
going on?'

'I didn't like the accommodation,' she replied.

'So where did you move to?'

She hesitated. 'A private house.'

God, she felt awful. This obfuscation.

'Who was the guy who answered the phone?'

'Sheriff Fuscante.'

'You're living in his house?'

'Right.'

'Let me get this straight. He's a cop who runs a bed
and breakfast on the side?'

'No, it's not like that.'

'I don't get it, Andrea.'

She said, 'Things are a little difficult here.'

'I'm coming up,' he said. 'That's why I'm calling.
I'm booked on a flight to Albany tonight.'

'I don't think—'

'I'll find some way down from Albany to Horaceville.'

'It's snowing again.'

'Screw the snow,' he said.

'I honestly don't think this is wise, Patrick.' She
hadn't expected to feel this bad. Unhappy, sure, but
not this great cloud that filled her mind.

'I had a horrible meeting with Seymour Stein.'

'I'm sorry to hear that.'

'Guy's a monomaniac. The way he talks, you'd think
it was his script, his idea. Change this, change that, this
character has to go. Goddam *auteur*. I can't hack that.
I need to come up there and be with you.'

'What time does your flight arrive in Albany?'

'Seven-thirty,' he said. 'Listen. Can you hold a
moment? There's somebody at the door.'

'Right.'

She looked at Fuscante. He looked up from the map he was studying. He understood. She could see it in his eyes. She shook her head slowly. 'He says he's coming.'

'You can't dissuade him?'

'Not when he's this determined. And not when he's feeling bad about his work.'

'What will you tell him when he comes?'

She chewed on the tip of her thumb. 'Christ, I don't know.'

'I'll help any way I can,' he said.

'One thing I won't do is lie to him.'

'I'd be disappointed if you did.'

Listen, Patrick, I don't know how to tell you this. She held the phone to her ear and heard Patrick's voice far off. It seemed to her some kind of argument was going on between Patrick and whoever had come to the door of his apartment. And then she heard him say, 'Hey, wait a minute, fella.'

'Patrick?' she said. She raised her voice. *'Patrick? What's going on there?'*

Nothing. He was too far away from his phone to hear her, and too involved in whatever the squabble was.

She heard him shout, 'What the *fuck*?'

Then he was back, sounding weird, breathing hard. 'You're not going to believe this – there's a guy here wearing a ski-mask and holding a gun to my head.'

'A gun? What guy?'

'I don't know what guy, he didn't introduce himself. All I can tell you is he's holding a fucking ugly big gun to the side of my goddam head.'

Andrea looked at Fuscante, gestured for him to pick

up the extension. He left the kitchen. She heard him hurry down the hallway.

She tripped over her words, flustered and panicked all at once. 'What does he want?'

She heard a thump, Patrick moan.

'Patrick? Are you there? Speak to me.'

A click. Fuscante had picked up the bedroom extension.

'Patrick? Talk to me,' she said. 'Talk to me.'

The voice that answered was high-pitched and familiar. She was back beneath that farmhouse again, in the crawl-space, smelling the bad air. 'Hey, Andrea, how's it going?'

'Patrick isn't involved in this,' she said.

'I got news for you, kid. He is now.'

She heard a clattering, then Patrick's upraised voice: 'For Christ's sake, that hurt.'

Jimmy said, 'Shut the fuck up, Paddy. I'm talking on the phone here. You make another sound, you get worse than that. Understand me, you fuck?'

'He doesn't know anything about this,' she said.

'I give a shit?'

Fuscante said, 'Whoever you are, I suggest you put the gun down and do yourself a favour and walk out of there.'

'Hey, am I speaking to the cop?'

'Yeah,' Fuscante said.

'Well, cop. Here's the way it is. I count to ten. I reach ten I blow this sucker's head all over his fucking computer. You got that?'

'Don't do it,' Fuscante said.

'Aw. Don't do it. Whatcha gonna do? Come busting in the front door and stop me? Beam yourself all the way down to Manhattan? Hey, Andrea. You still there?'

'I'm here,' she said. She felt a great wave of help-lessness. 'Please don't hurt him. Don't do anything to him. I'm begging you, don't.'

Jimmy said, 'Two three four. I'm counting, Andrea. You hear me counting? Four five six. Now what comes after six?'

'What do you want from me?' she said.

'Guess.'

Fuscante said, 'Spell it out. Now. Before you get in too deep.'

'Before I get in too deep? You make me laugh, Fuscante. In too deep. Heh-heh. Seven and counting to the big One Oh.'

Patrick was groaning. She heard him say, 'Please, Andrea, please, for the love of God.'

'I'll do whatever you ask,' she said. 'Anything. Anything at all. I swear.'

'We want everything,' Jimmy said. 'All of it. Everything you got from Malle.'

Andrea felt as if something had lodged in her throat. She had nothing to give. Absolutely nothing.

'Eight. Eight and a half. Heh-heh.'

'I already told Hal—'

'Hal don't believe you. Eight and three quarters.'

'Please, wait, wait,' she said.

'I'm waiting,' he said. 'Nine.'

She heard a sound in her head like the unbro-ken beep of a life-support system. A flatline. 'Please,' she said.

'Nine and a half. Nine point five. Tickety-tick-tick. Save your boyfriend's life, Andrea.'

Fuscante said, 'She doesn't know a goddam thing. Can't you understand that? What does it take to make you see, you fucking maniac?'

'Nine point nine. I'm getting the feeling nobody's listening to me.'

Andrea thought: *A lie. Anything to stall this maniac. Anything to save Patrick.* She couldn't force her head to work. The beep went on and on.

She heard herself say, 'Let me speak to Patrick. Let me speak to him!'

'I don't think you're concentrating, Andrea. Patrick can't come to the phone. Now we're just about at ten. Got anything to tell me? Got words for me?'

Fuscante said, 'One last time. Put the goddam gun down and walk out of there—'

'Ho hum, cop,' Jimmy said. 'Time's up. Say goodnight, Paddy.'

'*No!*' she said.

The next sound was like a single clap of hands, short and abrupt. She knew what it was, and she felt herself sway a little and saw the room tilt around her and the window shift to a strange angle.

The phone slid out of her fingers.

Fuscante came hurrying into the room and she slumped against his shoulder, and he held her.

'Patrick didn't do anything,' she said. 'He wasn't involved in any of this. He didn't know the first thing about . . . oh Jesus. They just do what they want. They don't give a damn, they kill, they don't care who, they kill and they kill, and Patrick,' and she fell into that place where language breaks down.

She stared beyond Fuscante's shoulder, seeing that the afternoon had given way, without the intermission of twilight, to darkness, and she thought of the small rooms of Patrick's apartment and heard his doorbell ring, saw him go to answer it, saw the man with the gun step inside, and then.

And then.

She imagined him lying on the floor a few feet from his desk and maybe his computer was switched on and a subdued grey light from the monitor fell against his face and all the cramped rooms were thick with silence.

chapter *Thirty-Two*

She walked up and down the kitchen. She had a headache that raged and a tight band of iron in her chest. Fuscante was talking into the telephone to a cop in Manhattan called Sharkey. 'No, I don't know what condition he's in,' Fuscante was saying. 'I only know he was shot.' When he hung up he placed a hand against her forehead as if checking for a fever.

'Sit,' he said.

She did so. She looked up at him.

'Sharkey will get back to me,' Fuscante said. 'Soon as he checks out Patrick's apartment . . .'

She kept getting pictures of Patrick and flickery little images of the gunman in a ski-mask, but she couldn't shove them into some cubbyhole of her brain where she wouldn't have to see them. Stanley and Irene, okay, they were connected, they were in this thing, whatever it was, and she could just about deal with that. But not Patrick, not poor Patrick.

She wished suddenly that she had the means to hunt down Hapsky and his associates and make them kneel down in the snow and hear them beg for mercy before she shot them; she'd do it, she knew she would, even if she'd never entertained murderous thoughts before in her life. But she'd been changed in a way she couldn't quite grasp yet, an emotional eruption that had blown away those little struts that keep you on the right side of being civilized.

I want to kill, she thought. *I want to track them down and kill them*. She thought of the snowy countryside, deserted hotels, distant houses half-buried. They could be anywhere.

She felt powerless. The landscape and the weather conspired against her. She rubbed the side of her head as she stood up, unsteady and reached for the support of Fuscante's arm.

'I need a drink.' She opened the Jack Daniels, poured a shot. She held it in both hands, sipped, shut her eyes. 'You know what I'm thinking? He'll never see one of his scripts get made. He worked and worked and he was always just this close to his big break, and now it's not going to happen for him. And I think that's heartbreaking—'

'We won't know anything for sure until Sharkey calls back,' Fuscante said. 'You can't jump to conclusions.'

With her eyes still shut, she heard Fuscante absently move one of the chess-pieces. The room pressed in on her. She could feel its density, as if it had shrunk around her, and its gravity intensified. Tap tap, Patrick's keyboard, tap tap, she couldn't let that play through her head. No jumping to conclusions. No leaps into the darkness. Just wait for a phone call from Manhattan from a

guy you never heard of until ten minutes ago, somebody
called Sharkey.

She looked at the phone. Beige and silent. 'I keep
thinking I could have saved him, I could have come up
with a lie that might have stalled the gunman, but my
head was empty, I wasn't thinking straight—'

'Don't put yourself through that. The gunman wasn't
in any mood for listening, Andrea.' He touched her hair,
watched her with sympathy and concern.

She asked, 'What's the point of shooting Patrick? I
don't see what it achieves. What can I give them? What
can I do?'

'Nothing. Stay here where you're safe.'

'Nothing! How can I just do nothing, Rick? Everything's fallen to pieces. You tell me. *Tell* me how to cope.
And why doesn't that goddam phone ring?'

Before Fuscante could make any response, there was
a sound from the hallway. Meg's voice – loud and
demanding – carried towards the kitchen. She was in
full flight, bustling through, snapping at O'Hanlon and
Millie, who were following her.

'She's *my* daughter and I want to see her. And no
pissant smalltown cops are going to stop me. Something's going on around here and I intend to find out
what it is, so get the hell out of my way!'

Not now, Andrea thought. *Please not now.*

Meg, bundled up in her white fur coat, appeared
in the kitchen doorway: a theatrical materialization –
enter stage right, jewellery rattling and shimmering –
O'Hanlon and Millie dragged along in her wake like a
couple of stage-hands.

O'Hanlon said, 'This woman just barged in, Rick.
Said she was Miss Malle's mother.'

'It's okay,' Fuscante said.

'You sure it's okay?' Millie asked. She glanced at Rick, then out of the corner of her eye looked at Andrea. It was an acid little look that said, *Who are you and are you fucking Rick?*

Fuscante said, 'It's fine, fine, really. You can go back to your car, Millie. Joe, just go back in the living-room. Okay?'

Both cops retreated reluctantly, O'Hanlon grumbling.

Meg said, 'Exactly what the hell is going on? I just heard some story about your father's house blowing up. The fat guy that runs the hotel says it was a propane leak, then another guy in the bar tells me there's all kinds of crap floating around Henrysville and he starts muttering about terrorists—'

Fuscante interrupted, a brave act, because nobody ever interrupted Meg. 'Whoever your source is, he's way off about terrorists, I can tell you that.'

Meg gave Rick the full stare, eyes like cast iron. 'Suppose you tell me who broke inside Andrea's room and rifled her stuff and stole a bunch of documents? Huh? Can you tell me that, *Sheriff*?' She turned to Andrea. 'As for you, why didn't you tell me anything about this? I might not be the greatest goddam mother in the world, but I came all the way up from Florida to be with you in this dismal hole, which counts for something in my book.'

Andrea wasn't sure how to respond to Meg, but Fuscante was patient and calm, admirably so. He pulled a chair out from under the table. 'Why don't you sit down. Please.'

Meg hesitated before she took one of the chairs as if it were a minor defeat to accept Fuscante's offer. 'Okay,' she said. 'I'm all ears, Rick. Shoot.'

Fuscante skimmed across the story, an expurgated version. He mentioned the murders of Stan Thorogood and Irene Passmore, but he withheld the fact that Andrea had been a witness to them – presumably to prevent an emotional outburst from Meg. *You saw it happen? Oh my God. What were you doing there?* He mentioned Hal Hapsky, but skipped over the incident of Hapsky breaking into the house and menacing Andrea, because by now he'd clearly assessed Meg's volatile nature. Throw no fuel on this woman: if you do she explodes. He couldn't avoid the subject of Patrick.

Andrea found her gaze straying to the phone – why didn't Sharkey call? What was keeping him?

Meg got up from her chair and stood directly behind Andrea, hands on her shoulders. 'What I'm hearing is a goddam nightmare,' she said. 'I'm taking you home with me, sweetie. I'm taking you out of this goddam place if I have to drag you screaming. You don't need this crap. Let the cops deal with it. Let the cops deal with everything. That's what they're paid to do.'

'I can't leave now,' Andrea said.

'The hell you can't.' Meg noticed the Jack Daniels and poured herself a glass. 'I need this, God do I need this.'

She took a long pull of the drink, then said, 'I'm hearing this tale of mayhem and murder and you're in the middle of it and you *insist* on staying here?'

'I can't go,' Andrea said.

'It's Rick, right? It's this thing between you and him, is that it?'

'No, it's not that—'

'My ass it's not. I know lust when I see it.'

'Oh Christ, Mother.'

'Why else would you stay? You think you can help? Supergirl, huh? Let me tell you, sweetie, the water's way over your head and you'll drown. Your father's dead. Stan. Irene. And Patrick . . . you know who's going to be next?'

Fuscante said, 'I don't think she's going to be safe wherever she goes.'

'Listen, buster, I can look after her. Don and me. We know places where nobody goes. We know Caribbean islands where Don has some holdings.'

'If they want her, they'll find her sooner or later,' Fuscante said.

'Because they have this bug up their ass about her knowing something,' Meg said. 'You're talking about Dennis Malle, and Dennis Malle never told anybody anything unless it suited him. He was the most secretive sonofabitch I ever knew, and this girl, my daughter, doesn't know the first goddam thing about what her father did.'

'Hey, you don't have to convince me, Meg,' Fuscante said.

'Okay, he got up to some weird stuff. I don't doubt that for a minute. But he loved this kid, and he wouldn't want her to suffer on his account. He wouldn't want to land her in the shit. No way.' Meg wagged a finger in the air. She was in full flight now, throttle open, all cylinders firing. She filled her glass from the bottle, waved the glass in the air. 'These characters are mistaken. And if Dennis could come back from the dead, he'd tell them so. He'd say, look, lay off the girl, she doesn't know a damn thing about anything, so take your act down the road, assholes. That's what he'd say.'

'He isn't here to say anything, Mother,' Andrea said. 'He's not going to come walking through that door and make everything all right again. And I don't believe you can dismiss whatever he did as "weird stuff", because I think we're looking at something a whole lot more than just weird. If it was only that, Stan and Irene wouldn't have gone into hiding the way they did. Patrick wouldn't have been shot and I wouldn't be sitting in this house protected by cops.'

Meg subsided just a little, lowered her voice, then looked at Fuscante. 'Listen. Dennis was a clam, okay. I don't know what he got up to. And I didn't stick around long enough to find out. But there's no way he'd have been involved in the kind of stuff you say Hapsky did. Sure, they were associated somehow – I don't doubt that, I saw them together with my own two eyes – but that was years ago, and Dennis, Jesus, Dennis wouldn't know anything about Hapsky's . . . unsavoury dealings. He wouldn't have been into shit like that.'

'Did you ever ask him about Hapsky at the time?'

'No, I didn't. Why should I? I didn't have any reason.'

'So you've got no idea what connected them?' Fuscante asked.

Meg shrugged. 'None.'

'Think.'

'I've thought already, Sheriff. And I'm coming up empty.'

'There's a possibility you could be in danger also. You know that.'

'Not if I'm on some Caribbean island surrounded by all that blue water and high solid walls and maybe a couple of Don's old hunting buddies who happen to be expert shooters.'

Fuscante sighed, then looked at Andrea. 'It's up to you. Stay here. Go to Florida. The Caribbean. It's your call.'

'I've already made my call,' she said.

Meg slammed her glass down. 'I take it that means you're staying here.'

Andrea nodded. 'Right.'

Meg said, 'God, you're as stubborn as your father. He could be a mule when it suited him.'

'I can take care of her,' Fuscante said.

'For now maybe. Maybe. But for how long?'

Fuscante said, 'As long as I have to.'

Meg sat down. 'Okay. Okay. It's your decision. It's not my life. It's your life.' She ran a fingertip around the rim of her glass. 'I suggest we talk practical then. I've been in touch with an undertaker—'

'Already?' Andrea said.

'It has to be done and somebody has to do it, Andrea. I don't notice you making arrangements.'

Andrea didn't respond to this. She might have said she had other things on her mind, but she didn't. Meg was picking up the rhythm she'd lost a couple of seconds before. She'd been defeated in her attempt to talk Andrea out of this place, but she never dwelled for long on her losses. She just changed the subject and went in search of a victory.

'This was a nice guy called Rubinstein,' she said. 'He told me he'd take care of the whole thing, no problem, we didn't have to worry. Leave it all to him. He asked if we wanted a service.'

'That's the last thing Dad would have wanted,' Andrea said.

'You think so?'

'I'm sure of it.'

'Fine. I'll tell Rubinstein that. Something simple.'

'Nothing religious,' Andrea said.

'Right, nothing religious,' Meg said. 'That's settled.'

The telephone rang. Fuscante hesitated only a moment

before he picked up the handset. He looked at Andrea as he spoke. 'Sharkey?'

She clenched her hands together very tightly. *Patrick is dead*, she thought. *And I never got the chance to be honest with him about the situation with Rick. It never happened. There wasn't time. The tide went out.* She gazed at Fuscante and tried to read his expression, but she couldn't. His words floated to her '. . . Okay . . . I got it . . . fine, yeah, fine.' He put the handset down. 'He took one bullet in the thigh, but he's going to be ok—'

'He wasn't killed? Is that what you're telling me?'

'He's lost a lot of blood but Sharkey put him in an ambulance and he's on his way to hospital and he's going to be fine, Andrea—'

'He wasn't killed,' she said again.

'Right.'

Relief made her curiously light-headed. Things in the room seemed very bright, pulsating. 'You're absolutely sure he's going to be fine?'

'That's what I'm told,' Fuscante said.

'You know what hospital he's in?'

'Next time Sharkey calls, I'll get that information.'

'I want to phone Patrick. I want to hear his voice.'

Meg said, 'He's probably out cold on morphine or something, sweetie. You can talk to him all you want later. Just be thankful the gunman didn't blow a hole in his head.'

Thankful. That wasn't the word. She'd thought him dead and he'd been brought back to life and the realization astonished her. She reached for Fuscante's hand and held it. They hadn't killed Patrick because they didn't need to. It was enough to show her they could go into any corner of her life they chose, that no place was sacrosanct. Her life lay open, plundered.

O'Hanlon came inside the kitchen. 'Rick? I don't mean to disturb. Jonah Peabody's here with the material you requested.'

'Tell him to wait in the living-room, Joe.'

'Gotcha.'

'What material is this?' Meg asked.

Fuscante said, 'Something from Boston.'

chapter Thirty-Three

Jonah Peabody was standing by the fire-place. Somebody – O'Hanlon maybe – had lit a fire, and flames flicked up into the chimney. Andrea sat by the fire, spread her hands towards it. The room was chilly.

Peabody had a brown envelope in his hand. He gave it to Fuscante, who ripped it open and took out an audiocassette tape.

Peabody said, 'I've only listened to a couple of minutes, Rick. The quality's poor. There's a lot of static and interference.'

'I expected that.' Fuscante went to the stereo system, slipped the cassette into the play-slot.

Meg placed herself on the arm of a couch and said, 'What's happening now? A musical evening?'

'This is a sample of covert recordings made of Hal Hapsky's conversations over a course of three months in 1992 that were played for the Grand Jury. I had them transmitted by phone from Boston.'

'Hal Hapsky's greatest hits,' Meg said.

'Maybe so. But I doubt you'll hear anything you want to sing in the shower,' Fuscante said, and looked at Andrea.

She hadn't realized he'd asked for this material. She thought about voices on a cassette sent down a phone-line from Boston and re-recorded here in the Horaceville PD.

She understood. He wanted her to listen. He wanted to know if she could identify any of the voices.

No, there was more. More than that. She knew what he was looking for.

'You ready?' he asked, and looked at her.

No, she wasn't ready, she didn't think she could ever be truly ready, but she nodded and sat back and gazed up at the ceiling. She heard Rick press the PLAY button and immediately the room was filled with a hissing sound. It was several seconds before a voice emerged from this background.

'I got two really bad autos' [inaudible].

'. . . yeah, I heard . . .'

'They're not roadworthy.'

'. . . tell me about it.'

'Things rust here, so I need to unload them.'

'. . . yeah, I can see that' [inaudible].

Fuscante paused the tape and looked at Andrea. 'The first voice is Hapsky.'

She said, 'Yeah. I don't recognize the other guy.'

He started the tape again.

'They'll be at the game. They'll show.'

'. . . you want, what, I should call you after . . .'

'Yeah. The usual.'

A silence after that. And then more hissing, followed by the sound of crockery, knives and forks,
somebody eating.

'These [clack clack] hot . . . indigestible.'

'. . . can't hear you, man . . .'

'I'm telling you these huevos rancheros, Christ.
Whooee.'

'. . . this is a fucked connection, I'll call later . . .'

'I don't know where I'll be.'

'. . . you want me [inaudible] . . .'

'Yeah, that place. I know.

'. . . this sucks, this phone . . .'

It was like listening to weirdly disjointed poetry,
Andrea thought, in which the spaces and silences meant
more than the words.

Fuscante stopped the tape and said, 'The first guy is
Hapsky again. You know the second?'

She shook her head.

Meg said, 'Cars, huevos rancheros. I assume this is
leading somewhere?'

'Maybe. Maybe not,' Fuscante said.

Meg folded her arms over her chest. 'Then it might
be a waste of time.'

'A lot of cop work turns out that way,' he replied.
'I have low expectations that conflict with my natural
optimism.'

He played the cassette again. Andrea felt tense listening to these voices, which seemed to issue out of
nowhere. Utterances in a void. Hapsky must have
known he was being bugged. Otherwise, why the coy
language, the lack of anything direct?

'These two particular vehicles are real losers.'

'. . . Yeah . . .'

'So what they need is to be trashed.'

'. . . I got that much, yeah . . . only it's a problem . . .'

'I don't want to hear about problems.'

'. . . see, there's more than just two to trash . . .'

'What are you saying? More than two?'

'You got it . . .'

'You need help, that what you're saying?'

'Yeah, you got it. It's too many.'

'You know [inaudible] call.'

'. . . Yeah, right . . .'

'I'll get back to you after I call the wholesale guy.'

'Pause it,' Andrea said. 'That's Falco.'

Fuscante looked at her. 'You're sure?'

'I'm sure. Falco and Hapsky.'

'Talking about cars?' Meg said.

Peabody made an impatient sound, a long sigh. 'This is Department business, Rick. I don't think it's wise having outsiders here.'

Fuscante said, 'Don't get so uptight. Meg's an interested party.'

'Oh yeah, I'm agog when it comes to cars,' Meg said.

'See?' Peabody said. 'I don't think certain parties should be involved in it, especially since the lady here seems to treat it so lightly.'

Fuscante made a gesture of dismissal. Peabody glared into the fire and tapped one foot angrily. *If I was running the Department things would be different.*

Meg said, 'What I'm wondering is how come you recognize these voices, Andrea?'

'It's another story,' Andrea said.

'I'm being kept out in the cold. I see.' Frost in Meg's voice. 'People go around talking about cars and God knows what, but nobody's going to let me in on the full story, is that it?'

Andrea said nothing. She watched Fuscante press
PLAY again.

'How many in total?'

'Five, maybe six.'

'That's a bunch.'

'. . . five that's definite . . .'

'Ah shit.'

'. . . call the wholesale guy . . .'

'Yeah, I been trying.'

Hapsky and Falco again. More hissing followed. It
suggested a meaningless sound emitted by a random
radio pulse in another galaxy. Andrea watched the green
digital counter on the cassette-player and thought about
vast distances, worlds too far away to reach. She felt
a pulse beat in her throat and remembered suddenly
one time when she and Meg and Dennis had gone to
Coney Island and she'd spilled onions out of her hot
dog and down the front of her blouse and Dennis had
dabbed at the damp spots with a tissue and Meg had
laughed because it had been that kind of day, a silly
giggling buoyancy had affected them all – how long ago
had that been? Twenty-five years? Something clouded
the recollection, though. Dennis had an appointment
somewhere, she remembered this, and he'd left Meg
and her to wander Coney Island on their own, and the
mood changed abruptly, and Meg had said, 'That's just
so typical of your father. He promises us a day out and
then abandons us.' Why had this come back to her now?
The sun had been bright and the late summer afternoon
humid and she remembered the Ferris wheel and how,
when she sat huddled against her mother at the highest
point in the wheel's arc, she'd scanned the crowds for a
sight of her father, but she hadn't seen him – and now
she realized she was listening to these tapes in much the

same way as she'd searched the Coney Island crowds that afternoon, expecting to see him, expecting to hear him: 'I'm over here, Andrea. Look! This way!' But he hadn't come back that afternoon . . .

She caught herself falling ever more deeply into the smells and sounds of that afternoon. Cotton-candy burning sweetly on the air. Onions simmering in water. Brine. The tape hissed. Her memory made the same sound. She didn't want to listen any more, either to the memory or to the cassette-tape.

The hissing quit.

There were voices again.

Rambling conversations. Hapsky talking to people she couldn't identify.

After a quarter of an hour Meg said, 'This is about as interesting as the phone directory. Men babbling. Making no sense.'

Fuscante said, 'Patience.'

'I'm not blessed in that department,' Meg said.

Andrea wished Meg would shut up.

'I got five or six autos.'

'Yeah?'

'I need [inaudible] off my hands.'

'Yeah?'

'I mean, the usual discount for a preferred customer.'

Laughter.

'. . . more than' [inaudible].

'What's up? Getting greedy in your old age?'

'. . . ha . . . [inaudible] . . . expenses.'

'Okay, I'm in no position to haggle here. I'm over a barrel.'

'. . . you want to tell me the pick-up?'

'I'll call.'

Andrea sat forward. 'Rewind,' she said.

Fuscante pushed another button.

'. . . you want to tell me the pick-up?'

She looked at Meg, who'd stiffened a little on the arm of the sofa, her body locked, her hands pressed together.

'Again,' Andrea said.

Meg said, 'No, don't. You don't need to.'

'Again,' Andrea said.

Meg said, 'Jesus Christ.'

Fuscante rewound, played back again.

'. . . you want to tell me the pick-up?'

'Let it keep playing,' Andrea said.

'No,' Meg said.

'I asked to hear more, Mother,' Andrea said.

'Why? You know that voice.'

'Please, Rick. Let it play.'

Meg said, 'There's no need. Don't you think I recognize Dennis's voice when I hear it?'

'It's not his voice.'

'Goddammit, you know it is.'

Andrea lit a cigarette.

'. . . you want to tell me the pick-up?'

She looked into firelight, then turned her face toward Rick.

'Is it, Andrea?'

Why fight it? Why go through that conflict? She relented and said, 'It might be.'

'. . . I'll get back to you after I call the wholesale guy.'

'There's no might,' Meg said.

Fuscante said, 'I'll play some more if you like.'

'It's Dennis, for God's sake,' Meg said.

The wholesale guy, Andrea thought.

She was aware of Fuscante studying her. She thought: *A voice comes from beyond the grave.* The cassette-deck was a medium. It raised the dead. This was why Fuscante had asked for the tape. He wanted to find one incontrovertible truth about her father, and here it was, the Demolition Man talking with the Wholesale Guy.

She heard herself say, 'I don't think that's conclusive. Okay, it sounds like my father, but what does it prove?' She was clinging to some small thread that might redeem the man. Even now. Even after everything that had happened. She was still holding on. It was instinctive, in her blood. She was his child.

'It didn't prove anything to a Grand Jury,' Fuscante said.

The tape was still rolling.

'You'll come to this part of the world?'

'. . . can do . . .'

'I got it set up so you can' [inaudible].

. . . [inaudible] 'hotel room . . .'

'This is in and out.'

'. . . good . . .'

'Hey, I heard about some real estate, a bargain.'

'. . . nice nice . . .'

Fuscante said, 'You see the tactic, of course. It's confusion. Hapsky talks about cars. Then he mentions real estate. Billy Dee or some other investigating officer checks it out and finds Hapsky has actually acquired some cars he decides to off-load. Hapsky makes the code fit the reality. Sure, there are cars, but he's not talking about cars, is he?'

Andrea thought: *A bunch of beat-up cars. Cars meaning people. People to be disposed of.*

'And there would be some parcel of real estate too. You can bet on it. If Hapsky was being followed, any

report of his movements would have mentioned the fact
he visited an apartment complex or a building of some
kind, talked with a realtor, discussed a price. That kind
of thing. Nobody can come back and accuse Hapsky of
making it up. He covers his ass.'

Andrea flashed on her father's house. The wrecks
that sat up on cinderblocks. The cars he said had come
with the property. Props in the masquerade. Two of
Hapsky's vehicles. What else? Two of the battered,
useless cars Hapsky had been keen to get rid of, and
they'd finished up at the back of her father's house,
and he'd never got round to having them removed.
What had happened to the others Hapsky had mentioned? Maybe Dennis Malle had sold them for scrap
or dumped them elsewhere or simply abandoned them
in a concealed place – what did it matter? The tape was
evidence enough of a terrible collusion. Cars. It had
nothing to do with cars or real estate.

It had to do with death.

She got up from the sofa. She had a sudden urge to
rush from the house and go out into the street and run
and keep on running until she'd reached the edge of
the world.

Fuscante said, 'I'm sorry.'

'You don't have anything to be sorry about.'

'I didn't know what might be on the tape, Andrea.'
He made a hopeless little gesture with his hands.

'Now we know,' she said.

Meg put an arm round her shoulders. It felt heavy
to Andrea, and possessive. 'Come with me down to
Florida, sweetie. Put all this behind you. Say you'll
do it. For your own good. Forget the man.'

'I can't just forget him,' she said.

'Hey, don't you think this pains me too?' Meg said.

'I'm sure it does.'

'It's like a goddam arrow in my heart, honey. I don't *want* to believe, I don't want to think for a *minute* that Dennis was involved in anything like this . . .' Meg looked pale. 'But you heard the tape.'

Hapsky's words, 'I'm not in the business of telling children there's no Santa Claus', rolled through her head. She didn't want to go to Florida. She wanted to find Hapsky. That killing urge again. That need for blood. She moved from her mother's touch and walked to the cassette-deck and pressed the STOP button and the room was silent except for the sound of wood burning.

'I hate him,' she said.

Nobody else spoke. She was aware of movements in the room, Meg parting her lips, Fuscante shifting his weight, Peabody taking off his glasses and blowing on the lenses.

'I hate him,' she said again. 'And I'm not talking about Hapsky.'

Meg threw cellophane from a cigarette pack into the flames and it went up in a flutter of purple-red smoke and Andrea, as if mesmerized, watched it burn. Hatred and rage, purple and red.

The door opened and Millie stood on the threshold of the room, slipping the rubber band from her hair and letting it fall loose upon her shoulders as if to remind Rick – and Andrea – that underneath her uniform she was a good-looking woman.

'Rick,' she said. 'Got a minute?'

chapter *Thirty-Four*

*A*ndrea watched Rick Fuscante step out into the hall with Millie. She was conscious of Meg observing her, hovering nearby as if she were an attendant at somebody's sickbed. Unspoken sentences hung in the room: *Come with me now, we'll just blow this place. There's nothing for you here.* Meg was exercising a restraint completely foreign to her.

Andrea listened to the voices in the hallway.

Millie said, 'It might be nothing, Rick.'

'I'm not taking chances,' Fuscante replied.

Andrea peered round the half-open door, and saw Fuscante's broad back and Millie's face, her serious expression. 'Gann drinks a lot of that shit he brews himself. He's inclined to have whacky visions. You know that.'

Fuscante was quiet a moment. 'Yeah, but I can't afford to ignore him on the grounds he might be out of his head. He might be on the ball with this one.'

'It's getting up there's the problem,' she said.

Andrea opened the door the whole way, moved into the hall.

Fuscante turned to her. 'A guy called Fred Gann who lives about a mile from the Dover Point Hotel claims he saw a couple of jeeps at the place, which is shut until April first. Nobody ought to be up there.'

Millie looked at Andrea. 'This is the same guy who said he saw a flying saucer one time over his house. You gotta put his statement in perspective.'

'He's been known to make his own moonshine,' Fuscante said. 'It's inclined to give him hallucinations.'

'But you'll check it anyway,' Andrea said.

'I'd be a fool not to,' Fuscante said.

Millie said, 'It's a crap road even at the best of times.'

'We can make it,' Fuscante said.

Millie looked doubtful. 'You can't take the snowmobiles. Too noisy – assuming there's anybody up there.'

Fuscante said, 'I wouldn't even consider the snowmobiles. I figure we can four-wheel as far as Grogan's Ridge, then go the last half-mile on foot.'

'With drifts up to your neck and the temperature below zero,' Millie said.

'I can't do anything about the weather.' Fuscante had a slight note of irritation in his voice. 'Snow doesn't faze me. I've lived with it all my life.'

Andrea said, 'Take me with you.'

Fuscante shook his head. 'Don't even ask.'

'I want to go,' she said.

'No way,' Fuscante said. 'Absolutely no way.'

'I can't just sit around here.'

'You'll be looked after—'

'I don't think you're listening to me, Rick.'

'Lady wants to go,' Millie said.

Fuscante said, 'I don't want any arguments here. I'm leaving O'Hanlon and Rosen and you, Millie. Caskey's out back. That doesn't change. I'll take Peabody and I'll round up some other guys and we'll go out.'

Andrea caught his sleeve. 'I've got a right to go.'

'I don't have time for an argument,' Fuscante said. He called out to Peabody, who emerged from the living-room. Then Fuscante was moving towards the front door, grabbing his coat from the rack, taking his cellular phone out of the coat pocket and flipping it open, dialling a number as he opened the door. Peabody went after him. Icy air entered the hall. The dark of the street intruded.

Left behind, Andrea thought. *A woman's place.*

She shouted at him, 'This is my business as much as anyone else's.'

He didn't even turn. 'It's cop business. It's out of your hands,' and he was gone, slamming the door.

Millie said, 'I guess he really values your safety, lady.'

Andrea looked at the closed door, the pane of stained glass set into the wood. She heard Fuscante's vehicle roar to life. She thought, *I could go after him. I could follow him.*

Millie, as if she'd deduced Andrea's intention from the look on her face, walked to the front door and stood with her back to it, arms folded. She had an imposing quality. 'At least it's warm,' she said. 'There's a nice fire inside. Out there you'd freeze your buns off.'

'Terrific.'

'And you'd only be in the way.'

Andrea went into the living-room. What was she supposed to do now? Wait here with Meg and O'Hanlon?
The cop was standing close to the window, every now
and then parting the curtains and looking out.

Christ, she hated waiting, living in a state of suspen-
sion. She had every goddam right to be out there with
Fuscante.

Meg was in front of the fire, hogging the flames.
'Something happening?'

Andrea said nothing.

'You look like a little kid fuming,' Meg said.

I am *fuming*, Andrea thought.

Meg smiled at O'Hanlon. 'Would you mind going to
the kitchen and grabbing that bottle of Jack Daniels?
Joe, isn't it?'

'Joe. Right.'

'Thank you, Joe.' Meg spoke, sweetly, as if to a
servant.

O'Hanlon went out, returned seconds later with the
JD and a couple of glasses. Meg poured, handed one of
the glasses to Andrea, who took it but didn't drink.

Meg looked into her glass and sighed and there was a
slight bitterness and maybe some sadness in the sound.
'I still can't believe it. You're married to a man, sleep
with him, carry his child – and when you get right down
to it, you don't know who he is. You've been making
love with a stranger. All those intimacies. All those rev-
elations. I find it impossible . . . You know something,
sweetie? I don't even give a damn about his funeral. I
couldn't give a shit. I'll let that undertaker do anything
he wants with the body, because I wash my hands off
it. Bury it. Burn it. Bastard doesn't deserve . . .'

Andrea wasn't listening. She was imagining four-wheel-drives travelling snowy back roads, Rick leading a group of men through great drifts. At a level just below her annoyance she was concerned about him, and she didn't want to be. She wanted to hang on to the anger she felt towards her father, she didn't want to dilute or adulterate it with whatever sentiments she might feel about Fuscante. She had to keep these men and her feelings about them separate in her head.

She listened to the creak and spit of the logs and drank her JD. Meg was going on about how little you ever really knew another person. Especially one like Dennis Malle. Don, now, you could practically read his mind, there wasn't a secretive bone in his body. But Dennis, he had a dangerous edge, and those were the kind of men you had to be careful about, the kind who looked like they kept secrets, the kind that told lies. Unfortunately, they were also the kind you fell head over heels for. They made you lust after them. And they made love like there was no tomorrow.

Andrea wondered about playing the tape again, making sure – but what was there to be sure about? She'd been through this, denying and denying and denying. Truth was a tidal wave. It flattened all your intricate little sandcastles. It dumped detritus dredged from the ocean floor on the beach. Bones. Hanks of hair. Things that had once been human.

The man who'd pushed her higher and higher in a swing all those years ago and said, 'Trust me' – that man had been capable of killing other people.

More than simply killing.

She didn't want to think. She was burned out.

She walked into the hallway, where Millie stood smoking a cigarette.

'Don't report me for smoking on the job,' she said.

Andrea looked at her. Big-boned, wide-hipped, with a Nordic complexion She had a face that could be either rock-hard or baby-soft, tough or seductive. It was the former she showed Andrea.

'So. You and Rick. Serious?'

'I hardly know him,' Andrea said. How to get past Millie and out the goddam door? How to slip away?

'He had a tough time with Cathy.'

'He hasn't talked much about her.'

'Cathy slept around.'

'That's too bad.'

'Looking at her, you'd swear she sang in the church choir. Pale blue eyes, yellow hair, ringlets even. Goddam ringlets down to here. You'd put butter in her mouth and it wouldn't melt.'

Andrea looked at the gun strapped to Millie's hip, the handcuffs that dangled from her belt, the night-stick, the canister of mace. The woman was a walking arsenal. She had a fat black cellular phone stuck to her side, like a second pistol.

Forget it. There's no way past this sentinel.

'Yeah, Cathy was a piece of work all right.'

'It must have been painful,' Andrea said.

'I'll tell you what was painful. Everybody in town knew about her except Rick. Who's gonna tell him, "Hey, did you know your wife's screwing around?" Then he walked in on her one afternoon and there she was, getting it on with some salesman guy. Not a pretty sight. Opened his eyes wide, though. He used to tell me he wished he'd paid her more attention. Guys say that when it's too late.'

'Are you saying it was his fault?'

'It takes two to fuck things up.'

'Did he, you know . . . have another woman?'

Millie pushed a hand through her thick hair. 'He didn't have time for another woman. Married to the job. An old story.' She hitched up her belt. 'Play straight with him. If there's anything between you and him. Don't fuck with him.'

'I don't know what's between us,' and she drifted to Patrick. Her mind was cluttered all at once. Where was that sense of order she'd prized? That feeling of control? An illusion. She'd listened to married couples talk about their problems and she'd felt in control, aloof even, but none of that was left.

'I seen a certain look in his eyes,' Millie said, 'and the same kinda look in yours, lady. I have a real soft spot for the guy, in case you haven't noticed. A word of advice. You treat him right. He's a damn good man.'

'I'm transparent.'

'Transparent? You're an open book. One of them oversized books for the vision-impaired.' Millie smiled. 'And, no, there's no way outta this house. So you can put that right outta your mind.'

'Psychic.'

'Just observant.'

And smart, Andrea thought. *Not to be underestimated. Okay, so I'm stuck here until Rick comes back.* 'Will he phone?' she asked.

'He might. Depends.'

'He'd want to keep you informed, wouldn't he?'

'Rick? Keep *me* informed? Rick doesn't have to keep me posted on his comings and goings. Where would you get that idea?'

'Us, I mean. He'd want to keep us informed.'

'Us? Uh-uh. You mean *you*. You're the one who

wants to hear from him. Christ, you wear it all on your sleeve, don't you? You'd be shit at poker.'

From outside there was the sound of a vehicle, a vibration in the air.

She wondered if it was Rick, if he'd come back for some reason, maybe something he'd forgotten. Maybe he'd even changed his mind about taking her along. *Don't get your hopes up. He doesn't want you along.*

Millie turned, opened the door an inch or two, looked out. She took her gun from the holster, a precautionary move.

The blasts were deafening and deadly and shattered the wintry silence of the night and the stained-glass panel in the door flew out and wood splintered, and Millie was kicked backwards, as if she'd been struck by an enraged stallion. She travelled two or three feet as she was propelled, dropping beside Andrea, head tilted back, mouth open, eyes wide. Andrea glimpsed through the open door a flat-bed truck and a guy at the cab window with a shotgun, and another lying flat in the back, also with a shotgun. She ducked to one side, out of their line of vision and heard the sound of more gunfire, not the rumble of a shotgun this time, but a pistol, which she assumed was Dave Rosen firing from his car parked out front. O'Hanlon came into the hallway, gun drawn. He pushed Andrea to the floor with such force she struck her head against the wall. In the living-room Meg was shouting, '*Jesus Christ!*' in a voice distorted by panic and fear. O'Hanlon stepped over Millie and slid along the hall with his spine to the wall. He fired once, twice, and then the shotguns exploded again and the door was blown back off its hinges and O'Hanlon, clutching an arm that was suddenly spurting blood, screamed at her, 'Get back, get back the living-room,' and she crawled on elbows and knees through the door and into the room, where Meg was still shouting, covering her ears with the palms of her hands.

More gunfire. The windows imploded. The drapes blew back. The flames in the fire twisted and danced sideways as cold air stirred them. She grabbed Meg and dragged her to the floor and covered her mother's body with her own, an act she didn't stop to think about, an instinct. She raised her face, looked into the limited segment of hallway that was in her line of vision and saw another cop – this was Caskey, who'd been parked out back – come into view. He was bent at the knees and firing his gun towards the street without any apparent regard for his own safety. Where was O'Hanlon? What had happened to Rosen? The shotguns went off again – *boom boom, boom boom* – and what remained of the windows was finally destroyed and the curtains ripped and slid from the rings that held them in place. Andrea flattened her face against Meg's back and wondered if she should make an effort to get out of this room, which lay exposed to the street and the gunmen in the truck. But where? Where to go? There was only the hallway, also brutally exposed.

And Millie lay out there. Millie.

The gunfire went on. Shotguns answered by pistols, a one-sided argument, like a loud man shouting down a meek one. She wondered how long this battle could rage. She raised her head a little and glanced through the window at the street and saw the guys in the truck fire again. The noise was thunder roaring in her ears. She had the feeling of being caught up in a terrible storm. She heard the wall beyond her crack, plaster flying, an electric wire sizzle as it was struck and severed. The lights in the living-room and hallway went out suddenly. Blackness. Meg was shivering and crying underneath her and digging her fingernails into the back of her hand and saying, 'Oh God God God, get me out of here!'

Outside, the truck turned so that its full beams flooded the room with the sharp white terrifying effect of searchlights. She felt trapped inside a compound where a watchtower cast a merciless light. She heard gunfire come from the driveway and the rattle of bullets against the panels of the truck, but another round of fire from one of the shotguns overpowered the sound of the handguns, and the light, stark and revealing, continued to dazzle the room. She imagined the truck was going to clamber over the snowpiles on the sidewalk and rumble through the front yard and keep on rolling like a tank through the windows and into the room itself, crashing past what remained of the window-frames, crushing everything in its forward motion.

In the far distance was another sound. Sirens. Wailing.

The truck moved back. She heard tyres squeak on ice. She watched the lights withdraw from the room, a pulling back of white, a re-emergence of black.

She didn't move. She lay still, holding her breath, trying all the time to comfort Meg with her body.

Somebody stood in the doorway with a flashlight.

She didn't want to look.

She heard O'Hanlon say, 'Are you hurt?'

She gazed into the beam. 'Millie . . . ?'

'Millie's dead,' O'Hanlon said quietly.

'The others . . . ?'

'Rosen too.'

She heard pain in O'Hanlon's voice and was glad she couldn't see his face.

'But Caskey's okay,' he said. 'Yeah, he's okay. Caskey. Just a young kid.'

'You?'

'I'm bleeding. I don't think it's too bad.'

Andrea got to her knees. Although the living-room was as dark as the hallway, she could see a pale square of light falling from the kitchen beyond O'Hanlon. She needed this light. She was drawn to it. Light and life.

Meg said, 'They've gone?'

O'Hanlon leaned against the jamb of the door and groaned. 'They've gone.'

Andrea stepped toward the cop, reached out, touched him. He sucked in his breath swiftly. She dropped her hand to her side. Her fingers were wet with his blood. He turned away from her and headed towards the kitchen, holding his arm. She walked behind him.

She stumbled against Millie.

She swayed a little, entered the kitchen. O'Hanlon was running water at the sink. He'd taken off his jacket and rolled up the sleeve of his shirt and was bathing the red gash in his upper arm.

'Let me look at that,' she said.

He shook his head. 'You don't want to see this.'

She stepped back from him. 'I'll call Rick.'

'Call an ambulance before you do anything else,' O'Hanlon said, and just kept running water over his wound like a man in shock. On and on, working pink-tinted water with his big red hands and making a quiet humming sound, as if this might keep his pain and loss at bay.

Outside, the sound of sirens grew louder, puncturing the dark. She thought that she might be listening to the inside of her own head, and the sirens were the voices of all the people who'd died as a consequence of Dennis Malle's life.

And her presence in this small town.

chapter *Thirty-Five*

*T*here were cops everywhere in the house, paramedics carrying stretchers. All the chaos attendant on death. In the kitchen a paramedic was examining O'Hanlon's wound. The big cop was pale, losing blood. Another paramedic administered a shot to Meg to calm her. Andrea refused the offer. She wanted clarity and focus. She didn't want her brain numbed and senses deadened.

She could see, through the space where the front door had been, two guys with stretchers pick up Rosen's body from the snow. *The snow is always red in Horaceville*, she thought. The street was slashed with blue and red and white lights. Somebody placed a sheet over Millie in the hallway. A white sheet illuminated by flashlights. Caskey, young and unaccustomed to havoc, was moving here and there in the manner of a man who needs to do something, only he isn't sure what, he hasn't been trained for this. Just move, go from room to room, keep busy, look for something to do, don't think, people are dead.

Inside the kitchen, Meg was looking glazed.

'You should go back to the hotel,' Andrea said.

'Don's probably wondering.' Meg's voice had a flat, druggy tone.

'I'm sure somebody can drive you.'

Caskey, lingering in the doorway, volunteered. 'Where's she staying?'

Andrea told him. He helped Meg out of her chair.

'What about you?' Meg asked.

Andrea said, 'I'll stay here.'

In different state of mind, Meg would have argued against this decision. Drugged and traumatized, she lacked an edge. 'Who's going to look after you now?'

'I'm surrounded by cops, Mother. Look around.'

Caskey said, 'I'll be right back,' and led Meg outside. Andrea watched. There was blood on the pine floor around Millie's body. A couple of cops were standing over the corpse with flashlights. She didn't recognize them.

She went back inside the kitchen to O'Hanlon. The paramedic was applying a tourniquet.

'How bad is it?' she asked.

'Bad enough,' the paramedic said. He was a young guy with a shaved head and intense blue eyes. 'He needs to be hospitalized.'

O'Hanlon said, 'I can't leave the woman in this house on her own. Fix me up as best you can right here, boy.'

'I can't work miracles, Joe.'

'Just keep me from leaking to death, for Christ's sake.'

'I'll call Rick,' Andrea said. 'You know his mobile number, Joe?'

O'Hanlon winced as the paramedic adjusted the tourniquet. 'Slipped my mind. Somebody's sure to know it. Ask any of the other guys. Listen, has anybody gone after that truck?'

'I don't know.'

'Find out, would you,' he said.

She went out of the kitchen again. The two cops hovering over Millie glanced at her, looked away, said nothing. She entered the living-room, which felt like a box of ice. Four cops, each with a flashlight, stood among the debris. She recognized Gomez.

'Miss Malle,' he said.

There was something less than friendly in his voice. *He blames me*, she thought. *It comes down to that. He holds me responsible for all this. And why shouldn't he? I come into all their lives and suddenly there's disaster and chaos. Carnage.*

The loss of colleagues. That would be the worst of it. Friends, associates, people who shared one another's lives.

She said, 'O'Hanlon wants to know if anybody's chased the truck.'

Gomez said, 'We got a couple of roadblocks up. But nobody's reported anything yet.' She could tell from his voice that he was straining to maintain a certain level of politeness. 'God knows how Rick's going to react.'

'Has anyone called him?'

Gomez gestured to one of the other cops. 'McPherson just tried. No answer.'

'No answer. What does that mean?'

'Out of range maybe,' Gomez said.

'But he's only a few miles away at most.'

'Sometimes there's interference. The snow. Or maybe he's in a blind spot. Like a dip in the land, something. We get that sometimes. We'll keep trying.'

Even as Gomez spoke, McPherson, an overweight man in a great marquee of an overcoat, was punching numbers into his cellular phone. Andrea watched him, wondered about Rick out there. This place called Grogan's Ridge where he was headed. The Dover Point Hotel. Going through drifts on foot. She thought about the flat-bed truck. Maybe it had already cleared town before the roadblocks were in place.

Exhaustion coursed through her, a reaction to the attack, like being drained after a vicious electric storm that left you shaken and trembling, but she wasn't going to give in to that. Too easy in a way. Sleep. Just sleep. No, she had to do something, she wasn't sure what.

'Nothing,' McPherson said and stuck his phone in its pouch. 'I'll give it another couple of minutes, try again.'

Gomez said, 'Fuck. Millie and Rosen. Fuck fuck *fuck*.'

McPherson said, 'It's shit.'

Gomez said, 'I had three years in the NYPD. All that time, I never saw stuff like this. You know that, Mac? Never even had to draw my gun down there. New York, Christ's sake. You come to Horaceville, you think, this is like extended leave or something. Boy, was I wrong.'

McPherson made a small clucking sound. Disapproval. Disbelief.

Another cop turned his flash on Andrea and said nothing. Like he just needed to look at this woman who'd come sailing into Horaceville as if she was the angel of death. She wanted to apologize. She wanted to say, 'Blame me.' It didn't matter that Fuscante had asked her to come to his house. It didn't matter that her father's life had led her to this awful point in time. She wanted to say, 'I didn't mean for any of this to happen. I once had another life and it was okay, fine in a humdrum kind of way, I wasn't going to change the world or anything, but it was all right. I mended the broken pottery of marriages. I quick-fixed relationships. I handed out platitudes. Got marital problems, guys? Ask me, I'm offering freebies, let me help, make it up to you.'

She turned her face away from the harsh flash. Inside her head was a desperate babble: *My life turns to this. A frozen house. Shotguns in the night. Death. And Patrick doped up in a hospital bed.*

She heard a familiar voice in the hall. She saw Wallace appear, flashlight in hand. He stooped over Millie and whipped back the sheet and turned the beam on the corpse. Andrea moved to the doorway and looked at him and he raised his face to her without expression. Then he turned his attention back to Millie, reached down and closed her eyes. He remained in this stopped position, his back hunched. He drew the sheet over Millie.

'It's not worth all this,' he said. 'Nothing is.' He made a gesture with his hand, taking in not only Millie's body but the broken front door, the shotgun holes, the entire house, the devastation, the world in general.

She had the feeling he was trying to tell her something, but she wasn't sure what. At least his tone of voice wasn't one of censure. He wasn't laying culpability of this catastrophe on her doorstep. She watched light from his flash glisten in his beard and long hair. His eyes gleamed. He inclined his head and drew a hand in a weary manner across his face and just for a moment she experienced pity for him, although she really wasn't sure why. He was carrying a weight she couldn't see. He was being pressured by a force invisible to her. Maybe it was death. Maybe it was an accumulation of all the years he'd spent probing corpses, cutting through bones, examining organs – all these years had finally caught up with him. And Millie was one body too many.

He stood up slowly. 'I looked for that ring, you know. I looked all over for it.' He came very close to her. He emitted a smell of damp hair. She thought of a dog coming in from the rain.

She said, 'It's lost. I accept that. It doesn't seem important any more.' She glanced down at the sheet, drawn to it against her will. A few feet from the body lay something that glowed dull and metallic. She realized it was Millie's gun, knocked out of her hand when the first shotgun blast had blown through the door.

Wallace stretched out an arm, gripped her shoulder. For a moment she wondered if he'd been drinking, but there was no scent of alcohol on his breath.

'You know, according to a Maori legend I once heard, there's a valley where everything lost eventually turns up,' he said. 'Maybe that's where the ring is.'

She stared into his eyes and thought, *Drugs? Did he dabble, write the occasional script for himself? He didn't seem the type.*

'People sometimes get this look on their face when they speak to me,' he said. 'Parents who have to identify their dead child, a husband who has to look at his wife after a road accident. They show grief, they can't hide that – but there's always something else in their eyes. Do you know what it is?'

She said she didn't.

'It's hope. It's the look of people who wonder, just for this one bizarre microsecond of time, if I have the power to restore life to their loved one. If I have access to magic. Or a potion, a wonder-drug. Or even an unholy talent, perhaps. And I don't. Of course, I don't.' He released her and took a step back. He smiled at her thinly. 'Why am I telling you this? Maybe you're just an audience for the ramblings of a man who's dog-tired, Miss Malle. That's all.'

'Then you should get some sleep.'

'An eminently practical suggestion,' he said. 'But lately I've been having bad dreams. There's one where I'm trapped in this strange lab and I don't recognize the instruments, which are rusted and ancient, and the bodies just keep coming and coming. There's no end to the procession of them. What makes this dream a blue-ribbon nightmare is that some of the cadavers aren't dead. I'm sawing the rib-cage of one, and he opens his eyes and screams. I wake up sweating . . .'

He was off-centre, she thought. A man out of balance. A professional slipping out of the straitjacket of every-day protocol, failing to check his behaviour, to shield his feelings. She'd misjudged him when she'd called him cold. He wasn't that. He was only a man with a frail defensive system, working in a job that gave him nightmares.

She wanted to comfort him. And she might have done, might have reached out to touch him, but Gomez was calling her name from the living-room. She turned, saw him hold out a telephone to her.

'For you,' he said.

She took the phone. She heard Rick's voice through the crackle of static.

'I'm told it's total disaster back there,' he said.

'They came in a truck soon after you left.'

'Gomez said . . .' His voice was carried away on an electronic wind and she lost his words for a moment.

'I can't hear, Rick.'

'You know what this means,' he said. 'They've finally decided you don't know shit about your father's secrets . . . you don't have anything in the way of documentary evidence, or any other kind. If you had, you'd have told them when Patrick was being threatened. I think that clinched it for them as far as you inheriting anything from Dennis Malle. So that particular game's over. Unfortunately, we have a whole new game now.'

'I know what it is, Rick. It's open season on me, because I can place Hapsky at the scene of the murders in New Dresden.'

'Right, and . . .' His voice was sucked away again, riddled with static.

Open season, she thought. She looked at Wallace, who was beginning to back off from the body of Millie.

'Did you make it to the Dover Point?'

'We got to Grogan's Ridge . . .'

'This goddam line is breaking up.'

'. . . Gann says he never saw any vehicles parked at the hotel.'

'So why did he tell you he did?'

'Somebody had a gun at his head, that's why.'

'You were lured away,' she said.

'. . . shout, you're fading!'

'It doesn't matter. Are you coming back?'

'Yeah, I'm coming.'

The line fuzzed and spluttered and finally disconnected. She gave Gomez back the phone, then she went towards the kitchen. Lured away. Misled by a man with a gun to his skull. One cop fewer in the house to protect her. Two, counting Peabody.

Wallace had gone now. She looked around for him, didn't see him. She entered the kitchen, lit a cigarette. Her hand wasn't steady. O'Hanlon was sitting at the table, and the young paramedic was washing his hands in the sink.

'Rick's coming back,' she said.

'Did he find anything up there?'

She shook her head. 'How are you doing, Joe?'

'Better than some,' he said.

Was that an accusation? she wondered. Or had she reached that last sorry stage where she'd begun to misinterpret even the most simple statement? Was she finding resentment where none existed? No, because there was definitely hostility towards her, she'd felt it from the cops in the living-room, she couldn't escape it.

She looked at O'Hanlon. His bare arm, bandaged above the elbow, was tattooed with a single pale-pink generic flower. A strange adornment, unexpected in its delicacy. But everything was strange and distorted now. The night had been sent crashing out of its axis – Wallace's behaviour, the fragile phone connection with Rick, the voices that had issued from the cassette. Everything had cartwheeled. The world was upside-down and her place in it tenuous.

'Let me ask you, Joe . . . Is all this my fault? Am I to blame? Tell me honestly what you think.'

O'Hanlon said, 'Don't ask me questions like that.'

'Why? Because you don't want to answer them?'

'I don't have an opinion, Miss Malle. I do my job and I see what I see.'

'And what is it you see, Joe?'

He stared glumly at the wall. 'I told you. I don't have an opinion.'

'So you think I'm responsible—'

'I didn't say that.'

'You didn't say the opposite either, Joe.'

'Things happen,' he remarked. 'Once they happen they're history.'

The paramedic dried his hands on paper towels. 'Well, Joe, ready for a painkilling shot now?' he asked.

'I'll wait until Rick gets back.'

The paramedic said, 'You're a stubborn old fart. What's Rick got to do with it?'

'I'll see what he says,' O'Hanlon said. 'He might have something he wants me to do.'

'With *that* arm?'

'I'll wait anyhow, if you don't mind.'

'It's your arm,' the paramedic said.

O'Hanlon said, 'I wouldn't say no to a shot of brandy, though. For medicinal reasons.'

'I look like a liquor store, Joe?'

'You're like one of them St Bernard dogs. I know you got a stash in that bag.'

'You know too much for your own good.' The paramedic fumbled inside his bag and came out with a vacuum-flask of brandy. He poured a little into the cap and gave it to O'Hanlon, who sniffed it before tasting.

Andrea propped her elbows on the table, hands held to either side of her face. *Open season on Andrea Malle. You're the dead centre of the target.* She crunched her cigarette out in the ashtray that lay on top of the map Rick had been studying earlier. She gazed at his crosses and asterisks. The names of hotels. Farmhouses in the landscape. Lonesome places in the drifts.

O'Hanlon said, 'One thing. Seems to me we don't get to choose our fathers.'

'Thanks for saying that much, Joe.'

'Hell, it's true.'

True. But it didn't change anything in her mind.

She thought of the people who'd been detailed to protect her, and how they'd died. The anger built inside her again. This killing frame of mind. This rage. It was a barbed-wire knot in her head. She thought, *It's not a way I ever felt before.*

Now you have it in your heart to do murder.

She placed her hands on the map. She looked down at the asterisks and crosses Rick Fuscante had made on the paper. Dover Point Lodge, Smucker's Inn, The Homestead Resort. Her eye travelled the map, and she imagined she was flying over the landscape like a bird of prey, seeing the great white stretches below her, the frozen rivers and lakes, the thin ribbons of impassable back roads, the farmhouses and empty hotels. And then she stopped in flight, and hovered, her attention caught by a certain place-name on the map, and she felt the same hot violent surge of recognition a hawk might feel on seeing a hapless squirrel scurry across open space.

She folded the map and got up from the table. She grabbed her coat from the back of a chair.

'Going somewhere?' O'Hanlon asked.

She didn't stop to answer him.

chapter Thirty-Six

She moved down the hall, paused a moment, picked up Millie's gun from the floor, the keys from her belt, then walked past the two cops who stood on the porch and stared at the street. Neither of them looked at her. Maybe they assumed she needed to get out, distance herself from what had happened in this house. They didn't speak, made no attempt to stop her, and by the time she climbed inside Millie's four-wheel-drive Bronco and turned the key in the ignition, it was too late. She saw in the wing-mirror one of the cops raise a hand, and maybe he shouted something at her, something like 'Where the hell do you think you're going?' but she didn't hear and she wasn't in any mood to stop and listen.

She reached the end of the street and turned in the direction of the main road. A feathery snow was falling, soft flakes sliding down the windshield. Go. Just go.

Keep going. She buckled her seat-belt when she hit the main road, pausing for a moment to spread the map on the passenger seat. She flicked on the reading-light and left it burning.

Six miles west out of Horaceville she'd reach Zion Road, no more than a thread on the map.

She hoped the snow-ploughs had worked that territory. If they hadn't—

She wasn't going to think about that possibility.

Unpredictable. This whole undertaking, this grinding drive across icy surfaces and new snow beginning to cover the old, a gun and a map on the seat beside her – it was all unpredictable. She'd lost her mind, control, this was freakish behaviour. She thought of Fuscante, imagining his anger and anxiety when he discovered she'd gone, but—

This is what you have to do. Something *you* have to do.

Six miles beyond the limits of Horaceville she slowed as she approached Zion Road, which was badly signposted. She wasn't used to the vehicle and she hit the brakes a little too hard and it skidded a few yards beyond the intersection. She stopped, reversed, turned into the narrow road, which climbed up into darkness. It was the kind of road where lovers came on long summer nights and parked at the summit and gazed down at the lights of the town and sat in mute contemplation of love and sex and the universe – but in the grip of winter it wasn't a place for romantic interludes. Snow had been banked on either side of the road, but the surface was glassy-white, treacherous. You had to respect this surface. You couldn't take chances. A wrong move and you'd go crunching into a bank.

She pulled on the emergency brake, checked the map.

She ran a fingertip the length of Zion Road. What if she was wrong? Then she'd have lost nothing. She'd have accomplished nothing either. She'd just turn around and go back to Horaceville.

It was there on the map, where Zion Road snaked into a series of bends.

Skytower Lodge.

Skysomething, Hal Hapsky had said. 'I'll go back to Sky' – something.

Skytower. None of the other hotels or resorts on the map had a name anything like that. It was worth checking, wasn't it? It was worth the trip to make sure, right?

And the gun, the gun was simply a precaution, a little extra insurance, even if she had no experience of pistols, and she remembered the Browning 9mm her father had kept under his bed, because of the prowler he'd written about in his uninformative diary.

She released the brake and gave the vehicle a little gas and began the climb again and saw her headlights come back off the road as if they'd been bounced off mirrors. She drove another half-mile. There were tyre-tracks in places, barely visible under the new snow. But these might have been left behind by the plough that had come this way. They hadn't necessarily been made by Hapsky and friends.

She went into a sharp bend, struggled with the wheel. The angle was unexpectedly acute, and no sooner had she negotiated it than she hit the next sharp switchback, and this time the vehicle slithered thirty or forty yards before she had it under control again. A prickling moment, a little edge of panic, but it was okay now, it was fine.

She only had another five miles, maybe a little more, to travel on this stretch. According to the map, Skytower was located about three hundred yards off Zion Road, along a drive marked by a thin dotted line. The driveway would probably be blocked, but even if it were clear she wouldn't want to take the vehicle close to the hotel. Too much noise. She'd alert anyone there. She'd leave the Bronco and get as close as she could on foot.

She'd look for signs of life. She'd look for that flat-bed truck parked nearby, maybe snowmobiles, a jeep. She'd make sure this was the place Hapsky had chosen to hide. And then—

The sound of the car-phone surprised her. The quick little electronic *buzz-buzz*. She braked, picked up the handset. It was Fuscante, of course.

'Where the fuck are you?'

'I had an idea.'

'What idea?'

'It's something I want to check.'

She knew he wouldn't leave it at that, and he didn't. 'Just tell me where you are.'

She hesitated.

'I don't know what it is with you,' Fuscante said. 'You fly out of the house, steal a Department vehicle, and you don't say where you're headed. What's your problem, Andrea?'

I owe, she thought. *There's a debt to the dead, and I want to give something back. I want to start making some amends.* She might have said these things, but she didn't, because Fuscante would have criticized her, maybe even ridiculed her. And she was in no mood to take it.

'Remember what happened last time you just took a

hike, huh? New Dresden? New fucking Dresden? You might have been killed.'

She stared ahead into the stretches of her headlights. The strip was bleak and the lights enhanced this quality. She was high up on the crest of some narrow back road and alone. Completely alone.

'Tell me your location, Andrea.'

'Okay, *okay*. I'm on Zion Road.'

'Why? What are you doing up there?'

'There's a place called the Skytower.'

'What about it?'

'I think there's a chance Hapsky might be there.'

'Is this instinct? Or more of that lateral thinking?'

'It's something I heard Hapsky say.'

'And you didn't think to mention it before?'

'I wasn't sure I'd heard him right, it was only a fragment.'

'Which you didn't deem important.'

'Not until I looked at a map. All I'm going to do is check the place out.'

'The hell you are. You stay right where you are and I'll drive up. It's going to take me forty-five minutes.'

'I wait, is that it?'

'Absolutely. You wait. No two ways.'

'I'm a good little girl and I do what you tell me? Pity I didn't bring my knitting with me, isn't it?'

'Oh, give me a break. I'm not buying into that one.'

'A ball of wool, a pair of needles, I might have run up a pair of socks for your Christmas present—'

'I'm not listening to this,' he said.

'Fine,' she said, and cut the connection.

The phone buzzed again immediately.

She picked it up.

Fuscante said, 'I'm worried about your goddam safety.'

'I know you are,' she said.

'All I'm asking is you wait.'

'You don't see it, Rick. I can't wait.'

'What is it I don't see? Is this your personal war or something? Your private vendetta? Is that what I'm missing?'

'Put it that way if you like.'

'Andrea—'

She shut off the phone. It rang against immediately. She didn't answer it. She was tempted, certainly, but no, why should she be told what to do? He expected obedience. He demanded compliance. Sit there and wait for me, Andrea. You shouldn't be up there on your own.

Screw it.

She'd come this far.

Just keep going. She felt a curious jolt of exhilaration. A certain liberty. Okay, she couldn't raise the dead, she couldn't give them the kiss of life, she didn't have what Wallace had referred to as 'an unholy talent' – but she could do this one thing without assistance, because she was sick of death and determined to contribute in some way of her own to the fate of the men who traded in that lethal commodity.

And because she had that quality Meg had attributed to her father. Stubbornness.

She saw a sign at the side of the road, a post buried in a snowbank. Skytower Lodge, an arrow, a bleached-out logo with the letters S and L linked together.

This is where I get off, she thought.

She went a few yards past the sign, then killed the engine, cut the lights. She stuck the gun in her pocket.

It was heavy. She got out of the Bronco and walked back to the sign. The silence of the night was intense, something you could practically taste.

She stood at the entrance to the driveway. The lodge wasn't visible. It was back some way, hidden behind trees and drifts. She saw no reflected light in the sky, heard no sign of life. What had she expected? The sound of a TV playing in the distance? Music from a stereo? Hapsky and Falco sitting in front of a fireplace enjoying a glass of port?

The drive was hard-packed frozen snow. Somebody had shovelled in places at a time when the snow was fresh. Patches had been dug out half-heartedly and mounds arranged here and there along the edges of the drive. And she noticed other details now, barely visible in a darkness alleviated only by the dullest suggestion of moon beyond the heavy cloud mass – tyre-tracks, and black stains made by the exhaust of a vehicle.

A wind, picking up in the east, shuffled around her face and chilled her. The branches of the trees stirred and shook. She followed the tracks. The driveway made a bend to the left and she stopped. The hotel, a two-storey wooden structure in the style of a Black Forest hunting-lodge, was a hundred yards away.

In a downstairs window a very pale light flickered. She realized its source wasn't electrical. She was looking at candlelight. Of course, why would the hotel owners keep the power turned on during the winter when there were no guests? They'd turn it off. It would be one of many things they'd do before they abandoned the place for the dead season. Drain water from pipes to prevent them bursting in a freeze, close the storm-windows, disconnect the phone, a whole list of things to do.

She saw the flat-bed truck behind a stand of bare

trees near the front door. A jeep was parked about ten feet from the truck.

She'd found the place.

Now all she had to do was turn and hurry back to the road and wait for Fuscante. He wouldn't come alone, she knew that. He'd bring other officers with him.

And then what? They'd go in, make arrests. No, too simple. They'd meet resistance.

How many were there inside the lodge? She'd assumed two – Hapsky and Falco. She didn't know for sure.

She watched the light flicker in the window and wondered about going in a little closer and maybe making a head-count. If she could do that, it would be vital information for Fuscante. He'd know the strength of the enemy and he'd be prepared. She stood motionless in the softly falling snow. She was beset by frustration. Had she come up here just to sneak a look inside a goddam window and then slink away?

No. Too passive. Snow clustered on her eyelashes and melted and ran cold into her eyes as she turned possibilities around in her mind. If she knew how to use the goddam gun, if she had that kind of confidence, she'd just – Just what? Become the executioner?

She was thinking insanely again. You don't know about killing. How it might feel. How it might affect you afterwards. Taking another life, no matter how unworthy you thought that life might be – could you do that?

She took a few steps closer to the lodge, saw somebody's shadow pass in front of the light a moment.

Go back to the road now. Wait for Rick. Get away from here.

She moved into the trees along the edge of the driveway and worked her way a little nearer to the

lodge. She stopped suddenly when the front door
opened and a figure emerged. She couldn't tell if it was
Hapsky or Falco. The man stood very still. Feet apart,
he whistled quietly and tunelessly. Then she realized
what he was doing – he was peeing in the snow. He
shook himself, bent over a little to zip up, gazed in
her direction, and just for a second she thought, *He's
seen me*. But apparently he hadn't, because he turned
round and went back inside and shut the door. She
waited a minute and then moved closer until she was
about twenty-five yards from the vehicles.

She heard laughter from inside the building, a stac-
cato Har-har-har. Then silence. She stepped forward
again, reaching the flat-bed truck, where she crouched.

The front door opened a second time and somebody
came out of the house and his footsteps made harsh
crunching noises. He approached the jeep, opened the
passenger door and tossed something in, then went back
inside the house. She waited a moment before she rose
from her position behind the cab of the truck and looked
at the jeep. The door hadn't been shut and the interior
light burned. A backpack lay on the passenger seat. A
suitcase had been jammed between seat and dash.

She understood: they were leaving.

They knew it was only a matter of time before they
were discovered, that any cops searching the area for
them would come to this place sooner or later. She
wondered if Hapsky and his associates had moved from
one empty hotel to another over the past few days. She
thought, *Do nothing. They'll drive out of here, they'll run
into Fuscante on the road.*

Unless they went in the other direction, turning right
on Zion Road and moving in the opposite direction from
Horaceville. That was the logical move. Why head back

towards town? The wind shuttled around the building in a quick burst and flapped at her coat and she heard the front door open again. She drew herself down behind the cab of the truck. The man who emerged from the lodge opened the back door of the jeep and stashed something inside, whistling as he did so.

She thought, *If they go now, they stand a chance of getting away. So you stop them. You think of some way to stop them.*

She took the gun from her pocket. She thought of Fuscante. By this time he couldn't be very far away. Maybe he was already coming up Zion Road. All she'd have to do was prevent them from leaving. Stall them. Somehow stall them.

She listened to the guy shift things around in the back of the jeep.

She felt giddy, confused by possibilities. She was outside herself. Looking down at herself concealed by the truck. A woman in a heavy overcoat with a gun in her hand and snow in her hair. No longer Andrea Malle, counsellor to marital basket cases. Somebody else. Somebody she didn't know any more.

One move. One quick move. It wasn't anything you analysed beforehand.

You just did it. You just acted. Go. Now. Do it.

She felt herself rise and suddenly everything was hard and sharp and real, the cold air and the snow and the weight of the gun in her hand, even her words were brittle as icicles.

'Stand still. Don't move.'

The man turned his head and looked at her. He wasn't Hapsky.

'Hey,' he said. He was casual, seemingly indifferent.

This angered her. 'Just don't move.'

'Or you'll shoot,' he said. The voice was Anthony
Falco's. He had a thin face and a long jaw and one
eyelid that drooped very slightly, making a half-moon
over his eye.

'I'll shoot,' she said.

'Well, *hot dog*,' he said. 'We were looking for you.
Strange the way things turn out.'

It wasn't supposed to be this way. You hold a gun
on somebody, they're supposed to be scared. They're
supposed to crumble. Falco looked like he didn't give
a damn about the gun or anything else. She wanted
to shoot him. The thought burned in her brain. She
could almost hear it sizzling the way a branding-iron
sizzled on the hide of an animal. She felt a dryness in
her mouth. She had the ridiculous urge to smoke.

He was grinning at her. He had one of those slightly
crooked grins more malignant than merry. 'So you come
all the way up here to throw your weight around,'
he said.

She didn't say anything. She just tried to hold the gun
level. She was wondering about Hapsky. She thought, *I
should have waited until they were both outdoors* – but she
hadn't. She'd acted without thinking the consequences
through, another impulse. In the best of all possible
worlds, Hapsky would just come strolling out of the
house, suspecting nothing, maybe carrying some luggage, and he'd see her with the gun trained on Falco
and he'd drop the luggage and stick his hands in the air
and say, 'You got me cold,' but things apparently didn't
work like that. Falco, for instance – he wasn't scared the
way he was meant to be, the gun didn't faze him, he
seemed to regard her presence here as something to be
taken lightly, a chick with a weapon, no big deal. She
was nervous and unsettled and wondered about Rick

and what ran through her mind was the idea that he
might have had an accident coming up Zion Road, or
a puncture, and he was stuck halfway here—

'So,' Falco said, and nodded at the gun. 'You know
how to use that?'

'I know,' she said.

'And you'll pull the trigger,' he said. 'You're full of
shit, is what I think.'

'Push me,' she said. She wanted to destroy that idiot
grin on his face.

'Let me clue you in, honey. Fire the gun off and
that's gonna warn Hal and then what do you do when
he comes outta the house blasting away with a shotgun?
Or maybe he already knows you're around because he's
heard this little conversation we're having? You don't
think he *hasn't been listening*? *Huh*? HUH?' Falco was
beginning to raise his voice. She saw what he was doing:
a strategy of unnerving her. He wanted Hapsky to know
he wasn't alone out here. He was sending a warning.
She looked at the front door, then back at Falco. She
had a sense of things being awkwardly balanced. Falco,
Hapsky, she'd done this the wrong way and she wished
she could go back a minute or so in time and get it right,
but the clock had moved on.

'*Lookeee*. Over here, sweetheart.'

She spun around when she heard the voice behind
her. She fired the gun and it kicked violently in her
hand and jerked her arm up, and she fired a second
time, but she had neither aim nor control and she shot
without purpose into the darkness. Falco, who moved
quickly, punched her on the back of the neck and she
fell into the snow, looking up at him, seeing red flares
in her line of vision. The gun – but she no longer had
it, she'd dropped it somewhere.

And now Hapsky, a shotgun under one arm, was bending over her and smiling. 'The Lone fucking Ranger,' he said.

She had snow in her mouth and the pain in her neck was savage. She wondered if Falco had dislocated something. She looked at Hapsky's face, his cheeks dark pink in the chill air, his black hair layered and neat. The Demolition Man.

He bent down and held her chin in his gloved hand. She thought of the tapes. Her father's voice. She imagined Hapsky ordering the shooting of Patrick. 'This writer boyfriend, go down to the city and squeeze the fucker, Jimmy.'

'A pointless act, you coming up here,' he said, and squeezed her chin.

'Dad's blood runs in her veins,' Falco said.

'Yeah, and it was Daddy's blood rushed to her head,' Hapsky said. He squeezed her chin harder. His fingers were like iron clamped round her jawbone. She smelled his damp leather gloves. She couldn't move her lips. She tried to wrench her face away but he was too strong. He laughed that strange, sucking laugh of his and she remembered the touch of his hand on her spine in Fuscante's house and the recollection made her squirm. She wondered again how far away Rick was.

He had to be close. Had to be.

She bit into Hapsky's glove. Her teeth sank into soft leather. She couldn't have hurt him, but he pulled his hand back and slapped her anyway and her head rang like a bell at a boxing-match.

'Determined and headstrong,' he said. 'She's Dennis reincarnated, Falco. That's what she is.'

'Yeah, she's the Surgeon's daughter all right,' Falco said.

The Surgeon? She held a hand to her face where her skin was stinging. 'The what's daughter?' she asked.

As soon as she uttered the question, she realized she didn't want it answered. She remembered what Fuscante had said: 'We're looking at torture, mutilation, dismemberment.' She stared at Hapsky. She wanted him to say, 'Kid, we're only joking,' but she knew he wouldn't.

'I don't think she knows, Falco,' he said.

Falco said, 'For damn sure Daddy never told her. He was the bigtime security expert, that's all she knew.'

'You think she ought to know?'

Falco nodded. 'Yeah, why not.'

'I hate to be the bearer of bad tidings.' Hapsky looked mock-solemn, but there was no regret in his voice. 'This close to Christmas, it's a goddam shame really.'

She tried to lose herself in the patterns of snowflakes. She tried to enter the white drift and the way the wind swirled crystals haphazardly through the air. Hapsky, bending close to her ear, whispered, 'He was the best in the business, sweetheart. He was like the fucking Paganini of surgery. He could take his knives and he could work them like a fucking artist. Now this is the kind of work that might turn some stomachs. But not the Surgeon's, sweetheart. The guy was ice.'

'I'm not listening,' she said. She thought of picking up snow in her hands and stuffing it inside her ears and deafening herself. But Hapsky had raised his voice.

'He'd make people fucking vanish, sweetheart.'

She tried to say 'no', but it didn't come out as a sound.

'A whole person dismantled in a flash. Small packages.'

Falco said, 'Never left a mess, did he, Hal?'

'We're not discussing your average butcher here,' Hapsky said.

She wanted to say, 'He installed security systems. That's what he did.' But she was lost in Hapsky's eyes, and the awful light of truth in them.

'Unfortunately,' Hapsky said, 'his nerve kinda snapped. He was getting up there in years, maybe he'd lost – pardon the pun – the cutting edge.' Hapsky gave his weird laugh. 'Didn't enjoy the work any more, wanted out. But you don't get out. We tried to dissuade him. I mean, we really tried to accommodate him in the nicest way. We paid him some hefty money – nominally for his company, in reality for his continued cooperation in what had been a long-term highly profitable fucking association. But Dennis had ideas of his own. He kept records, sweetheart. Said he'd place them in the hands of quote "the appropriate authorities" if we didn't let him out. Anyhow, he leaves this threat hanging in the air and he fucks off. Him and that sidekick of his, plus the girlfriend with the big tits. But this is America, God bless her, and you can't hide for ever when you got computers spitting out data twenty-four hours a day three sixty-five days a year and then some.'

She felt mute. She pulled off her gloves and pressed her hands into the snow. She'd crossed a boundary into a world that had at best only a tangential relationship with the one she knew and now none of her directional instruments worked, her gyroscope was broken.

'So, in a phrase, he had to be wasted,' Hapsky said. 'You see that, don't you? I mean, our business depends on secrecy. A client comes to us and says there's a few knuckleheads zoning in on his private territory, he wants them removed. You wouldn't believe these foreign fucks, think they can just come in and grab a hunk of the pizza. So the customer – maybe a guy who's been doing business for twenty, thirty years – doesn't want this crap fouling his turf. He wants rid of it. You see what I'm saying? Dennis blows the whistle – we're all down the toilet, sweetheart.'

'Completely,' Falco said.

'And when somebody wasted him, my first thought was revenge, somebody had found out about his past employment and wanted to even a score – and if that was the case, then obviously it made me feel kinda exposed. Anybody knew about Dennis, they might know about me. See what I mean?'

She shook her head. She was thinking of Fuscante. She was thinking, *Hurry, hurry.*

'But now I figure it was just some itinerant thief, a jackass with a shotgun came by and things got out of hand and there was a struggle. Like the cops see it. Because if it was somebody who knew the score, they'd be coming after me also. But I'm not getting that kind of vibe, sweetheart.'

She looked beyond Hapsky at the sky. The moon broke through the clouds for a second, a silvery illumination that made the snow light up.

Falco said, 'I think we better split, Hal. If she's found us, her cop pals can't be that far behind.'

'You've got a point.'

'What about her?'

Hapsky looked at her. 'What about you, Andrea? What do you think we should do about you?'

He wasn't really asking a question, she knew that, because he'd already decided the answer.

She'd die, like Dennis Malle before her, in the snow.

chapter Thirty-Seven

She said the only thing that came to mind. 'You're right, Falco. Fuscante's on his way. And he's not alone. He should be here any moment.' She tried to keep her voice under control. She was hypnotized by Hapsky's shotgun. If he fired it she wouldn't have time to feel a thing. She couldn't take her eyes from the weapon, the solid dark enormity of it.

Where *was* Fuscante? How much time had passed since he'd spoken to her on the phone? She couldn't calculate that. Twenty minutes? Twenty-five? Her systems of measurement were malfunctioning. Why didn't she hear the sound of his vehicle, that comforting drone of an engine, in the distance? He'd told her he'd be there in forty-five minutes.

'Like the fucking cavalry,' Hapsky said.

'Just do the thing, Hal. I want out of here.'

Hapsky was quiet a second before he said, 'I'm thinking a hostage.'

'No way,' Falco said.

Hapsky said, 'Listen, if her friends are coming up here, we're seriously outgunned. We need a bargaining chip.'

'She's baggage,' Falco said. His voice was acid. He looked down at her and kicked at the snow with a vicious gesture.

'We'll take her and if it turns out we don't need her, fine, we dump her.' Hapsky leaned down and yanked her by the hair and drew her to her feet. Her body was cold, limbs numb. She didn't feel the pain in her scalp.

Hapsky pushed her towards the jeep.

'I don't like this,' Falco said.

Hapsky rammed the shotgun into her back. Falco, deeply irritated, kicked at the snow some more, like a petulant kid.

'I say execute her now, Hal. I never once heard of a hostage situation going smoothly. Something always goes wrong.'

'Nothing's going wrong,' Hapsky said.

'This whole situation's *wrong*, man.'

'I'm getting pissed off with your whining,' Hapsky said.

'Yeah? Let me show you what I'd do with this bitch.' Falco grabbed her by the shoulder, spun her round, flattened the palm of his hand into her face and pushed her down into the snow and stood over her. He took a gun out of his coat pocket.

Hapsky said, 'Where's the percentage in you and me arguing? We're taking her along.'

'No way.' Falco aimed the gun at her. 'You run too many risks, Hal. Blowing up that fucking house. That assault on the cop's place. And you should never have

let Malle get away like he did. And now you want to
drag this cunt along with us. Dumb and dumber.'

Hapsky said, 'You're out of line.'

Falco said, 'I'm blowing this bitch's brains out.'

She gazed into the eye of the weapon. It was a small
black hole, an avenue into an alternative universe. A
barren, silent one.

Where was Fuscante? What was keeping him? This
confrontation between Hapsky and Falco was going to
turn out badly for her, because Falco might think that
by shooting her he was asserting himself. The junior
partner takes a step up. A career move. Hapsky had
been at this game too long. It was time for new brooms.
A different strategy all round.

It was going to turn out badly no matter what.

She looked toward Hapsky, hoping he'd react, that
he'd become her unlikely saviour. She thought of her
father's life intricately involved with Hapsky's and it
was like walking a hallway of bevelled mirrors where
all the reflections were grotesquely deformed. The
Surgeon: 'A blade in his hand. He'd make people
fucking vanish, sweetheart.'

Hapsky levelled his shotgun at Falco. 'Put the weapon
away, Anthony.'

Falco kept his gun pointed at Andrea. There was
a history of conflict here – Falco forever doing what
he was told, asking no questions, yessir yessir, and all
the while building up a serious catalogue of resentments against Hapsky. Falco kept the gun trained
on her and his hand was steady and his whole body
inflexible.

'Put the gun away, Anthony,' Hapsky said.

'I'll put *her* away.'

Falco pushed the weapon against her forehead, his

arm rigid. She felt the metal against bone, saw flakes of snow on the barrel.

Hapsky said, 'I'm holding a shotgun, Falco.'

Falco didn't look at Hapsky. He kept staring at Andrea. She thought about this tense, triangulated situation. Suddenly the conflict between these two men was obviously more important to them than the idea that cops were heading for the lodge. Face was involved, position was at stake. It was a small self-contained world in which only Hapsky and Falco existed, and she'd become a satellite orbiting their planet. Maybe they'd forget she existed. Maybe she'd be allowed to drift unnoticed in space. But the pressure of Falco's weapon upon her forehead reminded her that she was still attached to the configuration of things.

She heard a noise in the distance. She couldn't identify it. It was motorized, raspy, and she couldn't judge how far away it was. Its source wasn't the road. It came from a place behind the lodge, so far as she could tell. But that might be an acoustic trick. The snow, the wind, distortions.

'What the fuck is that?' Falco said.

Hapsky tilted his head, listened. 'A snowmobile.'

He was right. A snowmobile. Unmistakably so.

Fuscante had chosen another mode of transportation. She thought, *He comes cross-country on a snowmobile, and meantime his back-up officers are driving up Zion Road in their four-wheel-drive vehicles. A flanking action. Clever, Fuscante. Smart move.* But she had a sense of sands falling inside a glass, time filtering away. The gun was still pressed to her forehead, nothing had been settled about her life or death.

Hapsky said, 'We get the fuck out of here.'

'Without the woman,' Falco said.

'Do whatever the fuck you like, Falco. I'm outta this place.'

Falco grinned down at Andrea.

She felt her throat lock. Her heart beat as if it was inside her skull. She no longer heard the roar of the snowmobile and wondered if she'd imagined it, but she hadn't, Falco and Hapsky had heard it too, but now it was silent and the night was a void and Falco was grinning as if to say 'Goodnight, sweetheart' and she thought, *Raise a hand and shove the gun away*, but there was no time for that because one chambered bullet propelled the length of a barrel was faster than any move she could make, faster than anything in the world, faster than light or sound. Death travelled at a velocity you couldn't measure.

The sound was crisp and quick and cracked the delicate skein of the night. At first she thought Hapsky had turned the shotgun on Falco.

But that wasn't it.

Falco dropped in the snow like a man felled by an axe. He lay flat on his back, his mouth open. The side of his head was gone. Hapsky, shotgun raised, looked in the direction of the lodge, then grabbed Andrea and dragged her to her feet and shoved her closer to the jeep. A second shot split the air and pinged off the hood of the vehicle and Hapsky said, 'Jesus Christ.'

Fuscante, she thought.

Hapsky fired one air-pounding blast towards the lodge, then pushed her into the jeep and clambered in behind her and twisted the key in the ignition. He backed up, churning ice and snow.

'Your cop friend,' he said.

'You can't get away,' she said.

'Watch me, sweetheart. Watch me.'

She saw the snowmobile emerge from behind the lodge. She saw Fuscante, in long coat and boots and black visor, speed across the space that separated him from the jeep. Hapsky gave the jeep gas and it lurched toward the snowmobile. Just as a collision seemed inevitable, Fuscante spun to the side. Hapsky braked, turned the wheel, swung the jeep round, drove it once more towards Fuscante. The vehicle rocked and rattled over ice and snow the texture of cement and there was a sudden eye-smarting flash as the lamps of the jeep melded with the beacon of the snowmobile, and the two vehicles raced toward one another as if this was a daredevil sport, a test of nerve, and Fuscante whipped the machine out of the jeep's path with only a couple of feet to spare. The air was filled with flying ice, white chips that glistened, exhaust fumes, the stench of fuel.

'I'll nail that fucker,' Hapsky said, and he braked, picked up the shotgun from his lap and rolled down the window. He took aim at Fuscante, who was swinging the snowmobile around for another assault. She felt dazed and realized she'd struck her head at some point in all the manoeuvring and blood was running from her forehead down to the corners of her lips. She heard the great din of the shotgun and clapped her hands to her ears. Snow was kicked up around the snowmobile but Fuscante was still in his seat, he hadn't been hit. He drove off about fifty yards and then turned the vehicle and directed it at the jeep. She thought, *He's behaving in a crazy, kamikaze way, he's a moving target, vulnerable.* And where was all the backup? Why hadn't they arrived?

Hapsky said, 'Guy has a death wish.' He reloaded the shotgun and stuck it out the window again. He took careful aim and she thought, *It's inevitable, he's going to hit Rick sooner or later*, and she threw herself against Hapsky and made him misfire. He swung one hand and smacked her in the face with his knuckles, and her neck snapped back.

'Stupid bitch,' he said.

She had a sense of the world spinning, the night in wild disarray. The snow wasn't falling from the sky, instead it seemed to be rising from the ground, an inversion of gravity. Dimly, she saw Hapsky take aim again, and she was aware of the lamp of the snowmobile forty or fifty feet beyond the windshield. She heard the detonation of the shotgun and the way it reverberated inside the jeep like the aftershock of a crack in the earth's crust. She saw the snowmobile list to one side and Fuscante collapse from the seat and drop to the ground, and she reached for the door handle, she had to go to him, she had to check on him, she couldn't just sit here if he was lying out there bleeding.

'Shut the goddam door,' Hapsky said.

She didn't. He had to reach across and restrain her.

She struggled, but he wouldn't release her. She slumped a moment, staring at the skewed angle of the snowmobile light and the still figure of Fuscante lying beside the vehicle.

'He's hurt,' she said.

'If he's not dead.'

'No, he's just hurt. He can't be dead. He *can't* be.'

Hapsky said, 'Let's check. Let's see how he is.'

She heard it in his voice: if Fuscante wasn't already dead, Hapsky would finish him off.

She walked in front of Hapsky towards the fallen snowmobile. The engine was still running stutteringly. She was dizzy and her movements were unbalanced.

She reached the place where Fuscante lay. She couldn't tell if he was breathing or not. She'd have to slide open his visor, remove his helmet. She'd have to look at his face.

Hapsky stood alongside her, shotgun poised, ready for the one last cartridge if it was needed. 'He's dead,' he said.

She didn't want to do it, didn't want to open the visor and look at him.

'Check,' Hapsky said. 'Make it fast.'

She reached out, her hand unsteady. She touched the dark visor.

She didn't see it coming.

Neither did Hapsky.

Fuscante had his pistol in his pocket and fired it through his coat and Hapsky made a strange moaning sound and lifted one hand to his throat and then slid down to his knees and remained in that position for several seconds before he pitched face down in the snow. He didn't move again. The shotgun lay a couple of feet from his body.

She looked at Fuscante and said, 'Thank God. Thank God. *Thank God.*'

He said nothing.

'You play dead pretty well,' she said.

He still didn't speak.

'Are you hurt?' she asked. 'You must be hurt. I'll make it better. I promise.'

He removed one glove, which she saw was damp and dark with blood.

'Your hand,' she said. 'Let me look at it.'

There was blood on the ring on his right hand. Blood on the tiny emerald, on the gold band.

'I'm sorry,' he said. And he took off his helmet.

She was kneeling in the snow the way she'd done when she'd found his body alongside the log-pile. She was seeing that same sky and the dead trees and hearing the sounds of her own grief. She was kneeling, swaying just a little. She opened her mouth to speak but language collapsed inside her. He reached out to touch her and she recoiled.

'I know,' he said.

She tried to speak again. But nothing happened. She looked across the stretches of snow. This was the land of the dead. The valley of lost things.

'I don't think I have a whole lot of time to spend here,' he said.

She didn't want to hear his voice. She didn't want the dead to get up and talk: 'You play dead pretty well.'

She felt a pain in her chest like a clenched fist behind her ribs. *This isn't happening.*

'I'm sorry,' he said again.

The wind scattered snow around her face. She couldn't *look* at him. She wanted to close her eyes and count to ten and when she opened her eyes he'd be gone, back to whatever place he'd come from. Her head was filled with a jumble of remembered smells and images – brine, candy apples, the sails of a small boat bloated by a breeze, the texture of pebbles and shells picked from a beach. Save it that way. Freeze it all in time. Protect it. Pretend.

But it was too late for that.

'You killed people.' She hadn't looked at him yet. She didn't intend to. 'You made your living that way.'

He didn't respond. He was watching her face. She could feel it. But she was damned if she was going to look at him.

'Why?' she asked.

'Why? That's too complicated a question. I was good at it. You do what do you best. It paid well.'

'How can you *say* that so calmly?'

'You think I'm calm?' He sighed. 'I was never calm.'

'You killed people, Jesus Christ.'

'They weren't good people.'

'Is that supposed to be a justification?'

'It's a statement of fact. They weren't good people. And I wasn't a good person either.'

'I can see that.' She got to her feet and walked a few paces away from him. She stood with her back to him. The snowmobile motor chugged and whined.

'Heartless when I had to be,' he said.

'Which was most of the time.'

'No, not always. I had my better moments. I have some good memories. You and me . . .'

She turned to look at him. The lamp illuminated his face. He looked gentle, kind, fatherly. She half expected him to take out a pipe and light it and start mumbling about how civilization was ruining nature or launch into one of his other favourite speeches. But these were illusions.

'At least I didn't let any harm come to you,' he said.

'How the hell can you say that?'

'I watched you. I kept an eye on you. Ever since you discovered the body, I haven't been very far away from you.'

'Thanks,' she said. 'Thanks a million.'

He didn't reply.

She realized something. 'It had to be Wallace, right? You couldn't go anywhere without that ring, could you? Your lucky charm. No, you had to have it back, didn't you? Why didn't I see that? He must have cost you. He performs a post mortem. He signs your death certificate. Nobody questions the coroner. Why should they? He meets you somewhere, gives you back the ring. And the body, I guess he provided that too. What was it? A stock item? A John Doe whose face Wallace worked out of shape?'

'I can't talk about that,' he said. 'I can't tell you Wallace had anything to do with this.'

'I don't think I want to hear it anyway. This life you led up here – the antique mandolins and the oil-paintings and the little nature-trail rambles, and all the time you were hiding because you'd taken two million bucks from your associates.'

'I wanted out,' he said.

'Why? Conscience bothering you?'

'You say that mockingly. But maybe it was. And maybe I was tired. You want simple answers. Even as a little girl, you always wanted simple answers. No, you'd say, that's too difficult, that's too confusing. Simple answers. But there aren't any. Not really.'

'The planning. The diary. The prowler. Crafty misdirection. And all the documents of your life in order. The meal you never finished cooking. Nothing out of place. All the angles accounted for. Including me.'

'I didn't let you down when it really counted,' he said, and nodded at Hapsky lying nearby. 'You'd be dead if it wasn't for me.'

'How can you *not* see it? I wouldn't have *been* in this position if it hadn't been for you! Do you know how many people are dead? People who didn't even know you? People who'd never met you? People who had absolutely no connection with your . . . life. If that's what it was. It wasn't much of one, was it? A massive structure of lies and stories and covering up what you really did. The trips overseas when you came back with gifts and tales. Did you practise your specialty abroad too?'

He didn't answer this. He said, 'I don't worry about those people. I can't allow myself to feel guilty.'

'Not even Stan?'

'Stan was too slow to move. I knew Hapsky was getting close. There were some ominous signs. The broker who handled my investments told me somebody phoned him from the IRS saying an agent needed to talk to me about a tax matter. When the broker checked it out, the IRS knew absolutely nothing about any inquiry. Then I heard somebody had been asking about my address at the post office in Horaceville where I had a box number under an assumed name. Something vague about delivering a parcel. You can understand that this stuff worried me. I'd developed a fugitive's instincts . . . I wanted to warn Stan, but he didn't turn up for an appointment we had. Maybe he was too scared to show himself. He hated leaving that ruin of a farmhouse. He felt too vulnerable. But I can't afford the luxury of emotions about Stan.'

'I'm not hearing this,' she said.

'There's a lot you're not hearing,' he said. He studied his wounded hand a moment. That characteristic little downward motion of his head, the set of his mouth in concentration, the pose brought back a flood of memories. She didn't want them. She didn't want heartache.

'You're damned,' she said.

'Only if you believe in damnation, Andrea.'

'I forgot. You don't believe.'

'I'm not sure what I believe any more, I'm not sure

if I ever genuinely believed in anything,' he said. 'I'm sorry you had to be the one who discovered the body.'

'You needed it to be me, didn't you?'

'I had the body. I needed somebody to discover it. Who else was I going to ask? I couldn't leave it lying outside on the chance somebody might *eventually* find it. That could have taken months. And I had to be reported dead sooner than that. I didn't have neighbours. I didn't encourage friendships. I summoned you.'

'And I came running. You knew I would.'

'Yes,' he said. 'I saw you find the body.'

'You *saw?*'

'I was flying the chopper. I watched you.'

The chopper. The black machine. He'd been looking down from the cockpit. In some way, this was the worst discovery of all. He'd seen her grief. He'd seen all the strength go out of her and watched her kneel in the snow beside the body.

And still – he'd flown away.

'I felt for you,' he said.

'Bullshit.'

'Believe it, don't believe it. But I did.'

'When you lie most of the time, how can anyone know when you're ever telling the truth?'

'That's a real problem.'

She heard a vehicle in the distance. Far off, barely audible.

'But I think I have more pressing problems than that,' he said. He got to his feet. He winced. His wounded hand dangled at his side. Blood dripped into the snow. 'For one thing,' he said, 'I'm going to have to stay dead.'

'I might tell the truth.'

'Or you might go through with my cremation.'

The sound of the approaching vehicle was growing louder. Fuscante at last.

She said, 'You killed people. I can't get my head round that one.'

'I'm your father. You're my daughter.'

'You really imagine there's some *loyalty* left?'

'I don't know for sure, do I?'

He approached her. He came very close to her. He brought his face within an inch of hers. She knew a kiss was coming. She moved her head aside, and he stepped back, and the kiss died in the cold air.

He smiled and sighed, touched her cheek with the tip of a finger, and she drew away from him because she had a terrible image of his hands, and the implements they'd held and what he'd used these tools for, and she refused to go down that road.

Then he turned, walked towards the lodge, stopped, looked back.

She saw him raise one hand before he vanished round the side of the building.

She imagined him going on foot across snow-covered fields and through thick drifts. Maybe he had a destination in mind. Maybe he had another vehicle somewhere nearby. Maybe the chopper wasn't far away.

She watched Fuscante's Dodge come up the driveway. A second vehicle travelled behind it.

Fuscante got out. Other cops milled around, looking at Hapsky, the flat-bed truck, the snowmobile, the body of Falco.

'You're safe,' he said.

'I'm safe.'

'I was worried. I mean, *deeply* worried.'

'You took your time getting here.'

'The roads,' he said. 'It doesn't matter. What's important is you're safe. Jesus, this place looks like a battlefield. What the hell happened here?'

'I'll tell you,' she said. 'But not now.' She thought of Dennis Malle trudging across fields. A lonely trek. A lonely man. He was always going to be alone. For the rest of his life.

Do nothing. Let it go. Let the coffin slide into the flames.

She said, 'I think I just lost something.'

'Something I can help you find?'

'Maybe you can. Or maybe I never had it in the first place.'

'You want to explain that?'

'I don't know if I can.'

'You've got blood on your face.'

He took a Kleenex from a pocket and dabbed it against her forehead and she closed her eyes and remembered the first time he'd touched her. The wind, picking up force in the secretive landscape, stirring through woods and swirling across fences, blew snow against her. She pressed her face into Fuscante's shoulder, a secure place where she wouldn't have to think for the moment about Dennis Malle, his hand bleeding, his heart a mysterious stone chamber, going down and down through the drifts on a journey with no destination.

chapter *Thirty-Eight*

At first light she went with Fuscante and several uniformed cops through the fields and snow-blasted woodlands that lay beyond the Skytower Lodge. The bodies of Hapsky and Falco had been removed but the vehicles remained, including the overturned snowmobile. She didn't want to look at it, but she did anyhow. She remembered her father's words: 'You'd be dead if it wasn't for me.'

Overnight, the snowfall had been scant and short-lived, a few flurries. The landscape under the grey sky was miserable and sullen and freezing: nature in its most surly manifestation. She trudged alongside Fuscante, thinking of the hours they'd sat in her hotel room drinking cup after cup of coffee while she explained – slowly, in the manner of somebody reluctantly describing a nightmare – what had happened at the lodge. He'd listened without interruption, absorbing everything, and then they'd lain down together, hands held, bodies close. No love-making, no passion, just a sense of nearness and security and waiting for the darkness to pass. She was drained, but hadn't felt any need to sleep.

'You could have lied,' Fuscante had said, 'protected him.'

'I thought about it.' And she had. She'd argued with herself, an inner conflict that tore at her. She'd half convinced herself that she should have concocted another story altogether, one that hadn't involved Dennis Malle. A fantasy in which Hal had killed Falco, and she'd killed Hal. But how could she have maintained this fabrication? She felt the truth was a preferable road to take, even if was a hard one. Even if it meant telling Fuscante that she knew her father was alive and that Wallace had probably been an accomplice in the masquerade.

Even if, in the end, she thought it was a kind of betrayal.

Fuscante had said, 'He's a killer. And I need to find him. You know I can't leave it alone, don't you? No matter what.'

She'd watched the first pale film of light against the bedroom window and remembered Dennis Malle shooting Hapsky, and if she felt any gratitude she understood she had to work to suppress it. Because if she gave into it, if she yielded even an inch, she'd be condoning all the acts of his history. *You may have been a ruthless killer but you're still my father and daughters are supposed to love their fathers, right? They're supposed to be bonded to them, correct? They're meant to love unconditionally.*

But she couldn't. Dennis Malle had rewritten the rules of love in a language she was unable to read.

'I'm going back out there to look for him,' Fuscante had said.

'And I'm going with you,' she'd said. 'No argument.'

He hadn't said no, but he hadn't said yes either. They'd left the hotel together and she'd wondered about Meg, if she should tell her what had happened – but no, she couldn't face a highly strung scene with her.

And now they were out in the white fields and barren woods at dawn, herself and Fuscante and four of his officers. Roadblocks had been established on the highway that ran through Horaceville in case Malle had made his way back towards town during the hours of darkness, back to whatever means of transportation he might have. But Fuscante was convinced that Dennis would have headed away from town and gone deeper into the countryside, seeking a retreat in an empty house or hotel.

His tracks led from the Skytower Lodge across a field and through a stand of trees. Here and there the snow was bloodstained. She thought of his damaged hand, wondered how badly it had bled, and despite herself she felt a flutter of concern.

In the middle of the woods she paused, conscious of Fuscante's officers spread out on either side of her. They moved silently. They carried rifles and shotguns. She didn't want to think of those being fired.

'You don't have to be here,' Fuscante said. 'You can go back to my vehicle and keep warm.'

She leaned against the trunk of a tree, shivered. 'Don't ask me to do that,' she said.

He touched the side of her face with his gloved hand. 'You don't like being here. You don't *want* to be here.'

'It's not a question of what I want, Rick.'

'You feel guilty.'

She looked at him. 'Guilt. Regret. Maybe some other feelings I can't put names to.'

'He used you, Andrea. He lied to you. Keep that in mind. And if that doesn't do the trick, remind yourself of some of the other stuff he did.'

'You don't have to say it.' Rick's world, she thought. Straightforward. Black and white. No grey areas. Why couldn't her own world be that way?

She pushed herself from the tree and kept moving, a step or two behind Fuscante. Dennis Malle's tracks reminded her of hoofmarks left in the snow by a wounded animal. She wondered how far they'd lead, if somewhere along the way they'd simply disappear. *I want it to be like that*, she thought. *No sign of him. No sign he ever came this way. That he ever really existed.* Suddenly the landscape seemed a place of great tension. Iced surfaces, things buried, bones you didn't want to dig up. She'd done all the digging she wanted to do, and where had it got her?

Fuscante put his hand on her elbow. 'You okay now?'

She said she was fine.

'You sure?' He looked at her doubtfully.

She was sure. She kept walking, eyes to the ground. She listened to the crunch of her boots sinking in the hard snow. One of the cops sneezed, stifled the sound in his hand.

They moved out of the wooded area. The wasted landscape appeared locked in an endless winter. You might think spring would never touch this place again. Seasons would bypass this area. Nothing would ever change here.

The tracks continued into open country. Drops of blood had frozen on the trail. She bent at one point, took off a glove, touched a hardened stain, remembered cutting her hand on a broken bottle she'd found on the beach at Nantucket and how her father had applied a Band-Aid and then kissed her fingertips and said, 'There, it's better.' And although the cut throbbed, she believed him. Because she'd always believed him. 'There, it's better. Everything's better now, sweetheart.'

Memories. You put them in a box and you locked it for ever and hoped you'd forget where you'd left the key.

After a quarter-mile of open land there was another stand of trees, pine branches bent under the weight of snow. The tracks led directly toward the trees, which grew close together. Fuscante halted. The other cops also stopped, as if they were awaiting his signal to advance. Andrea took a few steps forwards, then stood still. Daylight hadn't completely penetrated the thickness of the firs. It was as if a mist hung in the air between the trees. She gazed at the footprints, imagining her father coming this way in the dark. Feeling what? she wondered. The pain of his wound, sure, but what else? Loss? Sadness? Did he feel anything like that?

I don't know him, she thought. *I can't read his heart.*

She moved closer to the trees. She heard Fuscante say something, a phrase she didn't catch. She kept moving, even as she listened to him come up from behind. She saw how the footprints were blurred, as if her father had made a fruitless effort to obscure them. Or maybe he'd blundered in the dark and walked blindly around in circles.

Fuscante said, 'You want to be the one to find him? Is that it?'

'He could be long gone,' she said. 'He might have had a vehicle stashed out here, a four-wheeler . . . He might be miles away.'

'That's what you secretly hope, isn't it?'

'I don't know what I hope,' she said. 'I don't know that I hope for anything.'

Fuscante looked at her a moment longer and then turned his face toward the firs and said sombrely, 'The prints are pretty erratic here. Like he'd stumbled. Maybe had to drag himself . . . I don't know, Andrea. It doesn't look good.'

She walked away from Fuscante, drawn between the trees.

Stumbled . . . had to drag himself . . . It doesn't look good.

The tracks were shapeless, no longer recognizable footprints but scuffmarks, tiny ridges, shapeless smears of blood. She heard Fuscante a few yards behind her. She didn't turn to look at him. She just followed the haphazard trail. Followed it down through the firs. Her breath made clouds on the air. She quickened her steps. Faster. Low-hanging branches brushed her face and hair. She pushed them aside, indifferent to the snow that fell into her eyes. Moving, tracing the zigzag marks left by her father, which were as crooked as his whole life had been. Wanting to find him anyway and not knowing why. *He's here*, she thought. *He's close.* She didn't have far to go now. His traces assumed the shape of pink-tinted swirls in soft white powder. He'd come this way on his hands and knees. She imagined this, she saw him crawl under the whispering flurries of snow, imagined him shuddering from the cold, bleeding. The picture made her anxious. She hurried, coat flapping, as if she were rushing to an emergency.

'Andrea,' Fuscante called.

But she didn't turn. She was following the tracks. She was hunting her father.

When the tracks stopped she stopped too.

He sat propped against a tree-trunk, his head tipped back upon the wood. He looked as if he'd fallen into a deep sleep. His skin was pale, almost the colour of the snow that had gathered on his hair and adhered to his face. She stared at him. *He's alive. That's what I want. I don't want him dead.* The collar of his coat was turned up under his chin. His hands were stuck in his pockets.

She was hardly conscious of Fuscante standing at her side.

'He'd lost a lot of blood, Andrea. And in this kind of temperature . . . I'm sorry.'

Fuscante put an arm around her shoulder. A protective gesture. Don't look. Don't punish yourself.

She stepped away from Fuscante and, reaching down, touched the side of her father's face gently, as if she expected to stir him from his sleep. His head turned slightly to one side, and then was still.

Goddam you, wake up. Wake up. Tell me who the hell you are.

She wanted to cry. She wasn't sure why. He didn't deserve tears. He didn't deserve her sorrow.

'Let's go home, Andrea,' Fuscante said.

She wondered what he meant by home. The small house on Docherty Street, or some other place she hadn't yet discovered. She didn't move. She gazed for a long time at the dead man until his features had changed completely and had shed all familiarity and he'd become a stranger, somebody she'd stumbled across in a forlorn wood, just a victim of a brutal season.